THE ACCLAIMED NATIONAL BESTSELLER

SIRO

"TOP-FLIGHT FICTION . . .
A SUBTLE AND ELEGANTLY CRAFTED TALE"
New York Newsday

"A TOUR DE FORCE IN EVERY SENSE
OF THE WORD,
a crackerjack story accurate
to the last arcane detail, honest to the core,
and utterly plausible . . .
A gripping story"
Charles McCarry, author of *The Tears of Autumn*

"EXCITING . . . ORIGINAL . . .
REFRESHING . . .
AN UNUSUALLY GOOD THRILLER"
Entertainment Weekly

"FASCINATING . . .
A tale of deception and disillusion . . .
Ignatius navigates sure-handedly through
the moral quagmire of an espionage operation
run 'off the books' and outside the law."
Cleveland Plain Dealer

SIRO

DAVID IGNATIUS

AVON BOOKS ◆ NEW YORK

"Our Gods," by Frederick Seidel, from *These Days* © 1988, reprinted by permission of Alfred A. Knopf, Inc.

AVON BOOKS
A division of
The Hearst Corporation
1350 Avenue of the Americas
New York, New York 10019

Copyright © 1991 by David Ignatius
Published by arrangement with Farrar, Straus and Giroux
Library of Congress Catalog Card Number: 91-7370
ISBN: 0-380-71820-0

First Avon Books Printing: January 1993

AVON TRADEMARK REG. U.S. PAT. OFF. AND IN OTHER COUNTRIES, MARCA REGISTRADA, HECHO EN U.S.A.

Printed in the U.S.A.

RA 10 9 8 7 6 5 4 3 2 1

For the memory of my grandparents
And for Eve, Elisa, Alexandra and Sarah

OUR GODS

Older than us, but not by that much, men
Just old enough to be uncircumcised,
Episcopalians from the Golden Age
Of schools who loved to lose gracefully and lead—
Always there before us like a mirage,
Until we tried to get closer, when they vanished,
Always there until they disappeared.

They were the last of a race, that was their cover—
The baggy tweeds. Exposed in the Racquet Club
Dressing room, they were invisible,
Present purely in outline like the head
And torso targets at the police firing
Range, hairless bodies and full heads of hair,
Painted neatly combed, of the last WASPs.

They walked like boys, talked like their grandfathers—
Public servants in secret, and the last
Generation of men to prefer baths.
These were the CIA boys with EYES
ONLY clearance and profiles like arrowheads.
A fireside frost bloomed on the silver martini
Shaker the magic evenings they could be home.

They were never home, even when they were there.
Public servants in secret are not servants,
Either. They were our gods working all night
To make Achilles' beard fall out and prop up
The House of Priam, who just by pointing sent
A shark fin gliding down a corridor,
Almost transparent, like a watermark.

FREDERICK SEIDEL, from *These Days*

I

AMY L. GUNDERSON

Washington / Samarkand

January 1979

1

$\blacklozenge$

ANNA BARNES COMPLETED HER TRAINING ON THE THIRD Wednesday of January 1979, a day after the Shah left Iran. It was not an auspicious moment to sign on as an American intelligence officer. The CIA was scrambling all over Europe and the Middle East that week, trying to save the thousands of Iranians who had been foolish enough to believe that the Imperium Americanum in that part of the world would last more than a few haphazard decades. And the agency was failing. America's friends (many of them less than admirable characters, it must be said) were being rounded up in Tehran; a few had already been killed.

That January was the sort of moment that intelligence agencies dread, for it seemed to call the entire enterprise into question. An intelligence agency is built around an implicit promise: We will keep faith with you. We will never betray you, or leave you to the mercy of your enemies. But who could believe such a promise from America now? It was always a lie, even in the best of times. Intelligence agencies betray people every day. But they don't like it to be quite so obvious as it was in those frantic weeks of early 1979, when the United States was on the run and its friends were being pursued like pigs in an abattoir. It looked bad. It frightened the new recruits.

Anna Barnes didn't have much of a graduation, as it happened. Late that Wednesday afternoon her instructor finished a lecture on agent development and said: "I guess that's it." He shook her hand and walked out the door of the motel room in Arlington where he had been holding classes for the past two weeks. And that was it. There was no diploma, no shaking hands with the director, no fond farewells to class-

3

mates, no plans to meet for drinks next summer in Vienna or Peshawar. Anna's only formal notice that she had completed her training came when she received a letter several days later, officially granting her a pseudonym—Amy L. Gunderson—which she would use forever after in agency cable traffic.

This can't be all there is to it, Anna told herself. But in her case, it was. She hadn't gone to "the farm" for training. She hadn't been near headquarters. She had not, in fact, attended a single lecture, briefing or orientation session that included any other recruit. Her training had consisted entirely of one-on-one meetings in motel rooms and safe houses around the Washington area. These sessions had covered the standard curriculum in tradecraft: the "flaps and seals" course in opening mail; the "crash-bang" course in high-speed driving and self-defense; the various lessons in recruitment and development of agents. But in every instance, she was the only student.

It was all very flattering. But for Anna, who a year before had been a doctoral candidate in Ottoman history, it was also a bit lonely. "You're special," an instructor had told her early on. That made it sound like a program for children with learning disabilities. But the mandarins knew what they were doing. Anna was in a kind of quarantine, whose purpose was to keep her work as close to secret as possible, even from most of her colleagues. That was because Anna Barnes was about to become a case officer under non-official cover, known in the secret language of the club as a NOC.

The closest thing Anna had to a real graduation was a meeting in late January with a senior member of the clandestine service named Edward Stone. He had been chief of the Near East Division for more than a decade, but Anna gathered from the person who set up the meeting that Stone was doing something different now, although it wasn't clear exactly what that was. All they told Anna was that Mr. Stone had heard about her unusual language skills—she had studied French, Turkish, Persian and German at various points during her training as an Ottomanist—and had asked especially to see her before she headed overseas.

Once upon a time, in the bad-old good-old days, such a

meeting would have taken place in a suite at the Madison Hotel, or a private dining room at Rive Gauche, or the drawing room of a retired ambassador in Georgetown. But this was 1979 and the rendezvous took place at a Holiday Inn off Interstate 270, next to a suburban office park and alongside one of those restaurants made out of derelict freight cars. It wasn't Stone's fault. That was the way they did things now. Some congressman might raise hell if word got out that senior CIA officers were meeting young recruits at French restaurants.

Anna wanted to make a good impression on Stone, but she was still not clear, after all the months of training, just what a woman intelligence officer was supposed to look like. Was she supposed to be sleek or bulky? Plain or pretty? Hard or soft? Anna wasn't sure, and she suspected that nobody else quite knew either. Women case officers in those days were still rather rare, and women NOCs were almost nonexistent. Which meant, Anna decided, that she could look however she pleased. She chose a sober outfit: blue suit and white cotton blouse. Almost a uniform. Even in this dull garb, she was an attractive woman, with luminous blue-green eyes and shoulder-length black hair, whose dark color was accented by a few strands in the middle that were prematurely turning gray. She had the look of a sleek animal: well bred, but with a distant memory of life in the wild.

Anna arrived first at the Holiday Inn and went straight to the room. It was as tacky and depressing as only a motel room on an interstate highway can be. She closed the drapes, then sat on the bed and looked around. It seemed possible that in the entire room there was not a single object made of a natural substance. Certainly not the brown fire-retardant drapes; not the green, fringed polyester bedspread; not the wood-grain plastic of the desk and bed tables; not the sooty tan rug; not the grainy bedsheets. Anna was gazing at this artificial landscape when there was a knock at the door and into the room walked a man who was all leather and wool and starched cotton.

"Hello, my dear," said Edward Stone, extending his hand. He was a courtly man in his early sixties, well groomed and well spoken.

"How do you do, sir," said Anna. She wanted to sound like a military officer, which in a sense was what she was.

"I do fine. But don't call me sir. It makes me feel old."

So he's a flirt, thought Anna.

"I brought you a little something," said Stone. He walked over to the bed, sat down, and opened a brown shopping bag. Inside was a bottle of French champagne. He forced the cork, which exploded noisily and hit the ceiling, just missing the automatic sprinkler.

"I didn't bring any glasses, I'm afraid," said Stone. He went to the bathroom and retrieved two squat motel-issue tumblers, into which he poured champagne up to the rim.

"Welcome to the club," he said, raising his glass.

Anna lifted her glass and took a long drink. The fizz of the champagne tickled her nose and throat.

"To success," said Stone.

"To not screwing up," replied Anna.

Stone smiled. "Don't worry. You'll find that the job is actually very easy. Absurdly easy, when things are going right."

They sat down in two Holiday Inn chairs by the window. Anna had pulled the drapes for security, but Stone opened them again. The winter sun was shining, glinting off the tile at the bottom of the empty pool. Stone took off the jacket of his gray pinstripe suit and unbuttoned his vest. He looked at once elegant and weary.

"Always close the drapes," said Anna, repeating a nugget of tradecraft that one of her instructors had dispensed several months before.

"We're in Rockville," said Stone. "Nobody cares."

Anna nodded. She felt like a greenhorn.

Stone had another drink of champagne and turned to his young companion. "Tell me a bit about yourself," he said. "I gather you were studying Ottoman history. That sounds exciting."

"Not to most people," said Anna. "My dissertation topic was 'Administrative Practices in the Late Ottoman Empire.' "

"And what was it about?"

"It was about how empires try to save themselves in their declining years."

"How timely," said Stone. "And how did the Ottomans try to save themselves, if I may ask?"

"By keeping their subjects at each other's throats. The Ottomans were masters at sowing dissension. It was one of the few things they were good at, actually."

"Not really an option for us, is it?"

Anna shook her head.

"Why did you leave this sublime work and decide to be an intelligence officer?"

"I was bored," said Anna. It was the truth, or at least part of it. After her third year of work on her dissertation, she had felt as dead as the Ottoman texts she was studying. She was falling out of love with an associate professor of English whose idea of a big time was buying an ice-cream cone at Steve's, and she wanted a change. She had delivered a paper on the Ottomans at an agency-sponsored conference, been approached afterward by a recruiter, and never looked back.

"Dubious motivation," said Stone.

"Why?"

"Because you'll find that the work of an intelligence officer, when performed competently, is also extremely boring."

Anna studied Stone's face. He didn't look bored. He just looked tired.

"More champagne?"

"Definitely," said Anna. He filled both glasses.

"And how did you learn all those languages?" asked Stone.

"I had to," said Anna. "It's sort of a union card for Ottomanists."

"Is it?"

"The Ottoman historians have a joke," she explained. "A young graduate student goes to the professor and says he wants to be an Ottomanist. 'Do you read Turkish?' asks the professor. Yes. 'Do you read Arabic?' Yes. 'Do you read Persian?' Yes. 'Do you read German?' Yes. 'Do you read Russian?' No. 'Well, come back when you learn to read Russian.' "

Stone laughed. "That's very funny," he said.

"I used to think so, too," said Anna. "Until I tried to study Russian."

"Well now," said Stone genially, finally getting around to the point. "You're probably wondering what this meeting is all about."

"Actually, yes. I was wondering that."

"If it's any relief, I don't intend to give you a lecture about how hard it is for a woman to be a case officer."

"Good," said Anna. "I've already had that lecture. Several times."

"And you shouldn't take any of what I'm going to tell you too seriously, because you won't be working for me. You'll be working for the chief of the London station, and through him for the chief of the European Division. Nonetheless, I did want to meet you myself before you headed out because, from your résumé, you appear to be a promising young officer."

Anna narrowed her eyes. "What are you chief of, if you don't mind my asking?"

"Good question," he said. Anna waited for a response, but it didn't come. Apparently it was not such a good question, or at least not one that Stone intended to answer. He sat in his chair, holding his champagne glass up to the light and watching the bubbles.

"This is not a very happy time for the United States," Stone continued after a few moments. "And it is an especially unhappy time for the organization you are joining. We're not supposed to say that. But it should be obvious to any intelligent person."

"I don't have much to compare it with," said Anna.

"Of course you don't. But take my word for it. How old are you?"

"Twenty-nine. Next month."

Stone sighed and shook his head. "As you'll soon discover," he said, "it's not much fun to operate in this sort of environment. It's much easier when you're on top of the hill and everybody wants to be your friend. When you're king of the hill, you don't have to recruit agents. They recruit themselves. They think that helping the United States will make them rich or powerful. Nowadays, people must worry that it will get them killed."

"Come now," said Anna. "Things can't be that bad."

Stone gave a thin smile. He looked so tired and gloomy that Anna felt she should try to cheer him up. He reminded her slightly of a philosophy professor she'd had at Harvard, a man who had concluded late in life that the world was such a mess that intellectual work was pointless. Anna had tried to cheer him up too, to encourage him to return to teaching and writing, until she realized one day that the despairing old professor was actually trying to seduce her. That made his angst somewhat less compelling, and she snubbed him. Stone couldn't be that demoralized.

"Personally, I can't wait to get started," she said cheerily.

"Glad to hear it," said Stone. "Glad to hear it. And you'll be going to London as a NOC, is that right?"

"Yes."

"And your cover will be as a banker with a firm called Halcyon Ltd.?"

"Yes." Anna wondered how Stone knew these details. They were supposed to be closely held secrets.

"And who are you supposed to handle, exactly?"

Anna thought a moment. "I'm not sure. People passing through London. Iranians, Arabs, Turks. They weren't very specific."

"Quite a handful."

"I guess so."

"What about Uzbeks?"

"Excuse me?"

"What about people from the Soviet republic of Uzbekistan? Did anyone suggest that you should try to make contact with them?"

"No."

"Or Azeris. Or Armenians. Or Abkhazians. Or Kazakhs? With your language skills, you would be an ideal person to work with such people. Anybody mention them?"

"Nope."

Stone nodded. "Of course they didn't. Why should they? People from the Caucasus and Central Asia don't travel much to London. Or anywhere else, for that matter. Which is a shame."

"Why?"

"Because, my dear, they are the key to the puzzle."

Anna studied him, trying to figure out what he was talking about. What key? What puzzle?

"We have a problem with the Soviet Union, as you have undoubtedly noticed from reading the newspapers," continued Stone. "But what, exactly, is this problem?"

Anna shrugged her shoulders.

"The problem is that the Russians appear to be strong and confident, while the United States appears to be confused and weak. And that seems to be especially true in the great disaster area that stretches from Turkey to Afghanistan, which the newsmagazines lately have taken to calling 'the crescent of crisis.' That is what most people perceive, is it not?"

"Yes," said Anna. Why, she wondered to herself, is he telling me all this?

"But the reality is quite different, if only we had enough sense to see it." Stone raised his index finger, as if he had just come to this conclusion. "It is the Soviet Union that is weak in that part of the world. Fatally weak. And it is the United States that has the leverage, if we would only use it. For the Soviet Union is, to put it bluntly, a vast house of cards waiting for a strong breeze."

"It looks pretty solid to me."

"Of course it does—at the center. It's all too solid there. But at the edges, it's falling apart. It's a mess. All anyone has to do is blow hard and the entire country is going to fall over. Just ask an Armenian, or a Georgian, or an Uzbek. He'll tell you."

Anna eyed him curiously. She thought she was beginning to get the point. "How am I going to meet any Uzbeks?" she said. "As you were saying, they don't pass through London much."

"Keep your eyes open."

"Is that an assignment?"

"Of course not," said Stone, drawing back in his chair. "I have no authority to give you assignments. Moreover, it would be against official policy."

"What policy?"

"The United States has a strict policy against encouraging secessionist feelings in any of the Soviet republics."

"Why? If I'm allowed to ask."

"Because it is thought to be too dangerous. It looks too much like going for the jugular. I rather like that aspect, myself. But our friends at the State Department seem to think it could lead to nuclear war."

"Oh."

"So it would be wrong for me to encourage you to do any such thing."

"Um-hum," said Anna. She couldn't help smiling.

"Quite wrong," repeated Stone. He smiled back at her.

"And in the unlikely event that I should ever meet one of these untouchable characters, who should I tell about it?"

"Oh, I'm probably as good a person to contact as anyone," said Stone, still smiling. He didn't look quite so tired anymore.

Stone drained his glass of champagne and glanced at his watch.

"Alas," he said, "I must attend a meeting back at headquarters. How much nicer it would be to spend the afternoon talking with you about the real work of intelligence. But that would offend the paper pushers, I'm afraid."

He rose from his chair and shook her hand. "You are a person of considerable talent. I expect great things from you."

"Thanks," said Anna.

"You must come see me on your next trip home."

"I'd like to," said Anna. "Very much."

She was going to ask Stone how she could contact him, just in case she ever needed to reach him in a hurry. But he was out the door and gone.

2

♦

THE NIGHT BEFORE ANNA BARNES LEFT FOR LONDON, SHE HAD dinner with her mentor, Margaret Houghton. It was a fitting send-off, since it was Margaret who in a sense had gotten the whole thing started. "Aunt Margaret," though not actually an aunt, was an old friend of the family, a slender, soft-spoken woman who came to dinner on Christmas and Easter and brought the children exotic gifts from around the world.

Anna had known for years, in the way that one knows something mildly scandalous about a relative, that Margaret Houghton did something mysterious for a living. No one would ever say what; apparently it was too awful to be discussed. Anna had forced the issue one Christmas and asked her father where Margaret worked. He had rolled his eyes and said: "You know . . . up the river." He might have been talking about the Amazon, for all Anna knew. But when she finally caught on, she found the idea quite titillating. Aunt Margaret worked at the CIA!

Margaret's cover had always been her gentility. She was a slight woman now in her early sixties, who wore her hair in a neat bun, and would occasionally brush an invisible wisp of it off her scarcely lined forehead. She had a fine, long neck and a graceful carriage, and a trace of an old southern accent in her voice. But there was something about her that hinted that she was a woman who at some point had lived a great adventure. A tragic romance, perhaps, or a fortune squandered. A hundred years ago, people would have described her as "European," and not meant it entirely as a compliment.

The two of them seemed an innocent enough pair as they entered Jean-Pierre restaurant on K Street: Margaret dressed in a brown tweed suit that hid her figure; Anna in a gray cashmere dress that flattered hers. Two generations of handsome, well-educated women. Mother and daughter, perhaps; or, more likely, a stylish maiden aunt taking her favorite niece out for dinner. A fellow diner would have taken them for anything but what they were. And that, as Margaret liked to say, was only one of the advantages that women had in the intelligence business.

Anna let the maître d' remove her coat. It had been chilly outside. She tilted her head forward to remove a silk scarf, and back, so that her long black hair fell free. She followed the maître d' and Margaret to a quiet table in the rear. Anna's movements were easy and uncontrived, but she caught the attention of several male diners in the restaurant.

"I still have one reservation about you," said Margaret when they were seated. "You may be too attractive for this line of work."

Margaret had made a similar observation a year before, when Anna first expressed an interest in joining the clandestine service. She was still a graduate student then, writing the dissertation that she couldn't seem to finish, living with the man she didn't quite love, and feeling ready to explode. Initially, Margaret had discouraged her from joining the agency. "If you have something to prove, stay away," Margaret had said. "We don't need women with chips on their shoulders, or slits in their skirts." Margaret's remark had seemed unfair to Anna then, but the point had been made. Beauty was insecure. It called attention to itself.

"I'm celebrating!" said Anna. She lit a cigarette.

Beauty aside, Anna had struck everyone as a natural for the CIA. Her father had been a foreign service officer, so she had traveled the world as a girl, learning languages and studying strange cultures. Her mother had died of cancer when Anna was in her early teens, so she had drawn even closer to her father. She was still the ambassador's daughter—still fascinated by his world, still peering through the door of his study to the smoke-filled room where he read his books and drafted his cables. Except now the door was wide open, and she could walk through. In that sense, Anna was part of the new line of succession that had begun to develop in the 1970s among children of the Establishment. The sons might be living at the summer house in Maine year-round, or studying astrology in New Mexico. But the daughters were there, waiting to take their places at the great law firms and banking houses. And yes, even at the CIA.

"Who's Edward Stone?" asked Anna, exhaling a big puff of smoke.

"Why on earth do you want to know that?"

"I met him a few days ago. He seemed like an awfully nice man, but I couldn't tell what he wanted."

"That's his style," said Margaret. "He never says what he wants. He lets you figure it out."

"So you know him."

"Of course I know him. You forget. I know everybody."

"What does he do?"

"I'm not entirely sure. He used to run the Near East Division. But I gather he has his own compartment now."

"What does that mean?"

"It means that I don't know."

"Does he have anything to do with the Soviet Union?"

"Shhh."

The waiter arrived. Margaret ordered a Tanqueray martini,

straight up, with a twist of lemon. Anna ordered the same thing. It was a celebration, after all. The waiter looked surprised. In the fraternity of waiters, women dining together are regarded as cheapskates. They don't drink, they order salads, and they tip ten percent. Spending money in restaurants does not ordinarily give them the same rosy glow of substantiality it does men. Margaret had discovered some years ago that if she ordered food and drink like a man, she would be treated like one, at least by waiters.

"What's he like?" asked Anna.

"Who?"

"Stone."

"He's one of the old boys. I suppose he's like the rest of them, only a bit smarter. To be honest, when you've been around them as long as I have, their personalities begin to blur a bit."

"What are they like then, the old boys?"

"You know very well what they're like," said Margaret. "They drink too much. They screw too much. They're smooth and confident and they like to talk loud in restaurants."

"Stone wasn't loud."

"He's quieter. But he's still one of the boys. You have to remember that I have spent a lifetime watching these men, usually from a quite subordinate position. So I know the sorts of things about them that they don't know about each other."

"Like what?"

"Their vanity. Their anxieties. Their weaknesses. The things that women know about men. Although in Stone's case, I must admit I've never heard him express a moment's anxiety or doubt about anything."

The waiter returned with the drinks.

"To London!" said Margaret, clinking her glass.

"To success!" responded Anna. She was beginning to like this idea of a secret club whose mission was to travel abroad, eat in good restaurants and save the world.

"He seemed sort of sexy," continued Anna. "For a man in his sixties."

"Who?"

"Stone."

Margaret laughed. "Of course he does," she said. "They all

do. That's the thing about secrets. They give a man a certain air of knowing what he's doing, even if he doesn't have a clue. I think that's why they all stayed in so long, actually."

"To get laid?"

"Really, Anna!" Margaret looked at the younger woman in mock horror. But of course that was exactly what she meant.

"What would he be like to work for?"

"Why? Did he offer you a job?"

"No," said Anna. "I was just curious."

"He'd be fine, up to a point. But what you have to understand about the old boys is that it is hard for them to imagine women as colleagues. They think of us the way adults think of children. They like us, enjoy us. Respect us, even. But we are in a different category."

"Stone looked tired."

"They all look tired," said Margaret. "And no wonder. They *are* tired. Exhausted. Things haven't been going too well for the old boys, if you hadn't noticed. Their world is collapsing, and they don't know what to do about it."

"What about the younger ones?"

"They're a mess."

"How do you mean?"

"They would like to be like the old boys, but they can't because the world has changed. The dumb ones still try. But the smart ones know it's impossible."

"So what do they do, the smart ones?"

"They get flaky. Or they quit."

The waiter approached again and recited the evening's specials.

"I'll have the string-bean salad," said Anna, "and the grilled sole, with no sauce." The waiter frowned.

"That's not much of a meal," said Margaret. She turned to the waiter. "I'll have oysters. And a rib-eye steak." Her tone conveyed the authority of the carnivore.

"I've changed my mind," said Anna. "I'll have the same thing. The oysters and the steak."

"Yes, madam," said the waiter, radiating the glow of his now quite substantial customers. "Would you like to see the wine list?"

"Of course," said Anna. And she picked out a quite respectable red Burgundy.

* * *

Anna had not been entirely honest with Stone, or with Margaret, for that matter. The factors that had drawn her toward working for the CIA were more complicated than simple boredom. She was afflicted with the disease, common and occasionally fatal among intelligence officers, of wanting to make the world better. She had, in that sense, a deadly ambition to do good. What had pushed her toward leaving Harvard was a growing sense of the disarray and misery in the world. She read about Lebanese being slaughtered on the streets of Beirut or the massacres by the Khmer Rouge and she wanted to do something about it. When people experience such feelings in their late teens, they join protest marches; when it happens in their late twenties, they—on occasion—join the CIA.

Anna had not been completely honest about her research either. Far from the dry investigation she had described to Stone, it was wet with the blood of generations of Ottoman victims. Her dissertation had brought her to the edge of one of the world's great calamities—the collapse of the Ottoman Empire in World War I and the slaughter of Armenians and Turks in eastern Anatolia. She had become interested in the subject initially through her freshman roommate at Radcliffe, an Armenian-American named Ruth Mugrditchian. Poor Ruth, with the unpronounceable name and the large, sad eyes. Her family lived in Worcester, and Anna—the Wasp princess from boarding school—had not been sure at first whether to accept when Ruth invited her home for Thanksgiving. But she said yes, and the tales she heard over those four days about the massacres of 1915 left a lasting impression. She heard how Ruth's great-aunt Ahvanie had staggered across the Syrian desert with a Bible in her hand, collapsed in a ditch exhausted and starving, and been left for dead—yet somehow summoned enough strength from her Bible to make it to Aleppo, and then America. She heard the story of Suren, the grandfather of Ruth's cousin, whose dying mother had bribed an Arab to take her little son and hide him in a well until the Turks were gone. Suren, too, eventually made it to America. It was like joining a private conspiracy, hearing these tales of suffering and redemption, and to a Radcliffe freshman from an old Yankee family, they left a taste as sharp as a ripe fig.

Anna's problem was that in addition to liking Armenians, she also liked Turks. She found them, on the whole, a rather attractive and disciplined people. That deepened for her the mystery of what had happened in Turkey in the late nineteenth and early twentieth centuries. It would have been simpler if the massacres had been conducted by utterly despicable people. But that would have made the moral dilemma too easy. What interested her, Anna decided, was when civilized people did monstrous things. Those were the events worth studying.

Once Anna became an Ottoman historian in earnest, her studies evolved into a search for the moment at which the world had jumped the tracks and the horrific history of the twentieth century—the two world wars, the slaughter of six million Jews, the death of twenty million Soviets during World War II and a like number in Stalin's gulags—could be said to have begun. Anna suspected that it was Ruth Mugrditchian who knew the true answer. The world went mad on April 8, 1915, the day Ottoman Turks began to march the Armenian population of Anatolia, more than a million people, across the deserts to their death. Like a good scholar, Anna began to look for the roots of that madness. And the search carried her toward the secret world where all great tragedies begin. Eventually, one of her professors approached her and made the necessary introductions. He saw in Anna the ability to work alone, which every scholar must have, and also an idealism and a need to act that could be harnessed to the purposes of the Central Intelligence Agency.

Anna took a big drink of her gin martini. "Here's to women in the business!" Her bravado didn't quite conceal the edge of anxiety in her voice.

"Shhh," said Margaret, clinking her glass.

"I probably shouldn't say this," said Anna, "but I'm a little nervous."

"Of course you are," answered Margaret. "I'd be worried if you weren't."

"Tell me something honestly," said Anna. "Can a woman really do this job as well as a man?"

"Absolutely," said Margaret. "I am living proof of it."

Anna smiled. She knew enough, by this time, to understand the limits of Margaret's experience and accomplishments. Margaret was a trailblazer, yes. But she had worked mostly at headquarters, mostly in administration. Her recruitments had largely been of American professors and businessmen, nice, gentle, patriotic fellows who traveled to conferences in the Eastern bloc. When she finally made station chief, it was in one of those nondescript little countries of Western Europe where the biggest threat to national security was that somebody might steal the secret recipe for making the national brand of cheese.

"I guess I need a little handholding," said Anna.

Margaret took Anna's hand in hers.

"I didn't mean literally," said Anna. But she left her hand in Margaret's for a moment.

"You must remember that women have some big advantages in our line of work," said the older woman.

"Name one."

"I'll name several. We can control our emotions better than men. We can be braver, more disciplined, more discreet. And we can be invisible where a man would immediately be suspect."

"How can a woman be invisible?"

"What is ordinary is invisible. And there is nothing on earth more ordinary than a woman meeting with a man. That's why an American woman can go to dinner with a foreign man, even in Moscow, without arousing suspicion. People will look at them drinking and talking, and assume they know what's going on."

Anna looked around the restaurant, at the tables of men and women talking. It was true. There was no better cover.

"But women *do* have one great disadvantage," said Margaret.

"What's that?"

"They must deal with men."

Anna laughed.

"It is a sad fact of life," Margaret continued, "that the people with secrets are likely to be men. And it is another fact that most men don't regard women as equals. Consequently, they don't trust women, and that means they don't feel comfortable putting their lives in the hands of a woman."

"They would rather hit on women."

"Excuse me?"

"It's a modern expression. When you say a man is hitting on you, it means he's trying to go to bed with you."

"Precisely my point," said Margaret. "And this presents an obvious problem in our line of work. Because in the early stages of any case, you will have to be alone with the man you hope to recruit. You won't have told him yet what you really do, but in his mind there will be just two possibilities to explain your interest. Either you want to sleep with him . . ."

"Or you're a spy."

Margaret nodded. "Either way, you have a problem. That is why it would help you professionally if you were less attractive. I don't mean to be a bore on this subject, and I certainly don't expect you to go out and gain fifty pounds for the good of the firm. But it would help."

"You're not fat," said Anna.

"No, but I'm old."

The oysters had arrived. Anna picked one off the plate, held it to her mouth, tipped it upward, and let the oyster slide gently down her throat. Margaret used her fork.

"Let me describe the perfect woman case officer," said Margaret when the waiter had left. "She would be attractive, but not sexy. She would be confident, without a chip on her shoulder. She would be comfortable about being a woman, but not a women's libber."

"What about the perfect male case officer?"

"He doesn't exist."

"All right then, the typical male case officer."

"There is only one useful generalization, from your standpoint. Your male colleagues will be tremendously tempting as sexual partners, because they will be the only people you can fully relax with. My advice is: Don't do it."

"Did you?"

"Did I what?"

"Sleep with them."

"Of course I did. Every chance I got. But I'm still single, and most of them are still married."

Anna thought about that. She had no interest in getting married anytime soon. Still, she didn't think she wanted to end life alone, remembering all the married men she had slept with.

"Would you like to hear some female success stories?" asked Margaret.

"Absolutely. The more successful, the better."

"You may not like them."

"Of course I will."

"All right, but I warned you." Margaret lowered her voice further, so that it was barely above a whisper.

"The most successful woman operator we ever had began as a secretary. Audrey, I believer her name was. She had no education past high school, and she was married to a mailman."

"A mailman?" Anna lit another cigarette. "No wonder she went into the business."

"The mailman divorced her, leaving her with three children to support. Audrey needed a larger salary. Everyone in the clandestine service liked her, so she was promoted to be a clerk in the registry. It turned out that she had a fantastic memory for names and dates, so she was promoted again, to be a research analyst in counterintelligence. And she was superb in that job, so we decided to give her a chance as a case officer overseas, in Europe. Are you getting my point?"

"I don't think so."

"Audrey's secret was that everybody liked her. You couldn't help it. She had a quality that you find sometimes in a good salesperson in a department store. The woman who's so warm and friendly that you can't help talking to her while you're trying on dresses, and pretty soon you're telling her your life story and buying something much more expensive than you planned. Audrey was like that. And she had those three children, which made her respectable and safe, and discouraged foolishness on the part of men. Even though she was quite attractive. Bosomy, with very blond hair, nail polish, that sort of thing."

"Cheap, in other words."

"No. Not cheap. Just down-to-earth. We sent her to Europe, as third secretary in one of our big embassies, and targeted her on an engineer who had access to very secret research. He was in his late fifties, with a wife back in the provinces, and he was quite lonely. So Audrey began seeing him in the evenings. They would go out to a restaurant, or a movie. But never to bed. Audrey made sure of that, and the three children helped reinforce it. If it got late, she would remind the engineer that she had to get home to her children. Or sometimes she would invite him over to dinner, and he would play with the kids. They became like a second family for him."

"So how did she recruit him? Or did she leave that to one of the boys?"

"I'm getting to that. Audrey encouraged the scientist to talk about his work, as any woman would with a man she liked. And at some point she said, 'Listen, someone in my office is very interested in this subject. Could you help us by pulling together some newspaper articles about it?' And then, a few months later, she asked if maybe he could write a little analysis of his own, and then, maybe a longer study? And before long, the engineer was bringing Audrey documents out of his safe. He loved her, you see, even though it wasn't sexual. It was a classic case, in its way."

"Very sweet," said Anna. "But I'd love to hear a success story that doesn't involve an ex-secretary with a heart of gold."

"Don't be a snob, dearie."

"I'm sorry. I didn't mean that the way it must have sounded. It's just that Audrey's approach—the three children and all that—doesn't seem very relevant for a single, childless Ottoman historian manqué."

"Fair enough," said Margaret. "I'll give you another example. But I'm not sure you're going to like it any better than the first one."

"Try me."

"I'm thinking of a woman whose background was very similar to yours. She was an economist, with a degree from Bryn Mawr and a doctorate from somewhere or other. A charming, cultivated woman from a good family. And she proved to be one of our better women recruiters."

"What was her trick?"

"She played to her strengths. She was an elegant, upper-middle-class woman who traveled easily in that world and used it to her advantage. We put her in the proper milieu in Western Europe, where she could make contact with foreigners of a similar background. We gave her appropriate diplomatic rank, high enough that she could entertain people who mattered. Eventually, she began to get access to real information."

"That's a marvelous story. Why did you think I wouldn't like it?"

"Because the woman in question was a bit heavy. That was probably one of her advantages. It helped her men friends feel more comfortable with her. The sexual tension wasn't there."

Anna frowned. "You make it sound as if men are only comfortable with ugly women."

"You misunderstand me," said Margaret. She finished the last of her oysters and laid the shells in a row. "What I am saying is that in this era of sexual freedom, it is more difficult than you might think for a young, attractive American woman to get a foreign man to think about something other than sex. There is a notion abroad in the world that American women are easy lays."

"Outrageous!" said Anna. She studied the neat row of oyster shells. For such a personal subject, the conversation seemed awfully impersonal. "Margaret?" she ventured.

"Yes."

"What did you do when someone you were trying to recruit made a pass at you?"

"Ah," said Margaret. She closed her eyes and brushed one of those invisible hairs away from her face. "What did I do? Generally, I would pretend that it wasn't happening. I would maintain distance in the thousands of subtle ways that a woman can. Some women, without realizing it, often seem to be saying yes—through the tone of their voice, the look in their eye, the way they sit in a chair. Generally, I tried to make sure that I was saying no."

"Generally?"

"Every case is different. Sometimes it's useful to show a bit of leg."

"Did you ever sleep with one of your agents?"

"Never," she said quickly. Too quickly. "Never for operational reasons," she added, in a tone meant to close the subject.

"What does that mean?" pressed Anna, but the older woman wouldn't be drawn.

The waiter arrived, opened the Burgundy and served the steaks with great ceremony. He seemed to think there was something quite grand about two women feasting on such a meal. And they did have a grand time, eating and drinking and talking. By the end of the meal, Anna was flush with food and drink and becoming positively boisterous.

"Let me at 'em!" she said exuberantly. "I'm going to kick ass! You wait and see."

"Don't say that, my dear."

"Why not? I'm going to do it the way the old boys do. Tough. Cool. No nonsense. Take no prisoners."

"Stop it!" said Margaret sharply.

"What's wrong? That's the way the game is played."

"No, it's not. Or at least it doesn't have to be."

"How would you know?" demanded Anna. It was the cruelest thing she could have said, and she regretted it the moment the words were out of her mouth.

The older woman brushed another of those invisible hairs off her face. "My dear Anna," she said, "I am going to give you one last piece of advice, and I hope you will remember it."

"I'm sorry. I'm listening."

"You don't have to play the game the way men do. They are always talking about kicking ass, and squeezing information out of people, and busting their balls and being a tough SOB and that sort of thing. And I suppose it reassures them, all that tough talk. But that is not the way the business works. Not unless you're a Nazi."

Anna eyed the older woman skeptically. "So how does it work, if you're not a Nazi?"

"Gently. You usually get more information from people by stroking them than by threatening them. Talk to them, flatter them, listen to their boring stories; occasionally, let them imagine you are seducing them."

"In other words, act like a woman." Anna said the last word derisively, but Margaret ignored her.

"Precisely. Don't be afraid to be gentle. All the locker-room talk is silly. And usually it doesn't work."

"I'll think about it."

Margaret smiled. "Well, there you are. Now you know everything I know." She reached out her hand to Anna, shook it firmly, and then kissed her young protégée on the cheek.

"No, I don't," said Anna.

"What have I left out?"

"You've told me how the game is played, but not to what end. And you haven't explained why you first got into the business."

"That's for another night, I think."

"I'm leaving tomorrow."

"Let's just say that I'm like Edward Stone. We're from the same generation. We went through the same war. We learned the same lessons."

"Come on! What were they?"

"We learned how to manipulate people. And we learned to like it."

Anna nodded sagely, but she had barely heard. "To London!" she said, raising her wineglass one last time. If she had been wearing a mortarboard, she would have tossed it in the air.

3

♦

Edward Stone's final crusade began that January in the city of Samarkand, in the Soviet republic of Uzbekistan. He was not there in person, of course. He was half a world away, in an office in Langley removed by several floors, and at least one generation, from the new crowd who imagined that they were running American intelligence. But Stone was certainly there in spirit, and he was there by proxy as well. For if there was one thing that Edward Stone had accumulated in a lifetime of work in the spy business, it was the friendly assistance of other spymasters, known in the trade as "liaison."

Stone had thirty-five years' worth of contacts upon which to draw—with British, French, Germans, Lebanese, Saudis, Iranians, Pakistanis, Afghanis. Indeed, he had practically built some of those nations' intelligence services himself. The resulting bonds of loyalty transcended mere agent relationships and became a web of obligation that was stronger, more pervasive, and far less visible. For liaison was the one form of U.S. intelligence activity that remained hidden from prying eyes—not subject to review by Congress, occasionally not even reported to the White House. And that gave Stone and his foreign friends considerable room to maneuver, even in the cosseted world of 1979, even in the dusty streets and alleyways of Samarkand.

The sun rose that particular January morning over a local landmark called the Gur Emir—the tomb of the great emir, Timur—illuminating its blue dome with the soft light of the Uzbekistan plain. A few Moslem pilgrims had come to the shrine at first light, to pray at the tomb of the conqueror, known to Europeans as Tamerlane. This sort of folk worship was frowned upon by the local viceroys of dialectical materialism. But the authorities could not stop it. And so the pilgrims came each morning: round-faced Uzbeks in four-cornered hats, their wives following a step behind in *aberband* silk dresses, bright as panes of stained glass; a few Turkmen, in long blue frock coats and powder-blue turbans, stroking the wispy strands of their forked beards.

The pilgrims sat under the mulberry trees that ringed the shrine, waiting for the guard to come and open the big padlock on the front door, take their forty kopecks, and let them in. They could have broken into the shrine if they had really wanted to. It was a large, open place, protected only by rickety wooden doors and a low wall that could be climbed by an Uzbek toddler; it was surrounded by a warren of private houses, each hiding its secrets behind plain, whitewashed walls. The Soviet authorities didn't even bother to post a blue-shirted militiaman to protect the place at night. What was worth protecting in this pagan shrine? It would have seemed almost a joke to any responsible official of the Samarkand Oblast.

Eventually a guard arrived, opened the gate and let the

faithful enter the tomb. They walked in cautiously under a crumbling brick archway, across the broad outer courtyard of the shrine and into the inner sanctum. It was musty inside, and so dark you could barely see the blue tiles on the walls. In the central chamber that held the sarcophagus of Tamerlane, even the sharp-eyed Uzbek pilgrims needed a few moments to become accustomed to the dark. The men shuffled and muttered; the women put their hands to their faces and whispered prayers. And then an old woman, a grandmother layered with the fat of a dozen childbirths, saw something amiss.

"Allah!" she cried, pointing to the tomb.

The other pilgrims looked toward the sarcophagus, made of jade that had once been green but was now almost black from age and neglect. The heavy jade lid of the sarcophagus had been pushed back several feet, opening the warrior's tomb.

"Allah!" said the old woman again, her voice trembling.

"The Prince of War has escaped!" whispered the oldest man in the group. He said it tentatively, hopefully, the way one of the disciples might have said, "Christ is risen!" on the first Easter morning.

The small room echoed, as others repeated the words. As these voices began to resonate in the small brick chamber, the old woman suddenly let out a shriek and pointed across the marble screen that surrounded Tamerlane's resting place toward a simpler mud-caked bier known as the Tomb of the Unknown Hajji. Embedded in that burial mound was the trunk of a poplar tree, tall as a telephone pole. Atop the poplar, suspended by a string, was a banner proclaiming in Arabic script: *"Allahu akhbar!"* God is great!

"Allahu akhbar!" cried the venerable old man, who learned to read the Koran as a boy, before the great modern darkness descended on Central Asia.

"Ahhhhh," gasped several of the Uzbeks.

"La ilaha illa-Llah," said the old man, repeating the Koranic injunction: There is no god but God.

"Allah! Allah!" chanted one of the Turkmen. He said the words quickly, with each breath of air, one after the other, like a Sufi *zikr.* Others repeated the chant, the sound surging louder and louder until it became a guttural rumble and the small chamber began to reverberate with the emotion of the pilgrims.

The noise aroused the guard, who came running into the mausoleum. When he saw the open tomb and the banner, he turned and ran from the chamber out into the courtyard, toward the telephone. The Moslem pilgrims rushed out after him, bellowing and chanting, disappearing down the small lanes and blind alleys that radiated out from the square. Ten minutes later the first contingent of militia arrived on their three-wheeled motorcycles, then a second detachment and a third, until they had surrounded the place. After thirty minutes, the army, too, had arrived from a nearby garrison. The troops, like the militiamen, were mostly native Uzbeks and they looked frightened. For already, on their way to the Gur Emir, they had heard rumors of what the pilgrims had found inside the tomb.

What thrilled the people—and frightened their keepers—was that every Uzbek knew it had happened once before, nearly forty years earlier. The tomb of Tamerlane had been opened then, and the Prince of War truly had been set loose upon the world. That earlier cataclysm had begun when the worshippers of Lenin, the apostles of science and progress, had come east with their charts and instruments to conduct experiments at the tomb. They came at the behest of a famous scientist, Academician Gerasimov, whose name and academic credentials were invoked before the natives like the incantation of a village headman. The holy academician, they were told, was an expert in reconstructing the face of a dead person from the surviving bones and dust, and he proposed to work his magic now on the face of the sublime conqueror Timur, the man who had razed entire towns—slaughtered every man, woman and child—if they so much as hinted at opposition. And now this Gerasimov wanted to measure the distance between the bridge of the great conqueror's nose and his occipital bone, reconstruct the set of his jaw, stretch artificial skin across the remains of his princely cheekbones. The Uzbeks had opposed it, had pleaded against it, but the academicians from Moscow paid no attention.

Gerasimov's men had come to Samarkand and pried open the great jade coffin and removed the noble remains of

Tamerlane. They said they wanted to find out if he really had been lame, as legend had it, so they measured his femur and his tibia and conducted other such worthy experiments. Perhaps they paused momentarily to read the inscription on the lid: "The Spirit of War Rests Within This Tomb"—which was surely a "Do Not Disturb" sign, left centuries before. But it can only have made them laugh. So they pressed down on their crowbars and pried open the heavy jade . . .

The day the academicians opened Tamerlane's tomb was June 21, 1941. History records that on that very day Hitler made his decision to invade the Soviet Union. It was a day on which the spirit of war truly burst forth—with greater savagery, perhaps, than at any time since Timur walked the earth five centuries ago. To the superstitious people of Central Asia, it had been obvious enough what had happened. Cause and effect.

And it would have been obvious, too, to any amateur student of Oriental ethnology; to any visiting American who happened to overhear several Pakistani friends narrate this astonishing tale, as Edward Stone did one evening during a visit to Peshawar. For such a person, it would have been almost impossible, once he had heard the tale, not to contrive an experiment that would test what might happen in the vast and silent lands of Central Asia if the tomb were to become open once again. It took so little effort—a few clever Uzbek operatives based in Peshawar—and it had the potential to cause so much trouble. But at first, for Stone, it was a game; a way of testing his liaison network, of oiling the machinery and making sure that it would work. And it offered, too, a modest test of his hypothesis that the Soviet edifice in Central Asia was frail and ready to crumble.

The easiest evidence to monitor was electronic. An hour after the open tomb was discovered, Radio Samarkand went dead. When it returned to the air a few minutes later, the announcer began reading propaganda material that had been scripted for such delicate moments by the Central Committee of the Communist Party of Uzbekistan. The voice was bland and unmodulated, the verbal equivalent of an eye that never blinks:

"Everything that is joyous and happy in the life of the people of Samarkand and of the Soviet East as a whole is associated with the heroic activities of the Communist Party and with the great leader of the revolution, Lenin," said the voice. "The Great October Socialist Revolution of 1917 marked the beginning of rejuvenation for the ancient city. Under the leadership of the Communist Party, the people of Samarkand realized revolutionary measures creating new schools, medical establishments, industrial enterprises and implementing agrarian transformation in the region. Comrades: At the hour of trial, the people of Samarkand gave a pledge to Lenin. They wrote: 'Dear Vladimir Ilyich. We swear to stand firmly and defend the gains of Soviet power. We shall rather perish in struggle than allow the enemies of the socialist revolution to overthrow Soviet power in Turkestan.' "

By noon, the news had spread throughout the city with the speed of fire burning through dry grass. The rumors traveled fastest along the several miles between the mausoleum and the bazaar, where the farmers gathered each day to sell the fruits and vegetables from their orchards and gardens. The bazaar was a wondrous place, nearly impervious to Soviet power. Farmers and merchants jostled against one another, beckoning in the same boisterous language as five hundred years ago, when the bazaar stood astride the Silk Road.

Now as then, the commodity traded best in the bazaar was rumor. The red-kerchiefed woman selling apricot nuts told the news of the open tomb to the woman selling almonds, who walked over to the spice table and told the old crone selling cardamom, whose husband overheard and shouted across to his friend selling onions; the news jumped a long aisle, toward the cabbage sellers, and the radish men, and the women stacking their carrots in neat pyramids; and it traveled back to the far reaches of the bazaar, to the sellers of fabric and shoes and books and hardware. People even went to the phone booths, covered by black metal roofs shaped like four-cornered hats, and called their friends.

By midday, the whole of the bazaar was in an uproar. At prayer time, a mullah climbed atop the roof of a coffeehouse at the far end of the bazaar and shouted, *"Allahu akhbar,"* in the wailing cry of the muezzin. Militiamen had been in the market since mid-morning and several of them ran after this impromptu mullah, but the chase was useless. Their way was blocked by burly Uzbeks and low, shambling Turkmen. They weren't deliberately resisting the militiamen; they just stood where they were, crowding the doorways of coffeehouses, slow and deliberate in their movements, the way people in Central Asia can be when they don't want to be rushed, when even the great god of history cannot move them out of the way.

Radio Samarkand continued to dispense its verbal balm:

"Comrades," said the radio. "There is an Uzbek legend about a golden book in a golden casket which was buried in the ground at the time of bloody invasions by evil tribes. Centuries passed and the people believed that a warrior would be born to find the book and return it to the people. There eventually came into this world a warrior whose mind was brighter than the sun, whose eyes were kind, whose smile instilled cheer and hope and refreshed the tired as a water spring in the desert, whose words were filled with great wisdom. This warrior was the great Lenin. He found the golden casket with the wonderful book and opened it to the Uzbek and other enslaved peoples of the world."

The Uzbeks began to turn off their radios, across the length of the bazaar, in the barbershops, even in the barracks of the militia. But the voice continued:

"Lenin transformed the legend into a long-expected reality. Under the guidance of Lenin, the Uzbek people joined the working class of Russia and their class brethren throughout the country and launched the struggle for freedom and socialism."

The radios were all extinguished now, but the unblinking voice continued to speak:

"The socialist revolution brought happiness into the home of every Uzbek. It meant freedom for the Uzbek people from social, economic and national oppression. Lenin died, but Leninism is alive—as firm and unshakable as a rock."

What Stone instinctively understood was that this fabric of lies would not last another generation. The revolt expressed itself that day, and every day, in small individual acts, as simple as the assertion that God exists in an officially godless state. The evidence of this Islamic revolt was as pervasive and invisible as the dust in the air. It was everywhere and nowhere; everyone was a believer and no one. It was as if the entire Uzbek nation were engaged in a genial deception of their Soviet overlords—friendly, smiling, taking whatever money and modern conveniences Moscow was willing to supply; wearing their war medals and party buttons on holidays and pinning Mother Heroine decorations on their wives when the tenth child was born, but believing not a word of the Marxist cant that surrounded their lives, and waiting always for a moment to speak the subversive name of God.

Had Stone been at the tomb of Qutham Ibn Abbas that day, alongside one of his far-flung correspondents, he would have seen one more small moment of the rebellion that he knew lay ahead. It was trivial in itself, but it was one of a thousand seeds of rebellion that were scattered across the plain of Central Asia, ready to sprout. This particular incident began early in the afternoon when a group of Uzbek farmers walked down the road from the bazaar to the holy shrine of Ibn Abbas, the Prophet Mohammed's cousin.

It happened quickly, almost as an act of guerrilla theater. The group climbed the long stairway up to the tomb. Inside, the small room was crowded with a busload of Russian tourists, listening to a lecture on native folklore from an officious Armenian guide. They tromped about the room in their heavy Russian shoes, with no thought that they were in a mosque, walking upon holy ground. To them it was a curiosity, a relic of the pagan past that made Central Asia a quaint tourist attraction.

The Uzbek group gave way and stood aside, staring reverently at the wooden screen that shielded the tomb—but blocked from it by the Russians with their cameras and their loud talk and their guide telling amusing anecdotes about the religious practices of the Moslems. The act of sedition came in the wink of an eye. As the Russian group began to leave the room, one Uzbek man motioned to his brothers and sisters to sit down. They squatted on their haunches with their backs against the north wall, the women in the group squatting just apart from the men, as the Koran commanded. The chant began the moment they were in place.

"Allahu akhbar," sang the mullah. He was in fact an ordi-

nary farmer, a graduate of no madrassah; almost certainly he
did not own a Koran; almost certainly he could not have read
it if he did. But that day, in that moment, he was a mullah,
calling his people to prayer.

"Ashhadu anna la ilaha illa-Llah." I bear witness that
there is no god but God. The tiny congregation, squatting
against the wall, murmured a response.

"Ashhadu anna Muhammadan rasulu-Llah." I bear witness
that Mohammed is the messenger of God.

He prayed quickly. The next Russian tour group would be
arriving any minute from the front gate, from the bookstore
where they sold atheist literature and anti-Islamic tracts. The
mullah hurried. The name of God was no less powerful if it
was said quickly.

"Allahu akhbar," he began again, repeating the call to
prayer.

"Ashhadu anna la ilaha illa-Llah."

The untutored mullah recited the fatiha, the first sura of the
Koran. He was racing now:

"Praise belongs to God, Lord of the Worlds,
 The Compassionate, the Merciful,
 King of the Day of Judgment,
 It is Thee we worship and Thee we ask for help.
 Guide us on the straight path,
 The path of those whom Thou has favored,
 Not the path of those who incur Thine anger
     nor of those who go astray."

The men and women put their hands to their faces, bowed,
put their hands to their faces again. In the small room the
sound echoed and reverberated so that it began to sound like
a great chorus of Moslems, rather than eight dusty Uzbek
farmers. An old Turkman appeared at the door in a blue coat
and white turban, his eyes alight with pleasure to hear the
sound of prayer. He put his hands to his face the moment he
entered the room and followed along. A few more old men
arrived and joined in the chant, but the sound of heavy shoes
and Russian voices was approaching.

It ended as suddenly as it had begun. The mullah broke off

at the last verse, stood up and led his little band out the door single file, into the world of God's grace, and Soviet power.

It was nearly a month before an account of these events in Uzbekistan—and a half dozen more that told the same story—made its way back to Edward Stone in Washington. The delay wasn't surprising, given the route the news traveled. It might have been borne by the Pathan horse trader Mahbub Ali, who roamed the strange land that Kipling called "the back of Beyond." A visiting trader in the marketplace of Samarkand made his way by rickety Russian bus down the road to Termez, at the southern border of Uzbekistan, stopping overnight in Karshi, and two nights in Sherabad. When he reached Termez, the man found his way to the back room of a particular coffeehouse, and chatted with a particular old Uzbek gentleman who had relatives living in Kabul. And somehow—better never to ask exactly how—the news traveled across the supposedly impermeable Soviet border, till it was the talk of Mazar-i-Sharif and Baghlan, and then down the great highway to Kabul. And from there it flowed steadily, like water tracing its course downhill, through the peaks and valleys of southern Afghanistan and across the frontier into Pakistan. And when the news reached Peshawar, it came to the attention of a very particular friend of Edward Stone's, a Pakistani gentleman who worked for an organization with the bland title Inter-Services Intelligence Directorate and who was, like Stone himself, a player of the Great Game.

And when it finally reached Stone's desk, the news brought a smile, a long moment of contemplation and the consideration of new ventures for the future.

II

AMOS B. GARRETT

Istanbul / Washington

January 23–26, 1979

4

◆

THE AMERICAN CONSULATE IN ISTANBUL AT LEAST LOOKED AS IF
it belonged to a superpower. It occupied a fine old marble
building in the center of town, and on a sunny day, with the
American flag flapping in the breeze off the Golden Horn, it
looked rather grand. Not quite as grand as the Soviet consulate, a salmon-pink palace a few blocks away. But entirely adequate to the American purpose in that part of the world,
which in the late 1970s rested on less secure foundations than
its diplomatic real estate.

The consulate building had been constructed in the 1870s by
a Genoese shipowner named Corpi. He had spared no expense,
importing marble and rosewood from Italy, and some of the
more high-minded members of the consulate staff still liked to
refer to the building as the "Palazzo Corpi." Signor Corpi had
died a few months after his dream house was completed, so he
never had much chance to enjoy the frescoes of nymphs and
satyrs cavorting on the dining-room ceiling. Neither did the
Americans, as it turned out. The United States purchased the
lavish building in 1907, frescoes and all, supposedly after
the American ambassador to Turkey bet the Speaker of the
House of Representatives in a poker game. But during the
1930s, a particularly prudish consul general's wife decided
the frescoes were pornographic and had them plastered over.

Every time Taylor looked up at that dull, whitewashed ceiling, he thought of the long-dead ambassador's wife and said
a silent curse. She was an American type, an example of our
national desire to paint over the world and blot out the dis-
turbing parts. Perhaps some people still regarded these Amer-
icanisms as harmless, but in 1979 Taylor had lost patience.

Alan Taylor was the CIA's base chief in Istanbul. He had

37

been assigned that post, rather than a larger station with more administrative responsibility, because he was what the agency liked to call a "natural recruiter." That wasn't quite a compliment. He was a handsome man, just under six feet, thin at the waist, with a barrel chest that occasionally made him look like a pugilist or a barroom bouncer, despite his dignified features. He had dark hair, which he combed straight back on his head, and although he did not appear to be a fastidious man, he never seemed to have a hair out of place.

Taylor was in his late thirties, in the foothills of middle age but walking backward. He had a vaguely continental look, and people on the street might have assumed he was English or French because of his clothes and manners. But he was in fact a distinct American type, just as much as that long-ago ambassador's wife: He was the rebellious preppy, the naughty boy from the good family, who loved nothing more than telling the world to go to hell. Men and women tended to say the same thing about Taylor: He was the most charming man they had ever met. He was, as they said, a natural recruiter.

Such people were a vanishing breed in the homogenized world of American intelligence. And the feeling back at headquarters was: good riddance. The hell with the macho Ivy Leaguers, the boys from Beacon Hill who swore like they were from South Boston. The new vogue at Langley was to hire salesmen as case officers. Not ordinary, used-car salesmen, mind you, but serious salesmen. The kind who graduated in the top half of their class at Penn State and went to work for General Electric selling million-dollar electric turbines, who could spend a whole year, cool and calm, preparing a customer for one big deal. The sort of men who could look you straight in the eye as they told their earnest American lies, and make you feel good about it. Whatever Taylor's faults, he was not a salesman.

Taylor did not refer to the consulate building, ever, as the "Palazzo Corpi." His wife had done so, in the months before she packed up and left Istanbul, and it had been one of the small things that had gotten on his nerves. She was the sort of woman who should had been married to a diplomat, to one of those sturdy fellows who spent their time drafting unreadable cables about visits by the POLOFF to the FORMIN of the GOT. Taylor's wife had loathed the CIA, which was another thing she shared with the diplomats. She called it "the Sandbox."

The State Department had a more elaborate code. They had become so skittish about the agency in recent years that even in secret cables they referred to it only euphemistically, as the "Special Reporting Facility." And then, when even that tame phrase seemed too specific, by a new four-letter code word— "SIRO"—which sounded like the beginning of something interesting, like "seraglio" or "sirocco," but in fact meant nothing at all.

Taylor entered the ornate chancery building only when it was absolutely necessary. His home was the shabby office next door, a grayish stucco building the color of Bosporus sludge, which housed the consular section and Taylor's office.

From his window in the annex, Taylor could see the walls of the old Pera Palas Hotel down the street, and when his mind wandered—which was often—he would imagine what it must have been like in the salad days of the spy business. A lobby full of absurdly conspicuous intelligence officers from all the capitals of Europe, smoking cigars and trading stories. Mysterious Oriental characters weaving among them, selling information. Exotic, ruined women taking the lift to assignations on the upper floors. It was said that Mata Hari herself had stayed in the hotel once. Taylor had never taken Mata Hari seriously until he read that despite her seemingly voluptuous figure, she was actually flat-chested and wore a padded bra even in bed. From that point on, Taylor had regarded her as a sublime espionage agent—a princess of deception—and when he wandered over to the Pera Palas for a drink after work, he would try to conjure up her ghost. But he was always disappointed. The bar tended to fill up with heavy-breasted German tourists and daffy American girls looking for a two-week adventure. They were not Mata Hari, but they helped pass the time.

Taylor's immediate concern that January was the Turks. Turkey was one of the loose timbers in the world, but in the general commotion over Iran, nobody quite seemed to have noticed. The Shah's departure and the turmoil in the oil market had shaken New York and London, and as the aftershocks radiated out toward Istanbul and Ankara, they grew larger and more violent, until the very floorboards began to creak and sway. The problem in Istanbul wasn't long lines at the gas pumps. Much of the time, as the winter progressed, there simply wasn't any gas to be had. Oil prices increased eighty percent at the start of the year and kept climbing. There were daily power cuts in Istanbul and bare shelves in the stores. The Turks were responding to these dark forces by doing the one thing that still seemed within their power—killing each other.

The Turkish winter had begun with a massacre at a place called Kahramanmaras, in eastern Turkey. The trouble there had started a few days before Christmas, with a march by local leftists to protest the death of two schoolteachers. The leftists painted slogans on the walls, shouted epithets against the regime, and began throwing rocks. The army opened fire. By Christmas Day, 109 people had died at Kahramanmaras, more than 1,000 had been wounded, and over 500 shops had been destroyed. The violence soon spread to other cities, and on December 26 martial law had been declared in thirteen provinces. The murder rate from terrorism was climbing into double digits, and it seemed entirely possible in early 1979 that Turkey was heading the way of Iran.

Why was America letting the string unravel? That was what the Turks wanted to know. Why couldn't somebody *do* something? The American ambassador in Ankara sent home a tart cable: "Turkish concerns about U.S. reliability as an alliance partner have deepened as a result of our inability to prevent the fall of the Shah of Iran and the perception that the U.S. is losing strength in relation to the Russians." That was about as blunt as they got in the striped-pants set, but it didn't do any good. When the subject of Turkey came up back home the only thing anybody seemed to want to talk about was human rights.

Taylor didn't know what to tell his Turkish friends, so generally he didn't say anything. The chief of staff of the Turkish Air Force sought him out at a party in Istanbul in late January and warned him that the Iranian situation was a strategic disaster. Why wasn't America doing anything about it? "I can't talk about it," said Taylor. The general looked relieved. Of course the Americans were doing something about it; they just couldn't talk about it.

* * *

Taylor liked opening the pouch every morning. It was a gesture of optimism, an expression of hope that among the endless sequence of bureaucratic directives and memos from headquarters might lie a rough gem of insight, a new plan of action, a sense that somebody back at the central cortex had a clue about what was happening out in the elbows and knee-caps of the world. He was nearly always disappointed, but he came back again each morning with, if not always hope, at least curiosity. He was waiting for something to happen, something that would force the issue, something that would order the puzzle of his life. And it finally did, one day in late January.

The day began badly, when the code clerk brought Taylor the latest missive from headquarters. At first he thought it was a joke, an elaborate parody of the bureaucratic morass into which the agency had been sinking in recent years. It was a lengthy dispatch from "Edward J. Ganin," the pseudo-nym of the new director of central intelligence, Charles (Chuck) Hinkle. It had been sent via the director's special communication channel, whose messages carried the crypto-nym LWSURF but were known informally as "Chuckgrams."

"Management by Objectives" read the heading. Taylor leafed through the long memo. It was written in the earnest gibberish of a Dale Carnegie seminar, with a list of ten rules for better management ("No. 6: Dare to Delegate!") and a brightly colored poster-size sheet that said: TOUGH BUT FAIR— THE MANAGER'S CREDO! Taylor skimmed the document and got to the "action plan" on the last page. It mandated every CIA station and base around the world to draw up a detailed list of its current intelligence "objectives" and confirm that they accorded with the master list back at headquarters. If taken seriously it meant days of drudge work. Taylor decided he had better call his boss, Stanley Timmons, the station chief in Ankara.

"Has someone back home gone crazy?" asked Taylor.

"I beg your pardon," said the station chief, a gentle man who was nearing retirement and had every reason not to rock the boat. Timmons spent most of his time worrying about the agency's listening posts on the Black Sea and playing golf.

"What the hell is 'Management by Objectives'?"

"Read it yourself," said Timmons.

"I read it. But I don't believe that anyone could take it seriously."

"Believe it. I need your list in a week."

Taylor groaned. "Where did Hinkle get this silly idea?"

"From the President."

"That's reassuring. Maybe I'm in the wrong business."

"Maybe you are," said Timmons. "By the way, don't forget about the Bulgarians."

"I'm working on it. But I'm not sure it's there."

"Work harder. The White House is convinced the Bulgarians are sending weapons into Turkey. They want evidence."

"Who told them?"

"The Romanians. The French. How should I know? Just do it."

Taylor was going to say "Fuck the White House," but Timmons had hung up. Taylor put down the phone and looked at the "Management by Objectives" directive. He read a passage at random: "The way to stay ahead of the competition is to think smart, and the way to think smart is to avoid making the same mistakes, which create a negative feedback situation that prevents you from realizing your objectives!"

"What an asshole," muttered Taylor. He looked at the memo and gave it the finger. It was a childish gesture, but there was a part of Taylor that had never quite graduated from high school. He was the sort of man whose moral code had not progressed too far beyond the conviction that rules were a bad idea and that people, in general, should do what made them feel good.

"Alan, you have a call," shouted Taylor's secretary through the door. Taylor insisted on first names in the office. One of the many things that disturbed him about the CIA was that people were beginning to call each other "Mister," just like the State Department.

"Who is it?"

"Wouldn't say."

Good for him, thought Taylor. Someone who refused to be objectified.

5

THE CALL WAS FROM A TURKISH INTELLIGENCE OFFICER NAMED Serif Osman. He ran the Istanbul office of the Milli Istihbarat Teskilati, the Turkish National Intelligence Organization. The Americans usually referred to it by the English acronym TNIO, just as they called the government of Turkey the GOT. Taylor stubbornly insisted on using the Turkish initials, MIT. Serif was Taylor's principal liaison contact in Istanbul, and he had been trying hard for nearly a year to cultivate him. "Cultivate" wasn't the right word, exactly. He had invited the MIT man to lunch twice and tried to get him drunk, once unsuccessfully, once successfully.

The Turk suggested they meet for coffee. Taylor proposed the Hilton near Taksim Square, about a mile from MIT headquarters in Besiktas. The Turk suggested a cheaper, less conspicuous hotel nearby. That whetted Taylor's curiosity. He called downstairs to his driver and departed several minutes later in one of the consulate's bulletproof Chevys—glad for a momentary chance to escape the bunker.

Serif was waiting in the lobby. He was a robust man, with high cheekbones and a neat goatee. Like many Turkish men, he had a limited range of facial expressions. When Serif didn't like something, he narrowed his eyes. Otherwise, his face gave nothing away. Taylor smiled and shook his hand warmly, but the Turk was squinting.

The Turks were an odd people, Taylor had concluded soon after his arrival. Prickly and difficult, like their language. They didn't crack jokes, they rarely laughed. They rarely talked to foreigners. They did their part in NATO, but they suspected they were being had.

It was said in the agency that Turks were notoriously hard to

43

recruit. Taylor hadn't believed it at first, but after a few months, he understood why. They didn't have handles or rough edges or secret dreams. They weren't mercenary, so money wouldn't do it. And they didn't have the sort of complicated mind, like the Arabs, that allowed them to rationalize betrayal. They were intensely patriotic. The only way to get them to do something was to convince them that it was best for Turkey.

Serif didn't speak until they were seated at a table in the corner of the coffee shop.

"I have something for you," he said solemnly. Despite the grave manner, he looked pleased with himself. "Something we cannot use."

"And what might that be?"

"You know Kunayev?"

"Of course," said Taylor. He was the Soviet consul general. Kunayev was a figure of some interest. His cousin was the party first secretary in Kazakhstan, and his wife was a beautiful blonde from Vilnius.

"This morning he went to the Bit Pazar in Horhor to look at some old furniture . . ." Serif paused for emphasis.

". . . He saw something he liked." He cleared his throat. ". . . An Ottoman chair."

Taylor didn't get it right away. Big fucking deal, he thought.

"A chair?" repeated Taylor dully.

"Yes," said the Turk. "An Ottoman chair. Kunayev asked the shop owner to clean it up. He is half Kazakh, Kunayev, from Alma Ata. We think he will come back tomorrow and buy it. For his office maybe."

"Oh Jesus!" said Taylor. He finally got the point. What Serif was describing so solemnly was one of those serendipitous moments that underemployed base chiefs dream about, when your adversary does something stupid and allows you to do something smart. Like install a microphone in a piece of his furniture. All Taylor could think of to say was "No shit?"

The Turk looked embarrassed. Like most of his countrymen, he abjured profanity.

"How did you come across this lovely piece of information?" asked Taylor.

"The owner of the store next door told us. He's a Circassian. He hates the Russians."

"Why are you telling me about it?"

"Because we cannot do anything with it," said the MIT man. "There is no time for us to install a proper microphone that would not be detected. We do not have the equipment. The Soviets would find it, and we would have a flap with Moscow. So we have decided to do nothing ourselves. But we feel it is some waste!"

"Definitely," agreed Taylor. "Much waste!"

Taylor pondered the situation a moment. Bugging a piece of furniture wasn't as easy as Serif seemed to think. There was also the possibility that he was being set up. "Does Ankara know you're seeing me?" he asked.

"Of course!" said Serif. "Do you think I am a crazy man? This is strictly above the boards!"

"Just asking."

"This is a present from us to you," said Serif.

"We are most grateful," said Taylor, putting his hand over his heart.

"We ask one thing," said Serif, returning to his initial solemn tone. "That you share with us the product of this operation. Otherwise, no deals."

"That shouldn't be a problem," said Taylor. In fact, he hadn't a clue what headquarters would say.

"You give me your promise?"

"Sure," said Taylor. What the hell.

The Turk smiled slyly and stood up from the table. As he did so, he removed from his pocket a slip of paper and placed it gently on the table. On it was written the name of the antique shop and a description of the chair the Soviet had admired.

"Be very careful, please," said the Turk. "If you get caught, we never heard of you." He turned and walked away. Taylor wanted to kiss him. Into the enervating, paint-by-numbers world of the Istanbul base had fallen something unexpected.

6

TAYLOR'S CAR LEFT THE HOTEL AND MOVED SLOWLY DOWN THE hill and along Dolmabahce Avenue toward the city. Ordinarily, Taylor didn't mind the traffic. It gave him a chance to watch women in the streets. But today it was a nuisance. He looked at his watch. It was after three, which meant he had about fifteen hours. He leaned out the window and shouted at a man driving a vegetable cart, then pulled his head back in. His eyes were stinging from the winter smog, which settled over the city in November, when Istanbulis began lighting their dirty coal fires to stay warm, and hung on until April. Taylor looked across the waters of the Golden Horn, toward the old city. He could barely glimpse the spires of the mosques through the haze—Aya Sofia and Sultanahmet and Suleymaniye—a forest of stone, lost in the fog.

Byzantium. The city where spying was invented, whose very name had become over the ages a synonym for deceit and double-dealing—for what Yeats delicately called "the artifice of eternity"; the city where, in Ottoman times, the very functioning of the realm had been secret, hidden behind the gates of the "Sublime Porte"; the city where, in the time of the penultimate sultan, Abdul-Hamid II, half the population was said to be employed spying on the other half; an infinitely exotic realm of janissaries and concubines and black eunuchs—and come to what? To monstrous traffic jams and a haze of sulfurous smog.

That was the shock of places like Istanbul. They were so ordinary. The land of the seraglio had become a typical Third World country, struggling to stay afloat politically and economically. It had a moderately left-wing prime minister, a mountain of foreign debt, a population so sharply split on

46

politics that left and right were becoming two separate cultures. Turkey, in short, was like too many other friends and clients of the United States in the late 1970s. It was an in-between country: between Europe and Asia; between capitalism and socialism; between the Third World and the First. The prime minister typified the national schizophrenia. An amateur poet, he had translated T. S. Eliot and Ezra Pound into Turkish and was said to love "modernism." Yet somehow he did not love America.

When Taylor finally got back to the consulate, he tried to reach Timmons in Ankara. Timmons had left the office. His secretary thought he had gone to play golf. Just as well, Taylor decided. Timmons would have gotten in the way. Taylor knew what he wanted to do and—more important—whom he wanted to do it. He drafted a cable requesting the immediate dispatch of George Trumbo from the Athens field office of the Technical Services Division. He sent headquarters and Timmons an information copy, to cover his ass. If they didn't like what he was doing, they still had a few hours to complain. It was now well after four; the antique shop would open the next morning at eight. Fortunately, George Trumbo was in the office when Taylor's cable arrived. More fortunately, there was still time for him to catch the last commercial flight of the day from Athens to Istanbul. And most fortunately of all, George was not drunk.

George was a technical genius who, by any reasonable measure, had wasted his life in the agency. His specialty was electronic surveillance. He believed, as a matter of professional pride, that there was no such thing as a conversation that could not be overheard—in the same way that a Broadway ticket agent might insist that there was no such thing as a sold-out play. George had proved the point many times over. The agency liked to place technicians like George in big stations around the world—London, Rome, Athens, Bangkok, Hong Kong—to be ready for emergencies. It was a good idea, except the TSD men tended to go to seed. Out in the field there were too few technical operations and too many bars.

George had most definitely gone to seed. That was part of why Taylor liked him. He had stopped taking seriously the things in life that are not serious. George was a big, friendly man—a former jock who had been recruited by the agency in the mid-1960s after a knee injury ended his athletic career at a Catholic college in the Midwest—who had become interested in electrical engineering as a sort of hobby, like fixing cars. In agency parlance, he was a "knuckle dragger," a term that ascribed apelike characteristics to anyone who did "manual" work, like installing bugs or running paramilitary operations. George did indeed look dumb—until he began taking apart a piece of electrical equipment; then, unless he was very drunk, he looked like a genius.

Taylor liked him. But then Taylor liked everybody, at least until they proved themselves incompetent or hopelessly dull. That was why he was a natural recruiter. He called George "Georgie," the wireman called him "Al," and together they burgled people's apartments and bugged their telephones.

Taylor passed the next few hours in a blur. He first arranged a support team of two Turkish agents and drove them to Horhor to case the site. Then he returned to the consulate and sent a second cable to Timmons and headquarters. The cable assessed in more detail the possibility that Kunayev was a KGB officer and stressed again the time constraints that had made it impossible to obtain normal operational approval. Taylor even threw in a reference to potential intelligence about Bulgarian weapons shipments into Turkey. He signed the cable with his pseudonym—Amos B. Garrett—and then drove to the airport to pick up George.

It was almost nine o'clock when the big, smiling American emerged in the arrival hall carrying the canvas overnight bag that contained his tools.

"You fucker," said George loudly as he shook Taylor's hand. "I had a date tonight. This better be good." Several Turks turned and stared at them.

"It is," said Taylor, holding his finger to his lips.

"As good as the last one?" He was still nearly shouting.

"Screw you," said Taylor. "And be quiet."

"The last one was a beaut!" said George, a little less loudly. "All my work, up in smoke."

It was true, quite literally. The last time Taylor had called on George's technical services, it had been to install a hidden microphone in an Ottoman dueling pistol. Taylor had ar-

ranged for a Turkish businessman to present the pistol as a
gift to the Bulgarian military attaché in Istanbul. Taylor and
George had gone off to a little shop in the Kapali Carsi, purchased the gun, and lovingly installed the bug. It was an in-
genious device—absolutely undetectable. And the Bulgarian
loved it. He placed it on the desk in his office and for a week
it broadcast a delicious flow of raw intelligence (not, alas,
concerning shipments of weapons into Turkey). But then the
Bulgarian colonel did something nobody had expected. He
took the gun home with him, bought some gunpowder and
bird shot, and tried to fire it. It was a natural enough thing to
do, but of course the ancient gun exploded. The Bulgarian escaped serious injury, but the microphone was mortally
wounded.

Taylor had sent George the tape of the last few minutes of
the bug's life: the officer talking happily to himself in Bulgarian; the sound of him cleaning the barrel, inserting the pow-
der and shot. The sound of him walking outdoors, a long
pause while he aimed, then BLOOOEY! A terrible explosion;
and then a ghastly, empty silence. Taylor thought it was
funny, but George was upset. His microphones were his children, sent out into the world with all the love and care he
could muster. He didn't like it when they died prematurely.

They walked swiftly through the airport terminal.

"Let's get to work," said George enthusiastically as they
got in the car.

"Too early," said Taylor, looking at his watch. It was just
nine-fifteen. The two Turkish agents would be waiting for
them on Horhor Street at midnight. They had nearly three
hours to kill.

"Have you eaten?"

George nodded.

"Eat some more," said Taylor.

They went to a fish restaurant in Kumkapi, a district in Old
Istanbul overlooking the Sea of Marmara. The area was inhabited by a rich mix of nationalities: Armenians, Georgians,
Bulgarians, Kurds. Taylor chose a restaurant called Ucler, run
by three Albanian brothers. They were a suspicious lot, and
spent much of the evening peering warily out the door,
watching for trouble.

"What's with these guys?" asked George when one of the

Albanians went to the door for what seemed the twentieth time.

"That's the way people are in this part of the world, if you hadn't noticed," said Taylor. "They don't trust anybody. The Albanians hate the Bulgarians, the Bulgarians hate the Turks, the Turks hate the Kurds, the Kurds hate the Armenians. So they all spend a lot of time watching each other. That's the secret of politics in this part of the world. Play the little buggers off against each other."

The Albanian restaurateurs, in fact, were so suspicious of what might be happening down the street that they all but ignored the two Americans seated in their restaurant. Which suited Taylor fine. He outlined for George the basic details of the operation: the incautious Soviet diplomat who had gone shopping for an Ottoman chair; the layout of the antique bazaar; the plan for entering the building; the support agents who would accompany them.

George nodded and grunted between mouthfuls of food. Despite the fact that he had already eaten, he proved to be surprisingly hungry, devouring most of a large bluefish and a dozen large shrimp that Taylor had ordered but couldn't finish. He washed this down with two glasses of vodka, followed by a half bottle of wine, followed by a last glass of vodka. Taylor didn't object. George was a professional. If he wanted to get shit-faced before installing a delicate microphone in a hundred-year-old piece of furniture, that was his business. The agency had enough nursemaids and nannies these days, and Taylor wasn't about to join them. But as it neared midnight, he did order George an extra-large Turkish coffee, which the technician dutifully drank.

"Georgie, my boy," said Taylor, "let's go buy some antiques." George said nothing. He was an artist, and his performance was about to begin.

Horhor Street was in a district called Fatih, a sprawling, dusty quarter of cheap apartment buildings and dimly lit workshops on the outskirts of the old city. Taylor knew the area all too well, for it had become in the past year a gathering place for Iranian émigrés and was the home of several of his putative agents. He parked his car several blocks from the Bit Pazar and walked silently with George.

For all his bonhomie, Taylor was nervous. He had a sensation in his gut that felt like knitting needles trying to knit with no yarn. They walked slowly up the street, passing rows of darkened apartment blocks.

As they neared the top of the street, Taylor turned right onto a small alley called Kirik Tulumba Street. In the shadows, he saw Hasan and Hamid, the two Turkish support agents, who were leaning against a building smoking cigarettes. Behind them was the antique bazaar.

"That's it?" asked George doubtfully, motioning toward a modern five-story building.

Taylor nodded. It was an unlikely spot for a flea market. Rather than the usual warren of small shops, this was a tidy establishment with elevators and modern door locks and a night watchman. Most of the city's best antique dealers had moved here a few years earlier when the old antique market in Kuledibi was torn down.

The Turks extinguished their cigarettes. Taylor whispered something in Turkish to the younger of the two. He disappeared into the shadows beside the building and returned several minutes later, motioning to Taylor that the way was clear.

"Hamid," whispered Taylor to the older Turk.

"I'm Hasan."

"Whatever, you ready?" The Turk nodded. Taylor motioned him to move out.

The Turk headed toward the main entrance. He was the decoy. It was his job to distract the night watchman—to engage him in conversation, to join him for tea, to ply him with whiskey, to offer him baksheesh, as a last resort to subdue him by force—for thirty minutes, long enough for the others to gain entry to the antique shop. Taylor waited until Hasan was near the main door and then followed Hamid to the alleyway at the side of the building. The only sound was the faint reverberation of Arab music from a tape player a block away.

Hamid turned on a small flashlight and pointed it toward the wall. In the faint light, Taylor could see the outlines of a rope ladder climbing to an open window on the second floor. Hamid had already done the hard work of arranging the clandestine entry. All Taylor had to do was follow the script.

Taylor climbed the ladder first, gently, a rung at a time.

The ladder swayed against the concrete wall of the building but made little noise. Taylor paused when he reached the window frame, moving his head up slowly till he could see into the building. It was dark, save for a faint light coming up the stairwell. Taylor eased himself over the windowsill and onto the floor. George clambered up behind him with surprising agility, followed by Hamid. When the Turk reached the top he pulled the rope ladder up after him, laid it on the tile floor, and closed the window.

Taylor took a diagram from his pocket. The shop they wanted was called Ozcan Is. It was about twenty yards across the hall. Taylor moved silently to the door. It was locked tight, with two dead bolts. Taylor heard voices from the floor below and froze until he recognized one of them as Hasan's.

George reached into his bag and removed a small leather kit that looked like a manicure set. It contained a set of thirty-two picks, each made of spring steel no more than a few hundredths of an inch thick. The picks were tipped with various irregular shapes—a diamond, a square, a ball, a jagged point—that could press against the pins of the lock while an L-shaped "tension tool" gently pushed it open.

The first lock was easy. George squirted in some graphite. Then he inserted the tension tool, selected a pick with a triangular head, pushed it in all the way, and then rapidly brought it forward. Locksmiths called it "raking" the pins. On the fourth rake, the lock opened.

George attacked the second lock the same way, but after several dozen rakes it hadn't budged. He studied the lock to see if it might be an exotic variety with a special architecture, but it looked ordinary enough. He tried picking it more gently with various tools and then sighed and shook his head.

"Mushroom pins," he said in a whisper.

"Is that bad?"

George nodded. Unlike normal pins, which were straight and smooth and slipped up gently to the shear line when they were picked, mushroom pins were H-shaped and tended to get stuck halfway up.

Taylor looked at his watch. It was twelve forty-five. George had been working on the second lock for nearly twenty minutes. Downstairs, Hasan and the watchman were talking animatedly about the local soccer rivalry—the rowdies of Fenerbahce versus the gentlemen of Galatasaray. It was a favorite topic in Istanbul, but Taylor knew they couldn't keep talking about it forever. Eventually the watchman would have to make his rounds. He looked at his watch again and then looked at George.

"I'll use the gun," whispered George.

Oh shit, thought Taylor. He's going to shoot open the lock.

George reached into his bag and pulled out a small black snub-nosed object with a large trigger. Taylor was reaching to stop him when George put his finger to his lips.

"Take it easy. It's just a Lockaid gun," he said. The gun in question was an automatic pick, sold under the name Lockaid, whose trigger activated a small, straight pick that snapped up sharply against the pins. The only problem with it was that it was noisy.

Downstairs, the voices were louder. Hasan's thirty minutes were almost up. The watchman was apologizing profusely. He had enjoyed the conversation very much, thank you, brother, and the whiskey, but now he must make his rounds. Hasan was offering him one last drink, but the watchman was declining. Taylor leaned toward George. "Now," he whispered.

George smiled vaguely. He inserted the gun into the lock and pulled the trigger. SPROING. George turned the tension tool and the second dead bolt opened.

There were footsteps below. The watchman was beginning his tour of the first floor. Taylor nudged George, who eased open the door. The three tiptoed inside and closed it behind them. The watchman was climbing the stairs. Taylor motioned for everyone to lie down on the floor, behind some large pieces of furniture, until the watchman had passed. They were lying there, listening to the watchman's footsteps, when Taylor remembered the rope ladder.

The footsteps grew louder. Then they stopped. The watchman was at the window. There was a creaking noise that Taylor didn't recognize at first. Then he realized that it was the sound of the window opening. Disaster. The watchman had seen the ladder; now he must be looking to see where the culprits had come from. Taylor listened to the rise and fall of George's breathing for ten or fifteen seconds. Then he heard something unmistakable. It was the thin, vaporous sound of a man urinating. The night watchman hadn't discovered the ladder after all. He was pissing out the window. He must be very drunk, Taylor reasoned. Urinating out a window was something a sober Turk would never do.

The rest was easy. Taylor located the chair in question. It was a magnificent old Ottoman piece, intricately carved and stained a deep, rich brown. Inlaid in the wood were pieces of mother-of-pearl in handsome Oriental designs. Say what you like about old Kunayev, thought Taylor. He has good taste in furniture. George set up his portable workshop. From the canvas bag emerged a small high-intensity light, a silent high-speed drill, a palette of varnishes in different shades, and finally a small metal box containing his electronic treasures.

Taylor watched him with genuine admiration. George executed each task gently and lovingly. First he drilled a small hole four inches deep into one of the legs of the chair. Into this hole he inserted the guts of the hardware—a tiny device, no more than several inches long, that, once activated, would transmit sounds to a receiver several blocks away. At a point near where the top of this transmitting device would rest, he drilled another hole. This one was almost invisible, no larger than the size of a small sewing needle. Into it he delicately placed a filiment microphone that would carry sound to the transmitter. It was a tidy little package, not state of the art, but still useful. The chair could sit dormant for weeks or months and then be switched on when needed, like an electronic sleeper agent.

"What's the frequency?" George whispered.

"Say what?"

"The Soviet consulate. What frequency do they broadcast classified traffic on?"

"How should I know? What difference does it make?"

"I need to set the frequency of our transmitter. Usually I like to slip in right next to the Soviet's own frequency. It's the one place on the spectrum they usually don't look."

"Sorry. Not my department."

George mumbled aloud. "They're lazy. They probably use the same frequency here as in Athens and Rome. I'll park alongside and tune the volume down real quiet."

George removed the transmitter, adjusted it, and put it back in the leg of the chair. Then he filled up his hole with a fast-drying wood compound, matched the varnish and painted over the scar. Hamid sat motionless, waiting for him to finish. At one point he took out a cigarette and looked at it lovingly, as if imagining how good it would taste when the job was done. Taylor looked at his watch. It was after two o'clock. They had to be out before dawn.

George was utterly absorbed in his work and seemed unaware of the passage of time. When he finished the first leg, he installed an identical backup device in the second. He did it just as painstakingly as the first one. At three-thirty, George was carefully applying the varnish.

"I hate to say this," said George as he waited for the varnish to dry, "but this is a pretty old-fashioned operation."

"What are you talking about?" whispered Taylor.

"You don't really need a microphone anymore, Al. You don't even need a transmitter inside the premises. You just need a resonator."

Taylor ignored him. "Is that dry yet?" he asked impatiently, pointing to the varnish.

"You see, anything that vibrates can be a microphone," continued George, by now quite absorbed in the technical point he was elaborating. "A window can be a microphone. A wall can be a microphone. Even the filament in a light bulb can be a microphone. All you need is a power source to read the vibration, like an accelerometer behind a wall, or a laser across the street, or a tunable antenna. Did you know that? Isn't that amazing?"

"Jesus," hissed Taylor. "It's got to be dry by now."

"So this is a very old-fashioned operation, when you think about it. But still nice."

"Fuck it," said Taylor. "Let's not wait for it to dry, okay?" George smiled amiably and collected his tools. Taylor and Hamid were already out the door and to the window when George motioned to them to stop.

"We have to lock the door," whispered George.

"Use the gun," said Taylor. George looked almost disappointed, like a fly fisherman who has been told to fish with a shimmering silver lure instead of a hand-tied Gray Ghost. George inserted the Lockaid gun.

SPROING. Taylor hoped the guard was asleep by now. One dead bolt closed. SPROING. The other bolt turned shut.

Hamid opened the window and unrolled the ladder. Down went George, then Taylor. Then Hamid emerged, dangling from a rope he had clamped to the window ledge. He collected the ladder, closed the window, and slid deftly down the rope to the alley.

It was nearly dawn when they finally left Horhor. A few yellow taxis were already beginning to shuttle the streets. The smells of fresh bread and Turkish coffee were in the air. Taylor felt intoxicated. Hamid offered him a cigarette, and although he hadn't smoked in nearly a year, Taylor eagerly took it. Why not? To refuse would have been metaphysically unsound.

Kunayev didn't visit the antique bazaar in Horhor all morning. In fact, he didn't stir from his office in the salmon-pink pile on Istiklal Avenue. Taylor was edgy. He sat in his office with George, eating doughnuts and drinking coffee, listening to periodic reports from the Turkish surveillance team in the observation post across from the Soviet consulate. As the morning passed, he began to doubt that the Soviet consul general would ever revisit Horhor Street. It would be a mistake to do so, a breach of security, and the Soviets didn't make mistakes. That was an American specialty.

Finally, just after three, the watchers reported that someone—Kunayev—was leaving the consulate in a big limousine and heading along Istiklal Avenue.

When the Turkish surveillance team reported that he was nearing the Fatih district, Taylor held his breath. The Soviet diplomat was turning left on Ataturk Street, radioed the watchers. He was turning left again. Onto Horhor Street.

"Say that again," Taylor barked into the radio.

"Horhor Street."

Taylor smiled. His eyes twinkled. The watchers reported that the Soviet diplomat had parked his car. He was walking toward the antique bazaar, accompanied by his bodyguard. He was entering the building.

"Now buy the chair, asshole!" said Taylor.

"I hope the varnish dried all right," said George.

"Shut up," said Taylor. He apologized an instant later.

Kunayev finally emerged twenty-five minutes later, empty-handed. Taylor held his breath until he heard the next squawk over the radio. Behind the Soviet diplomat was his body-guard, carrying a large brown chair.

"Owooooo!" wailed Taylor when the last report came over the wireless. "Kunayev, you are one dumb motherfucker!" He pounded his desk, kissed his secretary, and barked again, like a stray dog with something to brag about.

"I hope the microphone works," said George. "I didn't have much time."

"Of course it will work," answered Taylor. "Tomorrow we start listening. Tonight we celebrate!"

"What you got in mind?"

"Georgie, my boy, I want you to go back to your hotel and get a few hours' rest. Because tonight I am going to take you on a tour of Istanbul nightlife."

"Nightlife? What do you mean?"

"I mean Grade A, hundred-proof sleaze. Tonight, my friend, you are going to see varieties of the human experience that you have never imagined."

"I dunno. I've been to Bangkok."

"Trust me," said Taylor. "Bangkok is tasteful compared to Istanbul."

7

◆

A COPY OF TAYLOR'S CABLE DESCRIBING THE OPERATION ON Horhor Street reached Edward Stone in Washington late in the afternoon. Technically, Stone wasn't supposed to have a copy. He was not on the routing list of division chiefs and staff chiefs and desk officers who normally would see such a communication. But he had friends. And one of them, a little spark plug of a man named Harry Peltz, stopped by just as Stone was about to head off to one of that season's endless round of retirement parties. Peltz had worked with Stone thirty years earlier in Berlin and now held down a sinecure in the European Division.

Stone was always surprised when people came to see him, even the regulars like Peltz. For he was trying, in his way, to be invisible. His office was small and austere, far from the busy corridors on the seventh floor inhabited by Hinkle and his coterie of special assistants. Stone's office was like one of those London clubs that have no name on the door, so that you can't find them unless you already know where they are. When he moved into this hideaway from the grand office he had occupied as chief of the Near East Division, Stone had brought just one thing with him. It was his framed epigram from Nietzsche's *Beyond Good and Evil,* which read: "Gaze not too long into the abyss, lest the abyss gaze back at you."

"You busy?" asked Peltz.

"Not at all," said Stone. "I was just heading to Crane's party."

"You'll like this one," said Peltz with a wink. He entered the office, closed the door behind him, and handed Stone the cable from Istanbul.

Stone read the message and smiled. "This is a silly operation," he said. "Why should I like it?"

"Because it's enterprising."

"I suppose so. At least someone is having some fun. Who is Mr. Amos B. Garrett, by the way?"

"Alan Taylor. Nice kid. Actually, he's not a kid. He's almost forty."

"Still a kid in my book," said Stone. He handed the cable back to Peltz. "I'll wager you dollars to doughnuts his little foray won't produce anything. Is that still a good bet, dollars to doughnuts?"

"Yeah. If they're cheap doughnuts."

"Keep me posted, would you?"

"Absolutely. As long as I'm around."

Stone shook his head. "Don't tell me you're on the purge list."

"So I hear."

"I'm sorry. Maybe I can say something to someone. Although the front office doesn't seem to take my suggestions too seriously these days."

"Forget it," said Peltz. "Who wants to work for these assholes anyway, right?"

Stone shook his head again and looked at his watch. "Forgive me," he said. "I'm late for Crane's party. Are you coming? We'll have a drink on Hinkle."

"No way," said Peltz. "I've been to enough retirement parties the last few months to last a lifetime. Anyway, if I saw Hinkle I'd probably slug him. Where's everybody going later?"

"I don't know," said Stone. "Probably to Oak Hill Inn. That's where these affairs always seem to end up."

"Maybe I'll see you there," said Peltz. He opened the door and ambled back down the hall toward the operations center, cable in hand.

The party was for Alton Crane, who was leaving the clandestine service after twenty-five years. It was held in the executive dining room on the seventh floor, just down the hall from the director's office. In attendance were Crane's semi-alcoholic wife, Betty, and his two sons—one with long hair and a beard who was "into carpentry," the other with short, blow-dried hair who was selling stocks and bonds for the family firm. They were, in their genteel disarray, the standard Washington Wasp family of the late 1970s. The guests were all trying hard to be cheery, talking about what a great run Alton had had, and how much he must be looking forward to getting out of the business and doing a little sailing, or fishing, or whatever it was that he had been longing to do all these years. But everyone knew that Crane was being pushed out the door.

Hinkle made a brief appearance, thanked Crane for his many years of meritorious service, and presented him with an intelligence medal of the sort they give newly arrived KGB defectors to make them feel important. Then Hinkle left and went back to his office a few doors down the hall. He didn't even stop to shake hands. The new director seemed to understand that he was intensely disliked by virtually everyone in the room. He had that much sense, at least.

Stone scanned the room. It was a picture of a generation in retreat. In one corner stood a cluster of old China hands, who had broken their picks against the impenetrable wall of Mao's

China only to see it suddenly open to America in the early 1970s; it was still impossible for most of them to imagine that the United States now conducted joint intelligence operations with Beijing. Nearby was the small remnant still fighting the war in Southeast Asia, still haunted by memories of agents left on hilltops in Laos and street corners in Saigon during the last desperate days. In another corner were the Arabists, who had spent their careers trying unsuccessfully to contain the world's most intractable conflict and who had, in the process, taken on the elaborate politeness and deviousness of their agents in Beirut and Cairo. And in the middle of the room, embracing all the disparate factions, were the Russia hands; they counted it a blessing if they made it to retirement without being falsely accused of spying for Moscow. So much talent, so many bright careers, devoted to the task of treading water in the polar sea of the Cold War.

The only person in the room who seemed entirely at ease was Crane himself. He had already imbibed several gin martinis and was trying to enliven all the long-faced colleagues who wanted to commiserate with him. In fact, Crane looked immensely relieved that the whole business was finally over. Stone approached him after Hinkle had left the room.

"Congratulations," said Stone.

"On what?" he answered.

"Your medal."

"Forget it," said Crane. "You want to know the truth? I can't wait to get out. I feel sorry for you poor buggers who have to stay. You have to keep up pretenses. Not me. I've done my bit. *La guerre est finie.*" He was smiling as he said it, which made it almost believable.

"You had a good run, Alton," said Stone, echoing the party line. He tried to remember just what Crane had done. Germany, along with everyone else; Mexico City; Manila; Rome. No major triumphs, no major flaps. Perhaps it really had been a good run.

"Did you hear about the lawyers?" asked Crane, still smiling.

"I don't believe so," said Stone.

"New edict from Hinkle, just announced today. They're putting lawyers on permanent assignment in all the big stations in Europe so that they'll be closer to the action. Just to make sure nobody does anything creative."

"I once considered becoming a lawyer," said Stone. "Perhaps I made a mistake."

"Nonsense," said Crane. "You'd make a lousy lawyer. Anyway, you're all that's left around here. They need you."

Stone looked around the room at the collection of old boys, has-beens and hangers-on. "For what?" he asked.

Crane laughed. "You poor buggers," he said again. As he spoke, another well-wisher approached and Stone stepped back toward the door.

"See you later?" called out Crane.

"Where are you going?"

"Oak Hill Inn. Please come. My wife wants to talk to you."

Stone winced. "Maybe."

"I'm counting on you."

"I'll try," said Stone.

Stone did put in a brief appearance at Oak Hill Inn, a tidy establishment on a hill overlooking Route 123 whose virtues included proximity to CIA headquarters. By the time he arrived, Betty Crane was thoroughly plastered and arguing with whoever happened her way, while Alton was singing Cole Porter songs to his secretary, a Hispanic woman in her mid-twenties with chunky thighs and a big chest. To Stone's great relief, he saw Harry Peltz walking toward him out of a cloud of cigarette smoke near the bar.

"What are you drinking?" asked Stone.

"Double whiskey," answered Harry. "No water. No ice. No nothing."

Stone ordered one for Harry and one for himself. It was not a night to be abstemious. Stone took his drink and walked Peltz toward a corner, farther from the Cranes.

"Has Alton been banging his secretary?" asked Peltz, looking back toward the guest of honor and his Latin song mate.

"I'm not really the person to ask," answered Stone. "Until now, I didn't know that Alton had a secretary."

"He's going to hate retirement. All that time with Betty. He's going to go nuts."

"That's not what he says. He told me at the party how happy he was to be leaving."

"Bullshit. That's just because he hates Hinkle so much. None of the old boys likes the idea of leaving. Not even me."

Stone wanted to change the subject. He was tired of talking about retirement, tired of feeling as if he were attending a permanent wake. "What's happening in your shop?" he asked. "Heard anything more from Istanbul?"

"Nada," said Peltz. "Why are you so convinced that operation is a loser anyway?"

"Why?" said Stone, looking at his whiskey glass. He didn't usually answer questions about operations, even from old friends. He took a long drink of scotch and looked at Peltz. "Because it's so old-fashioned. Even if it succeeds, so what? Who really cares what they're saying in the Soviet consulate in Istanbul. It's not for real. Do you follow me?"

"Not really."

"What I mean is that it's static. That's our problem. We've been watching the Soviets so long that we've begun to see things their way. They say they're a superpower and we believe them, so we try to bug their offices and recruit their people. Why? The whole thing is a fraud. It's a house of cards. We don't need to spend any more time looking at it. We need to knock it over. That's somewhat heretical, but do you see what I'm getting at?"

"Honestly, no. You're over my head. What have you got cooking anyway?"

"Not much."

"C'mon."

"The usual. Playing games. Knocking on doors to see who's there. But honestly, it doesn't amount to much."

"Cut the crap. What's up?"

Stone smiled serenely. "Sorry, I can't tell you."

"That's okay," said Peltz. "Who cares. Let's have another drink."

"Do me a favor," said Stone. "If this fellow Taylor in Istanbul stumbles onto anything noteworthy, let me know. That is a part of the world that interests me a good deal."

"Definitely," said Peltz. He repaired to the bar and returned with two more double whiskeys.

"To the future," said Stone, raising his glass.

"No way," said Peltz. "To the past."

So they toasted the glorious past, and the sorry present, and a good many other things as well. When Crane's secretary announced that it was time to form a conga line and Crane lined up behind her and put his hands firmly on her ass, Stone decided it was time to leave. Bidding farewell to the noisy group, he had an odd sensation: Headquarters had come to resemble an aging and somewhat tacky cruise ship that was drifting aimlessly offshore; on land, in the outposts of what still passed for the real world, the imperial legions were trying their best to maintain order. It was pathetic. Stone had a plan, beginning to take shape in the neat compartments of his mind. But for now, the best he could do was watch the sorry spectacle—and wait for usable pieces of debris to drift by.

8

IT WAS NEARLY MIDNIGHT BY THE TIME TAYLOR COLLECTED George at his hotel, and Istiklal Avenue had filled with its nighttime population of pimps, street vendors, shoeshine boys, drag queens and political pamphleteers. Most of these night dwellers had the dark, intense features that marked them as Kurds: eyes so black they gave off no reflection; hair so black it seemed like animal fur. Istiklal was a narrow street, crowning the top of a ridge, and the hawkers and merchants clung to the gaudy strip of asphalt as if they feared they might fall off the edge of the world if they strayed too far.

What those Kurdish vendors found on Istiklal Avenue was a piece of the First World. It was like Hamra Street in Beirut or Connaught Road in Hong Kong, a place where the fashions and accents and ideas were foreign and liberating, rather than native and limiting. It had been the same a century ago, when the district was known as Pera, and all the wealth and arrogance of Europe was compressed into those few city blocks atop the ridge. It was more "Turkish" now; you were more likely to hear Bulent Ersoy in the cafés than Brahms, but the mystique was the same. If you were a poor Kurd from Erzurum in the East, any little bit of the West that rubbed off was a blessing. You might never drive a Mercedes car down the grand boulevard, but you could at least stand on the sidewalk at midnight and smoke a Marlboro.

"First stop, Giraffe Street," said Taylor when he greeted George.

"What's that?"

"You'll see," Taylor said, smiling. He noticed that George was still carrying his little bag of tools. "You won't need those on Giraffe Street," he said.

"Never travel without them," answered George. Taylor rolled his eyes.

The driver deposited them at Galata Tower, an ancient monument built by Genoese traders which in recent years had marked the edge of the red-light district. From there, they walked down a steep hill until they came to an iron gate manned by two scruffy-looking policemen. Through the gate was a narrow alley thronged with Turkish men of various ages and growths of mustache. The street sign said: "Zurafa Cadessi."

"Giraffe Street," said Taylor, smiling at the policemen and pushing George through the gate.

"Why do they call it that?" asked George as they walked down a slight hill toward the first cluster of men. As they neared the crowd, the answer became obvious. There stood several dozen Turkish gentlemen, craning their necks to look through the window of a small establishment at the bodies of two semi-clothed women.

"Let's look!" said George.

"All right," said Taylor, pushing his friend toward the front of the crowd. "You asked for it."

Before them was a shop, perhaps fifteen feet across, lit by a bright fluorescent light. And under this garish light were two of the most surpassingly ugly women Taylor had ever seen, posing for the assembled throng. One was tall and thin, wearing black panties and a cutoff T-shirt that revealed the bottoms of her droopy tits. The other was short and very fat, dressed only in a pair of pink panties. She had turned away from the window to give the crowd a view of her ass. What an extraordinary sight it was! Taylor studied the way the arc of pink fabric spread across the puckering flesh of her backside. It was a vast distance and the material was stretched so tight that the threads at the edges were beginning to fray.

"That's your gal," said Taylor, pointing to the fat one. "For a mere two dollars. Plus tips. Plus sheets."

The lady in pink was winking at George. He was smiling back, and for a moment Taylor thought he might actually open the door and engage her services.

"A little friendly advice," said Taylor. "Don't let her get on top."

"She's definitely my type," said George, "but I think we should keep looking."

A few yards down the cobbled street they came to the next establishment, as brightly lit as the first. This was an altogether better spot. The women were younger and prettier, but their breasts were covered, which somewhat reduced the crowd of gawkers outside. "Our Turkish friends tend to be lookers, not buyers," explained Taylor as he pushed toward the window. "A lot of them are just here for a free tit show."

When they reached the front, they could see two women posed against a cheap tile mosaic of a Mediterranean beach scene. One was dressed in a yellow leotard, cut low on the sides to reveal a bit of flesh; she looked as if she might have escaped from a Turkish acrobics class. The other was a young girl, no more than sixteen or seventeen, seated on a stool. She gazed out at the crowd in an icy splendor—not moving a muscle as the dozens of eyes stared at her face and body. It was, thought Taylor, a triumph of self-possession and self-disgust.

"Let's go in and do a little bargaining," he said.

"Mmmmm," agreed George.

As Taylor opened the glass door, the resident pimp emerged from behind the stairs. He was a short fat man, dressed in a sleeveless undershirt, with a stubby cigarette dangling from his lips.

"Hello, my brother," said Taylor in Turkish. "These are lovely girls, as fresh as flowers." The girl in the yellow leotard smiled and tittered. She was surprised to hear a Westerner speak Turkish.

"Thank you, *abi,*" said the pimp. "They are clean, thanks be to Allah."

"Perhaps I could talk to them?"

"As you like, *abi.*" He was looking at Taylor more and more suspiciously. In truth, other than rowdy sailors from the Sixth Fleet, few Westerners wandered down Giraffe Street.

Taylor looked back through the window and saw that the crowd had grown. Looking at the anonymous faces pressed against the window, wide-eyed and horny, he wished he could free these little Turkish birds from their cage.

"I like the yellow one," said George.

"Smart fellow," replied Taylor, steering George toward the girl in the leotard, who was by now batting her eyelashes quite furiously.

"Hello, pistachio," he said. In Turkish, the word for pistachio—*fistik*—was a term of endearment for shapely women. The girl smiled.

"What is your name?" asked Taylor in Turkish.

"Gungor."

"What did she say?" asked George.

"Gungor. That's her name."

"What kind of a name is that?"

"Turkish, dummy."

George laughed. The young lady in yellow laughed, too, although she hadn't a clue what they were saying. The Turkish pimp did not laugh. He appeared to be upset by the bilingual conversation, the laughter and the general confusion that had resulted from the entrance of the two Americans.

"We are under the Turkish flag here," he said in his most dignified tone. "We speak Turkish!"

"Kasura bakma," said Taylor politely. Pardon me. Don't make anything of it.

The dignity of the pimp appeared to have been assuaged, and Taylor was about to resume bargaining when he saw a sudden look of terror in the pimp's eyes.

"What is it?" asked Taylor.

"Madame Mazloumian!"

Taylor turned and saw a small, white-haired old spinster entering the room from a back door.

"She has come for the money," said the pimp, who looked genuinely distressed. The girl in yellow, also vexed, disappeared behind a curtain. The ice queen remained on her stool.

"We better go," said Taylor. "This looks serious."

"Who the hell was that?" asked George when they were outside again.

"An Armenian lady named Mrs. Mazloumian. She owns most of these places. Supposedly she's the biggest taxpayer in Istanbul."

"An Armenian?"

"They're sort of the designated hitters in this league. They're Christians, so they can do all the naughty things that are forbidden to good Moslems, like run whorehouses for good Moslems."

"Hey, Al," cut in George. "All this shopping is building up an appetite. I want to get laid."

"Fear not, my boy, Ms. Right awaits."

They continued down the street. Taylor looked in one window, glanced at the haggard women on display, and pushed George farther on, toward a large crowd—the largest yet—gathered in front of a picture window.

"What do we have here?" asked Taylor, elbowing toward the front.

What they had was an absolutely stunning brunette, naked from the waist up, with the most ample breasts Taylor could remember seeing outside a men's magazine. They were at once very large and very firm, and the areolae around the nipples were a rosy red, almost as if they had been rouged. She had long black hair that glistened like a horse's mane, and when she saw the two Americans approaching, she tilted her head back and shook her hair wildly and wantonly.

"My God!" said George. "What a piece of ass."

"Let's go inquire, shall we?" said Taylor, opening the iron door of the shop with George on his heels. Several of the Turks burst into applause—for the girl and her prospective patrons.

Taylor got right to the point. "How much is she?" he asked the resident pimp. George was still staring in wonder at the woman's breasts.

"Let us not talk of money, my brother," answered the

pimp, sensing that he had here a customer who might pay three or four times the normal price.

Taylor pressed him. "How much, please, my friend?"

"Twenty thousand Turkish liras."

"She is beautiful, but for that I could marry her."

"Fifteen thousand Turkish liras," said the pimp.

"Al," said George, still studying the woman. "Come here. I wanna show you something."

"Hold on," said Taylor. "Let me finish bargaining." He turned again to the pimp. "Five thousand Turkish liras," he said.

"Ten thousand liras," said the pimp.

Taylor shook his hand.

"Hal-lo, big boy," said the Turkish lovely to George. It seemed she spoke a few words of English.

"Al!" implored George. "Come here."

Taylor walked toward his friend, marveling again at the woman's bosom.

"You like my tits?" said the brunette in throaty-voiced English.

"Definitely," said Taylor.

"You want fuckee-suckee?" she said huskily.

"My friend does."

"Hey, Al, for chrissake, I mean it. I got to show you something."

As Taylor approached, George whispered urgently in his ear. "Look at her throat."

"Fuckee-suckee?" repeated the woman. "We go upstairs!" The pimp, too, was encouraging George to head up the stairs to one of the tiny rooms.

"My God, you're right," said Taylor. "She has an Adam's apple!"

"That's not all," whispered George. "Look at her wrists. They're as thick as yours."

"I don't believe it!" said Taylor. He was shaking his head.

The Turkish whore blushed and turned away. She realized that the Americans had discovered her secret.

"Upstairs," said the pimp more urgently.

"I don't fucking believe it!" said Taylor, still shaking his head.

"Five thousand Turkish liras," said the pimp.

"Go fuck yourself," said George.

The embarrassed "woman" disappeared behind the stairs. She returned with a towel draped around her. The crowd of men outside, still eager for the tit show, began hooting and booing, which attracted more people from nearby.

"Aptal yabanci!" shouted one Turk to George; it was a vulgar Turkish expression that meant: You stupid foreigner.

"Has siktir!" cried another, which meant, more or less: Fuck off.

"Shit!" said Taylor. "We better split before this gets nasty." He and George pushed their way out the door just as the crowd was pushing toward them, and they barely managed to squeeze through. Their departure seemed to further inflame the Turkish onlookers. A man in his twenties grabbed George's arm; another pushed sharply against Taylor's back. Taylor took George by the elbow and literally yanked him away from the crowd. They were walking quickly up the small hill toward the gate when a group of Turkish gendarmes, aroused by the commotion, trotted down the hill past them. Taylor nodded deferentially, but the policemen, in their haste, barely noticed him.

When they were safely outside, George turned to Taylor and put his arm around him.

"My pal!" he said. "That's the last time I ever let you take me to a whorehouse."

"Calm down, Georgie," said Taylor. "It's all part of your introduction to the mystic East."

"I wonder if she had her dick cut off."

"You'll never know. Unless you're prepared to spend five thousand Turkish liras."

"Give me a break!" said George.

They walked back toward Galata Tower, where Taylor roused the consulate driver, who had fallen asleep.

"Come on," Taylor said to George. "I'll buy you a drink. The night is young."

"I want some action! I mean it!"

"I know, I know," said Taylor, shaking his head. He was embarrassed by his incompetence as a procurer. He made a mental list of possibilities, weighing each one against the risk that it would produce another disaster. "I've got it," he said eventually. He mumbled a few words to the driver from the consulate motor pool and got in the car.

"What's next?" asked George. "A sheep ranch?"

"A place called Omar's," said Taylor. "An old girlfriend of mine works there. Great gal. Her name is Sonia. She'll like you."

9

OMAR'S HAD THE AMBIENCE OF A ROADSIDE COFFEEHOUSE IN Tashkent or Tbilisi. It smelled of tobacco and Turkish coffee and the sweet licorice scent of anise; and, of course, for its worldly customers, Moslem or otherwise, of beer and whiskey. It was located near the university, just above Kumkapi, in a district frequented by immigrants—Tatars, Kazakhs, Uzbeks, Azeris and a half dozen other Central Asian nationalities.

The bar was on the top floor of a cheap hotel that catered to Eastern travelers, and it featured a spectacular view of the harbor and its varied patterns of illumination: the bright lights of the Istanbul business district across the Golden Horn; the distant twinkling lights of the Asian shore across the Bosporus; the riding lights of the Russian freighters in the Sea of Marmara, waiting their turn to navigate the narrow strait to the Black Sea; and framing this scene, the moonlit spires of the five mosques that dominated the old city.

The owner, Omar Gaspraly, was a Tatar himself, from the Crimea, and he had made the place a gathering point for émigré intellectuals from the Caucasus and Central Asia. On a good night, you could hear people cursing in a half dozen different languages. They came to eat and drink, to read poetry in their native languages, to proclaim the inalienable rights of nations that no longer existed; most of all, they came to denounce the modern-day overlords of that part of the world—the Russians. In Istanbul, among intellectual Uzbeks and Azeris, the rule was: "Everybody meets at Omar's."

"Al-an," boomed a loud and heavily accented voice when Taylor entered the place. Gaspraly embraced him and kissed him on both cheeks. He was a large man, with crinkly gray hair and perpetual laugh lines creased on his face. Taylor kissed him back. Behind the affable Tatar stood a slender Circassian woman in her early thirties in a low-cut, sequined dress. She had the sad look of a cabaret singer who has sung "I Left My Heart in San Francisco" too many times. Except in her case it was probably "I Left My Heart in Sevastopol."

"Sonia," said Omar, pulling her out of the shadows. "Look who is here!" Taylor kiss her on both cheeks. It was a former lover's kiss, at once tender and distant.

"I want you to meet someone," said Taylor, walking her toward George. "This is my friend. His name is Henry, and he doesn't know anyone in Istanbul."

"Hello, Henry," said Sonia.

"Hi," said George. He was wide-eyed, dumbfounded. Perhaps it was the contrast with the vulgar women they had encountered earlier in the evening, but George looked as if he had fallen instantly in love. "Come sit with us," said George. It sounded almost like a marriage proposal.

"One more time I must sing," she said. "Then I come sit."

Omar led them to a quiet booth in the corner of the room, almost hidden from the other tables. The room was so smoky that you couldn't see, at first, that it overlooked the magnificent panorama of Istanbul. The bar, enveloped in cigarette smoke and surrounded by the city lights, seemed to float over Istanbul like a cloud.

"Wod-ka?" said Omar, and wod-ka it was, a full bottle, and three glasses. "I come back," he said.

"How do you know this guy so well?" asked George.

"He did some work for us after the war. We got a few of his buddies killed. Somehow, he still likes us." Taylor emptied his glass of vodka and poured another for himself and for George.

"We fuck up a lot, don't we?" said George.

"Of course we do," said Taylor. "That is our mission. To provide a benchmark of incompetence against which other intelligence services can be measured." They pondered that truth together in silence for a few moments, the cool, sharp taste of the vodka on their lips.

"We're going to solve your problem for you, Al."

"Which problem?"

"Leaving people hanging. Getting them killed."

"Oh yeah? How?"

"With rats."

"Are you crazy?"

"No," said George, leaning toward Taylor and talking in a whisper. "Back at TSD we have a new project to implant transmitters in the bodies of rats. Then we train the little critters to follow very precise routes, sometimes several miles long. If they make a wrong turn, we zap them by remote control, until they get it right."

"So?"

"So when the rats get to where they've been trained to go, we send out a signal that kills them dead—poof!—and activates the microphone and transmitter. The dead rat becomes a listening post. The idea is to release these little guys at a precise point in the Moscow sewer system and have them make their way to the Kremlin, into the walls of the actual building where the actual fucking Politburo meets! And our dead rat will be just on the other side of the wall, broadcasting away. Incredible, no? Like having a miniature agent."

"With fur and big teeth."

"Seriously, Al, this is what you guys need. Nobody's going to get bent out of shape about losing a few rats."

"So how are the little fellows doing?"

"Still a few problems, actually. The rats tend to get lost, despite all the training. Stage fright maybe. And sometimes they don't die when they're supposed to. They hate carrying the hardware, so they try to get rid of it by scratching it, or gnawing at it, which can get kind of messy. But the idea is quite promising, don't you think?"

"Quite," said Taylor. "Maybe one of them could do my job." He poured himself another drink. The band was beginning another set. Taylor scanned the room with a look of pure pleasure on his face. This was the point of it all: to have a drink with a friend in an exotic bar while the band played Crimean love songs.

"Why do you like bars and whorehouses so much?" asked George. "They don't seem like your kind of thing, exactly."

Taylor thought a moment. It was a good question.

"Because I'm a neggo," he said.

"What the hell is a neggo?"

"That's a long story. I'll tell you sometime. Let's listen to the music."

It was, in fact, the truest thing that Taylor could have said about himself. At the New England prep school he had briefly attended in the late 1950s, they divided the world into possos and neggos. The possos believed in things. They got to class on time, they studied diligently to make the honor roll, they wore their letter sweaters right side out. At the seminar tables, they sat without embarrassment in the "suck seats" closest to the teacher. They didn't get drunk, they didn't get laid; but then, they weren't sure they wanted to. They were fine young men; they looked at life without irony.

The neggos, in contrast, professed to believe in nothing. They spent their time in the dormitory butt room, smoking cigarettes under a sign that read: "Recreant in Pacem." They read Zen poetry and listened to Miles Davis records and could recite long passages of "Howl" by heart. When they studied hard, they pretended not to. They were in search of experience and "authenticity." What they feared, above all, was the nothingness of ordinary life. They were, in their way, professional malcontents. When a teacher encountered a student who had lately developed that telltale James Dean look in his eye, he might implore him: "Mr. Jones, you're not going to become a *neggo*, are you?"

Taylor was very much a neggo. So much so that he was ejected from school in the middle of his senior year. "Fired," in neggo lingo. The formal accusation was that he had been gambling on a bridge game in the butt room, but many people did that without getting fired. In Taylor's case, it was an accumulation of things: He had pissed out the dormitory window one afternoon during parents' weekend; he had refused to take a standardized personality-inventory test. He had, in a hundred large and small ways, signaled a dislike for the school and its traditions. And the school finally reciprocated.

Taylor returned home in apparent disgrace and finished out

his senior year at the local high school in his hometown in
Connecticut. His grades were excellent, his test scores were
brilliant, but because of the black mark of his expulsion, he
was not admitted to Harvard or Yale, and went instead to the
University of Chicago. Taylor's father was mortified. In his
mind, the University of Chicago was for Jews. But Taylor
like it well enough. Chicago was a neggos' paradise. Taylor
found new ways to get out of his skin and into other people's.
He would hang out at the blues clubs on the South Side, listening to Elmore James and smoking pot. Or he would drive
east along the shores of Lake Michigan toward the glowing
nightscape of Indiana Harbor and Gary, and play pool with
steelworkers getting off their shifts. To Taylor, it was all glo-
riously romantic—except for school, which was a joke. As an
act of nihilism and defiance, he majored in Near Eastern languages. Surely that would keep him out of law school, he reasoned. And it did. But it didn't keep him out of the CIA.

Taylor would never have joined the CIA if it hadn't been
the 1960s, and if he hadn't been even more contrary than
people imagined. There was the pressure of the draft, of
course, and Vietnam, which seemed to Taylor, even then, like
an especially dumb idea. But it was more complicated than
that. In the wave of generalized national negativism that followed the Kennedy assassination, the people Taylor had spent
his adolescence trying to escape were now embracing his
worldview. Disillusionment was setting in among the bright
young men. The possos didn't want to be spies anymore.
They wanted to join the Peace Corps, go on freedom
marches, hang out in jazz clubs. Even Yale men were having
second thoughts. It was too much for Taylor to bear. The
possos were invading the butt room. So Taylor decided to go
the other way. The rebel became a counter-rebel. And the
Central Intelligence Agency, already losing its annual influx
of the right men from the right schools, was only too glad to
have him. It was, in a way, a neggo's paradise. As Taylor
quickly discovered, you didn't have to believe anything at all.

George might have coaxed a little bit of this out of Taylor,
a hint of the sensualist's quest for experience that had made
him, as his colleagues said, a "natural recruiter." But just then

they heard the booming voice of Omar, who was approaching their table.

"I can join you, Al-an?" said the proprietor. "Not stay long. Just say hi."

"Of course," said Taylor, pouring him a glass of vodka.

"Some coincidence!" said Omar.

"What's that?"

"Another American man is here tonight at my bar."

"Oh yeah?" said Taylor. "Where?"

Omar pointed to a table across the room where a blond-haired man in his late twenties was talking to two older dark-haired men.

"I thought maybe some friend of yours, huh?" said Omar. "He come here two, three times last few weeks. He talk to Azeri men. Tatar men. Tonight I think he talk to Uzbek men. He remind me of you, maybe."

Taylor gazed at the man across the room with a mixture of curiosity and concern.

"I don't believe I know the gentleman."

"Too bad," said Omar, draining his glass. "Maybe Omar is wrong."

"Omar is never wrong," said Taylor.

They talked for a few minutes, about the wonders of the old country and the perfidies of Stalin, which pretty much exhausted Omar's range of interest. To hear him talk, you might think that old Joe Dzhugashvili was still running the Soviet Union. Eventually, a waiter arrived to solicit Omar's help—a quarrel had broken out in the kitchen between a Kurdish busboy and a Sudanese dishwasher—and Omar excused himself. As he walked off, Taylor's eyes turned back toward the American whom Omar had pointed out across the way.

"I have to go to the ladies' room," he said to George.

Taylor took another long drink of vodka, rose from his chair, and headed toward the bathroom. His course led him near the table where the mystery man was sitting. He was tall and tanned, with blond hair and an athlete's body. As Taylor passed the table, he noticed that the man was talking in Turkish—not perfect, but not bad either. He gestured when he talked, reminding Taylor of one of those slick young television preachers on Sunday mornings before the football games started. Taylor visited the men's room and then returned to his seat, curious for more information about the Turkish-speaking American but wary of tipping his hand.

"Georgie," said Taylor, putting his hand on his friend's shoulder. "Do some reconnaissance for me, will you? Find out who this guy is."

"Who am I, workwise?"

"An expat businessman based in Athens." George nodded and strode toward the American, grinning like a Shriner out for a night on the town.

"Hey, asshole!" said George as he approached the table. The blond-haired man bolted upright in his chair and whipped his head around.

"Who are you calling asshole?"

George broke into a broad smile. "Sorry, pal," he apologized. "Just wanted to see if you were a fellow American."

"North America," said the blond.

"How's that?"

"I'm a Canadian."

"No kidding. Wow!"

"Who the fuck are you?"

"Take it easy. My name's Henry. I'm just in from Athens." George extended a meaty hand, waiting for the younger man to introduce himself. He didn't.

"You visiting, too?" asked George, compulsively friendly as only an American traveling abroad can be.

"I work here."

"No kidding. What do you do? I'm a salesman myself. Electronics, from Korea."

"I make films," said the young man, obviously hoping that George would go away. He nodded apologetically to his two Uzbek guests.

"Oh yeah? What kind?" asked George, leaning on the table.

"Documentaries. I'm working on a film about Soviet refugees in Turkey."

"Hey. Wow. No kidding. Who are these guys?"

"Some of my subjects. They are Uzbeks."

"Hi, fellas," said George. "Can I buy you guys a drink?" The Uzbeks smiled and nodded uncomprehendingly.

"No," said the filmmaker abruptly. "I have to leave soon.

We were just finishing our conversation when you interrupted us."

"Oh, sorry. Hey, I'll leave you alone then. You got a business card?"

The Canadian grudgingly handed him a card, hoping to get rid of him. It identified him as one Jack Rawls, employed by a concern called Filmworks, with an address in Vancouver.

"I'm from Ohio myself," said George.

The Canadian cut him off. "Nice meeting you, asshole," he said. He gave George a thin smile and turned back to the Uzbeks.

George returned to the dark booth, where Taylor, sitting alone, had nearly finished the bottle of vodka.

"He's a Canadian," said George. "His name is Jack Rawls. Or at least that's his work name. He says he's a filmmaker." He handed Taylor the Filmworks business card. Taylor studied it a moment.

"Bullshit," he said. "Whoever heard of a Canadian filmmaker in Istanbul? It's ridiculous."

"Definitely."

"What's he like?"

"Spooky," said George. "He talks a little funny. Like a Canadian, I guess."

"Company man?"

"Maybe," said George. "He does sort of have the look, doesn't he? What's he doing here anyway?"

"Beats me. But if someone back home is running a NOC into my territory, I want to know about it. I'm sick of being jerked around."

"Calm down, Al."

"Fuck you," said Taylor. He was drunk and angry, and looking to make trouble. It was a mood like the one twenty years earlier when he had stood up in his dormitory room one Saturday afternoon, unzipped his fly, and urinated out the window. Across the room, Rawls was getting up from his table and going to the bar to pay his bill.

"Listen," said Taylor, his eyes lighting up. "Why don't we find out where Mr. Jack Rawls lives when he's not in Vancouver."

"How?"

"Follow him."

"He'll catch us."

"No, he won't. My driver is a pro."

"Not *now*," pleaded George. The lights were dimming. It was almost time for Sonia's last set of the night. The band was beginning to tune up.

"Yes, now," said Taylor. "Come on. This is important. It's for his own good. Rawls could get in trouble. He doesn't know the neighborhood."

Taylor looked over his shoulder. Rawls was near the door.

"Come on, goddammit! I promise I'll make it up to you. I introduced you to Sonia, didn't I?"

George moaned at the mention of her name.

"Move it!"

George was a soldier. He dutifully picked up his canvas bag and walked out behind Taylor, who was weaving slightly from the booze. As they neared the door, George caught a glimpse of the chanteuse in her stage costume, looking even more beautiful than before. "Come back," she said, blowing him a kiss.

Rawls was already in the street, hailing a taxi. Taylor waited in the shadows until Rawls was safely off, then summoned his driver and told him to follow the taxi at a discreet distance.

The trip confirmed Taylor's suspicions. Rawls took the taxi back across the Galata Bridge to Pera, then pulled over when he reached the divided highway that ran along the edge of the Golden Horn. He then crossed the median strip and caught another taxi—a Murat sedan with a dented door—heading in the other direction. Taylor watched carefully as this little street ballet was played out. He didn't think Rawls had detected them, but if they continued to follow him in the same car going the other way, he surely would.

"This guy is definitely a spook!" said George. "I learned that same trick at the farm."

"Fuckin' A.'

"Now we're screwed."

"No, we're not," said Taylor.

"Why not?"

"Because I got the tag number of the second cab."

Rawls's cab had almost certainly headed back across the Ataturk Bridge to the old city. Taylor told his driver to wait several minutes and then head for the taxi stand in Sultanahmet Square, across the water, which was a gathering spot for cabbies at this hour. When they arrived, Taylor wrote the license number of Rawls's taxi on a piece of paper. He gave it to his driver along with five thousand liras and told him to make some inquiries. The inquiries turned out to be rather brief. For just then a yellow Murat sedan with a dented door cruised to the end of the taxi queue.

It took just a thousand liras to encourage the taxi driver to confide that he had just dropped off a tall blond man at an address just off Yeniceriler Street. When they arrived there several minutes later, Taylor realized to his chagrin that they were back almost to where they had started, in the immigrant district near the university.

"This guy is beginning to piss me off," said Taylor. He had the driver continue on another two blocks and park the car. Then he and George returned on foot to Rawls's apartment building.

The only light on in the building was the one in the right-hand apartment on the third floor. That must be Rawls's place, reasoned Taylor. Now they knew where he lived. So what? Taylor was standing in the shadows, wondering what to do next, when the light on the third floor went out.

"Night-night," said George.

But Rawls wasn't going to bed just yet. A few seconds later he emerged at the front door and, after glancing quickly up and down the street, set off again, heading back toward Yeniceriler Street. Where the hell was he going? What was he doing in Istanbul?

"Now what?" queried George. "Follow him again?"

But that wasn't the right answer. An odd look had come over Taylor's face, a smile so wide that the moonlight seemed to glint off his teeth. It had dawned on him that for the second time in forty-eight hours he had been presented with one of those moments of serendipity—so inviting that it almost compelled a mischievous response.

"Let's piss on this guy," said Taylor. He meant it as a term of art. George nodded. It would not have occurred to him to question Taylor's judgment. Second-guessing was for lawyers and congressmen.

"You got your tools?"

George nodded again. Of course he had his tools. He had lugged them along all night long, from whorehouse to Central Asian cabaret.

"What else have you got?"

"Everything."

"Mike?"

"Yup."

"Recorder?"

"Yup."

"Then let's wire this son of a bitch up and teach somebody a lesson."

"Are you crazy?"

"Absolutely," said Taylor.

Taylor and George crossed the street. The front door was unlocked, which seemed like a further provocation. Taylor looked for a doorman, who might be trouble, but there was nobody in the dim and dusty hallway. So he led George gently up the stairs to the third floor and stood guard while George once again tuned his little orchestra of electronic gadgets. It was absurdly easy to bug the room. He drilled a hole and inserted a contact microphone that could pick up sound from the other side of the wall. It had a built-in transmitter, and when George had covered the hole, it was invisible from either side. All that was left was to put the receiver-recorder somewhere out of the way. George put it under a floorboard on the stairs heading up to the roof of the building.

"This one is a beauty," said George. "It should be good for a month, unless this guy talks in his sleep."

"That's nice," said Taylor. By this time, he had sobered up. The pleasure of this last, entirely unauthorized adventure had given him a second wind. They found the car, awakening the poor driver from a sound sleep. Taylor told him to go back to Omar's. But by the time they got there, it was almost five o'clock. Sonia had left long ago and the only person still there was the night watchman. Taylor suggested other possibilities. He knew a call girl in Cihangir who liked to work mornings. He knew a club on the Asian side that never closed. But George wouldn't hear of anyone but Sonia.

Besides, admitted George, he was getting a bit tired.

* * *

George flew back to Athens the next day. Taylor hadn't planned it that way. He had instructed George to spend the day in bed, dreaming of Sonia, with whom he would absolutely, positively have a date that evening. But Taylor called just after eleven to report that the chief of station in Athens was grumbling about what he claimed was George's unauthorized absence and wanted him back immediately. Taylor didn't mention that he had received a similar call from Timmons in Ankara, in which the good name of headquarters was invoked.

Taylor gathered he was in the doghouse. Apparently he had not covered his ass quite enough to suit the paper pushers. Probably best not to make matters worse, he advised George, by telling anyone about the little caper the previous night with the mysterious Mr. Rawls. They would keep that to themselves, wouldn't they? Of course they would. George told Taylor how to retrieve the tape from the recorder outside Rawls's apartment, and he gently reminded Taylor that he would at some point need another microphone and recorder to replenish his inventory.

"No problem," Taylor assured him. And he was sure it wouldn't be. The little flap over George's not quite authorized visit would pass like a summer rainstorm. The management-by-objectives crowd might be momentarily peeved. But wait until they began reading the take from the bugged chair in the Soviet consulate and the tales of Bulgarians and smuggled guns. Someone might even get a promotion.

10

THE OTTOMAN CHAIR, IT TURNED OUT, WASN'T FOR KUNAYEV'S office at all. After three days in the basement of the Soviet consulate, where it transmitted the sound of rodents and blackbeetles, it was moved to Kunayev's residence in Bebek, a suburb of Istanbul just up the Bosporus. Taylor took the news stoically. The operation wasn't a total loss. Kunayev seemed an interesting fellow. Perhaps he was screwing the maid at home. Or better yet, the chauffeur.

But Kunayev unfortunately was not such an interesting fellow, after all. The Soviet diplomat appeared to lead an ordinary and relatively blameless existence: He liked to drink whiskey, he shouted occasionally at his wife, he played Benny Goodman records on a scratchy phonograph, and he entertained a string of Eastern bloc diplomats who were surely among the dullest people in Istanbul. His Lithuanian wife listened to a better class of music, but otherwise her life seemed as unexceptional as her husband's. She was a busy woman, who left the house often to go shopping or run errands. But there was no reason to suspect that she was seeing a lover.

Kunayev's real problem was the company he kept, Taylor decided. That first week, he gave two formal parties at his home. One was for a visiting delegation of metallurgists from the Ukraine who were attending a conference at Istanbul Technical University. The transcript went on for pages of obscure shop talk about the latest trends in international metallurgy. Eventually one of the Ukrainians got drunk and insulted another member of the group, bringing the evening to an abrupt close. The other big event of the week was a dinner in honor of the Yugoslav consul general and his wife. Kunayev turned out his version of the A list: The East Germans were there. So were the Romanians, and the South Yemenis. Kunayev did his best to try to elicit information from the Yemeni diplomat, but it was evident that the poor man had no idea what was happening back in Aden. Taylor felt sorry for Kunayev. His work seemed even more boring than Taylor's own.

After two weeks, Taylor reluctantly concluded that the Kunayev bugging operation was unlikely to rewrite the history of the Cold War. Indeed, despite Taylor's earlier claims to headquarters, it seemed doubtful that Kunayev was even an intelligence officer.

The Turks didn't seem to mind. Taylor delivered to Serif Osman, with great ceremony, a compilation of the first two weeks' material. Serif was pleased. He made reference to the historic friendship between MIT and the CIA and promised to study the material with the utmost care. Headquarters didn't seem perturbed either. Quite the contrary. Timmons was delighted. So were his bosses, and so were their bosses. Processing the transcripts gave them something to do back home, it seemed. They were "product." It didn't matter that it was gibberish, because no one with any common sense—no one who might dare to ask: "Who *cares* about Ukrainian metallurgy anyway?"—would actually read it.

They assigned Kunayev a cryptonym, CKJACK, and began asking all kinds of questions about him. Did he gamble? How many glasses of water did he drink in an ordinary day? How many children did he have and where were they studying? Did he appear to have any unusual sexual interests? The more questions they asked, the more paper they generated, which in turn enhanced the status of the operation. Timmons suggested that one of his men in Ankara, a Russian speaker, take over the case and Taylor happily complied. The whole business had begun to embarrass him.

The only thing that struck Taylor as the least bit interesting about the Kunayev household was the wife's evident interest in Islam. She spent hours listening to tapes of what sounded like sermons, in a Turkic dialect that Taylor couldn't understand. She talked often about the subject at home. Kunayev himself, half Kazakh, sounded uninterested. Taylor assumed at first that she was trying to impress him, trying to learn the culture and become a good Central Asian wife. But it was more than that. One day she actually put on a headscarf and went to see a local mullah, who was said to be friendly with the Iranian ambassador. Another day she went to a lecture at the Islamic Literary Society at Yildiz Palace on the rites of the various Sufi orders, also known as the dervishes.

Taylor tried to read the agent's report with a straight face. It seemed there were whirling dervishes, howling dervishes, barking dervishes, weeping dervishes, moaning dervishes. One order of dervishes instructed its followers to repeat the name of Allah 78,586 times to achieve enlightenment. Alternatively, the word *wahid,* expressing the oneness of God, could be repeated 93,420 times. Or the word *aziz,* expressing God's preciousness, could be repeated 74,644 times. In addition to these

eccentricities, the lecturer at Yildiz Palace had explained another interesting fact about the Sufi brotherhoods. They
formed an invisible chain stretching from Turkey east across
Central Asia, the lecturer said. And for that reason, the Soviet
authorities had been working unsuccessfully since the 1920s to
eradicate them. Through his long discussion, the Soviet consul
general's wife had taken careful notes, according to the surveillance report.

An unusual woman, Taylor concluded. There was one more
interesting fact about Silvana Kunayeva. She had a habit of
disappearing. The Turkish watchers would be following her
into a crowded store, or down a sidewalk jammed with people at rush hour, and they would lose the track. She wasn't
doing anything suspicious. She wasn't doing anything at all.
They simply lost track of her.

Then, one day in late spring, it ended. A Russian workman
arrived at Kunayev's residence and put the Ottoman chair in
a wooden crate. The sound of hammer and nails was almost
deafening for the poor transcribers. The crate was taken back
to the consulate, where it waited for several days. Then it was
put on an embassy truck, taken to the airport, and loaded
aboard a Soviet plane.

Taylor at first assumed the worst: The bug had been discovered and they were shipping the chair back to Moscow
Center for more study. But he was wrong. Inquiries at the airport revealed that the chair wasn't bound for Moscow at all,
but for Alma-Ata. And accompanying it was Kunayev himself. Discreet inquiries by several friendly diplomats revealed
that the Soviet consul general was returning to his native republic for a brief home leave. He had even boasted to an Indian diplomat that when he went home he would be meeting
with his cousin, the party first secretary of Kazakhstan. The
chair, Taylor finally understood, was a gift—an elaborate
piece of baksheesh. At last, Taylor felt a measure of respect
for Kunayev. The corrupt little man was trying to kiss the ass
of his political patron.

Taylor sent home a detailed cable summarizing these de-
velopments, but the front office was not amused. Continuing
the surveillance in Alma-Ata would be a practical impossibil-
ity. The operation was finished. The CKJACK transcripts

would no longer feed the maw of analysts and taskers and estimators. A "product" would disappear from the shelves; the sum of intelligence would be diminished. It was all very sad. The only person back home who seemed genuinely pleased by this course of events was Edward Stone. A regular reader of the CKJACK traffic, Stone saw another small piece of his mosaic falling into place.

III

SDROTTEN

London / Istanbul

February–March 1979

11

♦

Anna Barnes arrived in London the day the Ayatollah Khomeini returned to Tehran. The agency was in a generalized state of panic. All the big stations in Europe had been altered to look for assets who might be able to do something, anything, to help patch together contacts with the new regime. The files of old prospects who had been rejected years before as uninteresting or unreliable were now being reopened. They were turning over every stone—wild-eyed Kurdish nationalists, money-grubbing Iranian journalists, French leftists—nobody was so weird that the agency wasn't willing to give him a look now, when it was in trouble.

What possible interest could any of this have for the young dark-haired American woman arriving on Pan Am Flight 106 from Dulles? None, evidently. She had been immersed in a copy of *Institutional Investor* on the way over, and when she arrived at Heathrow, she bought herself the latest issue of *Euromoney*. She was a banker, apparently. A young career woman on the make. They were everywhere that year, the women lawyers and bankers fresh out of Oxford and Yale and the Ecole Nationale d'Administration, queuing up for their seats on the global gravy train.

Halcyon Ltd. had its offices in one of those forgettable squares near Holborn Circus. Anna showed up the first day in a dress-for-success pinstripe suit, light makeup, all business. She spent the morning filling out forms for a Mrs. Sanchez, the head secretary, who was the only person there until nearly eleven o'clock.

"You're PCS, aren't you?" asked Mrs. Sanchez.

"Excuse me?" asked Anna.

"Is this a permanent change of station, or are you here on TDY?"

"It's my first station, actually," said Anna.

Mrs. Sanchez rolled her eyes as if to say: I guessed that. She showed Anna to her office, gave her a key to the ladies' room, pointed out where they kept the paper clips and pencils, handed her some cable forms, and generally did her best to make Anna feel like an idiot. Apparently Mrs. Sanchez was not entirely comfortable with the notion of a woman case officer entering her domain. Eventually other co-workers arrived and gave Anna at least the semblance of a real welcome.

Presiding over Halcyon Ltd. was a twinkle-eyed and slightly dizzy man in his fifties named Dennis Rigg. He had been a NOC for more than twenty years, and his manner suggested that all the years of concealment and anxiety had devoured the interior of his personality, leaving only the cheery, giddy shell. The firm's two other associates worked for the agency as well—both young men in their early thirties, who tried very hard to look like Ivy Leaguers but were actually from state schools in the Midwest. Mrs. Sanchez and the other secretaries were CIA, too. The only non-agency person on the premises was a retired military man, Admiral Hawes, or Dawes—Anna could never quite get the name because he swallowed his words—who was nominally the chairman of the firm and was trotted out to impress visitors and putative clients. The Admiral took very long lunches. Sometimes they lasted for days.

Halcyon Ltd. was a nest of NOCs: a small group of case officers working under non-official cover. It was a tidy arrangement. The Halcyon NOCs reported to the London chief of station, just like embassy officers, but they met their handlers at safe houses. Like all NOCs, they had some obvious advantages over the inside people. They could spot and develop agents without disclosing official U.S. government interest. They could gain access to people and places that would be denied to an embassy staffer. They could meet unobtrusively with agents. All in all, they had less flap potential. Unless, of course, they got caught.

Halcyon was a product of the agency's endless wrangle over cover. Everybody knew that embassy cover—as a political or commercial officer—was the same as no cover. It was transparent. If the Russians couldn't figure out for themselves who were the spies by looking at the Diplomatic List, they had help from State Department wives, who complained endlessly at cocktail parties about the better perks that CIA officers received: bigger apartments, larger allowances for entertaining, more frequent travel. The State Department had tried to help by developing something called "integrated cover," in which CIA officers going behind the Iron Curtain would train and study alongside ordinary foreign service officers—seemingly indistinguishable. But once people got to the embassies, cliques started to form, and they gave the game away.

The answer was more NOCs. That, at least, was the recommendation of several of the task forces that had examined the cover problem since the 1950s. The argument for more NOCs was always the same: They were truly clandestine. The argument against them also was always the same: They were a pain in the ass. Halcyon illustrated both sides of the debate. Since the firm nominally specialized in Third World investment projects, especially in the Near East, its "employees" could travel widely and meet a range of people without arousing suspicion. The drawback, from the London station chief's standpoint, was that running NOCs was almost as complicated as running agents.

It was assumed that NOCs were neurotic. They had to be, living out there in the cold. They would come back after a half dozen years of pretending to work for an advertising agency or an airline all messed up in the head. Sometimes the cover job would have taken over so completely that the NOC would imagine it was all for real—the big car, the trips to Nice—and forget he was still a GS-14. It was hard, even for men. And for years, it had been assumed that it would be impossible for women. They would get too lonely, too isolated, too weird. They would fall in love with their agents, or their case officers, or any old Joe who talked to them in the street. Those old assumptions were slowly changing. Even so, the mandarins probably wouldn't have sent Anna Barnes forth so eagerly that year if the world hadn't been so obviously going to hell.

* * *

The real problem with being a NOC, Anna decided after her first week, was that there wasn't enough to do. The gang at Halcyon wasn't allowed to operate on its own, assigning itself targets and levying requirements. Everything had to be cleared through the London station, then through Langley, then back through the station, and back finally to Halcyon. That multiplied the paperwork and delays.

At first Anna thought it was just because she was so new that she had so few real things to do every day. But she noticed that it was the same for the others. They spent an awfully long time reading the newspapers each morning. At twelve forty-five the men would all stride off to lunch, for fancy meals in Mayfair restaurants that were allocated variously to "spotting" and "development" of prospective talent. They returned around three o'clock, usually looking a bit flushed, and occupied themselves with paperwork for several hours. Sometimes they even did a little merchant banking business, to keep their cover intact. But the impression remained that they were somewhat underemployed. Anna remembered what Edward Stone had said about intelligence work and boredom. Perhaps he had been right.

Anna busied herself the first week with moving into a flat in the newly fashionable district of Notting Hill Gate. ("Yes," Dennis had said, "that's where you would live.") She also reacquainted herself with London, a city she had passed through a half dozen times before, often with her father. During her lunch hour—at Halcyon it was more like two hours—she took to visiting her father's old haunts. She paid calls to his favorite shirtmaker on Jermyn Street, to the store where he bought his hats on St. James's Street, to his favorite shoe store on King Street. After two days of visiting the stations of the cross, she got tired of it—there wasn't much to see in a men's shoe store, after all—and went shopping for herself along New Bond Street.

Several times that first week Anna told her twinkle-eyed boss that she worried she wasn't getting much accomplished. Dennis answered such queries with aphorisms culled from a lifetime in the spy business. "Keep spotting!" he would say. "Always be on the lookout!" At the end of the first week, sensing that all was not entirely happy with the new girl, Dennis sent her off to a seminar on Saudi development planning, thinking that would make her feel better.

Anna needn't have worried quite so much. The wheels of the bureaucracy, although invisible to her, were indeed turning. At the beginning of her second week on the job, she received a telephone call from a man at the embassy named Howard Hambly. He was nominally a second secretary in the economic section, but he was in fact the officer assigned to supervise the care and feeding of Anna Barnes. He was calling from a phone booth to arrange a meeting.

They met at a safe house in Stoke Newington. It was a small workingman's house on a quiet street called Carysfort Road, a block from Clissold Park. It was a street where milkmen and minicab drivers lived, a street where people went out to eat at the fish-and-chips shop around the corner. It struck Anna as a silly place for a safe house, a place where an empty dwelling occupied briefly and occasionally by Americans would stick out rather obviously. But she was new to the business.

Howard was waiting at the door. He was a balding man in his mid-forties, harried-looking, not quite put together, the sands running out in the hourglass of his career. He had been sent to London as a reward for many years in sub-Saharan Africa, and he seemed to regard his tasks in the London station as a diversion from the important work of attending plays and visiting pubs. Running a NOC was the last thing he wanted to be doing. They were notoriously fucked up. Even the men.

"So how are you settling in?" Howard asked solicitously. Meaning: Are you cracking up yet?

"Fine!" said Anna cheerily.

"Got an apartment?"

"Yes. A really nice one. Above an antique shop."

Howard surveyed her. She certainly didn't look neurotic, which to Howard meant homely. She was dressed neatly, attractively even, in a skirt and cashmere sweater. She seemed perky enough. She wasn't complaining.

"I have a little job for you," said Howard.

"Great!" said Anna. "What is it?"

"We have a guy who's been trying very hard to make contact with us. He's an Iranian. He keeps calling the embassy, leaving messages. Claims to be part of Khomeini's secret intelligence service, which is weird, because we don't think Khomeini has one. He also claims to have some very hot poop. We haven't known what to do with him, so we haven't done anything. He's kind of an oddball, to be honest. I don't suppose that would have any interest."

"Are you kidding?" said Anna. "Of course it would. When do I start?"

The embassy man smiled. There was something about Anna that made people remember their own first blush of enthusiasm. "Listen," he said. "I ought to warn you. This guy may be a big nothing. In addition to being weird."

"No problem," said Anna. "What's his name?"

"Ali Ascari. At least that's the one he's using with us."

"When can we arrange a meet?"

"Hold on, sweetie. We need traces. We'll ask headquarters and Tehran whether they've got anything on Ascari, any past connections with us or anybody else. For all we know, we've already got a 201 file on him back home, under some other name."

"So how am I going to meet Mr. Ascari?"

"That shouldn't be too hard. We'll use SDFIBBER."

"Who's SDFIBBER?"

"He's an Iranian journalist here in London. His real name is Farduz, or Marduz, something like that. He knows everybody, sees everybody. He's a perfect access agent. We'll have him arrange a lunch with you and Ascari."

"SD is the prefix for Iran?"

"You got it."

"What's my rationale for being there? If you don't mind my asking a dumb question."

"That's not a dumb question. That's a good question. Let's see. You're a pretty woman, a friend of SDFIBBER, like to meet interesting people."

"No way," said Anna. "He'll take me for a hooker."

"Okay. You're a terribly serious young investment banker with a passionate interest in the Iranian economy. Like that better?"

"Much better."

"I'll see what headquarters has to say and get back to you.

But they ought to buy it. They've gone Iran-crazy back home, now that everything has turned to shit. They'll approve almost anything." Anna barely heard him. She was going to handle a case. She was going to swim in the big pool.

12

◆

As Anna lay awake that night, tense with the anticipation of her first assignment, she thought of Dr. Marcus, the agency psychiatrist. He had been Anna's instructor for a two-week tutorial, "The Psychology of Agent Recruitment," conducted in one of those crummy motel rooms back in Arlington. And in the way that psychiatrists do, even when they're making conversation at a cocktail party, he had asked her questions and nodded gravely and said "Um-hum" as she tried self-consciously to answer. Anna hadn't been sure at first whether she was Dr. Marcus's pupil or patient, and then had realized that she was both.

When she first met Dr. Marcus, she had been surprised that someone like him could possibly work for the CIA. He looked like an aging graduate student, tall and shabbily dressed, balding with a fringe of matted red hair and dark circles under his eyes. It was the face of a man who had had too much caffeine over the years and too little sleep. He looked, in fact, like a walking illustration for one of his theories about recruitment: a man who hadn't achieved all that he might have in life, and was therefore vulnerable to an approach. Except in his case, he wasn't vulnerable. He asked all the questions.

The first few sessions had been like psychotherapy. The point was simply to talk, Dr. Marcus said, and cover any personal details that might have been skipped during the initial screening. Anna soon discovered that Dr. Marcus had a habit of pausing in mid-conversation, often for a very long time, and she found herself blurting out odd things about herself to fill the dead space. She wanted to be helpful. Dr. Marcus would ask a simple question about her graduate work and Anna would volunteer: "My father never wanted me to go to graduate school."

"Um-hum," Dr. Marcus would say in his flat, affectless voice. "And why was that?"

"I think he wanted me to go into the foreign service."

"Um-hum."

"But probably not the CIA."

"And why not?"

"I don't know. Maybe he was afraid of it. Foreign service officers don't usually like the CIA."

"And does that make the CIA more attractive for you, Anna, the fact that your father didn't approve of it?"

At this point Anna would want to punch Dr. Marcus in the nose. But he looked so hungry for words, and so harmless, that she was soon offering up some other morsel. She would talk about her useless brother in New Mexico, or her ex-boyfriend in Cambridge, or her brief and laughable experience with marijuana in college. Anything to keep poor Dr. Marcus from looking so forlorn. He seemed especially interested in Anna's life as a woman. "Would you describe yourself as a feminist?" he asked during their second session.

"Yes, of course," answered Anna.

"Why do you say 'of course'?"

"Because for a woman my age it's like saying you're a woman."

"Um-hum. And why is that?"

"Because. It just is. If you live in America and believe in your country, you say you're an American. If you're a woman and you believe in yourself, you say you're a feminist. It's no big deal."

"Why not?"

"Okay. It is a big deal, to some people."

"But not to you."

"Yes, it is to me, too."

"And what does it mean to you to be a feminist?"

"It means you stand on your own. You make decisions for yourself. You don't just do what men tell you."

"What if men are telling you to do something sensible?"

"Then you do it, of course. Give me a break, Dr. Marcus."

"I see. And do you like men?"

"Yes, of course I do."

"What do you mean 'of course'?"

"I mean I like men. I like talking to them. I like going to the movies with them. I like sleeping with them. I like men. Get the picture?"

"And do feminists like men?"

"Jesus Christ! How should I know? Some do. Some don't. It all depends on their personal experience."

"I see. And what has your personal experience been?"

"Good, mostly. Occasionally bad. But I'm careful."

"Careful of what?"

"Careful not to get too involved with the wrong man. Careful not to let things get out of control."

"What do you mean by 'out of control'?"

"You know. Scary. Vulnerable. Like a roller coaster with no brakes."

"Um-hum," said Dr. Marcus, nodding gravely.

And so it went, hour after hour, these meandering analytic dialogues. At first Anna had been curious about Dr. Marcus and wanted to please him by giving appropriate answers. Then she began to find his questions intrusive and boring and decided that she disliked him. Finally, by the third day, she found herself relaxed and floating on a tide of self-revelation, saying whatever fell into her head without the slightest embarrassment. Whereupon Dr. Marcus seemed at last to grow tired of the exercise, and began focusing the sessions more closely on matters of tradecraft.

Anna had not realized, until these meetings with Dr. Marcus, the extent to which CIA operations were shaped by psychology. The more he talked, the more obvious it became that modern intelligence work was about understanding vulnerabilities and predispositions, about knowing how to spot the particular traits that made one person a perfect recruit and the other a walking disaster, and ultimately about using the positive and negative reinforcements that allow one human being to condition the behavior of another.

"The Soviets teach their case officers that there are four methods of recruiting an agent," Dr. Marcus had said one day.

"They use an acronym: MISE. It stands for Money, Ideology, Sex, Ego. But the Soviets are wrong, Anna."

"Why?" Anna had asked. It sounded sensible enough. Money, ideology, sex and ego seemed as inescapable as the four points of the compass.

"Because there is only one motivation that really matters, and that is ego. That is what leads someone to become a spy, to defect, to betray his country. He may rationalize it in other terms. He may see himself as serving a higher cause. Or he may think he wants to screw teenage girls in California for the rest of his life. But these are merely the conscious expressions of something deeper. Ideology is not a deep motive. It may be how an agent rationalizes his defection, but the real motivation is something more basic, involving response to authority."

Anna remembered the lecture almost word for word. And as she lay there in bed in her little flat in Notting Hill Gate thinking about what she would do the next day, she went back through Dr. Marcus's advice the way a football player might review the play book in his mind the night before a big game.

"There is a life cycle of treason," Dr. Marcus had said. "Have you ever read *Passages?*"

Anna nodded. Everybody had read *Passages*.

"Then you know a lot about how to recruit an agent, because the same factors are at work. I've looked at the cases of dozens of spies and defectors, and I've found that the ripest time for someone to commit treason is when he's in his late thirties to mid-forties. The time when he's hitting mid-career and mid-marriage and taking stock. It's a passage, of sorts."

"So treason is the ultimate mid-life crisis," Anna joked. But Dr. Marcus didn't laugh. She had it exactly right. Treason *was* the ultimate mid-life crisis.

"If you spot a man who is doing well in his career," Dr. Marcus continued, "who's happily married and doesn't seem to be having any mid-life anxieties, he's probably not a likely target for recruitment. Treason happens when a man is frustrated. His ego is blocked. He decides he hasn't accomplished all he had hoped to in one system, so he chooses another."

"How can you tell if someone is ready to jump?" Anna had asked.

"You look for the indicators of mid-life blockage. A marriage that isn't working. A career that isn't rising as fast as it should. When you spot someone with those characteristics, you look more closely and try to find out what makes him tick, what he really wants out of life. Then you try to give it to him."

"How?"

"In whatever ways you can think of. The Soviets once recruited a Swedish military officer who was angry that he hadn't been promoted to colonel. The first thing they did when they had him on the line was to hold an elaborate secret ceremony where they made him a general in the KGB and gave him a medal. You do whatever it takes. Medals, plaques, testimonials. Whatever the ego craves. The point is to answer, in the mirror relationship you are creating, the particular need that is not being met in the man's ordinary life."

"But how do you know who will make a good agent?" Anna had wondered.

"You don't," the psychiatrist answered. "But you can make some good guesses. Treason is about rejecting authority, so you obviously need someone who is prepared to do that. But the particular form the rejection takes is extremely important, in operational terms.

"Some people want to confront authority directly. An extreme case is someone like Solzhenitsyn, who hates the system and wants to tell the world about it, regardless of the risks. That sort of person is very brave and admirable, and might make a good novelist. But he'd make a lousy intelligence agent, because he'd be so obvious."

So much for recruiting Solzhenitsyn.

"Then there's the sort of person who wants to break with authority, but who isn't quite so bombastic. Someone who would leave his wife or quit his job if he was unhappy. He'll be a good defector—he wants out—but a lousy agent in place."

"What kind of person makes a good agent in place?" Anna asked.

"Here's a hint. Consider two men, both with bad marriages. One has noisy fights all the time. The other is completely calm on the surface, doesn't tell a soul about his problems, but in secret is seeing a mistress. That man is your candidate for agent in place. He is showing you an ability to live with contradiction and a capacity for split loyalty."

"He sounds like a dreadful person."

"Perhaps, but in our game, he's your man."

13
—— ◆ ——

Anna's first thought when she saw Ali Ascari enter the restaurant was: What an ugly little man! He was short and stocky, with a big nose and bulging eyes that darted back and forth as he scanned the room. And he was very hairy—covered with hair, in fact—from his bristly back beard to the backs of his hirsute hands. It was a relief in some ways that he was so ugly. Anna had been half afraid that he would be a suave Omar Sharif type with bedroom eyes.

Ascari approached the quiet corner table where Anna and SDFIBBER were sitting. He gave SDFIBBER a big hello, kissed him on both cheeks, and then turned to Anna. He was wobbling his head slightly and rustling his bottom like a preening pigeon. SDFIBBER made the introduction, using false names, according to instructions.

"This is my friend who I mentioned to you on the phone, Allison James. She's a banker."

"Hello, miss," said Ascari.

"How do you do," said Anna, extending her hand. Ascari's eyes, she noticed, were no longer meeting hers. He was looking at her chest. She moved her purse under her arm to partially block his view.

"Mr. Farduz tells me you are interested in Iran," said Ascari as he sat down next to Anna on the banquette, head still wobbling slightly.

"Yes," said Anna. "Very interested. We represent several

large clients who have substantial interests in the Middle East. We're looking for new business. Economic development. Especially now, with oil prices rising and development plans likely to change."

"Um-hum," said Ascari, taking out his worry beads. He didn't seem to be listening.

"And loans," Anna continued. "Some of our clients are commercial banks."

"That's nice," said Ascari. "Mr. Farduz didn't tell me you were so pretty."

"Thank you," said Anna courteously.

Ascari turned to SDFIBBER and rattled off something in Farsi. Anna strained to listen to the conversation and, as she caught the drift of it, her temperature rose.

"Look at that ass!" said Ascari.

"And those long legs," said SDFIBBER.

Anna bit her tongue.

"Her breasts are nice," continued Ascari. "Not too big, but nice."

That's enough, thought Anna. She cleared her throat and spoke carefully in Farsi.

"Excuse me, gentlemen," she said, "but be careful what you say. You wouldn't want to insult a lady."

There was a great commotion of embarrassment and apologies, mostly from SDFIBBER, who looked worried that Anna might do something to cut his retainer. They ordered drinks. Ascari, despite his mullah's beard, requested a gin and tonic. SDFIBBER tried to be charming. He passed along the latest gossip about the Shah. The Empress Farah, it seemed, wasn't liking exile in Morocco. She wanted to move on, to the United States. And the Shah's sister, the harlot! She was in Paris, entertaining all comers and spending money by the barrel. He went on like this for nearly thirty minutes of singsong chitchat. Ascari mostly stared at Anna and played with his worry beads.

Eventually SDFIBBER looked at his watch.

"What a nuisance!" he said. "I'm sorry, but I must go."

"No," said Anna firmly. "You should stay."

"I am sorry," said SDFIBBER. "But truly I must go. I have an appointment. Why don't you two stay and talk. About Iran."

"Can't your appointment wait?"

"I'm afraid not."

"Perhaps I should go, too," said Anna, looking at her watch, trying to think what proper tradecraft would dictate. What would an investment banker eager for business with Iran do? Stay, of course. But what would the same investment banker do if the client was ogling her tits? She rose from her chair.

"Stay," said SDFIBBER.

"Please stay," said Ascari. "There are some things I would like to tell you. About Iran." He looked serious. His head wasn't wobbling.

Anna slid slowly back into the chair.

"Good!" said SDFIBBER. "I'll leave the two of you to talk, then. Goodbye!" He shook hands with Anna, kissed Ascari three times, and headed for the door. Watching him leave, Anna made a mental note to do what she could to make life miserable for SDFIBBER.

When they were alone, Ascari turned to Anna with a look of great seriousness. He spoke in the nasally voice that Iranians seem to have in any language.

"Are you from CIA, lady?"

Anna sat up straight in her chair. Careful now. Nice and natural.

"No," she said. "I told you. I'm an investment banker. We're interested in doing business with Iran."

"You are not from CIA?"

"No." She had recovered her balance enough to try a little laugh. "How silly. What makes you think that?"

"You are not from CIA." He said it this time as a statement of fact.

"No," she repeated.

"That is big disappointment for me," he said. "Very big."

"Why?"

"Because I want to contact CIA. I have important things to tell them about Iran. I have been trying for three weeks, ever since Shah leave. I call embassy. I leave messages. No answer. So I thought maybe they send you."

He did look very disappointed. He was frowning and popping his worry beads back and forth on their string. Anna thought a moment. She couldn't remember anything in training that covered this situation. In fact, she couldn't remember anything in training that would apply to any aspect of this encounter. One thing did seem obvious, however. The goal in meeting Ascari was to find out what he had to say.

"Mr. Ascari . . ." said Anna, pausing.

"Yes, lady," he answered glumly.

"I do know a few people at the embassy. Would that help? Maybe I could pass your information along to them."

"You know embassy people?"

Anna nodded. "Yes. A few people. They're social friends."

"And these people, are they CIA?"

"I don't know," said Anna. "But it's all the same thing in the embassy, isn't it?"

"Yeah, maybe so. Okay. Let's talk." As he said this, Ascari smiled and put his hand on Anna's knee. She pushed it away but said nothing, pretending it hadn't happened.

"Okay, miss," he said. "We talk about Iran. Then you tell your friends in embassy. Yes?"

"Yes."

"Okay. I work with Khomeini people. Security people. Spy people. You get me?"

Anna was about to say yes when it occurred to her that she didn't, in fact, understand him. "No," she said, "I don't get you."

"What is the problem?"

"How can Khomeini have spies?" she asked quietly. "He just returned to Iran."

Ascari rolled his eyes and clucked his tongue. "Of course he has spies! What you think he been doing all these years? Just reading Koran?"

"You needn't talk so loud," said Anna. She looked around the restaurant. Nobody seemed to be eavesdropping, but you never knew. "Maybe it would be better to speak in Farsi," she said.

"No. English okay," said Ascari. "No problem." He seemed uncomfortable at the thought of an American woman speaking his language.

"Fine. Go ahead."

"So I work for Khomeini people. But I work for me, too. And I thought maybe Americans would like to meet a

Khomeini man like me now. Because Americans only know Shah man, and they are finish. But I know things."

"What sort of things?"

"I know some big terrorists work for Khomeini. They train with PLO men in Lebanon. They train with Syrian *moukhabarat*. They train with Russians. I know who they are."

"Um-hum," said Anna.

"You tell embassy that, okay?"

Anna nodded.

"I know who these big terrorists are. I know where they have training camps. Exact location. Maybe I find out some of their plans, too. Who knows. What you think of that, lady?"

"I'm sure the embassy would be very interested."

Ascari smiled. He put his hand on Anna's leg again, this time higher up the thigh. He seemed to be giving himself a reward for the information he had just provided. Anna pushed his hand away again, more forcefully.

"Keep talking," she said. "And stop touching me."

"Okay. Okay. I tell you something interesting. Next month Khomeini men will send out their own spies to Iran embassy in London, in Paris, in Brussels. Very dangerous, these men. But easy to spot."

"Why?"

"Because they all have beards!"

Anna smiled. She couldn't tell if he was joking.

Ascari wagged his finger at her. "Hey, lady. This is serious. You tell your friends at embassy to watch out for beards!"

Anna's smile vanished. "Right," she said. "Who else is Khomeini sending out?"

"He is sending men to buy guns. Arms dealers! One of them is my friend. His sister married to the brother of my sister's husband. He is the leader."

"What's his name?"

"You tell embassy?"

"Of course."

"Hussein Madaressi."

"Hussein Madaressi," repeated Anna, committing the name to memory.

"You have beautiful eyes," said Ascari.

Anna ignored him. "What else should I tell them at the embassy?"

"That's enough. What, you think I do this for free? You tell them what I told you. I know lot more things. Too many things. Big things. This is free sample. If they want to talk to me, they can contact me."

"How?"

"Here, come with me. I show you where I live." He took her hand and tried to pull her to her feet.

"Just give me the address," said Anna. "And the telephone number."

Ascari wrote the information out on a piece of paper. Cover, Anna reminded herself. "What about the Iranian economy?" she asked earnestly as Ascari was writing. "What can you tell me that would be useful for my bank?"

"I don't know economy," said Ascari. He looked bored again.

"How many of the Shah's big projects do you think the new government will continue?"

"I don't know economy," repeated the Iranian. He was staring at Anna's breasts.

"What about oil? How high do you think prices will go?"

"Hey, lady! You asking wrong man. How should Ali Ascari know what will happen to oil price?"

"It's very important to my bank."

"Hmmm," said Ascari, putting his hand on Anna's knee once more and stroking it. "I don't know. But maybe I could find out for you."

This time Anna slapped his hand and stood up. "That's enough," she said. "It's time for me to go. Waiter!" She called for the check.

"I pay," said the Iranian.

"Waiter!"

"Shhh," he said. "I tell you, I pay."

"All right," said Anna. At this point, she simply wanted out. "Thank you very much."

"Your friends will call me, okay?"

"Goodbye," said Anna. She didn't bother to shake his hand.

What a loathsome little man! thought Anna as she walked

out of the restaurant and into the gray chill of the London winter afternoon. What a vile toad of a man!

Anna returned to the safe house at Stoke Newington that evening. The milkmen were home. Their vans were parked on the street. She had calmed down considerably from that afternoon. In fact, she had decided to omit references to Ascari's appalling sexual behavior from her account of the meeting. It would only make her sound petty and bitchy, unable to control a prospective agent. She didn't want to get a reputation in her first month on the job as a whiner. Besides, Anna decided, if what Ascari said was true, he might be worth the trouble.

Anna summarized for Howard the main points of information that Ascari had passed along. The reference to Iranian terrorists and training camps. The warning that Khomeini's operatives would be arriving at European embassies in March. The identification, by name, of the man who would be buying arms for Khomeini.

"Not bad," said Howard. Anna suspected that, from him, that was a rave. "How'd you get him to tell you all this?"

Anna explained her little ploy about "friends at the embassy." Howard rolled his eyes.

"Not great," he said. "But not awful."

"I couldn't think of anything else."

"Does he believe that you're really a banker?"

"I think so," said Anna, remembering the feel of his hand on her knee.

"Good. At least your cover is intact, more or less. Which is important, because we don't want direct USG contact with this guy yet. We don't want Khomeini to think we're looking up his asshole. Pardon my French."

"Forget it," said Anna.

"What kind of guy is Ascari anyway?"

"A jerk."

"How do you mean?"

"You know, a Persian. Creepy-crawly. Touchy-feely. And he wants money."

"Of course he wants money," said Howard. "I'd be nervous if he didn't. Nothing so clean as money."

"Can we pay him?"

"That depends. We'll see how what he told you checks out with headquarters and Tehran."

"And then?"

"I dunno. Do you think you can work with him?"

Anna thought a moment. Could she work with this obnoxious pig? Not if he kept trying to feel her up. She would need to establish more distance. She would need to stop his lecherous behavior, period. The alternative was to admit failure in her first assignment as a case officer.

"Sure," said Anna. "I can work with him."

"Great," said Howard. "Because I think we ought to try for another meet."

"Terrific!" said Anna. "By the way," she added. "I'm not sure SDFIBBER is worth what we're paying him."

"Oh yeah? Why not?"

"He was very unprofessional today. Left after half an hour. Damned near blew my cover right off the bat. Bad news."

"Thanks for the warning," said Howard. "I'll put it in his 201."

Ali Ascari's information proved surprisingly accurate. A quick check by the Tehran station identified Hussein Madaressi as an Iranian businessman living in Stuttgart who had helped raise money for Khomeini while he was in exile. Headquarters queried the CIA base chief in Stuttgart, who checked with his local contacts and reported that an Iranian named Madaressi had, in fact, met during the last month with a prominent European arms dealer. As for the bearded Khomeini agents invading European embassies, Tehran said it couldn't confirm the report. But one of its local assets had mentioned during the past week that the mullahs might be organizing some kind of shadow foreign service.

"Headquarters thinks your man has possibilities," said Howard with a wink at his next meeting with Anna, several days later. "But they need more information to evaluate him."

"Do they want a PRQ?" asked Anna. That was how Howard and Dennis liked to talk, in the acronymic gibberish that, in this case, stood for the prospective agent's life history, known as a Personal Record Questionnaire.

"Slow down," said Howard. "We've got a long way to go before that. And we don't want you to break cover with him."

"What do you want?"

"Basic information. Date of birth, place of birth. How he makes his living. Who he has worked for in the past. Passport stuff."

"Isn't that going to seem odd? An investment banker asking him his birthday?"

"Tell him that your friends in the embassy want to know more about him. Tell him they were very interested by what he passed along at the first meeting, but they need to know more about him. Otherwise they can't evaluate him."

"Where should I meet him? A safe house?"

"Hell no. Where would a lady investment banker come up with a safe house, for chrissake? Just meet him in a restaurant. Call him on the phone and arrange to meet him in a restaurant."

"He may get the wrong idea."

"How do you mean?"

"He may think it's a date. You know, boy-girl, kissy-kissy."

"So what. Let him think what he likes. No matter what he thinks, you're holding the strings, right?"

"Sure," said Anna, nodding her head. It felt like a prison sentence.

Her concern must have been apparent even to Howard, for he stopped a moment and scratched his head. "How's the rapport between the two of you anyway?"

"What do you mean?"

"I mean, how do you get along? Does he like you? Do you like him? You know, rapport."

"It's okay. He can be quite manipulative. I've got to be a little tougher with him. Middle Eastern men look at an American woman and all they see is a cunt. Pardon my French."

Howard laughed at Anna's vulgarity. Maybe she was one of the boys after all.

Anna called Ascari on the telephone that afternoon and proposed that they meet for lunch the next day at a quiet restaurant off Edgware Road.

"I knew you would call," said the Iranian.

"You did?" asked Anna.

"Oh yes!" said the Iranian. "I knew it."

14

◆

Ascari showed up for the second meeting wearing a silk ascot and smelling as if he had bathed in cologne. He had trimmed his beard, from porcupine length to raccoon. He looked even more unattractive than Anna remembered. She was determined this time to be businesslike, tough, manipulative. She had dressed in the least flattering outfit she owned, a shapeless brown wool dress that looked like a carpet remnant. She had deliberately not washed her hair that morning and wore no makeup. For the first time in her life, she wished she had a pimple on her nose.

The restaurant was a rather dingy little place, tucked among the car-stereo shops and electrical-supply outlets that lined Edgware Road past Sussex Gardens. It was nominally an Italian restaurant, but in London that could mean anything. Greek, Turkish, Portuguese. It was the sort of place where people went when they wanted to hide, a place where the curtains were drawn and the waiters avoided eye contact. Dennis had recommended the restaurant, but it seemed to Anna, once she was seated, that it was all too obviously the sort of place for spies and whores. And it was no insult to Anna that the headwaiter treated her like the latter, even in her baggy brown dress.

"I love you," said Ascari when they were seated. He was leaning toward her with his hand on his heart.

"Shut up!" said Anna. She said it loudly. The restaurant was almost empty, and she didn't care if anyone heard. She was not going to take any more bullshit from the Iranian. "Let's get one thing straight, Mr. Ascari," she said. "I am a businesswoman, and I want to be treated like one, with respect. Is that understood?"

"Oh yes," said Ascari soothingly. "I know you American

women. You want to be just like man. Okay. I don't mind. I love you anyway."

"Shut up, dammit! I mean it!"

"Okay, miss. You can talk dirty with me. I don't mind. Whatever you like."

What was it about this man that made him so impossible? That allowed him to jump the tracks of ordinary conversation and go careening off in his own loony direction? It wasn't that he was intimidating. He was a fat, ugly little man with no appeal or charm, and Anna half suspected that she could break his arm if she had to. It was that he refused to play by the rules. He was the kind of man Anna loathed, the kind she had been smart and pretty and wellborn enough to have avoided dealing with her entire life. Now she hadn't that luxury.

"Listen to me," said Anna carefully. "I have a message from my friends at the embassy." At the mention of the word "embassy," Ascari seemed to cool off. He sat back in his chair. "My friends," she continued, "said they were very interested in the information you gave me when we met before. They asked me to meet you again."

"Interested?" He beamed.

"Yes. Very interested."

"Thanks be to Allah! How much money will they pay me?"

"They're not ready to talk about money yet."

"I am so sorry, then," said Ascari. "No money, forget it." He folded his arms and pouted, as if he had been cruelly insulted. I hate dealing with this man, thought Anna. I hate it! Yet she was a professional, or wanted to be, and he was a client.

"Calm down," she said. "I didn't say no money. I just said not yet."

"No money, forget it," repeated Ascari.

"I'll tell that to my friends at the embassy. But first, they say they need to know more about you."

"Yeah. Okay. Fine. What they want to know?" He adjusted his ascot. He was vain, for such an ugly man.

"When were you born?" asked Anna.

"In 1940, 1942. I don't remember."

"What does your passport say?"

"Which one?"

"How many do you have?"

"Two, I think. No, three."

"Where are they from?"

"One from Iran."

"Do you have it? Let me see it, please."

"Yeah, okay. Fine." He gave her the Iranian passport. She began copying the information in a small spiral notebook.

"Hold on!" said Anna sharply. "It says here you were born in Baku, in Soviet Azerbaijan."

"That is right. Baku."

"How did you get to Iran?"

"It was during the war. Everybody went everywhere. No problem."

"But what was your father doing in Baku?"

"He live there, lady. That was home, okay? But not now. Ali Ascari's home is Tehran. Understand?"

She looked at him dubiously. "Where are the other passports from?"

"One from Spain, I think." He fished around in the alligator-skin purse he carried and removed a Spanish passport. It looked brand-new. Anna wrote down the information, none of which matched what was on the Iranian passport. The Spanish passport said he had been born in Madrid.

"Nice job," said Anna, handing the passport back to Ascari.

He looked at her strangely. "Thank you," he said.

"What's the third?"

"Greek," said Ascari. "But I keep this one. I have to have some secrets, even from you, lady, and your friends at embassy."

"They'll be upset when I tell them that you wouldn't show it to me."

"Eh. So what."

Anna decided to let it go. Two passports were enough for now. Baku was a potential problem, but let headquarters worry about it.

"I like that dress," said Ascari, leaning forward in his chair again. "Brown is very nice color for you."

Ignore him, thought Anna. Don't answer. Stick to your game. "What do you do for a living?" she asked.

"Business," said Ascari.

"What kind?"

The Iranian leaned closer to Anna, so that she could smell the garlic on his breath, not quite covered by the mint smell of his mouthwash. She cocked her ear, thinking he would confide the nature of his work. But no.

"Lady," he said, "I know that you want to sleep with me."

Anna pulled back with a start. "You're wrong!" she said. "Flat wrong! And I told you, I am not going to permit this kind of talk."

"You know how I know?" continued Ascari, oblivious to Anna's protest. "I know because you call me back. After I put my hand on your knee. So I say to myself, if this American lady not CIA lady, and she let me put my hand on her knee, then she must like me very much. Or she want money. Do you want Ali's money?" He winked as he said it.

"No," said Anna through her teeth. "I do not."

"Then you must like me very much. Then you will sleep with me. I am happy. We will drink champagne."

"No! We will not drink champagne. And I certainly will not sleep with you. That is out of the question. Do you hear me?"

Anna worried that she was beginning to sound hysterical. But even the waiter didn't pay any attention. The few people in the restaurant seemed to assume that any Western woman with a man like Ascari was asking for trouble. Hold on, Anna told herself. Keep cool.

"I have surprise for you," said Ascari sweetly. "For your friends at embassy, I mean. Big surprise."

"That's nice," said Anna. "But first let's finish with your background. What is your occupation?"

"Business. I told you."

"But what kind?"

"You know, business. Any kind. If you want to buy, I sell. If you want to sell, I buy. You know. Business."

"Why don't we just say 'trader,'" said Anna. She opened her little spiral notebook again and wrote: Trader. As she did so, she noticed that Ascari had leaned over and was looking at her legs.

"You know what?" he asked.

"No. What?"

"I hate panty hose. Hate them."

"Shut up!" said Anna. Her voice was almost a shout.

"You know why?"

"Shut up! Stop it!" She could feel herself losing control.

"Because," he said with a giggle, "you can't get finger inside!"

"You slimy bastard!" She slapped him, hard. Then she walked to the ladies' room.

Anna doused her face with cold water and considered the situation. She was furious, as much at herself as at Ascari. It was her fault that she had lost control, first of him, then of her own feelings. She felt humiliated and abused, but worse than that, she felt incompetent. After a few moments of sober reflection, she decided it was time to cut her losses. For some bizarre reason, Ascari had her number. She would drop the case—walk out the door of the restaurant, call Howard from a pay phone, and tell him to get someone new. She was brushing her hair when she remembered Ascari's "big surprise." He had said he had a big surprise for the embassy. What the hell was that about? She probably should find out. At least ask the question. That would be her last contact with Ascari, absolutely the last word. Then she would leave. Anna finished brushing her hair, took a long look at herself in the mirror, and returned to the table.

Ascari was sitting contentedly when she emerged, smiling and drinking a whiskey. He looked slightly sheepish, if it was possible for a pig to look sheepish.

"Don't ever do that again," said Anna. "Do you hear me?"

Ascari nodded. There was a long silence, broken by the Iranian. "I am sorry that I treat you like a prostitute," he said. "You are not a prostitute. You are CIA lady."

"I told you where I work," said Anna evenly.

"Of course you are CIA lady!" said Ascari again. "I am not so stupid."

Anna didn't answer. Let the little prick think whatever he wants, she thought.

"You should have told me. Then I would not be so sure that you want to go to bed with me."

"Drop it," said Anna. "What is your big surprise?"

"Ah! My surprise. Okay, CIA lady. Listen very careful, because this is big stuff. Big stuff."

"I'm listening." Finish your business, she told herself, and get out of here.

"Khomeini men hate America," began Ascari. "You know that? America put in Shah. America made Iran its little whore, dress it up like cheap woman. So Khomeini men hate America."

"Yes. I know that. I know they hate America."

"They have plan for revenge. Next year is American presidential election, right?"

Anna nodded.

"So Khomeini men planning to kill presidential candidates."

"What?"

"You heard right. Kill. Boom! Bang-bang."

"Which ones?"

"The President, all the other candidates. And people who work for them."

"Say that again," said Anna. Her head felt as if it were spinning.

"What I said. Khomeini men have plan to kill all presidential candidates next year, and other big people."

"Where? At the conventions?"

"I don't know. Yeah, maybe at conventions."

"How do you know this?"

"That's all I tell you now. For the rest, you pay money."

"Who is involved? Do you have any names?"

"Hey! I told you. No more unless you pay money. You tell friends at American embassy. No more bullshit."

"How can they reach you?"

"Same number I gave you. Except I am going away on business trip tomorrow."

"Where?"

"Turkey."

"Where will you be staying?"

"In Istanbul. At Hilton, of course. Best hotel."

"What passport?"

"Iranian. I have others for tricky business."

"When will you be back?"

"A week. Two weeks. I don't know."

"Thanks for the information," said Anna. "But you're still a skunk." She rose from her chair.

"Hey, wait, lady!" said Ascari.

"Let's skip lunch, shall we?" said Anna, heading for the door. She had never been more happy to end an engagement in her life.

"Dynamite!" said Howard several hours later when he finished debriefing Anna. This time she gave him a thorough summary of the meeting. She omitted nothing, narrating every loathsome gesture, every filthy insinuation, every demand for money, every nasty assertion that she worked for the agency. It was all supposed to lead up to her demand that she be taken off the case. But she never quite got there. Howard was too excited about the assassination plot.

Anna tried to slow him down. "He's blown my cover," she said. "He knows I work for the agency."

"Naaa," said Howard. "You didn't confirm it, did you?"

"No," said Anna. "Of course not."

"Then don't worry about it too much. Iranians are spook-crazy. They think everybody works for CIA, so what does it matter?"

Anna frowned. "Okay," she said, still unconvinced.

"Did he really say that about panty hose?"

"Give me a break, Howard. I'm not in the mood."

"Okay. Sorry. We have work to do anyway. We've got to get this little item moving to headquarters, pronto. Which means that you get to help prepare your very first field intelligence report."

Howard removed a printed form from his briefcase and showed it to Anna. "You know how the grading system works?" he asked.

"Not really," said Anna.

"Okay," he said, going into his professor voice. "We rate every intelligence report according to two standards. The quality of the source and the reliability of the information. We grade the sources A to F. A means completely reliable. B means usually reliable. C means fairly reliable. D means not usually reliable. E means not reliable. F means reliability can't be judged. Got it?"

"Sure," said Anna. "I mean, it's not very complicated."

Howard looked slightly disappointed. "No, not very," he said. "We grade the content the same way, from one to six. One means confirmed by other independent and reliable sources, two means probably true, three means possibly true, four means doubtful, five means probably false, six means can't be judged. Easy, right?"

"Easy," said Anna. "It's like a color scale. Except it's mostly gray."

"You got it. In practice, there's no such thing as A-one. At least not in this world. Most of what we get is C-three. Possibly true information from a fairly reliable source. Middle gray, in other words."

"My favorite color," said Anna.

"So the question is: How do we rate your pal, Mr. Ascari?"

"Do you have a category called 'total, complete asshole'?"

"Afraid not."

"I'd have to call him an F-six. I don't know if he's reliable, and I don't know if what he says is true."

"I agree," said Howard. "F-six he is." He looked at the form. "Next item: When and where acquired. So I'll write: London. What's today's date?"

"February 25," said Anna.

Howard wrote the place and date acquired. "Now," he said, "we need a byline."

"A what?"

"A brief description of him for the report, right here where it says 'source.' "

"I don't know," said Anna, thinking back to the grading exercise of a moment ago. "I guess we ought to call him 'an Iranian source who claims links with Khomeini's circle, whose reliability is unproven.' "

"Lovely," said Howard, writing her description word for word. "Now, the juicy stuff."

"There isn't much. The source reported a plot by Iranians close to Khomeini to assassinate presidential candidates in the 1980 campaign, including the President and members of his staff, possibly during the presidential nominating campaigns. That's it."

"That's enough, sweetie," said Howard. "Believe me, that will wake them up back home."

"What about the fact that he was born in the Soviet Union? Is that a problem?"

"Not with me. Azerbaijanis, Iranians. What's the difference? But put it down. It will give the CI people something to do. If it bothers anybody, they'll scream."

Ascari had indeed pushed the right button. It was almost as if he knew how the American government worked; as if he knew that once an agency of the American government received a threat involving assassination of the President or presidential candidates, the information achieved a different status from ordinary intelligence, so that it was no longer subject to the same standards of evaluation. After Kennedy in 1963, the one thing that no agency of the government wanted to have in its files was an assassination threat it hadn't acted upon because it seemed too implausible.

Headquarters came roaring back overnight. Immediate, London. Priority. Bells and whistles. They wanted more information as soon as possible from Ascari and authorized aggressive further development of him, including payment of a one-time cash reward of $1,000 for the information provided thus far. They gave him a cryptonym—SDROTTEN, picked at random from a dictionary back at headquarters. And they authorized immediate travel to Istanbul by the officer handling the case, Amy L. Gunderson, who should continue to describe herself as an intermediary to the embassy.

Anna suddenly found that she was a star. Twinkle-eyed Dennis gave her a big kiss when she walked in the next morning. Later in the day, a courier arrived with a "hero-gram" from C/NE, the chief of the Near East Division. "Wish congratulate Gunderson on professional handling of tricky case. Subject of high interest and very timely. Report used in DCI morning notes and in memorandum to director of NFAC." Best of all, Anna received a personal message from Margaret Houghton, relayed via the London station. How she had learned of the case Anna couldn't imagine. It said simply: "Well done!" All of which made it very difficult for Anna to do what she had planned—which was to dump Ascari.

The next day a package addressed to Anna Barnes arrived at Halcyon. It was delivered by a courier, but other than the address had no markings. Anna debated what it might contain. New paperwork to support her cover identify? Insurance claim forms from the personnel department? A new training manual? She opened the package eagerly. Inside, to her surprise, she found a dog-eared old book, whose bruises suggested that it had passed through many hands before reaching its current destination. She opened the cover. The book was in a Cyrillic Turkic language, but she wasn't sure what it was until she saw the publication data on the title page. It read: "Baku, 1967."

The book was titled *Islam din galyglary—Survivals of Islam*—written by someone called M. M. Sattarov. She leafed through the pages. It appeared to be a study of current Islamic worship in Azerbaijan, including detailed descriptions of holy shrines and Sufi cults in the Soviet republic. As Anna was turning the pages, a handwritten note fell from the book. She picked it up.

"This would make a handsome gift for your new friend," read the note. "Good luck in Istanbul." It was signed: "Stone."

"Bring me back some Turkish taffy," said Howard that night, when they met to plan the next phase of the case.

"They don't have Turkish taffy in Istanbul," answered Anna.

"Then bring me a Turkish towel."

"They don't have those either."

"Then forget it," said Howard.

He laid out the plan. "Travel arrangements are your responsibility. Have the administrative people at Halcyon make them. Economy class, please. Put together reasonable cover for the trip. Something economic. And then get your ass over there, pronto, before Ascari goes somewhere else."

"What about money?"

"Pay him the thousand dollars in cash."

"He may not think it's enough. He may want more."

"Stall him. Tell him you need to check with your friends at the embassy. And tell him that we're going to want to polygraph him when he gets back to London, if he wants any more money. It's time to begin reeling this guy in."

"Can I tell him that I'm CIA?"

"No. You're a NOC, for chrissake."

"Please, Howard. I really think it would be better. He already knows it anyway."

"He doesn't know it," said Howard. "He suspects it. Which is different. What does it matter anyway?"

"It matters to me," said Anna, struggling for a way to explain the special problems she had with Ascari without sounding like a whiner. "Look, I'll be honest," she said. "If he knows I'm agency, then maybe he won't try so hard to hustle me. He'll treat me as an intelligence officer, rather than as a sex object."

"Oh, that," said Howard dubiously. "I can check with headquarters, but they seemed pretty adamant about maintaining the fig leaf. They're not likely to change their minds. Unless there's a real problem." He said "real problem" as if it were a kind of disease.

"No," sighed Anna. "I guess it's okay." She put her head in her hands.

"What's the matter, honey?" asked Howard, trying to be supportive. "You got the jitters?"

"It's not that," said Anna. "I'm just not sure I should be handling this guy."

"Why not? You're doing great so far."

"No, I'm not. I'm doing a lousy job. The chemistry is wrong. What did you call it the other day? Rapport. There isn't any rapport."

"Meaning?"

"Meaning I hate the guy. I think he's an obnoxious prick, and I'd be happy never to see him again."

"Look," said Howard. "You're not marrying him. You're just developing him. And so far, you're doing great! Cheer up. You're a star."

"He gives me the creeps."

"Tell you what," said Howard, putting his arm around Anna. "If you still feel the same way after the Istanbul meet, we'll see about handing him off to someone in the embassy. Okay?"

"Okay," said Anna. She took a deep breath. "One more thing."

"What's that?"

"What do I do if there's an emergency?"

"Like. what?"

"I don't know. If there's a problem in Istanbul. With Ascari. If I need to communicate with you or headquarters."

"Call the base chief in Istanbul. His name is Taylor. We'll send him a cable letting him know you're in his neck of the woods. And we'll work out some kind of recognition code before you leave. But don't call him unless it's an emergency. It's insecure."

"Okay," said Anna.

"Don't worry, for chrissake!" said Howard. "You'll do fine. Just don't fuck up." He laughed heartily. Anna tried to join in, but she couldn't muster even a chuckle.

15
◆

ANNA ARRIVED IN ISTANBUL LATE IN THE AFTERNOON, LANDing in a bank of sooty gray smog that covered the airport and stretched across the Bosporus to Anatolia. The airport had the militarized look of the Third World: watchtowers and barbed wire lining the runways; poor enlisted men standing guard in the winter chill, freezing their asses off so that the generals could pretend they were in control of things. And everywhere, the dust and debris that settles in public places in the Third World, and the surging crowds that cannot be contained in orderly lines.

For a woman traveling alone, arriving in a Third World city is never easy. There are too many eyes watching, too many hands reaching out for your baggage, too many taxicab drivers barking for your fare. For Anna that day, these ordinary indignities were magnified. The tight little man at passport control spent too long examining her passport—studying the document, looking at her face, checking the passport again, consulting a watch list of passport numbers. Anna tried to remain impassive, to give nothing away—not even a nervous smile—but her knees felt weak. Finally he stamped the document and waved her through.

Anna collected her bag and headed for the green "nothing to declare" line. The customs man pulled her over. Was she so obvious? Had she inadvertently caught his eye, inviting examination with that guilty look that makes a customs officer's job so easy? Or was it just that she was a woman traveling alone, and therefore suspect? He searched her suitcase, pawing through her clothes, and then sent her on. A scrofulous old porter lunged for her bag and carried it to the door of the terminal; she didn't have any Turkish money, so she gave him a British pound note, and when he complained, she gave him another.

When she finally found a taxi and settled onto the fake leopard-skin seat, she wanted to scream. Her spirits lifted a bit on the way in from the airport. Through the smog she could recognize the outlines of the landscape: the rusty freighters riding at anchor in the Sea of Marmara; the jumble of cars and boats and people at the Galata Bridge.

Istanbul looked a mess. Anna was amazed at how much the city had deteriorated in the two years since she had been there. It had the weary look of a capital under siege; faded political posters covering every wall; the tinny sound of cheap loudspeakers broadcasting political propaganda in squares and intersections; security men who stared at you in lobbies and on elevators. Anna remembered the old saw. All Turkish men were the same: "Two eyes and a mustache." That much hadn't changed.

She checked into a hotel in Taksim—middle-range, not too fancy, not too seedy—and bought several Turkish newspapers on her way upstairs and read them in her room. The front page of each paper was dominated by stories about terrorism. *Cumhuriyet* decried the bombing of a leftist bookstore in Istanbul. *Tercuman* denounced a raid on a rightist coffeehouse in Malatya. It was as if the whole country had slipped a gear.

Anna decided against calling Ascari that first night. The timing had been left open in the operational plan, depending on how she felt. And she felt terrible. She didn't want to talk to a soul, not even the Turkish chambermaid who tried to be nice when she saw that Anna was alone. She ordered dinner from room service, watched a game show on Turkish television, and then turned to the book she had brought along: a copy of *The Rubáiyát of Omar Khayyám* that her father had given her years before, when she entered graduate school. She made it as far as the seventh quatrain before dozing off.

Anna didn't call Ascari the next morning either. She was still without her bearings. It wasn't that she didn't know the city. Anna had covered every inch of Istanbul two years before—when she spent the summer there doing thesis research in the archives—but that was in another lifetime, when she was still an innocent, if somewhat bored, graduate student and Istanbul was a playground.

Anna decided while eating her breakfast—still in her room—that she would visit one of her old haunts in the city. The Basbakanlik Archives, where she had done her research: perhaps the archival tea room, where she had picked up the Turkish professor. She might even do a little research on Ottoman relations with the princely families of old Baku. And then, with her feet firmly on the ground, she would call Ali Ascari.

"Topkapi Sarayi, Lutfen," she told the taxi driver. After twenty minutes of cutting and weaving through traffic, they reached the walls of Topkapi Palace, and from there she walked the few dozen yards to the gray pile that housed the archival records of the Grand Viziers, the prime ministers of the Ottoman Empire. This gloomy building had been Anna's favorite spot in Istanbul, for it contained the elements that made the city so mysterious, and so comical. Anna flashed her old reader's pass at the main door and headed for the reading room.

The Basbakanlik reading room was a scene that might have been imagined by a Levantine Charles Dickens. It was run by an old woman, inevitably dubbed the "dragon lady" by visiting foreign scholars, whose greatest pleasure seemed to lie in denying researchers access to archival materials. Often, she didn't have to bother, since the cataloguing was so haphazard and erratic that it was difficult to find things at all. The Germans had made a stab at cataloguing the archives during the several decades when they played Big Brother to the Turks, but even the Germans had given up. As a result, there were tens of thousands of documents, handwritten in Ottoman Turkish script, some of them dating back to the fourteenth century. But no one was ever sure exactly where they were. The only certainty was that anything politically sensitive— anything involving sticky moments with the Armenians or Bulgars or Greeks, for example—had been pulled from the shelves.

Not that a researcher could visit the shelves. That was against the rules. The dragon lady would send one of her minions to the storage depot where most of the records were kept to retrieve the requested volume, assuming it was permitted, assuming it could be found. Many other things were against the rules, too. Indeed, there was a formal list of twenty-one rules in legalistic Turkish posted on the wall of the Basbakanlik reading room. "It is forbidden to use pens in the reading room, only pencils; except for document-request forms, which must be signed in ink." "It is forbidden for researchers to leave Turkey for more than a month without permission." And so forth. But these weren't all the rules; there were others, which weren't posted. You had to guess at what they were.

Anna surveyed the reading room: It hadn't changed in two years. The twenty-one rules were still posted on the wall; the dragon lady was still in her booth; the closed-circuit TV camera still panned the room, with its uncanny habit of focusing on women researchers every time they uncrossed their legs. And at the library tables, as ever, sat a half dozen glassy-eyed foreign researchers, staring at Ottoman texts.

Basbakanlik had its contingent of Turkish researchers, too, and of all the strange characters in the reading room, these were Anna's favorites. They were mostly "professional" historians—old men who had mastered the nuances of reading Ottoman Turkish and hired themselves out to scholars. These Turkish researchers sometimes took years to complete their tasks. Part of the reason for the slow pace was that the old men spent much of the day sleeping. As Anna scanned the room, she could see four or five "professional" historians who had nodded off.

"Ufuk!" whispered Anna, spotting a familiar face walking toward her. It was Ufuk Celebi, one of the dragon lady's assistants. During Anna's three months at Basbakanlik, Ufuk had been Anna's page turner. (Foreign researchers were not allowed to turn the pages of Ottoman documents; that was another of the rules.) When Anna had left Istanbul at the end of the summer, she had bought her page turner a box of Belgian chocolates. "Ufuk," she said again. He turned toward her, still not recognizing her.

"Shhh," he said. "What do you want, please?"

Anna debated whether to introduce herself and decided against it. "I'm looking for a manuscript," she said.

Ufuk eyed her curiously. "Ask at desk," he said, pointing to the twenty-one rules.

"They take so long at the desk. Maybe you can help me. I want to see the Azerbaijan papers. The correspondence between the Sublime Porte and Baku."

"Sorry, closed. These papers are all closed."

"But do you have them?"

"Ask at desk," repeated Ufuk.

The hell with him, thought Anna. She decided that she would have tea in the Basbakanlik Tea Room. It was a jolly little room, with the ambience of a nineteenth-century Balkan railway station. Here, too, nothing had changed. It was the same collection of horny graduate students, balding professors, crackpot Armenians and sleepy Turks. Anna had a cup of tea and a sweet roll. There was no sign of the charming Turkish professor who had enlivened her summer two years ago. But a German man in his early thirties spied Anna across the room, sat down beside her, and tried to pick her up. The German was very earnest and boyish. Anna indulged him just enough to get a buzz, and then ignored him. He left looking stricken.

Anna returned to her hotel fortified to do what she had been dreading and call Ali Ascari at the Istanbul Hilton. She sat down on the edge of her bed, pen in hand, notepaper on the side table. The first time, Ascari's line was busy. The second time, she reached him.

"*Marhaba,*" he answered in Arabic. He must have been expecting an Arab caller.

"Mr. Ascari," said Anna. "This is Allison James."

"Who?" Maybe that was a good sign. He didn't remember her.

"Allison James, the banker from London."

"Oh yes! How are you, lovely lady? I am so glad to be talking to you. Where are you?"

"In Istanbul."

"Ya salaam!" he exclaimed. "Why is that? Have you come all this way to see me? To see your friend Ali Ascari? This is a great day! Thanks be to God! Where are you staying?"

"I would like to see you, on business," said Anna. She could feel her heart racing. "My friends in London have sent me with an important message."

"Why not," said Ascari. "Meet me here, at the hotel, tonight. I will be in the casino. At ten o'clock."

"No," said Anna. "I don't think that's a good idea. What about tomorrow morning?"

"Impossible. Tomorrow I leave for Dubai. If you want to talk to me, it must be tonight."

"Okay," said Anna. "But not the casino. That would be too crowded. We should meet somewhere else. How about the coffee shop?"

"You do not understand, lady," said the Iranian. "I am doing business here. My business friends are taking me to dinner. They will be in the casino with me after dinner. You come then. First you meet Ali Ascari's friends. Then we go talk."

"I'd rather meet in the coffee shop," said Anna.

"Then go back to London. You want to see me, you come when I say. Otherwise, forget it."

Anna thought a moment. He didn't sound like he was bluffing. Maybe having his friends around would improve his behavior. "All right," said Anna. "The casino at ten."

"Dress nice, my dear," said Ali. "My friends are very rich."

"Hey! Wait a minute!" protested Anna. But Ascari had hung up.

Anna waited until nearly eleven o'clock. She would be damned if she would sit in a Turkish casino, being propositioned by strange men and feeling like a tart, waiting for Ali Ascari to show up. She spent a long time trying to decide what to wear and settled on a simple black dress and the jacket from one of her business suits—an odd combination, but that was the point. Her fashion accessory for the evening was an attaché case containing a thousand dollars in cash and a battered book in Azeri Turkish.

Ascari was sitting at the blackjack table with his two pals. He introduced them with a flourish: Abdel-Aziz from Saudi Arabia, a rotund man dressed in a white robe that made him look like a walking marshmallow, and Sami from Lebanon, a sallow-faced man in a silk suit. Ascari himself was dressed in a black Nehru jacket that was apparently meant to look like a tuxedo. All three appeared to be somewhat inebriated.

What a crew! Three 1979-model petro-hustlers—gambling, drinking and whoring away their small share of the hundreds of billions of dollars that had, as it were, come bubbling out of the ground. You could have seen them across Europe that season—in Monte Carlo and Paris and London and Athens—taking five percent of someone else's five percent and still making out like bandits.

"Come play blackjack with us," said Ascari, throwing Anna $200 worth of chips.

"No, thanks," she said. "I'll watch."

They played with the enthusiasm of drunken men trying to impress a very sober woman. The Saudi hit everything. He hit 15, he hit 17, once he even hit 18. He lost nearly $1,000 in the brief time Anna watched. Ascari was more cagey. He split his aces; he hit 14 but not 15; he doubled when he had the cards. He was ahead $500 at one point but lost most of it. When he won, he would exclaim: *"Ya Salaam!"* When he lost, he would cluck his tongue and mutter a dark oath in Farsi. The Lebanese was the only one who won consistently. He actually seemed to be counting the cards.

"Mr. Ascari," said Anna sharply after they had been playing nearly forty-five minutes. She pointed to her watch.

"Yes, my dear," said Ascari. "I'm coming. I'm coming." He extended his arm to Anna.

"Bye-bye, boys," said Ascari. He winked at Abdel-Aziz and Sami. He winked at the blackjack dealer and gave him a $50 chip. They all rolled their eyes. The Saudi blew Anna a kiss. Let them think what they want, Anna told herself. Once they were out the door, she disentangled her arm and moved away from the corpulent Iranian.

"Let's have a drink," said Ascari.

"You look like you've had enough," said Anna. "I suggest we go to the coffee shop."

"It's closed," said Ascari, pointing to his watch. It was almost midnight.

"I need to talk to you," said Anna. "Privately."

"Then we go to your hotel room."

"No. Absolutely not."

"Then we go to my room. I have suite. Very comfortable."

"No," said Anna.

"Okay, then where?"

Anna thought a moment. She couldn't very well give him the thousand dollars in the lobby of the hotel.

"If we go to your room, there will be no funny business. Understood?"

"Please, please. You hurt my feelings," he said, putting his hand over his heart.

"No sex talk," continued Anna. "No hands on knees. Because if there is, I'm calling the police and the American consulate. And you'll be in more trouble than you've ever seen."

"For sure, lady. For sure. I am hearing you. Ali Ascari is a gentleman."

Ascari had a bottle of whiskey in his room, as it turned out, and promptly poured himself a drink. Then he excused himself and repaired to the bedroom. Anna surveyed the room. It was filled with the paraphernalia of the petrodollar circuit: packs of cigarettes on every table, opened but half smoked; the remains of gifts to be given and received: candy, silk ties, perfume, a box of Davidoff cigars. It was the messy room of a messy man. Anna checked the location of the phone. She measured in her mind the distance to the door. She moved from the couch to a chair so that Ascari couldn't sit next to her.

Ascari returned after five minutes with his hair and beard combed, wearing a silk brocade smoking jacket and bathed in more of that awful cologne.

"This shouldn't take long," said Anna.

"I am at your service."

"As you might expect, my friends at the embassy are very concerned by what you told me at our last meeting, about assassination."

"Oh, yes," said Ascari. "As I expect."

"They would like to thank you for your help in this matter."

"Very good. Okay." Ascari was looking at Anna's attaché case. "You have a surprise for Ali maybe?"

"Maybe," said Anna. "But first I have a few more questions."

"Okay. Why not?"

"My friends want to know who will carry out the assassinations."

"Khomeini men. I told you last time. They will be Khomeini men."

"Yes," said Anna. "But that isn't very helpful. There are thousands of Khomeini men."

Ascari paused, tilted his head, stared off into space. It was hard to tell whether he was searching his memory or his imagination. "They will be from Qom," he said.

Anna took out her spiral notebook and wrote: Qom.

"And from Isfahan maybe." Anna wrote: Isfahan. "And maybe from Tehran, too."

This time Anna didn't write anything. "All three places?" she asked.

"Yeah. Probably."

"Will they be working with contacts in America, these men? Will they try to enter the country themselves?"

"Contacts," said Ascari thoughtfully. "They will use contacts."

"Who are the contacts?"

Ali surveyed the room, then narrowed his eyes and said in a whisper: "Mafia."

"Mafia?" demanded Anna. "Who? The Italian Mafia?"

"Shhh," said Ali. "Not so loud."

"But that's absurd. Why would the Mafia work with a group of Iranian revolutionaries? I'm sorry, Mr. Ascari, but that doesn't make any sense to me."

Ascari drained his glass of whiskey, rose from the couch, and walked unsteadily to the phone table, where he had left the whiskey bottle. He poured himself another drink, spilling more on the table than in the glass.

"Let's have a drink. Okay?"

"You've had enough," said Anna. "No more whiskey."

"Hey, lady, you go to hell. Nobody tell Ali Ascari what to do." He took a long drink, spilling some of it on his chin.

"What evidence do you have that the Mafia is involved?"

"No evidence. Forget it. This is boring subject. We talk about something else."

"Wait a minute. This is important. I've come all the way from London to talk to you about the assassination plot. I want information."

"They have been caught!" whispered Ascari as he wobbled back across the room toward the couch.

"Who?"

"The assassins. The Khomeini men. After we talk before in London, they were caught. Now they are in prison."

"Who caught them?"

"Other Khomeini men. Good ones. My friends. They catch the bad ones. Thanks to me!"

"Why didn't you tell me that before?"

Ali sat back on the couch. There was a dreamy, drunken look in his eyes. "Do you like my jacket?" he asked. "It is silk. Very expensive."

"What about the Mafia? Did you make that up?"

"Ali Ascari make nothing up!"

"My friends have ways of finding out whether you are telling the truth or not. You know that, don't you? They have a machine. It is impossible to lie to them."

"Take off your jacket," said Ali. "Be comfortable. You worry too much. You will get a heart attack and die."

"Cut the crap, goddammit!" said Anna loudly. "I want information!"

"Please, lady. Do not take name of God for swear word. Don't ever do that. Please! Ali might get upset. Now relax, and I will tell you some real informations. Very big secrets! Take off your shoes. Maybe your feet are hurting."

"My feet are not hurting. What are the big secrets?"

"About Soviet Union," said Ascari with a calculating smile. "About Moslem people in Soviet Union."

"I'm listening," said Anna.

"Ah, see! I knew you would be interested. Now you listen good to what Ali tell you. A big problem is coming for Soviet Union. Big explosion! Moslem people are going to fight Russian people. Civil war maybe."

"What are you talking about?" said Anna. It sounded like more of Ascari's craziness.

"Hey! You listen. Ali Ascari knows what he is talking about. Moslem men in Soviet Union ready to fight! We send them guns. We send them Korans."

"Who sends them guns?"

"Khomeini men. Afghan men. Pakistani men. Saudi men. All Moslem men want to help brothers fight Russians."

"Hold on, hold on. What are you telling me? That Iran is sending guns across the border into the Soviet Union?"

"Oh yes! There is an army of Moslem brothers who move across the border. It is a great secret!"

"How do you know about it?"

Ascari leaned toward her and lowered his voice. "I told you before. I am an Azeri man! My father is from Baku. I have cousins across the border. Believe me, lady. I know."

"Guns across the border?" repeated Anna. As she said it again, she thought of someone who would be quite interested in this piece of information. Mr. Edward Stone, dean of the old boys, sender of obscure Turkic monographs, job title unknown.

"Yes, guns. And other things."

"What other things?"

"Oh, you know. Videotapes. Radios. VCRs. Why not? We are traders in our part of the world. So we trade."

"I know," said Anna. "I've noticed that, actually. Now listen, Mr. Ascari, this had better not be more of your lies. Because if it is, you're finished."

"Trust me!" said Ali indignantly. He put his hand on his heart. "Maybe not everything I tell you about assassination is true. Okay. Maybe not everything. But I want to get your attention. Because I know so many things. I have my own spies. Like tonight, my friends Abdel-Aziz and Sami. They know too many things. Whatever you want to know about Saudi Arabia and Lebanon, they can tell you. Who is new mistress of Saudi king? Who is paying who in Lebanon to make trouble. They tell me and I tell you. Easy pie! I can be your helper. And you need help, you know that? You Americans really make a big mess. Ali Ascari help you clean it up. What you say?"

"I don't know what to say," said Anna. "I have to talk about all this with my friends at the embassy."

"Uh-huh," grunted Ascari. "You messenger lady, I know." He gave a wink and looked at the attaché case again. "So what you bring me, huh? What surprise you have for Ali Ascari?"

Anna picked the attaché case up off the floor. She thought a moment. She wasn't sure anymore that Ascari had earned his money. She didn't know which version of the assassination plot was true, if any of them. She certainly didn't know if the business about arms shipments across the Iranian border was true. But she had brought the cash all the way to Istanbul to give to Ascari, and she wasn't about to take it back.

Anna clicked open the locks on the case. Ascari sat up in his chair like an attentive puppy. The prospect of receiving money seemed to have a salutary effect on his disposition.

"First, I have a gift for you." She flipped up the lid, removed the worn book on Azeri holy places, and handed it to Ascari.

"Oh, yes. What is it, please?"

"A book."

"Oh yes, very nice. What else you bring me?"

"My friends thought you would like the book. It's very rare."

"Very nice, thank you, lady. But Ali Ascari doesn't read too much." He opened to the title page, as much out of politeness as anything else. Then his eyes saw the Cyrillic type and caught the word "Baku." "Wait a minute, lady," he said.

"Yes?"

"This book is from Soviet Union. What the hell is this? Are you KGB lady?"

"No, of course not. The book is about Islam in Azerbaijan. My friends thought you would like it, because you are a religious man."

"Sure, lady. Okay. Fine. I read it later. What else you got for Ali?"

"I have also brought you a reward from my friends at the embassy in London," said Anna evenly. "They are grateful for the information you have provided. They will want to be certain that it is true, and back in London they may want to give you a test with the machine I mentioned, to make sure you are telling the truth."

"The money," said Ascari. "The money."

Anna opened the attaché case again, revealing ten thin little stacks of currency, each holding ten ten-dollar bills. Ascari peered in greedily, and Anna handed the case over to him. The money didn't even cover the leather bottom of the container. The Iranian assayed the thin stacks and, with a grunt of disgust, dropped the case on the floor.

"Bullshit!" he said, waving one of the wispy stacks in Anna's face. "This is bullshit. This is a thousand dollars."

"That's correct," said Anna. "It is a thousand dollars. A special bonus for the information you have provided. My friends thought you would be pleased."

"Pleased? Are you crazy? A thousand dollars? Ali Ascari spends this much in one night! I spend this much for my hotel room! This money is an insult. You are saying to me: 'Go to hell!'"

"Calm down," said Anna. But her words had no effect. The Iranian, convinced that he had been insulted, was working himself into a rage.

"A thousand dollars!" he shouted, throwing the bundle across the room. "Better you should give me nothing." The little stacks of tens scattered across the rug.

"There may be more money later, if your information is reliable," said Anna. But Ascari wasn't listening.

"Do you know how much you are insulting me, lady? I spend that much for a woman for one night! A good woman, too! Not a cheap CIA-KGB whore."

"I'm leaving now," said Anna. She rose quickly from her chair and headed for the door. But Ascari was quicker than she had expected. With the nimble feet of a fat man, he bounded to the door ahead of her, stood in front of it, and bolted the chain.

"Where are you going, lady? Ali Ascari not through yet. Ali Ascari want his money's worth!" He was breathing hard, sweating from his forehead, stretching his fat fingers toward her.

Anna froze. She was stopped by a combination of fear and astonishment that this pathetic little man imagined that he could have sex with her. She wanted to scream, but her voice wouldn't work. Ascari lunged toward her drunkenly, grabbing at her blouse and pulling it open, so that the lace of her bra was exposed. That unstuck Anna's voice.

"Get away from me, you fat little fuck!"

Anna reached for her purse, where she had a can of a chemical spray supplied by the tech shop in London. But again Ascari was quicker and knocked the purse out of her hand. Oh shit, thought Anna. Her head was spinning. All she could think to do was to scream for help, although she wasn't sure she wanted to explain to the hotel cops, let alone the Istanbul gendarmes, what she had been doing in Ascari's hotel room. Stay calm, she told herself. And for God's sake, don't cry.

"Let me go now!" she said, holding her blouse and trying to sound cool and in control. "The American consulate knows where I am. If anything happens to me, they'll come after you. I'm warning you. Stand away from the door and let me go."

"Shut up," said Ascari. The confrontation only seemed to have increased his recklessness. He moved toward a desk near the door, reached into the top drawer, and removed from it a stubby knife with a curved blade. It was a letter opener, but still an effective weapon. "Now," he said, "you better be nice to Ali Baba!"

Oh Jesus, thought Anna. What do I do now? Her eyes darted around the room, looking for some means of rescue or escape. The door was blocked. The windows were too high to jump. Then she saw the telephone, and on the table next to it, the half-empty bottle of whiskey.

"What does CIA lady look like with no clothes on?" said Ascari, moving toward her with his knife. "We see if you worth a thousand dollars." He waved his blade and made a warbling cry.

As Ascari moved toward her, Anna retreated toward the table. He was talking Farsi now, calling her a whore and the mother of a whore. Anna could feel her knees trembling as she backed toward the table. Do it! she told herself. When she reached the table she lunged, seizing the bottle in one hand and the telephone receiver in the other. Her body moved more decisively than her brain might have thought possible.

"Stand back!" she said, waving the bottle at him. The Iranian, surprised by her sudden motion, took a step back.

"Don't move!" she said. She tried to dial "O" with the same hand that was holding the phone, but her finger slipped out of the dial. Ascari saw her mistake and laughed at her. She was trying to dial again when he rushed toward her with his little scimitar, shouting something in Persian.

Anna dropped the phone and crouched instinctively into the fighting position an instructor had taught her several months earlier in an Arlington motel room. She leaned one way, then stepped aside as Ali lunged for where she had been. As Ascari went past her, Anna raised the whiskey bottle over her head and slammed it down. She missed Ascari's head, but hit his right arm hard, just above the elbow. Ascari fell to the floor, overcome as much by surprise as by the force of her blow.

Anna stared at him a moment, amazed by what she had done. Her arm, holding the whiskey bottle, felt as if it had electricity running through it. Ascari was groggily trying to get up. What was she waiting for? If she ran at that instant, she could probably make it through the door. But Ascari would still be chasing her, and Anna felt, in that moment, that she had done enough running for a lifetime. She raised the bottle again. Her whole body was surging with energy now, as if a switch somewhere had been flipped for the first time.

As Ascari turned his face toward her, Anna brought the bottle down. This time it hit him on the forehead, hard enough to bruise the skin, but not hard enough to break the bottle. Ascari screamed and fell back to the floor, dazed by the blow. Then Anna did something that her colleagues decided later was probably excessive. She kicked Ascari in his fat stomach. And then, as he was groaning, she kicked him again.

With Ascari collapsed on the floor, Anna moved quickly. She collected as much of the money as she could find, stuffed it in the attaché case, grabbed her purse from the floor, and headed for the door. She unbolted the lock and turned for a last look at Ascari. He wasn't moving.

"Don't ever do that again!" said Anna.

She closed the door and ran to the elevator. There was no sign of Ascari behind her. I hope he's dead, Anna thought to herself as the elevator headed down to the lobby. She walked quickly out the door and along the long driveway of the hotel. Still there was no sign that Ascari was following her. She walked down Cumhuriyet Avenue a quarter mile to the next big hotel and stopped at the door.

At first the doorman shook his head: No admittance. She realized how bizarre she must look—clothes askew, bathed in sweat, smelling of the half bottle of booze that she had accidentally poured on herself as she struck Ascari. It was only when Anna spoke English that the doorman relented. He pointed her toward a telephone in the lobby, from which she dialed the home telephone number she had been given for the Istanbul base chief, Alan Taylor.

It was nearly two o'clock when she reached him. Taylor answered the phone with a trace of annoyance in his voice. In the background was a woman's voice, speaking in Turkish.

"This is Vera," said Anna, using the recognition code that had been agreed on before she left London. He was supposed to answer: "Welcome to Istanbul," and then work out, in code, a time to meet.

"Who?" answered Taylor, fumbling through his mental Rolodex of real names, work names, cryptonyms and codes

"Vera," said Anna. "This is Vera."

"Should I know you?" asked Taylor.

"Damned straight!" said Anna. She was angry. "I'm a visitor."

"Right," said Taylor. He had a vague recollection of a cable that someone from London would be coming through Istanbul. "Whatever you say."

"The reason I'm calling," said Anna, "is that I've had a bit of trouble tonight."

Now Taylor was listening. "Whatever you need," he said. "Where are you? I'll come get you right away."

"No," said Anna. That would be insecure. What's more, it would mean surrendering herself to the care and protection of a man, which at this moment she powerfully wanted—and did not want.

"You sure?" pressed Taylor.

"It can wait. Let's meet at two o'clock."

"Say what?" answered Taylor. He knew she was talking in

code, but he had forgotten what this particular code meant. There were dozens of them, for different agents, NOCs, liaison contacts. In this case, "one o'clock" meant immediately, "two o'clock" meant the next day.

"Let's meet at two o'clock," repeated Anna.

"Oh, fuck it," said Taylor. "Let's just meet tomorrow morning."

"Right," said Anna. "Where?" Obviously if he had forgotten the part of the code dealing with the time of an emergency meeting, he had forgotten the part about place.

"My shop," said Taylor.

Anna hung up the phone. Meeting at the consulate was bad tradecraft, but at that point she didn't care. She was tired. It didn't make sense to go back to her hotel, where Ascari might somehow track her down, so she simply checked into the hotel into which she had stumbled. They overcharged her on principle—a single woman, arriving alone at that hour. She didn't care about that either. She felt unnaturally calm. An Iranian agent had just tried to rape her, and she had beaten him senseless and left him for dead on the floor of his hotel room. She felt as if she ought to be sobbing, or at least sniffling. But she was just tired. She took a shower, crawled into bed, and slept soundly until the next morning.

16

◆

Anna had been waiting nearly an hour when Taylor finally arrived at the consulate; he had the woozy look of someone who has had too much drink and too little sleep the night before. Anna was sitting in the reception room on the first floor of the Palazzo Corpi, reading a book, and at first Taylor walked right past her. Apparently she didn't look like his mental image of "Vera." The voice on the phone had been tough, sharp, controlled. The dark-haired, green-eyed woman on the couch looked younger and more vulnerable.

"Where the hell have you been?" asked Anna when the receptionist steered Taylor toward her.

"Rough night," said Taylor.

"Not as rough as mine. Believe me."

"Come tell me about it," said Taylor, taking her arm and leading her across the courtyard to his office in the annex. The office was piled with cartons of new visa applications from Iranians, which Taylor was sifting in the hope of finding people who might have some intelligence value. Taylor cleared one of the boxes from his couch, motioned to Anna to have a seat, and closed the door.

"Sorry about last night," he said. "I'm sure I must have gotten a cable about you, but I can't remember what it said. Who are you anyway?"

"Amy L. Gunderson," said Anna. "Does that ring any bells?"

"Nope," said Taylor. "But my memory for pseudonyms isn't too hot."

"I'm a NOC," said Anna. "Based in London."

"What's your real name?"

"Should I tell you?"

"Sure," said Taylor. "What the hell."

"Anna Barnes," she said. "I'm new."

"So what happened, Anna Barnes?"

"I had a bad time last night with an Iranian we're trying to develop." Her voice was calm, perhaps a bit tired. The electricity of the previous night had flowed out of her body.

"What's his name?"

"Ali Ascari. I had a meet with him last night in his room at the Hilton. He got drunk and abusive. I had to hit him, with a whiskey bottle. I'm afraid I may have hurt him."

"What was he doing?"

"He was trying to attack me," she said, avoiding the word "rape." She spoke quietly, almost clinically. "He had a knife. I didn't really have any other choice."

Taylor smiled.

"What's so funny?"

"You sound apologetic," said Taylor. "Obviously the son of a bitch had it coming."

"He did," answered Anna. "But it's sort of a mess, isn't it? I hit him pretty hard, especially the second time. For all I know, he may be dead. God only knows what they'll think back at headquarters. They'll probably think it was very unprofessional."

"Fuck headquarters," said Taylor.

Anna smiled. "That's easy for you to say. But I'm a new kid."

"Go ahead. Say it."

"Fuck headquarters."

"Excellent. Now, I seriously doubt your man is dead. Not to take anything away from your skill with a whiskey bottle, but it takes a hell of whack to kill someone that way."

"I kicked him, too. Twice."

Taylor squinted at her. She was full of surprises, Amy L. Gunderson. "Congratulations," he said. "But I still doubt you killed him."

"That's good, I guess."

"Don't be disappointed. Maybe you'll get another shot."

"Never," said Anna with a shiver. "I've had it with this guy. I should never have met him again. I'm the wrong person. The chemistry is all wrong."

"I'll say," said Taylor. Despite herself, Anna laughed. "Seriously," he continued, "I'll send someone over to the Hilton to ask a few questions. In the unlikely event they've found a dead Iranian, we'll get you out of Istanbul pronto and try to tidy things up. If he's gone to the doctor, we'll find out how bad he's hurt. If he's sitting in his room with a hangover and a lump on his head, we'll send up some aspirin. Whatever it is, we'll take care of it. So stop worrying."

"If he's alive, he's going to be angry."

"Tough shit."

"But he may want to take revenge, on the agency, or on me."

"Does he know who you are?"

"True name? No. He knows me as Allison James."

"Does he know you're agency?"

"Yes and no. He knows I'm in contact with agency people in London, and he calls me 'CIA lady.' But he probably doesn't think I'm the real thing. In fact, it's probably beyond his comprehension that a woman could be a bona fide CIA officer."

"You may have changed his mind last night," said Taylor. "Anyway, don't sweat it. We deal with bigger assholes than this guy every day of the week."

Anna smiled. She appreciated Taylor's little pep talk more than she wanted to let on.

"I'm going to need communication," she said. "I ought to cable London and headquarters right away and let them know what's happened."

"No problem," said Taylor.

"And I need somebody to go over to the hotel where I was staying before and pick up my stuff."

"No problem."

"And then I guess I ought to get out of here. When does the Pan Am flight for London leave?"

"In an hour. You'll never make it."

"I'll go tomorrow."

"Listen," said Taylor. "Maybe you want some company later, after you finish your cables. You're going to feel a little spooked, no matter how tough you are with a bottle."

"I'd love some company, to be honest. If you're not too busy." She didn't consider the etiquette of accepting his offer. Taylor was a colleague. He was initiated into the secrets of her world. Which meant she could relax.

"How about a brief driving tour of the Anatolian countryside, in a bulletproof Chevrolet?" asked Taylor. Anna didn't answer. She just closed her lids on those radiant, blue-green eyes.

Anna finished her cables just after noon. The act of writing them, confessing to her various bosses that her jaunt to Istanbul had been a disaster, made her nervous all over again. She looked pale when she knocked on Taylor's door.

"Good news," said Taylor. "Your Iranian friend isn't dead."

"Thank God!" she said. By now, her homicidal fantasies had disappeared. Drafting her cables, she had reflected on the prospect of being tried for murder in an Istanbul court and decided it was not to her liking.

"He's not even angry. He's contrite."

"You're kidding. How do you know?"

"Because forty minutes ago someone named Ascari called the switchboard with a message for Allison James. Which is you, correct?"

"Correct. What was the message?"

"Tell Allison James thank you for the book and that Ali Ascari is very sorry. What book is he talking about?"

"It was a gift. A guide to Moslem holy places in Azerbaijan. His family is from Baku."

"How thoughtful."

"What did the switchboard say?"

"They told him they didn't know what he was talking about. That they didn't know of anyone by the name of Allison James."

"This guy doesn't give up," said Anna, shaking her head.

"In this part of the world," said Taylor, "a man doesn't really respect a woman until she's hit him over the head with a whiskey bottle."

The car was ready at twelve-thirty. Taylor dismissed the driver and took the wheel. "Let's go to Asia," he said, gunning the car onto Mesrutiyet Street so that the tires squealed. Taylor's sense of style was better than his sense of direction, and he got lost on the other side of the Bosporus Bridge. "It's no use asking for directions," he advised Anna. "Turks can't bear to admit they don't know the way, so they make up an answer."

So Taylor, directionless, explored the back alleys of Beylerbey, Cengelkoy and Vanikoy. He found his bearings eventually in Anadoluhisari, up the Bosporus, at a familiar restaurant, where they stopped for lunch and shared a bottle of wine. Anna began to relax. She told Taylor more details about the odious Ali Ascari. She told him about the vicissitudes of NOC-dom in London; by the last glass of wine, she was telling him how, little more than a year before, she had decided to join the world's most exclusive men's club. Taylor smiled and drank.

Taylor's plan was to go to Polonezkoy, a bucolic little village about twenty miles east of the Bosporus distinguished chiefly by the fact that its residents all had blue eyes and blond hair. They were Poles, descended from Polish soldiers who had fought on the Ottoman side during the Crimean War, received land from a grateful sultan, and settled there with their wives and children (hence the name Polonezkoy). They had behaved like good Polish peasants—building tidy farms and copulating industriously with each other—with the result that the land was very green and the population was very inbred.

For generations, the yeomen of Polonezkoy had supplemented their farm income by providing food and short-term lodging (very short-term, by the hour) to wealthy Istanbuli gentlemen and their mistresses, who needed someplace out of the way—preferably run by heathen Christians—to conduct their illicit liaisons. It was a charming, Old World version of a hot-sheet motel, and a place where Taylor had more than once brought his own women friends.

The landscape changed radically a few miles inland. The suburban clutter of the Bosporus gave way to the rugged hill country of Anatolia—dry, dusty, and nearly empty of people. Europe lapped over the edge of Asia, at the eastern shore of the Bosporus, but went no farther than a mile or two. Taylor broke his rule and stopped just east of Beykoz to ask directions. "Polonezkoy?" he asked a gaunt Turkish gentleman. The man thought he meant Poland and pointed northwest, toward Warsaw. Eventually they found someone who pointed them in the right direction, and the car bumped along the one-lane dirt road while Taylor fiddled with the radio knob.

"You're not married," said Anna, looking at Taylor's left hand as he swung the steering wheel toward her.

"Not anymore," said Taylor. "She left me, six months ago."

"Why? If you don't mind my asking."

"We were incompatible."

"What does that mean?"

"It means we didn't fit together anymore. My wife wanted me to get serious, take a job back at headquarters, have children, be a normal guy. But she gave up."

"Why?"

"Because she finally realized I was a hopeless case. My wife was an improver. A fixer-upper. She never got the point."

"Which was what?"

"The point was that I wasn't going to change. I liked the way I was. It was wasted effort."

Anna nodded. She didn't know whether to sympathize with Taylor or his ex-wife. Taylor went back to fiddling with the radio knob.

"I'm trying to find police radio," he said. The static floated in and out, but amid the blur you could hear the voice of a Turkish announcer intoning the police slogans of the day. "Remember that the police are here to protect human rights," said the announcer. There was a vigorous police march, followed by the admonition: "You should be the kind of policeman that people will call 'friend.' "

"I love this station," said Taylor. "They should have police radio back home."

The radio announcer began intoning a summary of the day's terrorism incidents. His voice had the flat tone of a sportscaster reading the soccer scores. "In Izmir, one shooting; in Trabzon, two shootings and one bombing; in Ankara, four shootings."

"What's happening to this country anyway?" said Anna as the police announcer rumbled on. "It's a mess."

"The usual," said Taylor. "There's no political center anymore. Just extremes. So the whole country is going to the mattresses."

"In Konya," continued the police-radio announcer, "one shooting and one bombing. In Istanbul, six shootings and two bombings." Taylor turned police radio off.

"What are we doing about it?" asked Anna.

"Who? The boys and girls from RTACTION?"

Anna nodded. RTACTION was one of the CIA's cryptonyms for itself.

"You gotta be kidding," said Taylor. "We're not in the game."

The Chevrolet rumbled on. Every few miles they passed a cluster of cement-block houses, each with a muddy terrace and a collection of chickens, sheep and a lame cow or two. Dark-eyed children were everywhere in these settlements, more numerous than the farm animals. Each house had the standard adult complement—a heavy woman in a headscarf and a thin man in a worn coat—that seemed universal in the Turkish countryside. Anna looked at the women, lumpy and misshapen. That was one of the immutable cruelties of the Third World class system: It made poor women fat and rich women thin.

"Who was that cooing in Turkish in the background when I called you last night?" asked Anna.

"None of your business."

"Touchy, touchy."

"Her name is Tina. She's a blackjack dealer at the Etap Marmara. Actually, her name is Tuna, but she got tired of people making rude jokes, so she changed it."

"Is she in the business?"

"No. I told you, she's a blackjack dealer."

"What's the attraction?"

Taylor looked at her and smiled.

"Raw sex," he said.

Anna blinked.

"She's very pretty," he continued, "in a cheap sort of way. And as she tells all the blackjack players, she has the fastest hands in Turkey."

"Give me a break," said Anna. "That's not what I meant. I meant, isn't it hard to relax with someone who doesn't know what you really do?"

"Nope," said Taylor. Anna stared out the window at some pigs. "I've learned a lot from Tina, actually," he continued. "About Turkish women."

"Such as?"

"You really want to know? She's rather graphic."

"I think I can take it."

"Well, she told me quite a lot about what it's like to be a single girl in Turkey."

"Go on."

"Okay. For starters, Turkish men are virgin-crazy. They have to marry a virgin or they go nuts. So a woman tries hard to remain a virgin until she's twenty-five or so. During that time she'll do almost anything with her boyfriend. Blow jobs, anal sex, whatever. But no penetration of the vagina. Absolutely not. That, she saves for the wedding night. And if she gives it away to a man who doesn't marry her, she has a major problem."

"That's pathetic, don't you think?"

"I don't have an opinion. In these matters, I am simply an observer."

"And when she's older than twenty-five?"

"By then, a Turkish woman stops caring, according to Tina. She assumes the worst—that she's never going to get married—and starts to live for herself. She assumes that anyone who'll marry an old bag over twenty-five probably won't even notice whether she's still a virgin."

"How old is Tina?"

"She's twenty-three."

"So why does she sleep with you? Or are you a pederast?"

"Of course not!" said Taylor. "Tina has discovered the existence of a revolutionary medical technique that is going to change life in this part of the world."

"And what is that?" asked Anna, not sure she really wanted to know.

"Hymen reconstruction. The fancy gynecologists in Istanbul already have a fee schedule for it. According to Tina, the standard fee is sixty dollars. Two days before the wedding is ninety dollars. If you want it on the wedding day itself, God forbid, it costs a hundred fifty dollars. Of course, it's more for Saudis and Kuwaitis."

"Yuck," said Anna. There was a long silence as the car bumped and weaved the last few miles toward Polish-land. Eventually, they glimpsed the green fields of Polonezkoy, rising like a fair mole on the dark body of Asia.

Blond, blue-eyed men stood outside each of the big houses in the village, beckoning tourists to stop for food and rest. Taylor stopped at a house on the crest of a hill; it was owned by a sturdy fellow named Thaddeus. He welcomed them enthusiastically and hurried them inside.

"Upstairs or down?" asked Thaddeus.

Taylor looked at Anna, as if seeking guidance. But Anna, relaxed and unaffected, paid no attention. She was looking at the Polish airline posters tacked to the wall. "Why don't you give us the tour," said Taylor.

Thaddeus led them up a creaky stairway to a long hallway. He flung open the first door on the left. It was a small room, with a single bed at one end and a little table and two chairs at the other, next to a window that looked out over the mock-Polish countryside.

Anna entered the room first. She walked to the window, then back to the bed. It was a steel-frame bedstead, low to the floor, with a rough corduroy bedspread, a lumpy pillow and no sheets. What a sad little room, she thought.

"We can bring food up," said Thaddeus coyly, "or we can leave you alone."

Anna looked at Taylor. What was this all about? Could it be that Taylor—this man she had met several hours ago—was hoping to screw her in that dumpy little bed? Taylor said nothing. He was looking out the window, pretending not to be listening.

"Let's try downstairs," said Anna abruptly. "I think that's more what I had in mind." Taylor turned toward her. There was a sheepish, naughty-boy look on his face.

Thaddeus walked them back down the creaky stairs to the dining room, which had a half dozen tables. It was a low-ceilinged room that seemed too small to hold all the furniture it contained, and it felt cramped and hot.

"What about outside?" asked Anna, pointing to a garden with several small tables arrayed under a grape arbor. "Can we sit outside?"

"As you like," said the Turko-Pole. He escorted them out to the garden and, a few moments later, returned with two enormous bottles of beer.

"Is this where you bring your women?" asked Anna.

"Sometimes," he answered. He still had that sheepish look on his face.

"Do they like it?"

"Sometimes."

"Are you trying to screw me?"

"Not necessarily. I just thought you'd like it here."

Anna looked around. The air was cool and crisp and clean, unlike the dirty air of Istanbul. A red rooster was ambling around the garden, looking for crumbs.

"I do like it here," she said. "But I'm just passing through."

Taylor nodded. "Whatever you like," he said.

They smoked cigarettes and drank beer and talked. With the sex question defused for the moment, Taylor throttled back a few degrees. The muscles in his face relaxed; the rhythm of his speech slowed and softened. But on this calm, leeward side of Taylor, there was a whisper of restlessness, like a breeze blowing through an empty courtyard.

"How do you like the business?" he asked.

"I liked it fine, until last night."

"That's the good part, hitting people over the head with bottles. Wait until you get to the bad part."

"What's the bad part?"

"Filling out the paperwork to explain why you broke the bottle."

Anna laughed. "Seriously," she said, "what's the bad part?"

Taylor thought for a long moment. "You want the truth?" Anna nodded. "The bad part is feeling like you're wasting your time."

"How often do you get the bad part?"

"Lately? Most of the time."

"You can't be that disillusioned. You're not old enough."

"Or young enough. Cynicism is a young man's game."

"What are you going to do about it?"

"I dunno. Quit, maybe, if I can't find anything interesting to do on the inside. I'm becoming convinced there's a big problem back home, but I can't figure out what it is. It sometimes seems like they've sent everybody off to eunuch school."

Anna nodded. There was a pause. "Not that it matters," she volunteered, "but as a point of historical fact, there was no 'eunuch school.'"

"What are you talking about?"

"The Ottomans. The Palace School was for the janissaries. The eunuchs stayed in the harem. The head eunuch, the *kislar aga,* simply told everyone what to do. There was no school."

"What are you, a eunuchologist?"

"Ottoman history was my field, before I became a NOC."

"No shit," said Taylor.

"No shit."

"What sort of life crisis pushed you into the CIA? Too many overdue library books?"

Anna gave her standard answer. "No crisis," she said. "I was bored. That was the main reason."

Taylor looked skeptical. "Were you married?" he asked.

"No," said Anna. "But close."

"Too close?"

Anna nodded. "His name was Tom. He taught English at Harvard. Very smart, very gentle, very loving. When I met him, I thought I had finally met the man of my dreams."

"But he wasn't?"

"No, he was, actually. That was the funny thing. He really was the man of my dreams. He liked the same kind of music I did, the same places on Cape Cod, the same novelists, the same flavors of ice cream. And he took women seriously."

"A New Age man."

"Screw you. You can make fun of it, but those things matter. When I met Tom, I had been with so many half-baked, self-centered men, I couldn't believe how lucky I was to have found someone smart who was interested in me."

"Sounds like bliss. What happened?"

"Tom had a fatal flaw," said Anna. "He was an intellectual, a man who liked abstractions. I began to realize that he liked his abstract version of me better than he liked the real person."

"Mistake," said Taylor.

"And it turned out he was selfish, too. For all that gentleness, he was as self-absorbed as the others. He would listen to what I had to say, and then say what he wanted to say. I was just a prop. He liked me because I was smart enough to understand him. But that got boring. I wanted something different."

"What did you want?"

"I wanted a man who would connect, a guy who would walk up to me in a bar, look me in the eye and say: 'Hey, little lady, let's have some fun.'"

Taylor smiled. "Hey, little lady, let's have some fun."

"Don't flatter yourself." Anna pulled her coat tighter around her body. As the sun fell lower in the sky, it was getting chilly.

"So who have you found since Tom?"

"Nobody," said Anna.

"Nobody?"

"I've been too busy the past year to think about relationships. And its hard to be honest and open with someone if you're keeping as many secrets as we are."

"Who says you have to be honest?" said Taylor. "A lot of our colleagues are liars, and they seem to get laid all the time."

"Maybe," said Anna. "But that doesn't turn me on."

Taylor thought a moment. "I know one thing we have in common," he said.

"What's that?"

"We're both easily bored."

They drove back to Istanbul at twilight. The beer and the talk had left them both easy and mellow. Sex was in the air, like moisture before a rainstorm; not talked about, not acted upon, just there. As they drove back through Beykoz, Anna recognized one of the houses and nudged Taylor.

"I've been there," she said. "To that little house by the water, with the green shutters."

"When?"

"Two years ago. When I was here as a graduate student, doing research for my thesis."

"Who lives there?"

"A funny old woman named Natalia Temo."

"How did you happen to meet her?"

"A Turkish professor introduced me. He thought she might have some old documents that would be interesting. But it turned out she didn't."

"What documents? If you can explain it to a non-Ottomanist."

"They sounded pretty sexy, actually. This woman was the granddaughter of an Albanian doctor named Ibrahim Temo, who had been one of the founders of the Union and Progress Committee back in the 1880s."

"Known to non-Ottomanists as the Young Turks."

"Correct," said Anna. "I was interested in Temo because he had attended the group's first meeting in Istanbul in 1889, along with three other medical students: a Circassian from the Caucasus named Mehmed Resid, a Kurd from Arabkir named Abdullah Cevdet and a Kurd from Diyarbakir named Ishak Sukuti. That was the golden age for the Young Turks."

"How do you remember all this stuff?"

"I have a memory for historical trivia. That used to be my job. Anyway, what I wanted was the group's papers. They were revelant for a chapter in my dissertation about how the Young Turks lost their idealism. I wanted to find out what had gone wrong, how the members of this progressive organization turned into a bunch of killers by 1915. So I went to see Natalia Temo. And she told me an amazing story. A sort of detective story."

"Tell me," said Taylor. "I like detective stories. They're about my speed."

"Okay. But it's complicated. It began when the original members of the group decided they would send their papers to Sukuti, who would act as their archivist. Temo sent him his papers until he fled to Romania in 1895. Eventually Sukuti was forced into exile, too, and he took the papers with him to San Remo, on the Italian Riviera."

Anna looked at Taylor. "Is this boring?"

"No," he said. "Quite the contrary. You can't imagine what a pleasure it is to be talking about something other than tradecraft."

"Okay," she said warily, resuming her narrative. "Sukuti stayed in San Remo until 1905, when he became very sick. He knew that he was probably dying, so he arranged to send all the important documents to Temo, in Romania. He put them in a trunk and wrote Temo that they were coming. But before he could send them, he died."

"Delicious," said Taylor. "This is sounding like *The Maltese Falcon.*"

"Just wait. It gets better. The Ottoman consulate in San Remo had been watching Sukuti for years. When they learned of his death, they bribed the police, stole the trunk and sent it to Sultan Abdul-Hamid in Yildiz Palace in Istanbul. The trunk stayed there until 1909, when the Young Turks finally got rid of Abdul-Hamid. Whereupon Ibrahim Temo went to Yildiz, found the trunk, and took it back with him to Romania."

"Where it remains."

"No. That's the problem. When Ibrahim Temo died in 1945, he left the trunk to his son. And when the son died, the papers should have gone to his daughter, Natalia. In which case they would have gone to me, for my thesis, because she liked me."

"But she didn't have the papers?"

"Nope."

"Where are they?"

"Albania," said Anna with a sigh.

"Albania?"

"Somehow the Albanian government found out about the papers in the 1950s, after Natalia began trying to emigrate to Turkey. They wanted them for the Albanian national archives, presumably because Temo was Albanian. Natalia told me that two Albanians came one day to pick up the trunk and she never saw it again. It's probably in Tirana now, gathering dust."

"So you never found out what turned the idealists into the murderers?"

"No. That was part of why I gave up my dissertation. I decided I would never really know."

"What happened to Natalia?"

"The Romanians eventually let her out. She came to Turkey in the late 1960s and settled down in the little house with the green shutters in Beykoz. She's an old woman now. Tough, and sad."

"What was in the papers? Did you ever find out?"

"All I know is what Natalia told me. She had looked through the papers as a girl and talked to her grandfather about them. From what she said, they sounded fabulous. They included correspondence among the various branches of the Union and Progress Committee, written in code to confuse the sultan's spies."

"What kind of code?"

"I don't know. The only thing Natalia remembered was that each member and branch had a number. Let's say Paris was six, so if you were the ninety-first member of the Paris branch, your number was six/ninety-one."

"No wonder the Albanians were so interested. They're spy-crazy."

"There may have been another reason. From what Natalia said, the papers showed something that might have interested certain people in Moscow."

"Like what?"

"Like the fact that in 1905, when Sukuti died, the Young Turks were part of a network that stretched throughout the Caucasus and Central Asia. There were Young Georgians in Tbilisi, Young Bukharans in Bukhara, Young Turkestanis in Tashkent, Young Azeris in Baku, Young Armenians in Yerevan. All working together to topple the old empires."

"So what."

"So history didn't begin in that part of the world in 1917, the way the Soviets like to pretend. There used to be something else. There used to be another vision of Central Asia."

"Interesting," said Taylor. "But it's ancient history. Back home, they can't remember what happened last week. Who's going to care about what happened seventy-five years ago?"

"Nobody, sad to say. That's why I decided to stop being an Ottomanist. It was time to get out of the archives."

"Welcome to the real world, such as it is," said Taylor. His arm was on the back of the seat, and he let it drop casually over Anna's shoulder. He pulled her toward him and gave her a kiss on the cheek. As he held her, his hand touched her breast. Anna let it stay there a few moments, wondering what it would be like to sleep with Taylor, what his hands would feel like on her body. By now, Taylor was feeling the curve of her breast in his hand. He was evidently the sort of man who didn't stop until someone said: "Stop."

"Stop," said Anna.

Taylor smiled. No problem. He was easy.

Silence surrounded the car. In the winter chill, small clouds of fog were forming on the black waters of the Bosporus. As Taylor drove, he thought about Anna's tale of Young Azeris and Young Turkestanis and a network of Central Asians that had existed nearly a century ago. And as he thought, an odd notion fell into his head. He recalled an unlikely encounter a few weeks earlier with a Canadian who claimed to be a film-maker but showed unusual interest in Central Asian émigrés.

"Let me ask you a question," said Taylor. "Have you ever met a NOC named Jack Rawls?"

"No. But NOCs don't hang out together. We're supposed to be anonymous. Who's Jack Rawls anyway?"

"Probably nobody," said Taylor. "I saw him in a bar a few weeks ago. He's another Central Asia junkie. I thought maybe he might be a member of the brethren."

"Beats me. But I'm a new kid."

Taylor kept his eyes on the road as it wound along the Bosporus, still thinking about Rawls. No, he decided. It couldn't be. They weren't that smart back at headquarters.

"Forget Rawls," he said. "This crowd doesn't want to make trouble in Tashkent. They just want to stay afloat. Anyway, Central Asia is off-limits."

"So I've heard," said Anna. "But I'm not so sure everybody follows the rules."

"What's that supposed to mean?"

Anna didn't answer at first. Then she turned to Taylor.

"Let me ask you a question," she said. "Have you ever met Edward Stone?"

"The big shot, back at headquarters?"

Anna nodded.

"Nope. Heard about him, but never met him. Why do *you* ask?"

"Because he's interested in Central Asia, too."

"Is that so?" said Taylor, enunciating each word. "Is that so? Tell me more."

"I can't. I don't know any more."

"Son of a gun," said Taylor, shaking his head. Maybe there was life in the old corpse yet.

"I probably shouldn't have told you that," said Anna. She made a mental note to send a message to Stone, when she returned to London, summarizing what Ali Ascari had said about the shipment of guns across the Soviet border. It would be a way of making amends for her indiscretion.

"No," said Taylor. "You probably shouldn't have. But that's what I like about you." Taylor made a mental note, too. There was a certain item he should retrieve from an apartment off Yeniceriler Street.

They returned to Istanbul just after eight and had another drink in the hotel bar. Taylor leaned close to Anna and talked almost in a whisper. It was bedroom talk, but it never got to the bedroom. Anna said good night just before ten. She had a plane to catch the next morning, and the somewhat tangled strands of a new career to pick up back in London. It wouldn't do to fall for an outrageous character like Taylor on a one-night stand in Istanbul.

IV
RTACTION

Istanbul

March–May 1979

17

◆

TAYLOR RETRIEVED THE RAWLS TAPE THE DAY AFTER ANNA Barnes left Istanbul. He had no idea what it might contain, much less what he would do with it. The recorder was still operating after more than a month, just as George Trumbo had said it would be. But transcribing the tape was a bit awkward. Taylor didn't want to give it to one of Timmons's technicians in Ankara, who might begin asking questions. He decided against having his own secretary transcribe it, for the same reason. So with some cryptic telephonic advice from George in Athens, he struggled himself through the many hours of conversation recorded over the past month.

Once Taylor began reviewing the Rawls tape, he couldn't stop. He stayed up all one night and into the next morning, listening and transcribing in longhand the parts that interested him most. What he heard, as he sat listening on the floor of his apartment in Arnavutköy, surprised even a career neggo who had made it a practice never to be surprised by anything: Mr. Jack Rawls, the putative film producer from British Columbia, was organizing what sounded like a private army of Central Asian émigrés.

Rawls began each conversation the same way: He would thank the visitor for coming, talk a little nonsense about his documentary film on Soviet émigrés, and then move gradually into a discussion of the history and politics of Central Asia. He seemed to be trying to gauge the intensity and commitment of each of his visitors. As Rawls talked passionately in his TV preacher's voice and the visitors responded in kind, the sessions took on the air of a revival meeting.

The first meeting was with a man who called himself Abdallah. Taylor imagined him to be a short dark man with broad cheekbones and hollow eyes. Rawls began with pleasantries, invocations of Allah and talk about his movie. Then, when he had established that his visitor's family was from Tashkent, at the center of the vast expanse of Central Asia once known as Turkestan, Rawls began turning the crank.

"The Russians have dismembered Turkestan," said Rawls, speaking in his language-school Turkish. Taylor clasped the earphones tight, trying to hear every word above the hiss of the tape. "The Russians in Moscow took the great land of Turkestan, which stretches from the Black Sea to China, and what did they do with it? They colonized it!"

"Oh yes!" chimed in Abdallah.

"Yes, my friend," returned Rawls. "The Russians cut great Turkestan into little pieces. They took the vast and noble empire of Genghis Khan and Tamerlane and divided it into five little pieces they could swallow. Uzbekistan. Tajikistan. Kazakhstan. Turkmenistan. Kirgizia. Little lands, too small to fight. And then, when great Turkestan was weakened, the Russians destroyed the mosques! Stalin tried to keep his crime secret, but I have the numbers."

"You do?"

"Listen! In 1917, there were 26,000 mosques across Turkestan and the Caucasus. By 1942, only 1,312 remained!"

"Shame!" said Abdallah. His voice was trembling.

"And do you know what the Russians call the sons of noble Turkestan today? They call them *chernozhopy*, which means 'black bottoms.' "

"No!"

"Or they call them *churka*, which means 'wood chips'! Do you understand me? The Russians think your boys are as dumb as chips of wood."

"Allah!"

"The sons of your land! Black bottoms and wood chips!"

"*Yok!* We must teach them a lesson!"

"Yes. But we must be careful."

"What should we do?" The émigré's voice had the eager sound of a believer waiting for the good news.

"Perhaps my friends can help," said Rawls slowly.

"Who are your friends?"

"My friends in America."

"The CIA?"

"Do not mention that name, ever. I told you that you must be careful."

"Am I dreaming?" cried Abdallah. "Do you mean that you are ready to help us at last? I have waited my lifetime for this!"

"My friend, great Turkestan is the last colony on earth. When was Algeria freed? Twenty years ago. And Kenya and the Congo and all those little black African lands. Great Turkestan is still waiting, but its time will come."

"Allah!" thundered Abdallah. "You will help us at last!"

Rawls spent the remainder of that conversation swearing Abdallah to secrecy and warning him to tell no one— absolutely no one—about their contact. "Free Turkestan!" said Rawls as they parted.

"Free Turkestan!" repeated Abdallah.

Taylor moved the tape forward to another session. This time Rawls's visitor refused to give his name. But as the conversation progressed, it became clear that he was one of the so-called Meshki Turks, whose families had been deported from Georgia to Uzbekistan in 1944. Rawls played him like a virtuoso. Taylor listened to the tape with a mounting sense of Rawls's skill as an intelligence officer.

"Where was your family from, my friend?" Rawls began, oh so gently.

"From Akhalkali district, in southern Georgia."

"And you spoke Turkish there?"

"Yes, Turkish. Always Turkish. Until 1935, when they told us we were Azeris and made us learn the Azeri language. No one knew why. In those days, you did not ask."

"And what happened in 1944?"

"My family was sent away."

"And where were they sent?"

"To Uzbekistan, near Ferghana. They went by wagon."

"And many died?"

"Yes, very many. My aunt died. My brother died." He paused and took a breath. "My mother died. And for no reason. What had she done? What had any of us done? Why did they move us like that in the middle of the night, and take us a thousand miles away from our homes, for no reason?"

"It was genocide."

"Yes, it was," said the visitor. "But the world knows nothing of it."

"You are wrong," said Rawls. "We know, and we have not forgotten."

"Who?"

"My friends in America. We have kept records. We know that 200,000 people were deported from Meshketia on the night of November 15, 1944. We know that at least 50,000 people died on their way to Uzbekistan and Kazakhstan. And we know why."

"You do?" He sounded dazed, as if the American were suddenly offering to solve the riddle of his life.

"Your family and the thousands of other Moslem Turks of Meshketia were deported because Stalin was preparing to seize the provinces of eastern Turkey—Kars and Ardahan—that he claimed belonged to the Soviet Union. And he did not want your people, ethnic Turks, to cause trouble. So you were moved. Overnight. And if 50,000 of you died on the way, what did it matter to Stalin? You were just poor Turks! You were expendable."

"What a monster! What a crime!"

"My friends say there is an answer."

"What is that?"

"Free Turkestan!"

The Meshki Turk inhaled sharply, as if the idea were too dangerous and intoxicating to be breathed in normally. "Free Turkestan!" he said, repeating the two words as if they were the very essence of life.

"Perhaps that is the way to avenge the genocide of the Meshki Turks and protect their rights."

"Free Turkestan!" said the man once more.

"But only a powerful movement can free Turkestan from its Russian masters and provide safety for its people, from the Black Sea to Sinkiang!"

"Is such a thing possible?"

"I don't know. But perhaps my friends in America can help."

And so it went with each of the half dozen visitors to Rawls's safe house in Bayezit. He altered his pitch slightly for each one. He told the Crimean Tatar about Stalin's folly in branding a whole race—the sons and daughters of the Crimea—as traitors to the Soviet Union. He wept with a Chechen for the tragedy of their lost and plundered homeland. He raged with an Uzbek about the way the Russians from Moscow had plundered and destroyed the beautiful Aral Sea, the jewel of Central Asia.

One consistent theme, in each of the conversations, was that at some point Rawls would ask the same question: Are you a member of one of the Sufi brotherhoods? Are you a Naqshbandi, or a Qadiri, or a Yasawi, or a Kubrawi? Have you visited the holy places? Shah-i-Zindeh in Samarkand, the burial place of Qutham Ibn Abbas, the "living saint," who was decapitated in battle and carried his head with him into a well, from which he performs miracles for the faithful? Or the shrine in Kazakhstan of Ahmad Yasawi, the founder of the brotherhood that bears his name? Or the tomb of Ali at Shah-i-Mardan in the Ferghana Valley of Uzbekistan? Or the tombs of the great Bahaeddin Naqshband, near Bukhara, and Yaqub Charki near Daghestan? They always said no, Rawls's visitors, but that didn't mean much. Sufis always denied that they were members of any brotherhood. What mattered was that Rawls asked the question.

"What the fuck is going on here?" said Taylor aloud when he finished reviewing the tapes. He went first to Stanley Timmons. The station chief had scheduled a golf game that afternoon, but at Taylor's insistence he postponed it. Taylor flew to Ankara with the Rawls tape in his briefcase. Timmons was waiting in his office with his deputy.

"Can I see you privately?" asked Taylor.

"Gee, I guess so," said Timmons, apologizing to his deputy and escorting him to the door. He turned to Taylor. "What's the big deal? Why the crash meeting?"

"Stanley," said Taylor. "I want you to be honest with me about something."

"Sure," said Timmons. "If I can be."

"Are you running a NOC operation in Istanbul I don't know about? One involving a guy whose cover name is Rawls and who is pretending to be a Canadian filmmaker from Vancouver?"

"What's his real name?"

"How should I know?"

"Hmmm," said Timmons. "No. I don't think so. At least not so far as I can recollect. Of course, I probably couldn't tell you if we did have such an operation going. Because if you were supposed to know about it, you already would. But no, actually, it doesn't ring any bells."

"Then I have some bad news for you. I think someone is running an operation behind your back."

"Impossible."

"Are you sure?" Taylor's tone was sharp and skeptical.

Timmons scratched his head. "Well, no. Not completely. On rare occasions, I suppose I might not be informed."

"Such as?"

"Cover problems. If headquarters sent a NOC to do something extra sensitive, they might want to keep it away from the embassy. They might even want to keep it away from the station chief. That's possible. Or sometimes headquarters might want to send someone into the embassy under deep cover, as an admin officer or USIA man, and for security reasons, that person would have no contact with the station whatsoever. That happens."

Timmons coughed nervously and lit a cigarette. He was working himself into a state of some anxiety as he imagined the various scenarios in which he might be left in the dark.

"Perhaps," said Timmons, "you had better give me some details about this operation that you claim is being run behind my back."

"Gladly. But I want you to promise me something."

"What?"

"That you won't tell headquarters how I found out."

"How can I promise that? Maybe you did something unethical."

"I didn't."

"Okay, fine. I promise. Now tell me the story about . . . what did you say his name was?"

"Rawls. That's his work name at least. I first saw him a month ago in Omar Gaspraly's bar in Bayezit."

"Who's Omar Gaspraly, for crying out loud?"

"He's a Tatar whose family ran away from the Crimea a long time ago. His place is kind of a hangout for émigrés from Central Asia. They all go there and get smashed and pretend they're going to liberate the motherland."

"Go on, go on." Timmons, his curiosity aroused, was now eager for details. He was like a cuckolded husband determined to know precisely what his wife had done to him.

"I'm there late one evening with George Trumbo from Athens, who had come in to help me with the Kunayev operation."

"I remember," said Timmons dubiously.

"I'm trying to find George a girl when Omar tells me there's another American in the bar. And it's this guy Rawls, talking to a couple of wild-eyed Uzbeks. I'm kind of curious, so I send George over to check him out. He says he's a filmmaker from British Columbia, doing a documentary on Soviet émigrés, and gives George his card."

"Sounds like a company man. The Canadians don't have anything going in Turkey."

"That's what I thought. And it pissed me off. So I decided to find out what was going on. I was slightly drunk at the time, to be honest, so maybe that's why I did it."

"Did what?"

"I followed him home and had George bug his apartment. It was a stupid thing to do." Taylor tried to sound contrite.

"Is that all? Is that what I had to promise not to tell anyone?"

"Yes."

"Forget it. Who cares. Get to the good part. What's on the tape?"

"Some strange stuff. Rawls meets every few days with one of these émigrés—Uzbeks and Kazakhs and God knows what else—and jerks them off about liberating their homeland. He tells them how nasty the Russians are to Soviet Moslems, as if they needed to be reminded of that. And then he suggests, without quite saying so, that Uncle Sam may be able to help them."

"Help them do what?"

"He doesn't ever say, exactly. But tells them: 'Free Turkestan!' as if it's the slogan of some sort of underground movement."

"Forget it," said Timmons, shaking his head. "We don't do that sort of thing anymore. Strictly forbidden."

"That's what I thought. But listen to the tape."

"No way."

"Listen to the goddam tape!"

And he did. Timmons's plans for a golf game were abandoned, as he sat numbly listening to selected passages from the tape. Abdallah from Tashkent. The Meshki Turk. The Uzbek. The Tatar. Every time Rawls mentioned "my friends in America," Timmons would grumble, "Aw, shit!" When Taylor finished his excerpts, Timmons put his head in his hands. He looked crushed.

"I don't know what this is all about," said Timmons. "But it goes without saying that it's very sensitive. Whatever it is."

"Right."

"To be blunt," continued Timmons, "I don't really want to get involved in it. If someone had thought I needed to know, then I would know. But since I don't, it's obviously none of my business."

"But you do know, now."

"I don't need this aggravation," said Timmons evenly. "I'm due to retire next year and I intend to do so quietly and happily. If you want to make a fuss, that is obviously within your power. But I am staying out of it. It isn't my case. So it's all yours. Be my guest."

"Thanks," said Taylor. He couldn't help feeling sorry for Timmons, old and tired and afraid of anything that might rock the boat.

"Copy me on any cables, if you would," said Timmons. "Just so you'll know, I will be sending a cable of my own tonight informing headquarters that you have briefed me about a sensitive matter you appear to have stumbled across and that I have advised you not to pursue it."

Taylor thanked Timmons and shook his hand. He felt like he had been watching someone die of self-strangulation.

The urge to make trouble was for Taylor something akin to a biological instinct. And so, with a dim sense that the trouble he was making might be chiefly for himself, he drafted a cable that night for headquarters. His first thought had been to send an LWSURF message straight to the director, as a way of pulling the highest possible chain. But that was stupid. Hinkle would probably ignore it, or worse, give it to one of the congressional intelligence committees. Taylor's next thought was to send a message directly to the deputy director for operations. But that was stupid, too. It would look like he was picking a fight. And Taylor had a long-standing rule never to pick a fight when you didn't know who your adversary was.

All Taylor really wanted to do, he decided, was to needle the bureaucrats, to let them know he had discovered their little game in Istanbul and deliver a polite "Fuck you." So he drafted the most innocuous sort of cable—a simple request for traces, for any pertinent information in the registry—on one Jack Rawls, filmmaker, with a particular request that he be informed if said Mr. Rawls was a CIA asset, so that he could help protect his cover. Then he settled back into the routine of life in the Istanbul base and waited for the return mail.

18

It was a condition of CIA life in 1979 that you saw the fabric of American power unraveling around the world, perhaps even understood why it was happening, but were powerless to do anything very useful to stop it. If you were at all conscientious about your job, you began to feel bad, like a fireman who has to watch a tall building burn out of control because his horses and ladders won't reach the flames. And in the winter of 1979, there was most certainly a three-alarm fire ablaze in the world. Iran was burning. The fire was spreading. The agency seemed willing to do almost anything—except put out the fire.

New schemes were floated every few weeks. In early March, someone back home decided it would be wise to recruit more Kurdish agents, to threaten Khomeini with a revolt by his Kurdish population. Jolly good idea! So the call went out to the stations and bases of the imperial region, and a few days later Taylor was visiting a toothless old buzzard from Diyarbakir who had been suggested by the CIA base in Los Angeles (Southern California seemed to be the heart of the Kurdish diaspora) as a man who might lead a Kurdish exile army. The old man hadn't entirely lost his wits. He demanded as a condition of his participation in the Kurdish War of Liberation that a large sum be remitted immediately to a numbered bank account in Switzerland. Taylor duly relayed his message to headquarters, with an information copy to Los Angeles.

Taylor's biggest headache was recruiting Iranian agents. Headquarters decided it could trade visas for intelligence, so an edict went out that Iranians would receive special-status visas if—and only if—they could demonstrate clear intelligence value. By now, thousands of Iranian refugees had gathered in Istanbul, all clamoring to come to America and open beauty salons or manage 7-Eleven stores or drive taxicabs at Dulles Airport. And every one of them was prepared to tell whatever preposterous story was necessary to obtain the golden visa. Taylor couldn't bear the thought of listening to so many earnest lies, so he turned most of the interviewing over to his secretary. A more sensible procedure, Taylor suspected, would have been to require, as a condition of granting a visa, that every Iranian promise *not* to provide intelligence to the United States.

A minor flap developed in mid-March when it was discovered that an Iranian local hire in the visa department had been selling places in the queue to his compatriots for sums as large as $10,000. Investigators were dispatched from Washington, and they proceeded to interview everybody in sight. Evidently this was the sort of crime the bureaucracy could get really excited about—petty larceny. The Turks eventually agreed to prosecute the visa clerk; the poor Iranians who had given him payoffs were stricken from the roll of eligibility. Taylor, who knew nothing about the scheme but had unwisely told one of the investigators that the Iranian was the sort of entrepreneur who would do well on Wall Street, was officially found blameless. But unofficially it was clear that the bean counters back home were not pleased.

Taylor muddled on. What continued to interest Washington

most were the Bulgarians and their putative plot to smuggle guns into Turkey. Taylor had uncovered little evidence that it was true. The unhappy fact was that the guns flowed into Turkey from every direction—Lebanon, Syria, Iran, Greece and, yes, Bulgaria—but the problem was the demand for guns, not the supply. Yet every few weeks, another nagging message would arrive from headquarters requesting new intelligence on Bulgarian guns. Feed the goat, Taylor had concluded. He put out regular queries on the subject, which generated a regular flow of useless information.

Taylor worried about Turkey, despite his inability to do anything about it. His anxieties had started soon after he arrived in Istanbul, when he realized that he could tell young Turkish leftists and rightists apart just by looking at them. He had been walking out of the subway, known as *tunel,* at the lower end of Istiklal when he saw a group of teenage boys across the street.

"Leftists," he said to himself without thinking very much about it. They were wearing parkas, jeans and military boots. That was leftist garb. Rightists looked different. They wore long wool overcoats and dark glasses. Taylor had taken a closer look. Definitely leftists. They had leftist mustaches. All Turkish men had mustaches, of course. But the leftist version was like a bush, sprouting out over the lip and sometimes straggling into the mouth, while the rightist moustache was thin and closely clipped, like a string. And at that moment, when it dawned on him that Turkey was polarized even along sartorial lines, Taylor had decided he needed an agent in the student movement. Purely for intelligence purposes, he assured Timmons. No covert action.

What he got for his trouble, in that first fishing expedition, was a skittish young Turkish professor of political science whose cryptonym was EXCHASE/1. He had been assigned "1" in the hope that he would go out and recruit his own string of subagents, who would be known as EXCHASE/2, EXCHASE/3 and so forth. But in truth, he wasn't much of an agent. His "intelligence" didn't go much beyond what was in the newspapers, and his chief interest seemed to be staying alive himself. Taylor didn't mind. For all his shortcomings, EXCHASE/1 still seemed to know more than the Turkish police. If you heard an explosion somewhere in Istanbul and called police headquarters to ask about it, the captain would say: "Don't worry. It doesn't involve Americans." And that would be it. EXCHASE could at least tell you the gossip.

EXCHASE's real name was Bulent. The schedule called for Taylor to meet him once a month in a safe house in Kadikoy, on the Asian side. Taylor's deputy, who took care of such administrative details as renting safe houses, seemed to like the Asian side. Perhaps he thought it was more secure to meet someone there than on the European side, nearer the consulate. That struck Taylor as a dubious proposition, since the only Americans likely to be stumbling around Kadikoy on a weekday afternoon were drug dealers or spies. But never mind. The rents in Kadikoy were cheaper.

Taylor took the ferry across the Bosporus to Uskudar. The sun was out, momentarily poking through the haze and soot of late winter, and the trip reminded Taylor why Istanbul, for all its egregious faults, remained so lovable. The city was made to be seen from the water, and the view of the skyline as the ferry pulled away from the dock near the Galata Bridge was one of the most spectacular sights on the planet. Taylor stood on deck counting the spires of the five great mosques, pink in the morning sun, as the ferryboat churned through the inky black water.

"*Salep! Salep! Salep!*" cried a vendor making his way through the crowded afterdeck; he was selling a frothy hot drink of the same name, made of milk and salep root and flaked with cinnamon. "*Salep,*" ordered Taylor. He spent the rest of the trip breathing in the aroma of cinnamon and spice as the magnificent wreckage of old Istanbul receded in the distance and the jumble of modern Anatolia approached off the starboard bow.

EXCHASE was a rather sad fellow; an earnest young man with reddish hair and complexion and a dazed look in his eye. He had the leftist mustache, but it was a somewhat sparse version. His problem was that he was too thoroughly Americanized, having taken a doctorate in political science at the University of Wyoming several years ago. Now he was back home teaching at Istanbul University, and he felt uncomfortable and undignified. His way of reassuring himself that he wasn't really caught up in the squalid mess of Turkish life was to spy for the CIA.

"You're late, Bulent," said Taylor when the young agent arrived at the safe house. He was only fifteen minutes late, but Taylor chided him anyway. Agents were never supposed to be late.

"I'm frightened," said the Turk.

"Why?"

"It is getting very dangerous at the university."

"For who?"

"For everyone. My students are afraid even to go buy a newspaper. In some neighborhoods, I myself am afraid to buy a newspaper."

"What for?" asked Taylor. He wondered whether perhaps EXCHASE was losing his nerve.

"Because if I buy the wrong newspaper in the wrong place, there may be trouble. If I ask for the leftist paper *Cumhuriyet* in a rightist area, and a rightist sees me, he may attack me. So at the newsstand I just nod at the paper I want, and when the man gives it to me, I fold it up so that no one will see it. Better to play it safe."

"That's ridiculous."

Bulent looked hurt. "It happened just last week," he said solemnly, "near the campus in Bayezit. A rightist was buying a copy of *Tercuman,* and a leftist saw him and shot him."

"Shot him?"

"Of course. At the university, everyone has a gun now. Except the women."

"So I gather."

"Excuse me, I am wrong. Among the Maoists, the women also have guns. But they are strange women. They are short and ugly, and they have sex with other Maoists. We have a saying at the university: The further left you go, the uglier the women are—and the easier to get in bed."

"We had the same saying where I went to school," said Taylor.

Bulent didn't crack a smile. He was a very serious young man.

"What about the guns?" pressed Taylor. "I know I've asked you this before, but it's important. Where do they come from?"

"Bulgaria," declared Bulent. He had gathered from previous conversations on this subject that that was the right answer.

"How do you know? Have you collected serial numbers on the guns, the way I asked you to at our last meeting?"

Bulent shook his head.

"Why not?"

"It was not possible."

"Why not, goddammit?"

Bulent looked stricken. On his lower lip was the beginning of a tremor. "Because it is too dangerous for me," he said quietly.

"That's part of the deal."

"I know. But if I look too hard for the guns, the others will know that I am a spy, and they will kill me."

"And you're frightened."

"Yes. I am frightened. I am sorry."

Taylor felt sorry for the Turk. He was pathetic. "Chin up," he said, patting the Turk on the shoulder.

"Okay, okay," said Bulent.

Taylor changed the subject. The hell with Bulgarian guns. "What's new with your leftist friends at the university?"

"Ahhh!" said Bulent, pleased that at last he had some useful information to impart. "I have a big report for you. There is a new split between the Dev-Yol and the Dev-Sol."

"Remind me which is which."

"Of course. The Dev-Yol believes that the revolution will begin in the countryside and then spread to the cities. The Dev-Sol believes the revolution will begin in the city and spread to the country. Now they are very angry and shooting at each other."

"What are the police doing about it?"

"Which? The Pol-Bir or the Pol-Der?"

"Give me a break, Bulent."

"The Pol-Bir is the rightist faction of the police. The Pol-Der is the leftist faction."

"Right. So what are they doing about the problem?"

"Neither of them is doing anything about the Dev-Yol or the Dev-Sol. They both think the CIA is running things." He looked at Taylor expectantly. Even a well-educated person like Bulent still harbored the fantasy of American omnipotence, despite the obvious evidence to the contrary. Taylor didn't want to disappoint him.

"Shhh!" he said. He gave Bulent a wink. Bulent nodded. The thought of this powerful, faraway America—which had deigned to take him up in its hands—seemed to be all that kept him going. Taylor looked at his watch.

"One more question and then I'll give you your money," said Taylor. "What's the word on campus about Iran? Is anyone joining the Islamic Students Association?"

"A few people," said Bulent. "Mostly they are poor boys from the country and ugly girls. Do not worry about them. They are losers."

"How much money is the Islamic Students Association giving to its members?"

"Some. Less than the leftists give out. About the same as the rightists."

"Where does the money come from?"

"Iran," said Bulent. It was probably true, but he was just guessing. What a waste of time, thought Taylor. He reached into his coat pocket and withdrew an envelope.

"Here's your stipend," said Taylor, handing the envelope to the Turk. Inside was eighty dollars.

"Thank you," said the Turk. He looked absurdly grateful, given the meager amount that the agency was paying him. Meanness was good tradecraft, Taylor had long ago learned. The rule was never to pay someone so much that this new affluence might make him conspicuous. That was part of why spying was such a rotten business. You couldn't even make real money selling secrets.

The next day was Taylor's regular liaison meeting with Serif Osman of the Turkish intelligence service. The Turk looked haggard. The usual assured and dignified manner of the Byzantine spymaster was gone. Instead, he had the frazzled appearance of a Third World cop surrounded by a population he couldn't control. Even his goatee, usually precisely cut and combed, looked unkempt.

"What's wrong?" asked Taylor.

"The eastern provinces," said the Turk. That was a kind of code. It meant "Kurds," a word Turkish security men preferred not to speak out loud.

"What's happening in the eastern provinces?"

"Foreign elements are creating disorder." That, too, was a kind of code, a reference to the Soviet Union. It was an article of faith in the Turkish security service that Moscow was supporting the Kurdish rebels in an effort to destroy the Turkish nation.

"Anything in particular?"

"Another funeral. It was exploited by leftist agitators. The army was forced to respond."

"What are you going to do?"

"Crack down, of course."

Serif walked to the window of his office. It looked out over Yildiz Park, where Sultan Abdul-Hamid had hidden for several decades in the late nineteenth century from the problems of his decaying empire.

"I will say this for Abdul-Hamid," said Serif, gesturing toward Yildiz Palace. "He knew how to deal with the Kurds."

"He let them kill Armenians," ventured Taylor.

Serif narrowed his eyes.

"Just joking."

"The sultan had many faults," continued Serif, "but he was in many ways the first modern intelligence chief."

"Um," murmured Taylor. What a distinction. The truth about Abdul-Hamid was that he was a nut. He had been so afraid of conspirators that he rarely ventured from Yildiz. He kept a hundred parrots in cages around the palace grounds to warn of intruders. He kept a loaded revolver in every room of the palace so he could shoot assassins. He drank milk only from his own cows, which were guarded twenty-four hours a day. He had his brother, Izzet, try on his clothes first, to make sure they weren't poisoned. He was, in short, a lunatic.

"Do you know Abdul-Hamid's secret?" continued Serif. "His secret was technology."

Taylor's eyes widened, but he said nothing.

"It is true! Abdul-Hamid used the telegraph to control his network of spies in Europe. And to gather intelligence about his empire, he sent out teams of photographers. I have one of Abdul-Hamid's albums here in my office."

"Is that right?" said Taylor. Feigning interest was an essential aspect of liaison meetings with local intelligence officials—looking at photo albums, sending greetings on

Ataturk's birthday, listening to the hoary myths of independence.

"Would you like to see it?" asked Serif hopefully.

"Of course."

Serif removed from a desk drawer a thick album of old prints, each mounted in a frame bearing Abdul-Hamid's *tughra* in elaborate Ottoman script. It was a catalogue of neatness and order, just the thing to please a paranoid sultan. In the pictures, Taylor noticed, everyone seemed to be wearing a uniform: firemen, policemen, soldiers and sailors, all posing proudly in their distinctive costumes; schoolboys wearing tunics with gold buttons and child-size red fezzes; fencers and gymnasts at play; medical students in double-breasted cloaks, arrayed behind half-dissected cadavers. If nothing else, thought Taylor, the album illustrated the Turkish passion for order: catalogues and lists, neat rows all arranged the same way. It almost didn't matter what the object was, so long as it was arranged neatly. Visit a Turkish fishmonger and you would see the same thing: the fish displayed in a neat fantail, the big ones and little ones all in perfect rows, heads together, tails together, just so. They were a disciplined, strong-willed people, the Turks. But sometimes a bit paranoid.

"Beautiful photographs," said Taylor. "But bad intelligence. If that's all the sultan saw, he must have thought the empire was in great shape."

"He didn't believe any of it," answered Serif. "It only convinced him that his enemies were more devious than he had imagined. So he would recruit more spies!"

Taylor nodded. That was a standard Turkish response, even now. If MIT wasn't getting enough intelligence about terrorism, it would hire several dozen more informants to hang around in leftist coffeehouses. And it would "interrogate" a few more leftists and Kurds. That was the other constant in Turkish security policy. Interrogating prisoners now as in Abdul-Hamid's time, was what the authorities seemed to like best.

"We Turks have a saying," admonished Serif. "If you don't beat your children, you will end up beating yourself."

"I'll try to remember that," said Taylor. "Listen, before I go there's something I want to ask you about."

"Oh?" said Serif. "What is that?"

"Have you ever heard the slogan 'Free Turkestan'?"

Serif squinted his eyes. "Say it again."

" 'Free Turkestan.' Have you ever heard an émigré group that uses a slogan like that?"

"Of course. Dozens of groups. Once upon a time, every waiter at Rejans restaurant had his own group. Not so many nowadays."

"Do Turks still care about Turkestan?"

"Of course we do!" said Serif. His dignity had been offended. "My own family came from the Crimea. From Bakhchisarai."

"No kidding."

"There is no kidding at all about this. Every Turk remembers our lost empire. We have a saying."

"And what is that?"

"We say: A man can travel from the Mediterranean to the Pacific Ocean and speak only Turkish."

"And eat only kebabs."

"Excuse me, please?"

"Nothing."

"Why do you ask me about Turkestan?"

"Just curious. I heard the slogan the other day—'Free Turkestan'—and I wondered whether it was anything serious."

"For us? For MIT?"

Taylor nodded.

"I cannot tell you, of course."

"Of course not," said Taylor. "But if you could tell me, what would you say?"

"Hmmm," said the Turk. The corners of his mouth were turned up. It wasn't a smile, but it was close. "I would say that it is not serious. This is a game for old men and waiters from Rejans. We have nothing to do with it anymore."

In early April, amidst this routine busywork of intelligence, the return mail Taylor had been waiting for finally arrived. He received a unusual cable from headquarters. It was sent on the "Restricted Handling" channel, which meant that it was especially sensitive and treated separately from the agency's normal, top-secret cable traffic. The message was from

Edward Stone. Stone advised that he would be arriving in Istanbul in one week for an overnight stop and wished to visit with Taylor. They would need somewhere secure to talk, Stone said.

19
◆

EVERY AGENCY OF THE UNITED STATES GOVERNMENT HAD A few people like Edward Stone. They were the permanent under secretaries, the master bureaucrats who survived each wave of enthusiastic politicians and kept the agency focused on its historical mission. Part of what gave the Stones their power was that they were living monuments to the world in which their agencies had been created, embodying each one's bureaucratic culture, its myths and traditions.

For most federal agencies, that time had been the 1930s and the culture was New Deal liberalism. Visit the great domestic departments in Washington even now—Agriculture, Interior, Justice—and you will see the physical remnants: vast murals depicting ordinary Americans, workers and farmers, cops and shopkeepers, engaged in the pageant of American social democracy. If America ever finally decided to abandon the ethos of Walt Whitman and Felix Frankfurter and Franklin Delano Roosevelt, someone would have to paint the New Deal murals over.

The Central Intelligence Agency was the product of a subtly different time and ethos. Its founding myths dated to the 1940s—the years of World War II and its immediate aftermath—and its traditions were patrician, not proletarian. When the CIA mandarins built their headquarters up the river in Virginia, they decided it should look like an Ivy League campus—cool and austere, like one of the modern buildings at Yale or Harvard. No one at CIA would ever have thought of commissioning a mural of some sweaty laborer in the

vineyard of intelligence. Too vulgar. Too public. If the agency
wanted to honor its traditions, then have Tiffany's engrave a
nice silver plate. The CIA was different. It was the product of
an America that had grown up in a hurry, that had left behind
the idealism and confusion of the 1930s and become, in the
space of a few years, tough and confident and cynical. It had
come into being to save America, not from the nebulous
problems of poverty and injustice, but from Germans and
Japanese. And then, everlastingly, from the Russians.

That explained Edward Stone's special status in the agency.
By 1979, he was one of the last remaining veterans of the
founder generation still at Langley. He was one of the few
people who could still remember that "Q clearance" origi-
nally meant you had access to Building Q, one of the temporary buildings scattered around Foggy Bottom in which the
agency was first housed; one of the few who could remember
shuttling among those buildings in the little buses known as
"green beetles." And what mattered most, he was one of the
few left who remembered just how ragged things had been in
those days, when there weren't any rules and you had to
make things up as you went along.

Stone's lineage, in agency terms, was part British and part
German. That was the very best pedigree to have. He had
come to London at the beginning of the war as a young army
officer assigned to OSS and begun working with the British
to unravel Nazi intelligence networks. When the war ended,
he went to Germany and continued the work—looking now at
the Nazi networks that ran east, toward the Soviet Union,
rather than west toward Britain and America. From those two
spent empires, Britain and Germany, Stone and his colleagues
built an American intelligence agency. From the British they
drew the tradecraft and the élan; from the Germans they drew
many of their agents. It was an awkward mix, but there
hadn't been time, back then, to worry about it.

The lessons of that time were hard-wired on Stone's brain:
the Soviets were reckless and duplicitous adversaries; the Europeans were gutless accommodationists; the Americans and
British were the world's last and best hope—not all of them,
mind you, but the right kind, the tough-minded ones. By
1979, Stone had been out of the military for more than three
decades, but he still wore a kind of Anglo-American civil ser-

vant's uniform: neat English suits of tweed and flannel; sturdy shoes with waxed laces; a brown homburg hat for ordinary occasions and, for special events, a stiff-brimmed gray one. He was utterly uninterested in change: When one of his suits became so threadbare and shiny it couldn't be worn anymore, he had his tailor make an identical one, same style, same color. He felt the same way about the agency.

Stone had not made the "transition" during the great American cultural revolution of the 1970s. Indeed, he hated what the agency had become by the end of the decade. It seemed to him cheap and undignified—all those congressmen running around holding hearings and the agency people meekly complying—quite apart from the dangers it caused to the craft of intelligence. "Oversight" was the new cure-all. Perhaps the congressmen thought that if clean people, such as themselves, had their hands in a dirty business, it would perforce become clean. A charming idea. But it seemed evident to Stone, after thirty-five years, that the only way intelligence work would ever become clean was if people stopped doing it.

What Stone truly couldn't understand was why the agency went along with this preposterous charade. Of course, members of Congress would talk about oversight committees and legal charters and American values. That was what congressmen did. But why had the agency signed onto this sort of Fourth of July nonsense? Had people lost their minds? Every time Stone saw Charles (Chuck) Hinkle leading a new group of congressmen on a tour of the agency, he felt a knot in his stomach. The barbarians were at the gate. The walls of the temple had been breached.

Stone had decided in the mid-1970s, as the onslaught gathered momentum, that it was a good time to disappear. The great purge of the clandestine service was already beginning; scores of covert bureaucrats with names like Evan and Nevin were being fired every few months. The auditors and nannies all agreed that the Directorate of Operations had too many bodies, and in a sense they were right. The clandestine service, like any well-fed animal, had built up layers of protective fat over three decades, and there were too many aging, wellborn spies on the payroll, thinking up dubious schemes to keep themselves occupied. But that wasn't really what the great purge was about. It was about power—about a secret arm of the government that had run its own affairs (and those of a good many other people) unhindered for thirty years and in the process made too many mistakes and too many enemies. And now it was at the mercy of the very people it had kept at bay all those years. Congressmen, journalists, bureaucrats—all looking for scalps.

Edward Stone, who had headed the Near East Division for more than a decade and was a sort of dean of the old boys' lobby, was an especially obvious target. Better to get out of the way, he had decided. Better to lie low for a while and see if people came to their senses.

And so he did—vanished one day from his spacious office with the maps and safes and went somewhere else, most people weren't sure where. As Hinkle's purge of the old boys increased, it was rumored for a time that Stone had been fired, too. But that was wrong. Some of his friends imagined that, like the old stag in the forest, Stone had concluded that his time had come and had gone off to some bureaucratic mountaintop to die a noble death. But that wasn't quite right either. Stone hadn't died and he hadn't gone up to any mountaintop. It would be more accurate to say that he had gone underground, which in a secret agency like the CIA amounted to a kind of double negative.

Taylor's initial reaction when he received Stone's message was that he had made the biggest mistake of his career. He didn't know why his request for traces had come to Stone's attention or what Stone would do about it. But he had the feeling that he had unwittingly picked a fight with the wrong man. His immediate problem was finding a secure place to meet. The Istanbul base had a secure conference room, the infamous "bubble," but it was hot and cramped and utterly uninteresting. So Taylor ruled out the bubble. There were restaurants aplenty, but they were too easy to bug. So forget restaurants.

A boat, Taylor decided. A boat trip up the Bosporus appealed to his sense of the dramatic. If his career was about to collapse, then he would go out in style. But what boat? The ambassador had a magnificent yacht, the *Hiawatha,* which he kept moored in Istanbul. But he was so paranoid that some congressional investigator would find out about it and take it away that he never let anyone use it. So that was out, too. Taylor paid a visit to a navy chief petty officer, who was nominally part of the Turkish-U.S. Logistical command, TUSLOG, but whose real job was taking care of the ambassador's boat.

"Ali Kaptan's boat," advised the navy man.

"Who the hell is Ali Kaptan?"

"He skippers the *Hiawatha* when the ambassador's in town, which isn't too often. But he has a little boat of his own, the *Teodora*. Maybe he'll take you out."

"Is he trustworthy?"

"Better than that. He doesn't speak English."

"Sounds like my man," said Taylor. And a few hours later, he had engaged the services of the good ship *Teodora* and its skipper.

Taylor picked up Stone at the airport late one afternoon. Stone had arrived on a commercial flight from Frankfurt, and he was carrying his own suitcase. That was Taylor's first surprise. Senior CIA officers usually toured the empire like kings, flying in private jets and arriving with little armies of bag carriers and door openers. Local station chiefs competed to find the most exotic restaurants and nightclubs for their royal visitors. Careers had been made finding the right fish restaurant in Piraeus, or the best dim sum in Hong Kong, or the raunchiest strip show in Bangkok. But one look at Stone told Taylor to forget about strip shows. The old man was dressed in his habitual winter costume: a three-piece wool suit and a brown homburg hat. As Taylor greeted him, he studied Stone's face for a hint of the purpose that had brought him to Istanbul. But Stone's face was a pleasant, impassive mask.

"So you're Taylor" was all he said. Taylor took his bag and led him to a waiting limousine, which took them directly to the pier by the Dolmabahce mosque. Stone seemed pleased by the idea of a boat ride. He was coming from Berlin, he said, where it had been bitterly cold.

It was, for Istanbul, a pleasant early-spring evening. The sun had burned through much of the haze, and as it set, the sky took on a pinkish glow. Up the Bosporus, to the left of the dock, stretched the white marble of Dolmabahce, a palace so grand it had nearly bankrupted the Ottoman Empire. Sultan Abdul-Aziz had spent two million pounds a year running the palace and its staff of five thousand. It was said, apocryphally perhaps, that he had strapped pianos to the backs of his servants, so that music could follow him around his gardens. Like so much of Istanbul, Dolmabahce stood as a warning of the folly of trying to bridge East and West.

Ali Kaptan was waiting at the dock with his boat. He was a Laz, it turned out, from a village on the Black Sea, and like so many poor Laz boys, he had made his way in life as a boatman. As Taylor and Stone climbed aboard, Ali Kaptan gave them a firm salute.

"The *Teodora*," said Stone, admiring the boat as he climbed aboard. "What a lovely name. Did the good captain name her after his daughter perhaps?"

Taylor translated Stone's query for Ali Kaptan.

"*Hayir!*" snarled Ali Kaptan. No! He seemed offended at the thought.

"He says 'no,' " said Taylor.

"Who *is* your boat named after?" asked Stone amiably. Taylor duly translated.

"The Empress Teodora," said the Turk, wagging his finger at Stone. Taylor rolled his eyes. He explained to Stone that the Empress Teodora was a notorious libertine who, in Byzantine times, had reputedly fornicated with a dozen men at a sitting, occasionally with three at one time.

"How charming," said Stone. "I hope her holes are all plugged this time." And with that, they cast off and headed up the Bosporus in the soft glow of the dusk.

Stone didn't waste any time. "Tell me about your contact with Mr. Rawls," he said when the boat was under way.

Taylor repeated the story much as he had for Timmons. He explained how he and George had encountered Rawls at Omar's place; how he had followed him home; how he had bugged the apartment and what he had found on the tape. Stone nodded and stroked his chin throughout the recital. When Taylor finished, he sat silent for a moment. It was the evening rush hour, and the Bosporus was packed with boats—large ferries and tiny dinghies skittering across the water.

"From what you've heard and observed, what would you guess Mr. Rawls is doing?" asked Stone.

"Trying to organize a Russian émigré network."

"Um-hum. And to do what?"

Taylor thought a moment. "I suppose to make trouble for the Russians."

"Yes. Certainly that. But to what end?"

"He claims that the goal is to liberate Turkestan."

"Yes, but obviously that's balderdash."

"I agree. So what's the point?"

"The point is simple," said Stone. "Assess the anti-Soviet underground. Test its strength and conviction. Develop contacts."

Taylor nodded. "Okay. Understood." He noticed that as Stone ran through this explanation, he had a trace of a smile on his face, though Taylor couldn't imagine why.

"It's always good to have contacts in our line of work," continued Stone. "You never know how you might be able to use them."

"I know this is none of my business," said Taylor. "But isn't there a danger the operation could get out of control? Some of these Uzbeks and Kazakhs are nuts."

"A modest danger," said Stone. "But certainly a risk worth running." He was smiling again.

Taylor nodded. All this fencing was making him edgy. When was Stone going to tip his hand and explain what he was up to?

Ali Kaptan bellowed something from the bridge. The *Teodora* was making its way past the twin fortresses—Rumeli Hisar and Anadolu Hisar—that guarded opposite banks of the Bosporus at its narrowest point.

Taylor pointed out the landmark. "Europe and Asia are closest together right here," he explained.

"Not very close, is it?" said Stone. He studied the landscape for a moment and then resumed his interrogation.

"Did you follow Mr. Rawls again, after you had listened to the tape?"

"No," answered Taylor.

"Did you replenish the tape?"

"No."

"Why not?"

"For the obvious reason."

"What was that?"

"Because I assumed I had stepped into something I shouldn't have. Something I wasn't supposed to know about, even though it was on my turf."

Stone cocked his ear. "I beg your pardon?"

"Because I assumed," said Taylor with an edge of anger in his voice, "that I had stumbled into one of our operations."

Stone chuckled.

"What's so funny?"

Stone fumbled with something in his pocket, shifted his feet, stared into the distance.

"That's right, isn't it?" said Taylor, more loudly. He had a momentary desire to punch Stone in his wise, well-groomed face.

"You needn't shout."

"Isn't it?" repeated Taylor. "Rawls is a NOC, right?"

"Rawls?"

"Yes, Rawls, goddammit."

"No, actually. He's not."

"He's not?"

"No," said Stone, finally laughing out loud. "That's the interesting thing. It's not our operation at all. I have made a very thorough check, and I can assure you categorically that we have no such operation on the books."

"What about the Canadians? Or the Brits?"

"He's not their man either. I've checked."

Taylor drew a breath. He felt as if he had been slapped. "Rawls isn't our man?"

"No. Of course not. We haven't done that sort of thing for years."

"Oh, Jesus."

Stone chortled again. He thought it was all very funny.

"If Rawls isn't ours, or the Canadians' or the Brits', then whose man is he?"

"The Russians', I suspect."

"You're kidding."

"I assure you that I am not. I would wager a substantial amount that the Soviets are running a false-flag operation.

And the flag in question is our own Stars and Stripes, with a bit of Maple Leaf for camouflage."

"Why are *they* doing it, for chrissake?"

"I already explained it to you, but you weren't listening. Or rather, you weren't hearing what I was saying."

"Tell me again. I'm dumb."

"They are doing it for the same reasons we would, only in reverse. They want to develop contacts, test the waters, get to know the breadth and strength of the anti-Soviet underground. And then, of course, they want to control and manipulate it. They're really quite paranoid on this subject."

"But why the false flag?"

"How else would the Soviets penetrate an anti-Soviet underground? They certainly wouldn't announce they were the KGB. It's standard procedure. The Israelis want to recruit a spy in the Syrian Army, so the recruiter pretends to be a Russian military officer. The target will spill his guts; he may even feel patriotic about it. Same thing here."

Taylor shook his head. He was embarrassed. "Rawls is a Russian?"

"Probably, yes," said Stone. "A very well-trained one, it appears. North Americans are the hardest people to imitate. You can get the accent right, with enough practice, but we have so many nuances, and the whole world knows them by heart. They've grown up watching our movies and television shows. They know how we talk and walk, how we light cigarettes, how we laugh. But it sounds as if your Mr. Rawls did a creditable job."

"Crackerjack."

"Don't blame yourself. With a few more minutes—or a bit less booze—I'm sure you and your friend would have gotten suspicious. A word or a gesture not quite right. Rawls was very lucky. He thought he would only need to convince Uzbeks and Tatars."

"But why would the Russians go to all the trouble?"

"My dear boy, they are secret policemen. This is what secret policemen do. They go looking for enemies. In this case, they have some reason to be nervous. They understand that the only real threat to the survival of the Soviet Union is the stability of its ethnic republics."

"They can't be that frightened of a bunch of Uzbeks."

"It's not just the Uzbeks they fear, but what might lie behind them."

"Like what?"

"Like the United States."

"Why would they think that?"

"Oh, there have been a few little hints from Washington over the past year. A few straws in the wind. Just enough to worry a sensible KGB man."

"And what might those hints have been?"

"I can't tell you," said Stone sweetly. "Not for now, at least. Perhaps another time."

Taylor looked at Stone with a growing sense of astonishment. He seemed to be holding a hand that contained nothing but wild cards.

"The Soviets are prudent," Stone continued. "When they decide they have a problem, they look for a way to control and destroy it. And they have been playing this particular game of émigré politics since the 1920s. Have you heard of the Trust?"

"Of course," said Taylor. He wanted to say: Ad nauseam. It was the one Soviet counterintelligence operation that everyone in the agency had heard of. The research director of the counterintelligence staff had spent the better part of thirty years studying it. In the Trust, the Soviets had created an anti-Soviet underground network during the 1920s and through it fed false information to every intelligence service in Europe. The Soviets, in effect, had created their own opposition. And they had done the same thing again in the early 1950s, creating a phony liberation movement in the Baltic states that Britain and America both embraced.

"It's quite a sophisticated little operation," said Stone. "Rawls undoubtedly reports to a case officer, someone unobtrusive who can maintain contact with him and send his reports back to Yasenevo. Probably someone we would never think to look for."

"Oh shit," said Taylor, shaking his head.

"What is it?"

"I have a feeling I know who the Russians are using as Rawls's contact."

"And who might that be?"

"A nice Lithuanian lady who's married to the Soviet consul general and spends all her time studying Central Asia."

"Touching," said Stone.

"Very. She had a habit of disappearing on us, but we could never figure out where."

"Perhaps now you have the answer."

Taylor shook his head again. He rose and walked unsteadily to the gunnels of the little boat. "I feel like shit," he said.

"You shouldn't," said Stone. "The fact is that you have given us a rather extraordinary opportunity."

The sun had set and a light fog had settled over the black waters. The Bosporus was quieter now, with only a few small boats—water taxis—shuttling back and forth between Yenikoy and Beykoz. There was a chill in the air. In the distance, there was the horn of a big boat moving into the Bosporus from the Black Sea.

"Time for a drink," said Stone. Taylor brought out a bottle of whiskey and proposed a toast to their fictive colleague, Mr. Jack Rawls.

"By the way," said Stone when they had settled into their second whiskey. "Why did you do a damn-fool thing like bug Rawls?"

"Because I was curious. And because he pissed me off."

"But it was against the rules. You didn't have authorization."

"That's true," said Taylor. "But I have learned over the years that by the time you get authorization to do something, the something in question is probably not worth doing."

"You had better explain that to me," said Stone, eyeing the younger man. Taylor looked at him and wondered whether to be honest.

"I'm going to pretend that you and I are friends," said Taylor.

"No need to pretend."

"I'll tell you a story that will help explain what I mean. When I was in Somalia, before coming to Istanbul, I had an agent high up in the government. At the top, actually. He was the foreign minister."

Stone nodded.

"We had all kinds of information that would have been

useful to him about the Ethiopians and the Sudanese and the internal opposition in his own country. But technically I wasn't supposed to share any of it with him. It was all marked ORCON or NOFORN. That seemed ridiculous. So I just told him. It saved his ass a couple of times."

Stone remained impassive.

"Sometimes the case officer in the field just has to trust his judgment," continued Taylor. "Otherwise, what's the point of having us out here? You might as well run everything from the front office. Although I gather that sort of thinking doesn't sit too well with Mr. Hinkle."

Stone took a long sip of his drink. "I loathe Hinkle," he said after a few moments. "As for the Somali case, I read about it in the files before coming here. I think you handled it appropriately. Better than appropriately. You handled it the same way I would have."

Taylor was surprised, not for the first time that evening, or the last.

"I am tempted to pay you a vain compliment," said Stone. "Which is to say that you remind me of myself when I was younger. But it was easier in those days to trust your own judgment. You didn't really have any other choice."

Taylor looked at the old man: the smooth, impassive face, the tired eyes, the look of a man who had so thoroughly immersed himself in his work that he had, in some sense, become that work. He tried to imagine himself as a man in his sixties and his mind went fuzzy, and then blank.

"I'll tell you a little story of my own," said Stone. "Would you like to hear an old war story?"

Taylor nodded.

"When the war ended in 1945, I was twenty-seven years old. What a heady time that was. We were barely out of college, and we had the world at our feet. I was still in the army, working as an intelligence officer at the U.S. headquarters in Heidelberg. By that time we had already made contact with General Gehlen, and we had decided that we would try to maintain his network of agents in Eastern Europe. The funny thing was, we didn't ask anybody's permission to do it. Who could we ask? The war was over. Nobody back home really cared. So we just did it, on our own authority. But we had one problem."

"What was that?"

"How to play Gehlen's agents. Since we had no formal authority, we had no money."

"So where did you find the money?"

"The black market," answered Stone. He was beaming at the recollection of his sweet and reckless youth. "We had whole trainloads of coffee beans and cigarettes coming into Germany for the use of the U.S. troops there, you see. So we diverted just enough to sell on the black market and pay stipends for Gehlen's agents. That way, we didn't have to ask anybody for funds. It was the right thing to do, obviously, but it would have taken too much time to get all the necessary permissions. And I hated bureaucracy, even back then. So we just did it."

"What if you had gotten caught?"

"We would have been court-martialed probably. Or maybe not. It was a different time."

"When did you stop using the funny money?"

"Not until 1948, after the CIA was created," said Stone. "They sent out a lawyer and made us sign a lot of paperwork. That should have been a warning, I suppose."

Taylor poured another drink for Stone and for himself. Patches of fog were gathering over the water and then dissipating, so that the shoreline came in and out of view every few seconds.

"So what do you do now?" asked Taylor.

"Ah. What do I do now?"

"Yeah. If you don't mind my asking."

"What have you heard on the rumor mill?"

"Not much. One version had it that you got canned."

"Not true, obviously."

"Another version says you're doing something very strange and secretive somewhere in the DDO."

"That is closer to the truth."

"Mr. Stone, do me a favor. Either give me a straight answer or tell me to fuck off."

Stone laughed. "I am attached to the Soviet Bloc Division. My title is Director of Special Projects."

"What does that mean?"

"It means absolutely nothing. I report to the deputy director for operations, and with his blessing, I have access to cable traffic in areas that interest me. It makes me a sort of free-lance troublemaker."

"What trouble are you planning to make in Istanbul?"

"I'm not sure yet," said Stone. "I'd like to think about it overnight. Do you have anything planned for tomorrow morning?"

"Nothing that can't wait."

"Let's get together then and discuss it, shall we?"

"Yes, sir," said Taylor. Which was unusual, because Taylor never called anybody "sir."

They heard the sound of the horn again, much closer. Ali Kaptan revved the engine and steered the boat toward a cove on the Asian side. "Russian!" he shouted over the sound of the motor. Taylor and Stone looked up the Bosporus and saw a stunning sight. A Soviet cruiser was making her way down the straits from the Black Sea, flags flying, crew on deck. A small white boat from Turkish military intelligence was accompanying her, snapping pictures and taking measurements.

In the half-light, from the vantage of little *Teodora,* the Soviet ship looked even bigger and more menacing than normal. It was an immense and awesome machine—every cleat and turret ready for battle, every inch of space devoted in some way to the modern Soviet ambition of challenging the United States. The horn sounded again, deafening this time, as the cruiser made its way past them toward the Mediterranean. In the wake of this giant vessel, the *Teodora* and its passengers bobbed like a cork.

20

◆

THEY MET AT THE CONSULATE THE NEXT MORNING AT EIGHT, which was the earliest Taylor had ever been at work. Stone was waiting in the main salon of the Palazzo Corpi, which was known as the "Missouri Room" to commemorate a visit to Turkey in 1946 by the battleship USS *Missouri*. Stalin had been threatening Turkey at the time, and it was said that when the great ship steamed into port, its massive guns pointing toward Odessa, the Turks had broken into cheers. Another age entirely.

Stone, himself a sort of monument to that lost age, was sitting on a couch reading a book about Byzantine architecture that he had pulled off a dusty bookshelf. He looked older and frailer in the morning light. He was so engrossed in the book that he didn't notice Taylor at first. The younger man led him upstairs, past the wrought-iron satyrs and nymphs that decorated the stairway, to the gray stucco of the communications room, and from there into the bland translucent whiteness of the secure conference room. Waiting on the table was a pot of coffee and a plate of sweet rolls wrapped in cellophane.

"Are you married?" asked Stone as he unwrapped his pastry.

"No," said Taylor. "Not anymore."

Stone nodded. That apparently was the answer he had hoped for. "And do you like your present assignment here in Istanbul?"

"I'm not wild about it. I like it when it's interesting."

"And how often is that?"

"Not very often."

Stone nodded again. "I take it from what you say that you would be interested in something more challenging."

"You bet."

"Hmmm. And do you have a competent deputy who can manage the administrative details in your absence?"

"I think so. He likes that sort of thing. Paperwork, renting safe houses."

"Are you as restless as you seem?"

Taylor turned his eyes to the blank white wall of the bubble and thought of the useless secrets it normally contained. He thought of how he had been spending his days and weeks of late, planting bugs and meeting with agents like EXCHASE. "Yes, I'm as restless as I seem. Maybe more so."

That, too, seemed to be the correct answer, for Stone turned toward Taylor and looked him in the eye. "I'm sorry to ask you these questions. But I don't want to discuss this

Rawls business with you unless I'm fairly sure that you would be an appropriate person to pursue it with me. I take it that you would be interested."

Taylor made a mental inventory. He had a reasonably solid career that was leading up the ladder. But it was becoming increasingly obvious to him that it was a ladder to nowhere.

"Sure," he said. "Why not."

"Then I think you're my man."

"For what?"

"For the operation I have in mind. I've been doing some thinking overnight, and the more I think about your Mr. Rawls, the more convinced I am that we have been presented with an unusual opportunity. An almost irresistible opportunity, I would say."

"To do what?"

"That's the question, isn't it? To do what? Now what do *you* think we should do with Mr. Rawls?"

"You're asking the wrong man. Until last night, I thought he was working for you."

"Come now. Surely you have a suggestion."

Taylor thought a moment. The answer seemed obvious. "Burn him," he said. "Expose him to the Turks as a Soviet illegal. Have the Turks PNG him and his lady case officer and the consul general and anybody else they feel like."

"Well, of course. That's always the right answer, isn't it? Burn someone. Put him out of business. But what would that get you in this case?"

"It would embarrass the hell out of the Soviets, in addition to breaking up their little network."

"Tempting. But wouldn't they simply do it again? Not in Turkey perhaps, but somewhere else. And we'd have to start all over again, assuming we were lucky enough to find out."

"So what's the correct answer?"

Stone looked at his coffee cup, which was empty. "Is there any more coffee, do you suppose?" Taylor summoned the code clerk, who returned with another cup of coffee for Stone.

"What's the correct answer?" repeated Taylor.

"Do you mind if I answer you in a somewhat roundabout way?"

"No. I'm getting used to it."

"I'll begin with a question. Don't you find it troubling that the Soviets are so aggressive in this part of the world? In Iran, and Afghanistan, and even here in Turkey?"

"Of course I do. It drives me nuts."

"And haven't you wondered how we might be able to tilt the balance the other way? How we might be able to undermine the Soviets, and create a measure of strength out of our present weakness?"

"Yes, but I haven't come up with much, other than bugging Soviet diplomats."

"Well now," said Stone, banging the table lightly for emphasis. "Wouldn't it be nice if we could, in fact, do what your Mr. Rawls is pretending to do? If we could organize a true CIA-sponsored network in Central Asia?"

"Sure, if it would work."

"A network of agents that could organize clandestine cells inside the Asian republics, distribute subversive literature, smuggle guns across the border."

"Great," said Taylor. He still looked dubious.

"An underground that could put the fear of God into the Kremlin. Better than that, the fear of Allah. An underground network that would absolutely terrify the Soviets and make them worry that their country was in danger of unraveling. Wouldn't that be lovely?"

"Lovely."

"Unfortunately," said Stone, "we can't do it."

"Because it's illegal, I suppose." Taylor was getting exasperated.

"Not illegal, technically. But any such operation would require a finding by the President. In the unlikely event that he agreed, it would also require notification of Congress. And even if they agreed, we still couldn't do it."

"Why the fuck not?" Taylor was losing patience with Stone's riddles.

"Because it is beyond our capabilities, my friend. The sad truth is that we don't have the plumbing in this part of the world to pull off such an ambitious operation. Never have had."

"So we're back to square one."

"Not quite," said Stone with a smile. "Not quite. That's what I realized last night. It may be true that we cannot create an actual underground organization of our own. But we can create something almost as good. We can create the illusion of one."

"How, for chrissake?"

"Isn't it obvious? By using your Mr. Rawls. By feeding him, by putting information in his hands that will convince the Russians that we are doing the very thing they're afraid of, the very thing they're pretending to do themselves. If we're clever about it, we can convince them that they have stumbled across evidence that the CIA is running an anti-Soviet underground that stretches from Baku to Tashkent."

Taylor smiled. The idea was simplicity itself. "Will they believe it?"

"Yes, if we let them discover the evidence themselves, piece by piece."

"And what will we do with this imaginary network?"

"We will run operations. Or more precisely, we will create the illusion that we are running operations. We will let Rawls and his colleagues discover an underground organization that is sending guns into Azerbaijan. Then we'll let the KGB chief in Baku find the guns. We will tell Rawls the underground is smuggling thousands of religious cassettes to the underground mullahs of Uzbekistan. The KGB man in Samarkand will only have to find a few dozen cassettes to believe it's real."

Taylor tried not to sound snowed. "Not bad," he said.

"That's the beauty of it, you see. It doesn't have to *be* an underground network. It just has to look like one."

"Mr. Stone, you are a devious son of a bitch."

"Thank you. Coming from you, I take that as a great compliment."

"So how do we get started?"

"You'll need a small team. A half dozen people, at most. Contract hires, most of them, I should think. It's important that this be invisible, even from the clandestine service. Especially from the clandestine service. We'll talk about the details when we get back home. Can you be in Washington in two weeks?"

"I don't know. What will headquarters say?"

"Oh, I wouldn't worry about that too much. In a certain

sense, I suppose I am headquarters. I'll arrange whatever needs to be arranged."

"Then I'll be there."

"Anything else?"

Taylor thought a moment, about the life he was giving up, and the one he was beginning, and a thought fell into his head. He recalled a conversation several weeks earlier with a young woman case officer from London—a woman who appeared to be unusually knowledgeable about the life and times of the peoples of Central Asia.

"I have one personnel suggestion for you," said Taylor.

"And who might that be?"

"A NOC named Anna Barnes. Before joining the outfit she studied Ottoman history. She knows this part of the world."

"Anna Barnes," repeated Stone. He had that odd smile that came over him when he was caught in the midst of one of his games.

"That's right. Anna Barnes."

"How interesting that you should mention her. As it happens, Miss Anna Barnes is already on my list. As a matter of fact, I am planning to see her in London tomorrow. With any luck, she'll be joining us in Washington for our little planning session."

But Stone never left anything entirely to luck. The papers for Anna Barnes's TDY assignment to Washington were already in the works by the time he landed at Heathrow that evening.

V

KARPETLAND

Washington / Brooklyn
Athens

May 1979

21

◆

THE SIGN ON THE DOOR SAID "KARPETLAND," AND IN SMALLER
type: "The World at Your Feet." The office itself was a
second-floor walk-up in a commercial building just off the
Rockville Pike. It was in one of those small shopping centers
built in the 1960s that had since become derelict castoffs,
shunned by the newer chain stores and boutiques of suburbia.
Other establishments in the complex included an insurance
agency, a doughnut shop, a hardware store and a fabric store.
It was a place out of time, with no evident connection to the
larger environment of Washington, which was why Stone had
selected it. He wanted his new enterprise to be born under
cover, as far as possible from the physical and psychological
orbit of headquarters.

Anna Barnes arrived punctually at ten o'clock. She was
dressed for spring, in a bright silk dress gathered and tied
at the waist. She rang the bell, half expecting that Stone
himself would open the door to greet her. A middle-aged
woman came lumbering down the stairs instead, and after
giving Anna a careful look, opened the door. "I'm
Marjorie," she said, as if that explained everything. "Please
wait upstairs."

Anna walked up one flight and surveyed the office. It was
a small and somewhat dilapidated showroom. Three gray
metal desks stood in the front of the room, each bearing a
black telephone, a blotter, pens and stationery. Beyond the
desks was a thin stack of Oriental rugs and, on a table, samples of wall-to-wall carpeting. The wall decorations consisted
of a clock, a calendar from an auto-parts store and an old
TWA airline poster. At the back of the room were two
couches, a coffee table and a water cooler. The showroom

was lit by two long fluorescent fixtures hanging overhead, which gave it the seedy glow of a pool hall.

"Have a seat," said Marjorie, gesturing toward one of the couches. On the coffee table were copies of *People* and *Better Homes & Gardens,* all several months old. Anna skimmed an article about a lawsuit filed against a famous actor by his former girlfriend, Michelle. After ten minutes the doorbell rang, and Marjorie once more clunked downstairs. This time up walked Alan Taylor, looking tanned and sleek and wearing a double-breasted blue blazer with gold buttons.

"Fancy meeting you here," said Taylor. He had the same mischievous look in his eye that Anna remembered from Istanbul. Before she could answer, the bell rang once more. Someone apparently had been waiting for the rest of the group to arrive before making his appearance. This last visitor didn't wait for Marjorie to let him in. He had his own key.

"Hello, friends," called out Edward Stone, bounding up the stairs. He was in disguise, or at least his notion of it. In place of the usual gray flannel suit and brown homburg hat, he was wearing a red lumberjack shirt and khaki work pants, a pair of boat shoes and a cap that said "Redskins" on the brim.

"Welcome to Karpetland," said Stone grandly.

"What the hell is Karpetland?" asked Taylor.

"Didn't you see the sign? It's your new base of operations. I hope you like it, since you may be spending rather a lot of time here over the next few weeks."

"Delightful," said Taylor, picking a piece of Karpetland stationery off one of the gray metal desks. "Why did you spell it with a 'K'?"

"To discourage people from calling us on the telephone. Nobody in his right mind would think of carpets and ask the operator for the 'K's. And if anyone should be foolish enough to do so, Marjorie can take care of them." He gestured to the middle-aged woman. "Did you meet Marjorie? She is on loan to us from the SB Division."

"Not formally," said Anna, extending her hand. She was about to introduce herself, but Stone cut her off.

"Uh-uh-uh. No true names, please. Marjorie will know you two as Lucy Morgan and William Goode, the two employees of our modest enterprise. We'll have passports and other documentation ready for you on Monday."

Taylor scanned the room. "We're not actually going to have to sell rugs, are we?"

"Of course not," answered Stone. "Don't be silly."

Taylor looked relieved. He sat down at one of the desks and tried the phone. It worked.

"Come join me and we'll get started," said Stone, striding toward the couches in the corner. "Marjorie, we won't need you for several hours. Perhaps you could do some errands and come back after lunch. About two-thirty, say."

"Yes, sir," said Marjorie, taking her purse. Stone waited for the front door to close.

"Now then," said Stone when she was gone. "I'm delighted to see both of you. I trust your trips were pleasant, and that you have reasonable hotel accommodations."

"Motel," said Taylor.

"And you must be wondering, after coming all this way, just what we're planning to do in this charming establishment in Rockville. Before we begin, however, I must ask you both to sign something." He removed from the pocket of his lumberjack shirt two pieces of paper and handed one to each of them.

"What is it?" asked Anna.

"A secrecy agreement, of sorts. It applies to the particular compartment we're opening for this operation. The gist of it is that you agree never to reveal details of our activity except to someone authorized to receive the information."

"Who's authorized to receive the information?" asked Taylor.

"I am," said Stone. "I'm not sure who else is. For practical purposes, nobody."

"That's easy enough," said Taylor. He took out a pen and signed.

"Do you mind if I read it?" asked Anna.

"Not at all."

Anna perused the document. "It doesn't mention the agency," she said after a few moments.

"Quite right. It doesn't."

"Why not?"

"It's a technicality, really. This compartment is separate from the normal administrative procedures of the Directorate of Operations. It's easier that way. More secure."

"Need a lawyer?" asked Taylor. His tone was not quite mocking, but close.

"Nope," said Anna. She signed the form and handed it back to Stone.

"Jolly good!" said Stone. "Now let's begin. I have told each of you a bit about what I have in mind, and I would like to fill in some of the blanks this morning. The simplest introduction I can give is to say that our mission here will be to practice a form of alchemy."

"Alchemy?" asked Anna, not sure she had heard him right.

"Yes, indeed. But in our case we will be creating something much more precious than gold. We will be taking weakness—specifically the current political and military weakness of the United States—and transforming it into strength. And we will be accomplishing this magic by using the only real tool available to the alchemist, a calculated sleight of hand."

"Sorry," said Anna, "but I don't have the foggiest idea what you're talking about."

"Of course not, but be patient. I promise it will become clear. What I want to do, by way of beginning our dialogue, is explain to you how I normally spend my time. Is that agreeable?"

Anna and Taylor nodded their heads. Since they first laid eyes on him, each, in different ways, had been wanting to know what Stone actually did.

"I believe I mentioned separately to each of you that my title is Director of Special Projects for the Soviet Bloc Division. What does that entail? you have undoubtedly wondered. What 'special projects' might I be directing? The simple answer is that I do whatever suits my fancy. But what I have concentrated on, for some time now, is a particular variety of what might be called, for lack of a better term, deception."

"And what variety might that be?" asked Taylor.

"I'm coming to that. Patience, please. Let's not be in any rush. Would you like some coffee? Tea? Marjorie told me she would have some here for us."

Anna and Taylor both shook their heads. "Go ahead," said Taylor. "We're all ears."

"Very well. My sort of deception, to put the matter bluntly, has sought to convince the Soviets that CIA operations are broader and more aggressive than is actually the case at present. My mission, if you will, has been to camouflage the frail and demoralized American intelligence service we know all too well, and to paint an alternative picture of a service that remains robust and stout-hearted; and then to make the Soviets chase the robust-looking shadows I throw in their way."

"How on earth can you do that?" asked Anna. "The Russians aren't stupid."

"No, indeed. They are smart and thorough, but also quite paranoid. And those are precisely the qualities I have sought to exploit. The secret is understanding how they operate. Shall I give you an example?"

"Yes, please," said Anna.

"Take CIA operations in Moscow. The truth is that the agency has very little on the ground there these days. We have few real agents and few real operations. But it is possible to create an illusion that we are more active by pushing certain buttons. The Soviets actually make it easy. The KGB, you see, simply doesn't believe that we are as inert and incompetent as we appear. So they go to extraordinary lengths to try to discover what we're really up to, and in doing so, they operate by certain standing rules. You just have to know what they are."

"Such as?" pressed Taylor.

"Such as: If an American diplomat is seen entering an apartment building where a Soviet with real secrets resides, that Soviet citizen is automatically placed under surveillance for a minimum of one year. Sometimes he is simply transferred to a less sensitive job until the KGB is sure he has not been in contact with any Western intelligence service. Obviously this sort of surveillance adds to the difficulty we face in actually recruiting any Soviets. But do you see how we might use it to our advantage?"

"By flooding the system," said Taylor.

"Precisely," said Stone. He was beaming. "When officers of the Moscow station come calling on me in Washington, I suggest that they visit certain apartment buildings in Moscow from time to time. All they need to do is stick their heads in the door, or ring a bell, or linger by a dark alleyway for a few minutes, or make a meaningless chalk mark on a wall somewhere, and the alarm bells go off in Moscow Center. A new counterintelligence case is opened on poor comrade so-and-so who lives in apartment 3-B."

"Do they really fall for it?" asked Taylor. It sounded too easy.

"Yes. If you do it right. You can't be too obvious, and you have to mix it up with other techniques. Would you like another example?"

"Please," said Anna. Taylor was shaking his head and smiling as he considered Stone's ruse.

"The KGB has a similar standing rule with regard to dead drops. They know our people in Moscow spend a lot of time looking for potential drop sites. So they carefully track where Americans go. And whenever they see one of our people near someplace that might make a good drop—an irregularity in the brickwork along the side of a building, or a knothole in a tree in Gorky Park, or a loose stone in a wall somewhere up on the Lenin Hills—they stake it out."

"What do you mean?" asked Anna.

"I mean they maintain fixed surveillance on that spot—usually with a television camera—twenty-four hours a day for at least a year. They are tireless, you see. That is part of their operating style. So what does the Director of Special Projects do in confronting this vast and seamless web of surveillance? What would you do, Anna?"

"I'd send the CIA station on an Easter egg hunt, looking for phony drop sites."

"Yes, of course you would," said Stone. "And not just that. Sometimes you would fill those phony drop sites with phony messages for phony agents. And some of the messages would interlock, painting a picture of broader operations whose purposes Moscow Center could only guess at."

"It's very clever," said Taylor, "but what does all this get you? You aren't recruiting anyone. You aren't collecting a scrap of real intelligence. All you're really doing is throwing a monkey wrench into the Soviet machine."

"And what's wrong with that? The Soviets work very hard to maintain Moscow as a controlled environment, in which they can orchestrate every event to their purposes. Our job, sometimes, is simply to sabotage the machine. Unfortunately, our colleagues at the State Department have never understood this."

"Understood what?"

"How pervasive the system of control is. They don't realize that the KGB monitors every foreign diplomat and journalist in Moscow and plays them off against each other. The ones who are cooperative get rewards—a concession in negotiations, a special interview. The ones who resist get punished—they can't find an apartment; their toilets keep backing up; their car won't work. Eventually even the toughest-minded give up and go home. The saddest part is the way our diplomats play along with this theater of illusion. The liberal young foreign service officer imagines that he is succeeding in Moscow because he is a sensitive and reasonable fellow, and that his more stubborn colleague is failing because he doesn't understand the Russian people or speak their language adequately. Preposterous! These people don't seem to grasp that Moscow is a vast Skinner box, designed to condition certain types of behaviors. And the U.S. diplomatic corps is living proof that it works! So yes, I am a Luddite. I want to sabotage the machine. Frankly, I think that's all we really can do, for now."

"Do you run all this from Washington?" queried Anna. She was still having trouble understanding how Stone's operation worked bureaucratically.

"Yes," said Stone. "And I do business only in person, with individual officers from the Moscow station when they come to visit me. I insist that there be no discussion of these operations inside the station, and no cable traffic whatsoever."

"Why?"

"Because Moscow station is insecure. Even the supposedly secure communications areas are insecure."

"Why?" she asked again.

"I can't tell you that," said Stone curtly. "I'm sorry. All I can say is that I believe the Soviets are reading our mail in Moscow, and that the only activities that can remain secret are those that are run unilaterally from here, off the books."

"Does headquarters agree with you?"

"Sensible colleagues agree. Foolish ones do not. But I really cannot discuss this issue with you any further." Stone turned away from Anna and toward Taylor, who was clapping his hands silently.

"Mr. Stone," he said. "As I told you once before, you are a devious son of a gun."

"Son of a bitch, I think you said. But save your applause,

please. I'm just getting to what matters most for our purposes. About a year ago, it occurred to me that we could use the various language services of Radio Liberty to reinforce this pattern of shadows and feints. So with the help of an old chum in Munich I arranged to put a few odd things on the air."

"Like what?" asked Taylor.

"Curiosities. Variations in the normal pattern of operations. Things that a trained analyst might conclude were messages to one of these invisible spies we appear to be servicing in Moscow. For example, if you play the same musical theme to introduce the news every morning at nine, change it once—just once—and the clever analyst will be convinced it's a signal. Or you put nonsensical messages on the air. "The sky is green." "Tolstoy is alive." Or you have the announcer deliberately give the wrong time one afternoon. Whatever strikes your fancy. No matter how silly it is, you can be reasonably sure that it will have them scratching their heads back at Moscow Center. And that's when I got to thinking," said Stone, his voice trailing off.

"Thinking about what?" asked Anna.

"About Soviet nationalities, which are the rawest nerve of all in Moscow. I began wondering whether we might in some way play upon the KGB's abiding fear that the peoples at the extremities of the empire—the Uzbeks and Tajiks and Georgians and Armenians—despise the Soviet state, and that the United States may be prepared to help them gain their freedom."

Anna looked at him warily, remembering her first conversation with Stone a few months before. "How did you do that?"

"At first, simply by using the radios. My friend in Munich agreed to introduce some small changes in the format. Very small to us, but quite worrying to the Soviets. The reading of a prerevolutionary essay on the Uzbek service. An item on the Chechen-Ingush service commemorating the birthday of Najmuddin of Hotso, who fought the Red Army almost single-handedly in the North Caucasus during the early 1920s. That sort of thing. Little needles. Pinpricks that might, over time, bother Moscow enough that it might cut back on foreign adventures and spend more time minding its own backyard. There were a few other things as well."

"What other things?" asked Taylor.

"Oh, I mentioned to a senator I know how pleased I was that the agency was looking at the nationalities problem again. I'm sure he gossiped about it. As a matter of fact, there is no better channel for false information about CIA operations than conservative members of Congress. They're so eager, and so gullible."

Taylor closed his eyes. "So that's what you were talking about in Istanbul," he said.

"How's that?"

"When I asked you why the Soviets would ever think the United States might get involved with a bunch of crazy Uzbeks, you said there had been a few hints to make Moscow nervous."

"Did I say that in Istanbul? I shouldn't have. But yes, there were hints of new American interest in Soviet nationalities, and yes, the hints came from me. The odd thing is, I didn't really think it was possible to follow through on this project in any meaningful way. Not until I learned of your little encounter in Istanbul with this man Rawls. After that, of course, the rest was fairly obvious."

"Who's Rawls?" asked Anna.

"A KGB man," said Taylor. "Who I initially mistook for a CIA man."

"Oh," said Anna.

"Which brings us to where we are now," said Stone.

"Which is where, exactly?" queried Taylor. "This is all fascinating, Mr. Stone, and I'm definitely a member of your fan club. But I still don't understand what we're doing here in Rockville."

"You are an impatient fellow," said Stone. "That's what I like about you. But before proceeding, we have another important item of business." He looked at his watch.

"What's that?" queried Taylor.

"Lunch."

"Who's catering?"

"You are, I believe," said Stone. He reached into the pocket of his khaki work pants and removed a chain with two silver keys. "The motor pool is outside in the parking lot. It's a white panel truck with the word 'Karpetland' on the side. Here's a key to the truck, and one for the front door."

"So what'll it be, food-wise?"

"There's a wide range of options in the neighborhood," said Stone. "McDonald's. Burger King. Wendy's. Hardee's."

"I vote for Burger King," said Anna.

"That's quite acceptable to me," said Stone.

"Burger King it is," said Taylor. "Who wants what?"

"Whopper with cheese, no pickle, no onions. Small fries. Diet Coke," said Anna.

"A hamburger of some sort, with whatever condiments they have," said Stone.

"How about a beer? It's good for cover."

"Fine idea," said Stone. And so Taylor was off, cruising suburbia in his white panel truck, stopping to chat with the pretty woman in the parking lot at Burger King, shopping for beer at the 7-Eleven with the practiced eye of Joe Six-Pack himself.

22

"DON'T EVER BE A SPY," ANNA'S FATHER HAD TOLD HER A few months before he died. It was on a Sunday afternoon, not long before his second and final heart attack, and she was reading to him from a book she thought he would like, called *Ottoman Statecraft*. It was a sort of Levantine version of Machiavelli, written in the seventeenth century by a man named Sari Mehmed Pasha. Anna was showing off, translating from Turkish.

"In the matter of spies," Anna had read, "perfect watchfulness and caution are essential. Rewards should be given both to the spy who comes with joy-giving news and to the spy who comes with information that excites anxiety. He must not be harmed because of news that brings gloom, for it is essential that spies have no fear of reporting their news correctly and truly."

"Don't ever do it!" her father had said suddenly.

"What?"

"Don't ever be a spy." His tone was so sharp and emphatic that it puzzled Anna.

"Why not?"

"Trust me," Ambassador Barnes had said. "If you're interested in the world, try diplomacy." The conversation had seemed strange to Anna at the time. What in her father's long and seemingly charmed career as diplomat had made him so wary of espionage? And why on earth did he think that Anna would ever want to be a spy? She was an intellectual; she wanted to be a professor, not an intelligence officer.

"Why don't you take the foreign service exam," Anna's father had suggested that evening.

Anna had been flattered. But as she thought about her father's remark, she concluded that it probably just meant he had given up on her brother as the family standard-bearer. Anna's older brother was, in fact, a walking illustration of how the male line of the Establishment was self-destructing during the 1970s. He lived in New Mexico, getting by as a part-time artist and full-time guru to a string of New Age women who somehow found him irresistible. On the rare occasions when he came home, before his father died, he would make a point of doing something obnoxious, like throwing the I Ching on the living-room floor while everyone was having cocktails, or doing the family's astrology charts yet again, just to show everyone he hadn't mended his ways. Clearly her brother was not a suitable candidate for the foreign service, much less the CIA.

Which left Anna. But she was, at that time, determined to pursue what she regarded as her father's lost vocation—the life of the mind. She had loved browsing among his books, especially the ones he had taken with him on his destroyer during the war: the collected plays of Shakespeare, Machiavelli's *The Prince,* Freud's *The Interpretation of Dreams,* a very dog-eared copy of *Ulysses* by James Joyce, the collected poems of T. S. Eliot. The modernist canon, in short. The young naval officer had carefully annotated each one, as if cramming for the great exam of life that might come with the next wave of Japanese planes. "Contrast this with Jung's theory of archetypes," he had written in the Freud book. "But must the modern Prince be so cynical?" he ruminated in the margins of Machiavelli. And in the pages of *King Lear:* "Yes! Ripeness *is* all."

Every young woman, at some level, spends a part of her adolescence looking for her father and trying to connect with his world. But in Anna's case, that was especially true. All she had wanted, back then, was to browse in his library forever. It was only after her father died that Anna learned from a family friend that he had begun his government career, not as a diplomat, but as something else. Some sort of civil servant in Germany. The lost vocation, it appeared, had been something entirely different.

Anna thought of her father, the ambassador who didn't trust spies, as she sat under the harsh fluorescent lights waiting for Taylor to return with lunch. Stone had excused himself and gone to the bathroom, and Anna was sitting at one of the gray metal desks trying to sort out what was troubling her. She felt disoriented, though she wasn't sure whether it was because of what Stone had said that morning or the long-buried memory of her father it had provoked. She busied herself tidying the desk, rearranging the black telephone, putting the Karpetland stationery in a neat pile.

Eventually Stone emerged from the bathroom. He had combed his gray hair back slick against his head, as was his normal style. The combination of his blue-collar getup of lumberjack shirt and work pants and the patrician hairstyle was jarring.

"You shouldn't wear that outfit," said Anna.

"Why not?" said Stone. "I rather like it."

"Do you want a frank opinion?"

"Yes, indeed. Of course I do."

"It looks silly."

"How so?"

"Men's clothes are like uniforms. When a man is out of uniform—or wearing someone else's—he looks silly."

"Very well. I'll keep that in mind."

Anna returned to her busywork. Her face was downturned.

Stone watched her for a moment and then spoke up, as if he sensed that something was bothering her.

"What did you make of my little lecture this morning? I hope it wasn't too tedious."

"Not at all. It was fascinating. I just have a lot to learn, that's all."

"Did you hear anything that surprised you?"

Anna thought a moment. If ever there was a time to be honest, this was it. "Yes," she said. "There was something that didn't make sense to me."

"And what was that?"

"I know this will probably sound stupid, but I don't understand why it's so important that the CIA look more aggressive than it really is. Won't that just make the Soviets even harder to deal with?"

"Ah, Anna, I knew you were my sort of person," said Stone. "That's a very wise and subtle question. The answer is that in the short run, yes, it probably will make them more truculent. But in the long run, it will lead to their undoing."

"How can you be sure?"

"I'm not sure, in the sense that I can prove it. It's more a matter of conviction. I believe that, among nations, weakness brings disaster and strength yields success. That is the intellectual bedrock of my life. I could no more doubt it than doubt the rising of the sun. So, inevitably, I believe that if we cannot actually *be* strong at present, we should at least appear so."

"Maybe," she said. "But it still sounds like kicking a hornets' nest. Why make the Soviets anxious? Why not just walk away?"

"How can I make you see? Let me try a historical analogy, one that will probably be familiar to you. I've been doing a bit of reading in your area of specialization these last few weeks, and I have been pondering a question that strikes me as especially interesting—and relevant to our conversation."

"Fire away."

"My question is this: Why did the Ottoman Empire decline so rapidly in the seventeenth century?"

"Let me think," said Anna, suddenly drawn back toward the world of the library. "Various reasons. The sultans became weaker and less competent. The European nations became stronger. The janissaries became corrupt bureaucrats, rather than warriors. Tax revenues weren't sufficient to support the administrative apparatus of the empire. Take your pick."

Stone shook his head. "All part of the story, no doubt. But the answer I had in mind is much simpler. It can be summed up in just three words. 'The Prince's Cage.' "

"Go on," said Anna, curious to see where Stone's argument might lead.

"Now correct me if I'm wrong, but as I understand it, the Prince's Cage began as an instrument of enlightenment and progress. Until the early seventeenth century, each new sultan had made it a practice to have all of his brothers strangled—with a bowstring, was it not?—so they couldn't challenge his rule. By our modern lights it sounds horribly cruel. Yet it was actually quite an efficient means of checking the sort of rivalry and intrigue that has brought many an empire to its knees."

"It was outmoded," said Anna. "And that was also part of the Ottoman problem in the seventeenth century. They were still following their old practices, and Europe was becoming modern."

"Quite so. Fratricide was old-fashioned. So the enlightened modern sultans stopped strangling their brothers and put them in what amounted to a glorified prison in the grand seraglio. The Prince's Cage."

"Correct," said Anna. "They called it the 'Kafes.' "

"A civilized approach. The sort of thing that would have appealed to a member of Congress, had such people existed in those days. But what was the cost of enlightenment? Rather than knock around the empire learning to be warriors, as their forebears had done, the Ottoman princes now stayed out of harm's way in the cage. Osman III was in the cage for fifty years before becoming sultan, was he not? And didn't Suleyman II spend thirty-nine years in the cage, much of it copying the Koran over and over? When these poor fellows finally emerged, they knew absolutely nothing about the world. They were pathetic. But it wasn't their fault. The system virtually guaranteed incompetent rulers."

"You've been reading Lord Kinross, I see," said Anna.

Stone smiled sheepishly, like a schoolboy who has been caught with his crib sheet. "Well, he's right, isn't he?"

"Kinross is right as far as he goes, although the reasons for the Ottoman decline were much more complicated than he says. But let's assume that you and Kinross are right. What on earth does this have to do with what I was asking you about Karpetland?"

"Isn't it obvious?" said Stone. "The forces of enlightenment have decided that the CIA is an outmoded and inefficient relic of the past, so they have placed us in a modern equivalent of the Prince's Cage. And I am trying to find a way for you—for all of us—to get out of the cage before it's too late."

Anna nodded, if not in assent at least in deference to the power of Stone's vision. But she wondered to herself whether he could really mean what he had said. Did he truly believe that the world would be a better place if the princes of the CIA were freed from the "cage" to do whatever they wished—make the decisions, call the shots—without interference from people like judges and senators and presidents? He can't be serious, she decided. It was a crazy thought, and Stone wasn't crazy.

"Lunchtime," said Taylor. He had returned with the food and a six-pack of Iron City beer. Anna and Stone were silent, still holding in their minds the threads of the earlier conversation. An aura of earnest concentration hung over the room. Taylor wanted none of it.

"C'mon, gang, let's eat!" he said loudly, depositing the food on one of the desks. He popped the tab on a can of Iron City and handed it to Stone. "Hey, lady," he called to Anna. "How about you?"

"I ordered a Diet Coke."

"They didn't have any. Want a beer?"

"Sure," she said. "Why not."

Taylor handed her a beer and opened one for himself. *"Serefe!"* he said.

"What does that mean?" asked Stone.

" 'Kiss my ass,' in Turkish."

"What?"

"I'm kidding. It means 'cheers.' "

"Cheers," said Stone, raising his beer can.

"Cheers," said Anna.

When the squeezed-out ketchup packets and the french-fry and hamburger boxes had been cleared away, Stone took center stage once again. The food seemed to have focused his mind. He was no longer the meandering dialectician, tacking back and forth toward a glimmering goal in the distance. His tone was now that of an operational planner, moving straight ahead toward a set of specific objectives.

"We'd better get going," he said. "Marjorie will be back in just over an hour, and I want to give you some specific assignments."

Anna took out a pad to make notes. Taylor put his feet up.

"The basic elements of this operation should already be obvious to you. Because the fact is, the two of you were the ones who discovered them. My only contribution has been to suggest a creative way in which these elements can be used. That's the easy part. Now you two will have to go out and actually do it—invest this imaginary scenario of mine with real people, real flesh and blood, so that it lives and breathes."

"You're not checking out, I hope," said Taylor.

"Absolutely not. But I'm not an operator anymore. At best, I'm a planner."

"So what's the plan?"

"The operation, as I envision it, will have two interwoven strands. First, we will seek to create the illusion of an independence movement in Central Asia; second, we will attempt to place this illusion before the Soviets in a way that they will find credible. We will be aided in these endeavors by two blessed accidents: Alan's discovery of a Soviet false-flag operation that is seeking to penetrate a Central Asian underground movement that they suspect already exists; and then, Anna's discovery of an Iranian from Azerbaijan who claims to be part of just such an underground. We have the instruments. Now we must play them. Or more appropriately, we must find people who can play them for us.

"Alan," he continued, "your problem is complicated. You must find a way to convey information to a KGB agent who is posing as a CIA agent, without his suspecting in any way that he is being fed false material. Have you thought about how to accomplish this sleight of hand?"

"A little," said Taylor. "Obviously we need a cutout, a Central Asian who can feed our stuff to Rawls. But I doubt we can find the right person in Istanbul. The Soviets have the town pretty well wired."

"I agree," said Stone. "Recruiting the right cutout is crucial, perhaps the single most important aspect of this operation, and the person probably can't be found in Turkey. As it happens, I have a recommendation for you."

"Who's that?"

"Once upon a time, we had among our brethren a most extraordinary man from Uzbekistan. He had worked for the Germans during the war, and we picked him up in the early 1950s. He's a charming character. Speaks with an Uzbek-Russian accent, if you can imagine that. He's just your man, if he'll agree to do it. But that may be a problem. He and the agency parted company rather unhappily at the end of the 1950s. I suspect he still harbors a grudge."

"What's his name?"

"Munzer Ahmedov."

"How do I contact him?"

"It's a bit odd, I'm afraid. The registry lists his permanent address as a mosque in Brooklyn. That's his favorite hangout, evidently."

"I didn't know they had mosques in Brooklyn."

"Apparently they do," said Stone. He took a piece of Karpetland stationery and wrote out the address of the mosque for Taylor.

"4905 Fort Hamilton Avenue," said Taylor, reading the address aloud. "Where the hell is that?"

"In Borough Park, near Maimonides Medical Center, I gather," said Stone.

"You gotta be kidding," said Taylor. "That's a Jewish neighborhood."

"I assure you that I am not kidding. Good luck in finding Ahmedov. I'll give you a letter of introduction."

"From who? You?"

"Heavens no. From a Turkish mullah in New Jersey who's a friend of ours, and also of Mr. Ahmedov's. They're in the same Sufi brotherhood, I gather."

"Probably the same bowling league, too. Can I take the truck?"

"I don't know why not, unless Miss Barnes objects."

"It's all yours," said Anna. "I'm not the panel-truck type."

"Now then, Miss Barnes," said Stone, turning to Anna. "What you bring to our table is the worthy Azeri-Iranian gentleman who calls himself Ali Ascari. And the first question we need to discuss is who will handle him. Should that person be you, do you think?"

"Absolutely not," said Anna. "That would be a very serious mistake. I don't like the guy, to be honest. And it would be insecure."

"I'm inclined to agree with you. So you will need a cutout, too. And again, I have a suggestion."

"No more Iranians, please."

"The man I have in mind is an old friend of mine who worked with me in Germany in the 1950s. He was chief of station in Beirut until he retired seven years ago in a huff. He can be a difficult man. Prickly, irascible. He's the only case officer I ever knew who made it a practice to carry a side arm. But he's a brilliant operator, one of the best I've ever known. His name is Frank Hoffman."

"What does he do now?"

"He runs a private security business based in Athens. His clients are mostly rich Arabs, and he travels frequently in the Gulf, which will be helpful for your purposes."

"He sounds great," said Anna.

"He is," said Stone. "The problem with him, as with Mr. Ahmedov, is that he may not want to do it."

"Why not?"

"He's become something of a crank. He thinks we're all incompetent."

"Have you sounded him out?"

"No. That wouldn't be appropriate."

"Why not?"

"Because if I asked him, he would say no. The unfortunate fact, you see, is that I was part of the reason he resigned."

"Oh," said Anna softly.

"So you'll have to make the approach yourself. He won't be easy to recruit, but if he agrees, he'll be the ideal person to handle Ascari. He should be easy to find in Athens." He wrote out Hoffman's home and office telephone numbers and handed the paper to Anna.

"Okay," said Anna, "but I should warn you. I'm not convinced that Ascari will make a good agent. He's unreliable, in addition to being a little shit."

"Oh, he'll make a tolerable agent, especially if Frank Hoffman gets his hands on him. I'll tell you a little secret about recruiting which applies to people like Mr. Ascari. I call it Stone's Inverse Law."

"What's Stone's Inverse Law?"

"It states as follows: If you walk into a room and take an instant dislike to someone—a particularly sleazy or uninspiring character—then it is almost a certainty that this man can be recruited to become an agent of the United States of America."

"That's Ascari, all right."

"Well, there you are," said Stone. "You two may want to begin by contacting the people I mentioned. If they agree, we'll talk about what to do next. We'll certainly want to add more instruments to our little orchestra when we get further along, but this is enough to get you started. May I remind you, finally, of the importance of maintaining security. An injudicious word to anyone and the project may be ruined." Stone looked gravely at Anna and at Taylor.

"What about the cutouts?" asked Taylor. "How much can we tell them?"

"Oh, I'll leave that to you. You both have good judgment. The two people I mentioned are reasonably discreet, if it turns out that you're working with them. I have no objection to your telling them a bit about what we're up to. But you'll know what makes sense in terms of operational security. Anything more?"

"What about money?" asked Anna.

"All arranged. The accounts have been opened. Marjorie will give you the checkbooks. And you already have the keys."

"Yes, sir," said Taylor, fishing the key chain out of his pocket.

"Now then, I must go. I have to maintain appearances at my non-job back at headquarters. Marjorie will be here to assist you with whatever details I've forgotten. I will be checking in regularly, but don't hesitate to call me immediately if any problems arise. Marjorie has my home number."

He shook hands with each of them again and headed for the stairs. Anna had one last question, which had been nagging in the back of her mind all day. On whose authority was this operation being conducted? Who ultimately was responsible for it? The question embarrassed her, and now, enveloped in the web spun so elegantly by the old man, it seemed almost a technicality. And it was too late anyway. Stone was walking down the stairs and out the door.

23
◆

THE KARPETLAND SHOWROOM SEEMED QUITE EMPTY AFTER Stone had left—even after Marjorie returned from lunch at two-thirty. She offered to make coffee for Taylor and Anna, and when they said no, she sat down at the desk closest to the door and took out a fat paperback book. She read with great concentration, pausing every few minutes to look dutifully at the black telephone.

Taylor took the desk farthest from the door and put his feet up, as if he'd been working in a run-down rug store in Rockville all his life. That left the middle desk for Anna. She sat down squarely, centering her bottom on the chair as if to anchor herself in time and space. She wanted to lean back and put her feet up, too, the way Taylor had done, but she was wearing a dress and she suspected that Marjorie would think it unprofessional. Taylor leaned toward her, wanting to make conversation, but Anna ignored him. She was already making plans.

"Marjorie," she said. "Could you check the airline connections from Dulles to Athens for me, please."

"What day will you be traveling, Miss Morgan?"

"Tuesday night if there's a direct flight from Dulles. Otherwise, Wednesday night."

"Yes, ma'am," said Marjorie, putting down her book.

"I'll need a hotel room, too."

"Which hotel would you like?"

"The Hilton," interjected Taylor.

"Yes, I suppose the Hilton would be fine," said Anna.

"What size room?"

"I don't care. Whatever they have."

"A suite," called out Taylor.

Anna laughed. "Yes, why not. A suite please, Marjorie."

Marjorie began busily dialing and reserving and arranging. While these negotiations were going on, Taylor had abandoned his desk and flopped down on the stack of Oriental rugs in the middle of the showroom floor. He appeared at first to be asleep, but when Anna walked over to take a closer look, he propped himself up on one elbow.

"Let's get out of here," he said. "This is a drag."

"We can't. We've got work to do."

"No, we don't. Stone has already taken care of all the busywork. We're wasting our time sitting around here."

Anna couldn't disagree. "Where do you suggest we go?" she asked.

"I dunno. Take a walk. See the sights."

"Of Rockville?"

"Why not?"

"What about Marjorie?"

"She'll be fine. What does she need us for?"

It was true. Marjorie was running on autopilot. "I'll get my purse," said Anna.

Taylor walked over to Marjorie's desk. "We're going out for a while. You can knock off whenever you like."

"Oh no, Mr. Goode. I'm here until five o'clock every day, Monday through Friday."

"Fine. Whatever you say. If we're not back by then, you just turn out the lights."

"All rightie," said Marjorie.

The Rockville Pike was thick with Friday-afternoon traffic, the Toyotas and Datsuns and Hondas idling like smug little water bugs alongside their big, sulking American cousins.

The highway, in that respect, offered a snapshot of America in the late automobile age. It was one of those suburban strips that were homogenizing the American landscape, making the outskirts of every city look more or less identical. It could have been peeled up off the ground, with its fast-food restaurants and tire stores and L-shaped shopping centers, and stuck down somewhere else—Atlanta, say, or St. Paul—without anyone noticing much difference. That was the new America. The pieces of our national quilt—once rich and varied, marked by the particular quirks and obsessions of each region—were now all the same. Which made it easier to find your way, and harder.

"Let's look for a bar," suggested Taylor as they emerged into the noise and haze of the late afternoon.

"Out here?"

"Sure. They have bars in the suburbs. They're all called PJ's or TJ's, and they all have the same hanging plants and phony bric-a-brac on the walls. But the drinks taste the same. C'mon."

Taylor put his arm around her shoulder, friendly as could be, and she, just as gently, let it slip off.

A few more blocks and they came upon a place called McGillicuddy's. It was a restaurant franchiser's notion of an Irish pub, with old Guinness and Harp posters on the wall, brass ship's lanterns in the lobby and, above the bar, an incongruous moose head with a sign that said "Kiss me, I'm Irish" hanging from one of the antlers. The bartender was wearing a green leprechaun cap. His name tag read: Sadlowski.

"What'll it be, folks?" asked the bartender.

Anna looked at her watch. It was just four-thirty.

"Isn't it too early to start drinking?" she asked.

"Not if you're on Istanbul time."

Anna ordered a piña colada, no cherry. Taylor ordered a gin martini.

"So what do you think of Stone's little operation?" ventured Anna. It was a question she had been wanting to ask Taylor all day.

"I like it."

"You do, really?"

"Yup. This is the real thing. It's what I've been waiting for for years."

"You don't think it's too far-out?"

"Nope. I think it's just far-out enough."

"And what about Mr. Stone? Do you think he's cleared all this with the director?"

Taylor shook his head. "I don't know, and to be honest, I don't care. The director is an idiot. I'm sure Stone has cleared things with whoever he's supposed to. He's a pro. He doesn't make mistakes."

"But it sounds as if he doesn't have to clear things with anyone."

"So much the better," said Taylor.

The drinks had arrived. Anna's wary eyes were beginning to soften. "And you think we can trust Mr. Stone?"

"Why not?" said Taylor. "You have to trust someone. I'd rather put my money on him than most of the drones we work with."

Anna thought of Howard Hambly and Dennis and the boys back in London. The difference between them and men like Taylor and Stone was . . . what? Toughness. Irreverence. A willingness to take risks.

"I just want to make sure we're doing the right thing," she said.

"Don't worry about it. Of course it's the right thing. A hot project, working with a smart guy like Stone. No paperwork, unlimited expenses. A chance to impress the big shots. What more could you want?"

"That's not what I meant. I was thinking more in terms of right and wrong."

"That's not my department," said Taylor.

"What is your department?"

"Applied mechanics."

"Oh, come on. I don't believe you. You wouldn't deliberately do something you thought was wrong."

"Maybe not. But deep down, I'm a sensualist. I think people should do what makes them feel good."

Anna shook her head. "I didn't think there were any more of you Jack Kerouac types left. You've gone out of fashion."

"Sorry," said Taylor amiably. "I didn't get the word."

Anna closed one eye and tilted her head. "Buy me another drink," she said.

Taylor looked at her closely. For the first time all day, she appeared relaxed. As Taylor studied her, it occurred to him that she was dressed, not just elegantly, but expensively. The fine silk dress, open at the neck; the high-heeled shoes of Italian leather; the sheer stockings. In the late-afternoon light, her skin looked as soft as the magnolia blossom sitting in a vase atop one of the tables. He looked at her eyes. They seemed almost to match the green print of her dress, until she turned her head slightly; then, in a subtly different light, they seemed to become an impossible aquamarine shade of blue.

"You look beautiful," said Taylor. He wondered how she would respond—whether she would protest, or change the subject, or chide him for being unprofessional. But she did none of those things.

"Thanks," she said. She leaned against the back of her bar stool, crossed her legs and took out a cigarette. Taylor lit a match and Anna gently pulled the flame toward her.

"Definitely," said Taylor. He didn't have to explain.

They talked through the late afternoon, over several more rounds of drinks. As night fell and the bar's regular customers began to arrive, greeting Sadlowski the bartender with friendly obscenities, Taylor suggested that they move to a booth in the corner. He didn't try to put his arm around Anna this time. He just leaned toward her, enveloping her in the canopy of his attention. And she pressed in with him under this tent of words and gestures. Hours passed, and still they remained in the dark corner of McGillicuddy's, ordering dinner, and after-dinner drinks, and after-after-dinner drinks. Even the bar food tasted like a gift from heaven. And after a very long time, when they had become as intimate as two people sitting fully clothed in a bar can be, the inevitable question arose. And inevitably, it was Taylor who posed it.

"Let's go back to my place," he said. "Or your place."

"I don't know," said Anna.

"Why not?"

"I'm not sure I'm ready."

"Oh come on," he said dreamily. "You're ready. You're a big girl. You're thirty years old."

"Twenty-nine, and that's not what I meant. I'm not sure I'm ready for you. You frightened me a little that afternoon in Istanbul, when we went driving in the country."

"Why? I was just trying to cheer you up."

"It was what you said about Turkish women. You sounded like a predator. Like a Westerner who's been let loose in the harem and wants to fuck everything in sight."

Taylor tried to look apologetic. "I'm sorry if I sounded that way. I don't want to fuck everything in sight. I'm much more particular. And anyway, I'm not the harem type."

"How do you know?"

Taylor looked at her curiously, wondering if this was a come-on, or a setup. "Is this a trick question?" he asked.

"Not at all. It's a question of historical interest."

"Okay. So what was it like?"

"What?" Anna closed her eyes coyly.

"The harem. What was it like?" Taylor looked Anna up and down. "How did they dress, for example, the women in the harem?"

She leaned toward him. "They dressed," she said softly, "to please the sultan. Their clothes were all soft and filmy, with nothing to really cover the body. A loose blouse; loose linen drawers tied around the waist with a string; and a silk gown that was open in the front so they could never quite cover themselves."

"I see. And did they have any unusual customs? Historically speaking?"

Anna thought a moment. "They shaved their bodies."

"So? Women do that now."

"No. I mean all over. Everywhere."

"Everywhere?" said Taylor, his eyes falling to Anna's crotch.

"Everywhere," she said, with a look that was half smile and half frown. "Someone called the Keeper of the Baths would take the woman and shave her all over, and then apply some paste to remove any hairs that were left. Then a slave girl would examine her body, every inch, to make sure it was smooth. And then they would perfume her with rose petals. The woman would sit naked on the floor of the bath while slave girls rubbed her with petals—in her hair, on her neck and shoulders, across her breasts, between her legs, around her toes and ankles."

"Shocking," said Taylor softly. He closed his eyes and took a breath. He was imagining what Anna would look like naked in bed, covered with rose petals.

"But that wasn't the oddest thing."

"Oh yeah? What was the oddest?" Taylor wasn't sure whether she was expressing indignation, or being flirtatious, or perhaps some weird combination of the two.

"The worst thing was how they made the woman get into bed."

"And how was that, pray tell?"

"They made her *crawl*. The Ottomans thought it would be disrespectful if a woman just got into bed next to a man. She might get ideas! So the rule was that she would start at the foot of the bed, kissing the blanket, and then creep slowly up past the feet and legs toward the man's head. Isn't that bizarre?"

"Bizarre," repeated Taylor.

"But you're not like that, are you?"

"No. I'm not. I like women. I don't want them to be slave girls. I like women the way they are."

"Do you?"

"Try me." Taylor put his arm gently around Anna and pulled her toward him. Her body offered no resistance. He bent down and kissed her on the lips; not with his tongue, but tenderly. He could feel her body trembling as he held her. Then she caught hold of herself again and sat up straight.

"You want to screw me, don't you?"

"Yes," said Taylor. "Is that all right?"

"I don't know. We're supposed to work together."

"So?"

"So women have to be tough. They can't just give in to every attractive man who comes along. Otherwise they end up like those used-up women in the harem. You know where the old concubines were sent when a new sultan took over? It was called the House of Tears."

"Why? You'd have thought they'd be glad to get out of the racket."

"Not at all. These women weren't prostitutes, they were artists. They studied seduction and dreamed of bearing the sultan's child. But only the most beautiful and clever really captured his attention. The ones who did had power and status, and money. Some of them invested in real estate, or the silk trade, or the jewel business. But they were careful, these women. They knew how to wait."

"So they hated to leave the harem?"

"They hated to be powerless. And seduction was power. There was one famous harem girl named Roxelana who actually convinced the sultan she could read his mind. She could even make him laugh! He fell so completely in love with her that he gave up the rest of his harem and married her."

"Who was this sultan?"

"Suleyman the Magnificent. The greatest and wisest of all."

"What about the bad sultans? What were they like?"

"They were disgusting, some of them. You don't want to know."

"Sure I do. Maybe I'll pick up a few pointers."

"Don't joke," she said. "If you really want to know how crazy men can be, then I'll tell you a story. But it's not funny."

"Okay," said Taylor.

"Back in the seventeenth century, one of the sultans was said to have a favorite game. He would take his concubines to the gardens of the seraglio. The eunuchs would lay carpets over the nearby trees and bushes so that people couldn't see in, and the sultan would make the women undress and stand naked in front of him. And what do you suppose he would do next? He would take his musket and shoot pellets at the women, which aroused him. Then he would take the women and fuck them."

Taylor turned away. She was right. It wasn't funny.

"This same sultan had another game. Want to hear it?"

Taylor didn't answer.

"He would take his harem girls and make them stand naked in an empty pool in the gardens. Then he would have a eunuch open the water pipes and a torrent of water would rush in on top of the women. Most of them couldn't swim, so they would bob up and down screaming. The ones that didn't drown, he would fuck."

Taylor reached for her gently. At first she resisted, but her body gradually relaxed and she let Taylor hold her, and comfort her, and eventually kiss her sweetly on the cheek. As he held her, he sang a bedtime song in a thin, inebriated voice. She lay there in his arms for a long while, until they heard the bartender say: "Last call." Anna sat up like a fluffy cat and looked at Taylor with her big blue-green eyes.

"I'm not ready yet," she said. "But I'm getting ready."

"What are you doing tomorrow?" asked Taylor a half hour later at the door of her motel room.

"Nothing," she said. "Got a suggestion?"

"I have a surprise."

"What's that?"

"How do you feel about making love on the grass?"

"Good night," said Anna, closing the door.

"I'll pick you up at ten," called out Taylor. She didn't answer, and Taylor couldn't see the smile on her face.

Taylor arrived at ten-thirty in the white Karpetland van. He had been shopping. A new cassette deck was playing the sound of a Bach cantata; in the back of the truck was a hamper containing a loaf of French bread, some ham and salami, several varieties of cheese, a jar of mustard and a bottle of white Burgundy. And a blanket.

Anna was waiting outside the hotel, wearing a sundress—looking as ripe and ready as a bud that has been waiting all year to bloom. She greeted Taylor with a kiss.

"Hop up," he said. "Let's go for a ride."

"Where are we going, rug man?"

"To a secret hideaway, where even serious career women can do exactly what they want."

They drove to the Beltway, crossed the Potomac, and then headed west along Route 66, toward Winchester. The landscape was pure Virginia: low scrub brush along the side of the road, giving way to lush green fields and tall trees and, in the distance, the rolling hills of the Blue Ridge. They passed grand horse farms and dark hollows dotted with rickety shacks. Taylor seemed to know where he was going, and Anna no longer cared to ask. She put her feet up on the dashboard, let the wind blow through her hair, and hummed along with the Bach tape.

Just past a little town called Marshall, Taylor turned off the main highway and headed up a two-lane road. That became a one-lane road, and then, heading up much more steeply, a dirt road overgrown on the sides with wild shrubs and vines. The panel truck pushed through the brush like a stalker in an unmarked jungle. At the crest of the hill, Taylor stopped the truck. The place was so dense with overhanging trees and brush that it was almost dark.

"Where are we?" asked Anna.

"You'll see."

Taylor took the picnic basket and the blanket in one hand and Anna in the other. He led her into the brush, pushing it back as he went. After a few dozen yards they came to a chain-link fence topped with angry-looking barbed wire.

"Now what do we do?" she asked.

"You can climb a fence, can't you?"

"Sure. But not one with barbed wire."

"No problem," said Taylor. He reached into the picnic basket and removed a pair of wire cutters. Holding them in one hand, he climbed to the top of the chain-link and began clipping.

"You can't do that!"

"Watch me," he said, and he snipped away until a large hole was opened in the wire. Then he slid back down, picked up the picnic basket in one hand and climbed back up and over the fence. "Your turn," he said.

Anna was lithe and agile, and once she realized that the fence was to be climbed, she was over the top almost as fast as Taylor. The skirt of her dress got caught on protruding wire as she was descending, and Taylor climbed up a few feet and unhooked her. Then he held her by the waist and gently lowered her. As her feet touched the ground, he felt her breasts against his chest and the beat of her heart. They were both breathing heavily from climbing, and when Taylor held her close, he became aroused.

"Where are you taking me?" Anna whispered.

"Forbidden territory," answered Taylor. He took her hand again and led her up a low hill. The brush was still thick, so she couldn't see what was ahead until they came over the crest, and then, suddenly, she saw why Taylor had brought her there. Stretching out below was a small green valley, hidden away from the surrounding countryside. And on the downward slope stood a farmhouse whose windows and doors were boarded up.

"Who lives there?" asked Anna.

"Nobody, except us."

"What do you mean?"

"It's a safe house. The agency owns it. They keep dozens of these places on ice for defectors, but nobody ever uses them. I thought we'd just appropriate it for a little while."

"It's beautiful," said Anna. She moved quickly through the tall grass, breaking into a run when the downward pull of the slope took hold. Taylor followed her, blanket and picnic basket in hand. When they reached the farmhouse they were both out of breath. On the other side of the house was a small creek that flowed over a waterfall. Taylor laid the blanket down on the lush grass just above the waterfall, so that the sound of rushing water was in their ears.

"Come to bed," said Taylor. He had already taken off his shoes and socks.

Anna looked at him, sitting atop his blanket amid the expanse of green grass, the look of desire on his face mirroring the lush wildness of the place. "Should we really do this?" she asked.

"Yes. Of course we should."

"What comes next?"

"I don't know. It doesn't matter."

"But we have to work with each other."

"So what. I work with people I hate. Why can't I work with someone I love?"

"Don't say that."

"Why not? Stop fighting so hard. Let go, for once." He stood up and walked a few steps toward her, feeling the moist earth and the blades of grass between his toes. "Come to me," he said.

"I haven't made love in so long."

"Come to me," he said again.

Anna slowly walked toward him, kicking off her shoes as she went. By the time she reached Taylor, he was hard again. He unzipped her sundress and lifted the straps off her shoulders. She wasn't wearing a bra, and her breasts fell free against him.

"I want you," she whispered.

Taylor slid his hands beneath the elastic of her pants and slowly pulled them down over her thighs, his tongue tracing the path down to her heels. Anna was trembling now. As Taylor passed his gaze slowly up the entire length of her body, she said softly, "Now."

Taylor stripped quickly and pushed up her skirt.

"Gently," she said. "It's been so long."

She needn't have worried. She was so aroused that when he lifted her up and held her astride him, he slid into her easily the first few inches. She was breathing so hard now that Taylor thought she might faint if she stayed on her feet, so he laid her down on the blanket and slowly entered her all the way. With the ground firm underneath her, Anna moved in rhythm with him, enfolding him, trembling and crying out when he went too far; then gradually tightening around him like a membrane that was about to burst, so that he could barely slide in and out; and finally pulling him with her over the edge.

24

"GO AWAY!" SAID MUNZER AHMEDOV WHEN TAYLOR approached him on the street corner in Brooklyn the next Friday. The noon prayer service had just concluded a block away at a two-story brick building marked "Uzbek-Kazakh Fraternal Association, Inc.," and Munzer was walking to his car, threading his way among the Orthodox Jewish men in long black coats who filled the streets. Taylor had been sitting in a coffee shop across the street from the mosque for nearly an hour waiting for Munzer to emerge. He recognized him instantly from the old ID photo Stone had provided: He was a short, round-faced man in his late fifties, with the high cheekbones and narrow eyes that marked him as a son of Central

Asia. It was a face halfway between Turkey and China, one that hid its secrets like a hooded trader along the Silk Road.

Taylor handed Munzer his card. "My name is Goode," he said. "I'm in the rug business." As Taylor spoke, the D train rumbled by on the elevated tracks overhead, on its way to Coney Island.

"Go away!" said Munzer again. "I not interested in any rugs." He spoke from deep in the throat, with a guttural accent that was at once Russian and Uzbek, just as Stone had described.

"I'd like to talk to you," said Taylor.

"This America. Nobody got to talk to nobody. Goodbye." Munzer opened his car door.

"I have a letter for you," said Taylor as the Uzbek man was closing the door. "From Sheikh Hassan."

Munzer rolled down the car window. "Sheikh who?"

"Sheikh Hassan."

"Turkish Sheikh Hassan from Rahway, New Jersey? That one you mean?"

Taylor nodded. He handed Munzer the two-sentence letter of introduction, passing it through the open window. Munzer read it and handed it back, looking very apologetic.

"Ah! I am sorry, my friend," he said, getting out of his car and shaking Taylor's hand. "I did not know you was friend of Sheikh Hassan from Rahway, New Jersey. So now, what can I do for you?"

"I'd like to talk to you," repeated Taylor.

"About rugs?"

"No."

"What about then, Mr. . . ." He looked at the card. "Goode."

"Is there someplace quiet around here where we could talk?"

"Yeah, sure. Turkish restaurant. Very nice."

"Where is it?"

"On Ocean Parkway. Just before Avenue J. You know where that is?"

"I'll find it," said Taylor. "What time?"

"Now, why not?"

Taylor walked back to the white Karpetland van. As he passed the façade of the Uzbek-Kazakh Fraternal Association, it struck him that it looked like one of those old-fashioned bowling alleys where they set up the pins by hand. The brick building was sandwiched between a furniture store called Rubinstein & Cohen and a storefront with a hand-lettered sign in the window that read: "Eretz Realty." It was certainly an unlikely neighborhood for a mosque.

Taylor found the Turkish restaurant on Ocean Parkway, next to a car lot with a big sign that proclaimed: "Masada Used Cars, Inc." The restaurant's decor was spare and simple: a white linoleum floor; a glass case just inside the door displaying the day's collection of kebabs and appetizers; on the walls, posters of Izmir, Konya and other Turkish haunts. Indeed, the café looked virtually identical to one you might find in Izmir itself. Munzer was sitting at a table all the way in the back, smoking a nargileh. He waved to Taylor and motioned for him to sit down.

"You like to smoke hubbly-bubbly, my friend?"

"Sure," Taylor answered. In situations like this, he was always willing to do whatever the object of his attention suggested. Eat lamb's testicles in Mogadishu. Chew qat in Aden. Drink a bottle of arak in Erzurum. Whatever it took. Taylor pulled the mouthpiece of the pipe to his lips and breathed in deeply. The crackling in the bowl and the sweet aroma suggested that someone had put a few crumbs of hashish in with the tobacco. He took another long drag and put the mouthpiece aside.

"Good," said Taylor. "Where's it from? Afghanistan?"

Munzer just smiled. "So what you like to eat?" he asked.

"It's your restaurant. You pick."

Munzer called over the waiter and rattled off a string of dishes. As he did so, Taylor tried to think about how to make his pitch. He didn't want to be impolite and talk business before eating. But then, he hadn't come all this way to eat kebabs. So he said nothing for a while.

The trick in recruiting anybody to do anything, Taylor had learned long ago, was to go a step at a time. The first priority was to get your target to cross some sort of threshold. It almost didn't matter what it was at the start of a relationship, so long as you got him to cross a line. If he was a foreign military officer who wasn't officially allowed to entertain

Americans at home, then you pushed him to invite you home; if he lived in a country where he wasn't permitted to accept money from a foreigner, then you gave him a very expensive present that amounted to the same thing. If he was a Central Asian emigrant who didn't want to talk about a particular subject, then you found a way to make him talk about it. The barrier was psychological. Once it had been passed, the rest was largely a question of time and persistence.

"You're from Uzbekistan, is that right?" Taylor said after a while.

"Yeah," said Munzer, taking the pipe out of his mouth. "From Tashkent."

"But you left a long time ago."

"Yeah. Long time ago."

"When was that?"

"Oh, you know, wartime, 1939."

"Ever been back?"

"Where?"

"To Uzbekistan."

"Not possible. Too dangerous."

Taylor took the mouthpiece of the water pipe in hand again and smoked a few more puffs, not wanting to seem in any rush.

"Why is that?" he asked eventually. "What's so dangerous?"

"Many years ago I am doing some things that Russians not like. Freedom things. So if I go back, *zzzkkk.*" He moved his index finger across his throat like a knife.

"What did you do to make the Russians so angry?"

Munzer didn't answer. He just kept puffing away on the pipe contentedly, as if he hadn't heard the question. With the stem of the nargileh stuck in one side of his mouth, his round face had the look of a lopsided grapefruit.

Taylor tried another tack. "Tell me, Mr. Ahmedov, do you think the Russians will always rule Tashkent?"

Munzer looked at him curiously and put down the pipe. "Maybe. Maybe not. How do I know?"

"You must have an opinion."

Munzer shook his head. "Why you ask all these questions about Uzbekistan?"

"I'm interested."

"Psss." He waved his hand dismissively.

"Really, I'm interested in Uzbekistan. It's one of my hobbies. I'd like to learn about your people's struggle against the Russians."

"This is a very sad story, my friend. Too sad for me. We talk about something else, please." He put his hand over his heart, as if it hurt just to talk about his country.

Taylor said nothing. If Munzer Ahmedov really wanted to change the subject, he figured, he could do so himself. But the Uzbek returned to his pipe, and neither man said anything for what seemed like several minutes. A waiter brought the food, and still neither man talked. Finally Munzer broke the silence. He turned to the American, studying his face, his clothes, his hands.

"You not sell rugs," he said.

"No."

"You not real friend of Sheikh Hassan."

"No."

"You CIA."

"I work for the government," said Taylor.

Munzer shook his head. He took a deep breath, as if the wind had been knocked out of him.

"You people no good for me," he said. "You go back to Washington, my friend. Don't bother Munzer no more."

"I'd like to talk with you. It's important."

"Yeah. They say that thirty years ago, and what we get? Nothing. Now I smarter."

"I've come a long way to see you, Mr. Ahmedov. As I said before, it's very important. You must believe me. You'll be making a terrible mistake if you send me away. Not just for yourself, but for your people."

"Yeah. Sure. My people. I hear this before, too. Why you come back and bother Munzer now after so many years?"

"Because I need your help."

"What for, please?"

"To work for your people."

"Psss!"

"I mean it. This is serious. It's not the same as before. Things are changing in Washington."

"What is different? What you do for Uzbeks now?"

"Let's go somewhere private where we can talk about it. Not here."

"We eat now," said Munzer. "I think about it."

They ate in silence. Munzer chewed each mouthful slowly, as if chewing over the sad history of his people with every bite. His eyes were fixed on an unseen spot in the distance, out beyond Masada Used Cars. He didn't look at Taylor again until he was finished with his food, and his deliberation.

"You come to my house, please," said Munzer at last. "We talk there."

"When?"

"Tonight. Six o'clock."

"Where do you live?"

"2138 Sixty-eighth Street, Brooklyn. Between Twenty-first Avenue and Bay Parkway." He took out a pen and wrote out the address in the neat cursive script he had been taught a lifetime ago in a Russian school in Tashkent.

"Thank you," said Taylor, shaking the Uzbek's hand. "I am happy that you will see me."

"I see you, but that all. Tonight I explain story of my people, and you understand everything. Why I not want to work with you CIA ever again." He nodded and smiled politely and waited until Taylor had left, then sat down and lit the nargileh again.

25

◆

MUNZER'S HOME WAS A NEAT ROW HOUSE ON THE EDGE OF Bensonhurst. It had new aluminum siding on the front and a 1975 Cadillac sedan in the driveway. The lawn was mowed and there were chintz curtains in the windows. To Taylor, it looked pretty much like every other house in this neighborhood of middle-class immigrants.

For all his bitterness toward the U.S. government, Munzer

Ahmedov was in most respects an American success story. He drove his almost new Cadillac to work in Queens each morning, to a small storefront in Astoria where he sold electrical equipment. He was surrounded by other immigrants who, like him, had chosen American-sounding names for their businesses. "Delta Fashion, Inc." "Clover Jewelry Corp." Munzer had named his company "Utopia Trading Co."

Munzer had gone into business in the early 1960s, when his heart was full of pain and betrayal. His specialty was small, high-value items—batteries, film, small stereos and television sets—things that could get lost in the vast hull of a freighter or fall off the back of a truck. Munzer was scrupulously honest himself, but he didn't ask unnecessary questions. He had made it into a good business, buying at the cheapest prices he could find and charging what the market would bear. It was America.

He was, by now, a pillar of the Uzbek-American community. He had long ago become an American citizen, reading the books about Jefferson and Lincoln that his children brought home from school. He had sent his three sons to college, and two of them to graduate school. He went to the mosque each Friday and once a month gave an envelope full of cash to the mullah to accomplish good works. He had learned, above all, the American middle-class secret of keeping to himself, staying out of harm's way, nursing his wounds in private. And for nearly twenty years—until that very day, in fact—the strategy had worked.

Taylor rang the doorbell and Munzer immediately opened the door. He didn't shake the visitor's hand, didn't offer a greeting, didn't say a word. Instead he led Taylor silently down to the basement, closing the door behind him. The basement had the musty air of an old library. Bookshelves lined two walls; they were filled with volumes in Turkish, Uzbek Turkish, Russian, German and English. In the dim light, Taylor saw what looked almost like a shrine at the other end of the room. It was a large framed picture of an Oriental-looking gentleman with a thin mustache, dressed in a black frock coat, bearing the unmistakable Mongol eyes and high cheekbones of Central Asia. On each side of the portrait stood a lighted candle. Taylor walked closer to get a better look.

"Who's that?" he asked.

"The leader of our movement, Mustafa Chokay. A great man. Come, sit down and I tell you about him, and many other things. What you like to drink? Tea? Coffee? Beer maybe?"

"Coffee."

Munzer shouted a guttural word upstairs. A short while later, a heavyset woman clambered down the stairs bearing a pot of Turkish coffee and two small cups. Mrs. Ahmedov, apparently; Munzer didn't bother to introduce her. She poured the thick coffee into the cups with a practiced hand and then disappeared upstairs again.

"To Turkestan," said Taylor, lifting his cup. Munzer narrowed his eyes. He said nothing in response. He took his coffee, slurped some of the dark black foam into his mouth, and then pointed to the face flickering in the candlelight.

"Mustafa Chokay," he said, "was leader of all Turkestani peoples. Uzbek peoples. Kazakh peoples. Tatar peoples. All peoples. If you understand story of Mustafa Chokay, you understand everything."

"I would like to understand."

"So I tell you. You listen. You want cigarette?"

"Sure," said Taylor.

Munzer shouted upstairs again and the older woman returned with a new carton of Marlboros. A mere pack wouldn't do in an Uzbek household; it would seem inhospitable. Munzer took out several packs and pressed them into Taylor's hand.

"Thank you," said Taylor, lighting up.

"So, Mustafa Chokay was a Kazakh, from a very noble family of Middle Horde. You know Kazakhs? They have Greater Horde, Middle Horde, Lesser Horde, Bukey Horde. Chokay was Orta Zhuz, Middle Horde. Okay? So in 1906, when he young boy, sixteen, Chokay read famous poem of Mir-Yakub Dulatov. 'Wake Up, Kazakh.' It tells truth for all Turkestanis, not just Kazakhs. You know this poem?"

"No," answered Taylor.

"I have English translation. You read it." Munzer pulled

down a volume from one of the bookshelves and handed it to Taylor, who read the poem aloud:

" 'Every year our land and water grow smaller,' " read Taylor. " 'They are taken by the Russian peasants. The tombs of our glorious ancestors are now in the middle of the streets of their villages. Russian peasants destroy them, taking the stones and the wood for their houses. When I think about this, my heart is consumed by sorrow, like fire.' "

"That's a very sad poem," said Taylor when he was finished.

"Ach!" said Munzer, putting his hand on his heart. "So Chokay, he hear this poem, and like all men of Turkestan, he want freedom and independence. But still he hope maybe some good Russian men can help Turkestani become modern men, too. So he go to Russian *Gymnasium* in Tashkent and to *Rechtfakultät*, faculty of law, at St. Petersburg to be like Russian men. And later he join Russian Duma and serve as secretary for Turkestani affairs until revolution begin in February 1917.

"And that is first great tragedy of our Turkestani peoples. Because Chokay and others believe Russian men when they promise to help. Kerensky promise in 1916, during Great Uprising in Turkestan, that he will make reforms. But when Kerensky get power in February 1917, what do he do for our people? Nothing. So Chokay begin to look to Moslem men and Turkish men. He start newspaper called *Ulug Turkistan— Great Turkestan—*and another called *Birlik Tuuy—Unity.*"

"*Flag of Unity,*" corrected Taylor.

"Allah! You speak Turkish?"

Taylor nodded.

"Then you know story of Mustafa Chokay?"

"No. Until now, I didn't know a thing about him. Go on. Tell me more."

"Okay. So October 1917 Revolution comes and it is second tragedy of Turkestani people. Bolsheviks make Turkestan Council of People's Commissars in Tashkent. But all fifteen men on council are Russian! Not one Moslem man. How can this be? So one week later—famous day, November 22, 1917—Moslem men meet in Kokand in Uzbekistan for All-Turkestan Congress of Moslems. And they form government of free and independent nation of Turkestan. And Mustafa Chokay is elected president!

"But this great dream dies. This Free Turkestan last only two months. Bolsheviks send Red Army and Armenian militia to Kokand in February 1918 to destroy us. Turkestani nation have no army. Bolsheviks and Armenians slaughter all Moslem men and burn city three days. Half of Kokand die in this massacre. People wonder why we hate Armenians—what they ever do to us that we hate them so much? So now you know. But Mustafa Chokay—thanks God!—survive and escape to Tbilisi in Free Georgia. And when Red Army invade Free Republic of Georgia in 1920, Mustafa Chokay escape to Turkey to continue fight. He start new magazine in Istanbul, *Yeni Turkistan—New Turkistan.* And then he move to Europe and publish new magazine in 1929 called *Yash Turkistan.*"

"*Young Turkestan,*" translated Taylor.

"Yes, very good. They teach CIA man better Turkish now maybe."

"Maybe."

"So Mustafa Chokay living in exile, but in Turkestan his people dying. More than a million Kazakhs die during 1930s. You hear what I tell you? That is almost half of all Kazakh peoples! They kill everyone. All writers, all teachers, all noblemen, all leaders of all tribes. Nothing left. Poor Mustafa Chokay, his heart is bleeding and he can do nothing. At first British say they will help us fight Communists. In 1920s they send us guns from Kashgar in Sinkiang, to help Moslem rebels fight against Red Army. But British betray Turkestani people. They make deal with Russians—they not help Turkestani fighters no more if Russians stop making revolution in India. Nice deal for everybody, except my dear Turkestanis. So that is third betrayal."

"By the British."

"Yes, and we never forget how they stab us in the back. But finally, finally, someone give Mustafa Chokay a chance to do something to stop rape of Turkestani people, and he take it. And this begin fourth tragedy."

"What was that?"

"Germany. When war begins, Germans arrest Mustafa Chokay in Paris and bring him to Berlin. At first Nazis call us 'Asian Jews,' because Turkestani Moslem men all circumcised. But after they talk to Mustafa Chokay they decide maybe we Asian Jews not so bad. Maybe we can help them find back door to Moscow. So in Caucasus and Central Asia they organize national committees and legions for each region. They have Georgian Legion, Armenian Legion, Azerbaijan Legion, Daghestan Legion, Tatar-Bashkir Legion, Kalmyk Legion.

"And they have Turkestani Legion, with Mustafa Chokay as head of Turkestani National Committee. And they tell us that when Germans defeat Russians, we Turkestani people be free!

"But Mustafa Chokay die in December 1941, so he never live to see disaster of this war. New leader of Turkestan Committee is friend and deputy of Mustafa Chokay. But we make wrong bet. Germans never get to Moscow, and Stalin destroy millions more Moslem people. He call us traitors, because we help Germans. All Crimean Tatars he send away in night. All Chechen-Ingush people he send away in night. All Kalmyk peoples. All dead."

"What about you?" interjected Taylor. "Where were you when all this was going on?"

"I am fighting for freedom of my Turkestani people."

"With the German Army?"

"Yes," said Munzer quietly. "Turkestani Legion. I not like to talk about this much with American people, because they not understand. Maybe you understand?"

"Yes. Of course I understand."

"Good! So, after war, our people are ruined. Our great leader Mustafa Chokay is dead. We have nothing. Munzer especially have nothing. I am living in DP camp in Germany, in British sector. One day in 1947 British man come to see me in camp. He very nice. How are you, Mr. Munzer. Pleasure to meet fine gentleman like you, Mr. Munzer. He tell me British ready to help me fight for freedom and independence of Turkestan, if I come to England and work with him."

"What did you say?"

"I say hell no. British already betray us once, when they first help Turkestani fighters and then make deal with Stalin to destroy them. Why we need that again? So I say no, thank you, Mr. British man. We have enough tricks from you.

"But now I come to worst part of my story. Most saddest

part. Because it is about America. In 1950, I am still in Germany wondering what I am ever going to do, when I am visited by an American man. Very nice. Sincere. Combs hair. Nice clothes. Like you, maybe. And he tell me that America want to help Turkestani people fight for freedom. And I think this too good to be truth. Thomas Jefferson, Statue of Liberty, Empire State Building! This great country want to help little Turkestan? How can this be? But he tell me, oh yes. America very serious now. They form Committee for Liberation from Bolshevism, they form Center for Liberation of U.S.S.R. Americans very serious."

"But they weren't."

"No, mister. At first they *were* serious. They start Uzbek-language radio service, and Tatar-Bashkir service, and Chechen-Ingush service, and Azeri service. And they do other things. Secret things."

"What secret things?"

"They train agents. They find men in DP camps in Germany. Men who fought in Turkestani Legion, or in Vlasov army, who only want liberation of their peoples from Stalin. And they train them. And I help."

"What was your job, Mr. Ahmedov?"

"Secret."

"It's okay. You can tell me."

"I was spotter in camps. I help them find Turkestani people who are maybe good agents."

"And then?"

"They send these people into Soviet Union. CIA and British send them across Afghan border into Uzbekistan and Kazakhstan, and across Iran border into Azerbaijan, and across Turkish border into Georgia. And in the north, they send weapons to Forest Brothers in Lithuania, and to Stefan Bandera men in Ukraine. They fly little planes, so low that radar cannot see them. They drop agents and supplies. But you know story. You know how it turn out."

Taylor nodded. "Yes. I know the story."

"All agents dead. They captured when they hit the ground, or few days later hunted in forest like animals. Or they just give up and confess to KGB, they so scared. All dead. CIA say they are very sorry. Very sorry. They keep sending more men. Men keep dying. But you know story."

"Yes. I know the story."

"It turn out Russians know everything. They have spies in DP camps. They have spies in General Gehlen organization. They have spies in British intelligence. Maybe even have spies in CIA?"

"Maybe so."

"But honestly, Mr. . . . What your name, please?"

"Goode."

"Honestly, Mr. Goode, this not what break Munzer's heart, fact that all these agents die. Everybody makes mistakes, even CIA. American betrayal of Turkestani people was something else."

"And what was that, Mr. Ahmedov?"

"Betrayal was that CIA tell us it support great struggle of Turkestani people for freedom and independence. We believe this. Munzer believe this. Statue of Liberty. Thomas Jefferson. But it is big lie. What Americans really want is for Russians to rule Central Asia forever. Only difference is, you just want your own Russians running show in Tashkent, not Communists."

"You had better explain that. I'm not following you."

"Sure. You bet. I explain to you. In 1952, I am in Washington. CIA tell me to broadcast tribute to Kerensky on Voice of America. I refuse. I say: Kerensky, hah! He break promise to our leader, Mustafa Chokay, in 1917. He tell us he will help but when he come to power, he forget us. So I say: Forget Kerensky. Let us talk about Turkestani people on radios. Let us talk about Mustafa Chokay, and 1918 massacre in Kokand, and freedom and independence. But they refuse. They say sorry, no independence talk for Soviet nationalities. Except for Baltic peoples, them only. Not even Ukrainians can talk about independence. We Uzbeks not allowed even to use old Uzbek words on radio. They think maybe Russians get upset. And then they say sorry, big mistake, and they stop Uzbek service. Pfft. No more."

"I'm sorry," said Taylor.

"Sorry? They break my heart, these Americans. They break my heart. So now maybe you understand, Mr. Goode, what I tell you in Turkish restaurant. Whole world betray Turkestani people, five times. Munzer had enough. No more trust left. Only tears."

The Uzbek put his head in his hands. Taylor said nothing for a long time. He watched the candles flicker around the face of Mustafa Chokay; the neat mustache, the quaint Western frock coat and necktie; the narrow eyes looking expectantly toward the camera. Taylor rose from his chair and walked to the shrine at the other end of the room and blew out the candles. It seemed like giving the Turkestani patriot a decent burial.

"Thank you, my friend," said Munzer, looking up. His eyes were red. Taylor sat down again, thinking about what to do, and remained silent for a while longer.

"What could we do to give you hope again?" Taylor said at last.

"Nothing. I am sorry, my friend, but that is truth. Hope is finished."

"But the 1950s were a long time ago. Things have changed. We've changed. What would convince you of that?"

"Nothing. I tell you again."

"What if we could do something very specific to show you that we were serious, Mr. Ahmedov? Something that would prove to you that things have changed."

"You cannot. Impossible. So do not play games with me, my friend. I am too old and too smart."

Taylor lit a cigarette. He told himself to move very carefully now, for this was the essential moment. The wrong suggestion and Munzer was lost. The right one and he might move a first foot across the line he had drawn in the sand twenty-five years ago.

"Mr. Ahmedov," said Taylor slowly. "The poem that you asked me to read earlier from the book"—Taylor walked over and picked up the book in his hand—"the poem from this book, called 'Wake Up, Kazakh.' "

"Yes. By Mir-Yakub Dulatov, one of our great Turkestani patriots. What about this poem? You want book? Here, you keep it. I get another."

"Listen to me, Mr. Ahmedov. What if we were to read this poem on the Turkic services of Radio Liberty—in Kazakh, Uzbek, Tajik—read it so that all of Central Asia could hear? Would that change your mind?"

"Psst. It is forbidden."

"Who says?"

"I know the rules. It is forbidden. It is anti-Russian poem and it is forbidden to broadcast anti-Russian poem on American radios. VOA, Radio Liberty. I tell you before, those are rules. That is problem, my friend. Don't you understand? That is why I give up."

"But what if those rules don't apply anymore?"

"Ach! Please. Rules are rules."

"But we make the rules for the radios, Mr. Ahmedov. And if we decide to change them, they're changed. And I am telling you, the rules are changing. That's what I have been trying to tell you all day, but you've been feeling so sorry for yourself that you haven't heard me."

Munzer looked at Taylor warily, with a tiny glint of interest in his eye. "Okay, suppose you are telling truth and rules have changed. How would Munzer know, please?"

"Just listen to the radio. Or have your people listen for you."

"When?"

Taylor thought another moment, wondering if he could depend on Edward Stone and his mysterious unnamed friend in Munich, and then decided—what the hell—and plunged over the edge.

"I make you this promise, Mr. Ahmedov. Listen to me very carefully. Within the next week, the Turkic services will read the poem of Mir-Yakub Dulatov which is called 'Wake Up, Kazakh.' You have your people listen, and when this poem has been broadcast, as I have promised, then you call me on the telephone and we will talk again. Okay?"

Taylor handed Munzer his Karpetland card, which had the office phone number in Rockville printed at the bottom. "Is that a fair deal?"

Taylor didn't give him time to answer. He extended his hand and shook Munzer's firmly. Now it was a deal. They had shaken on it.

"And when we meet next time, Mr. Ahmedov, I will tell you how we will strike a real blow—you and I—at last, for the freedom and independence of Turkestan. All right?"

Munzer didn't respond. He looked disoriented. He had been minding his business, living an anonymous and relatively happy life, and suddenly this stranger had arrived, summoning him to arms.

"All right?" said Taylor again.

"Yeah. Sure," said Munzer.

"I think your man Munzer can be had," Taylor confided to Stone when he returned to Washington the next day. They met briefly in the parking lot of a drugstore on Wisconsin Avenue, near Stone's home in Georgetown. The Karpetland van was parked a few yards away. Taylor had driven straight down from New York that morning and called Stone as soon as he arrived.

"Well done," said Stone, shaking Taylor's hand. "He's not an easy nut to crack, as I recall."

"He's like most émigrés. Gaga about the old country, but otherwise a nice guy."

"So how can I help you," said Stone, "on this pleasant Saturday afternoon which I had intended to spend on the tennis court?"

"Sorry to bother you. But to close the deal with Ahmedov I need a favor in a hurry."

"What might that be?"

"I need to have something broadcast on the Turkic services of Radio Liberty. You mentioned you had a friend in Munich who had helped you put stuff on the radios in the past, and I thought maybe you could ask him for a favor."

"Of course I can. What is it that you want broadcast?"

"A poem. A nationalist poem called 'Wake Up, Kazakh.' I have a copy of it here." He handed the book he had brought from Munzer's house to Stone.

"That shouldn't pose a problem."

"It's on Ahmedov's list of all-time greatest hits. Since it's anti-Russian, Ahmedov thinks broadcasting it is a no-no. I told him we could change the rules. That was my recruitment pitch, to get him on board. So if we can't do it, I'm screwed. I'll have to look for another guy."

"Not to worry. As I said, it shouldn't pose a problem. Nobody checks these things very carefully. And even when they do, there are always ways of covering one's tracks. How soon should this epic be broadcast?"

"Right away. I told Ahmedov it would be on the air within a week."

"How would next Tuesday be? Three days from now."

"You can do it that quickly?"

"I don't see why not."

"That would be fine," said Taylor. "Just fine."

"Anything else?" asked Stone, looking at his watch. "I have my tennis game."

"Not a thing," said Taylor.

26
◆

ANNA CALLED FRANK HOFFMAN THE DAY SHE ARRIVED IN Athens, using his old agency pseudonym—Oscar D. Fabiolo. That was Stone's idea. He thought it would help shake off the cobwebs. Fortunately Hoffman was home, rather than on one of his regular trips to see clients in Saudi Arabia, Kuwait, Abu Dhabi—or, increasingly, to the homes these gentlemen maintained in pleasanter spots, like Monte Carlo, Geneva, Paris and London. Unfortunately, Hoffman was in a grumpy mood.

"Is Mr. Oscar D. Fabiolo there, please?" Anna asked.

"No," answered a gruff voice. "He's dead."

"Mr. Fabiolo?" pressed Anna.

"Who's calling?"

"A friend of an old friend."

"Bullshit. I don't have any more old friends. Just new friends. Who is this anyway?"

"Lucy."

"I don't know any Lucy."

"Good," said Anna. "That makes me a new friend."

"You obviously want to talk to me, whoever you are."

"Yes, sir. I do. I've come a long way to talk to you."

"Are you pretty?"

Anna thought a moment about how to answer. "Not bad," she said.

"Aw, shit," barked Hoffman. "You might as well c'mon

over, honey. I got a million-dollar view here and nobody to share it with." Hoffman was better at getting mad, it seemed, than staying mad. And "honey" said she would be right over.

Frank Hoffman was in the security business. He had understood, as the oil boom began in the early 1970s, that the one thing the newly rich princes of the desert would need was someone to help them stay alive and hold on to their dubiously acquired loot. So he had left the agency in 1972 and formed a security company; he had initially planned to call it AA-Arab-American Security Consultants, Inc., hoping to be first in the Riyadh phone book—not realizing that Riyadh didn't yet have a phone book and that when it did, it wouldn't be in English. By now, Hoffman was so rich that he didn't really have to care what anybody called him or his company. He lived in a vast apartment in the Kolonaki district of Athens, at the foot of Lykabettos. The apartment overlooked the Acropolis and had, as Hoffman liked to boast, a million-dollar view.

Perhaps in deference to his surroundings and his new wealth, Hoffman had in recent years come to resemble a Greek tycoon. He was a short, stocky man—a fat man, to be blunt—but he had stopped worrying about it. He had a fifty-dollar haircut, wore Gucci loafers and open-neck silk shirts and carried around his neck an immense gold ornament shaped like the letter "O." His only real link with the old days was that he still carried a side arm, having bribed an appropriate official in the Greek Ministry of the Interior for the necessary permit.

Anna rang the doorbell of Hoffman's apartment having no idea what to expect. Stone had explained that Hoffman was eccentric, and that he had left the agency in a huff over what he regarded as high-handed behavior by the former director—and, peripherally, by Stone himself—in a case involving a Palestinian agent in Beirut. Otherwise, Hoffman was an unknown quantity. He was one of the colorful characters the old-timers liked to reminisce about, but whom nobody really remembered very clearly anymore.

"C'mon in, sweetie," said Hoffman, opening the door of his apartment. It was early evening, and through the huge windows of the salon, Anna could see the pillars of the Acropolis, floodlit and magnificent. Next to the windows, vying for attention, was a large color television that was broadcasting an episode of *Starsky and Hutch.*

"Not bad, huh?" said Hoffman, walking her over to the window. "Did I lie to you? Is this a million-dollar view or what?"

"Maybe two million," said Anna.

"Nah. The dollar is still strong here. One million. Have a seat. What are you drinking?"

"White wine."

"Bullshit. I'm having a whiskey."

"Thanks, but I'll still have white wine."

"Suit yourself, honey."

He went to get her drink. Anna pointed to the television set, which was blaring noisily. "Mind if I turn that down? I can barely hear you."

"It's *Starsky and Hutch*. A good one, too. Starsky pretends to be a tango dancer to catch a ring of blackmailers."

"I'll catch it another time," said Anna.

"Leave the picture on, would you?"

Hoffman brought her the drink, sat down across from her, and leaned toward her. "So who the hell are you anyway?"

"My name is Lucy Morgan."

"Oh yeah? Is that a work name?"

"Yes," she said. "It is."

"Well then, what's your real name, sweetie?"

"I probably shouldn't tell you."

"Suit yourself." He leaned back against the couch and resumed watching the soundless *Starsky and Hutch.*

"Anna Barnes," she said.

Hoffman roused himself. "Is that another work name?"

"No. That's it."

"How do you know my old pseudonym?"

"I'm a case officer in London. I was given your name by a colleague at headquarters who said you might be able to help us with something."

"Which colleague?"

"I'd rather not say."

"Uh-huh. And why did they send you from London or Washington or wherever the hell you're coming from when they have a whole floor full of no-name case officers bump-

ing into each other over at the embassy? I could tell one of
them no just as easily as I can tell you."

"It's a sensitive case. They're running it from headquarters."

"So they sent you."

"That's right."

"And you're a female case officer." He used the word "female" as a qualifier, like "crippled."

"Yes. Obviously."

"Equal opportunity, right?"

"Right."

"Well, I think it's a terrific idea putting women in the field
as case officers. I just want you to know that. I'd hate to see
the national interests of the United States get in the way of
equal opportunity. Believe me."

"What's that supposed to mean?"

"Nothing," he said. He was either slightly drunk or very
rude. "Hey, listen. I'll tell you a little joke. You'll like it. It's
cute."

Anna said nothing. She was thinking, in the back of her
mind, about how soon she could get a flight back to America.

"The joke goes like this. We parachute an agent into the
Soviet Union, and the guy is absolutely perfect. He speaks
perfect Russian, with no accent. He's dressed in Russian
clothes, made of the same lousy fabric they use. He smokes
the same loopy cigarettes they do. And his identity papers are
perfect, right down to the rusty staples that leave red marks
on the middle pages. This guy has everything! So when he
lands and hides his parachute, he walks into town and goes to
a café and asks for a beer, local brand, just right, perfect Russian, no accent. And the lady behind the bar says: 'You must
be from the CIA.' "

"I've heard this joke."

"So the guy says: 'How can you tell? I'm a perfect Rus-
sian. Clothes, accent, papers, cigarettes.' And the lady says:
'Yeah, but we don't get too many black Russians in here.'
Funny, huh?"

"Not very. And I've heard it before."

"Women have no sense of humor."

"Look, I think I'd better go."

"Hold on. Don't go. It was just a joke, for chrissake."

"Listen, Mr. Hoffman. I didn't come here to listen to racist jokes or to debate feminism with you. Frankly, I don't give a damn what you think about those subjects. Or anything else."

"Okay, okay. Calm down. So why *did* you come to see Uncle Frank then? Call him out of the blue, using his old code name? Huh?"

"Because someone back home had the idea that you might want to help us with an important case."

"But why little old me? I'm retired. I've gone to seed. I don't give a shit anymore. Didn't they tell you that?"

"Yes, they did, actually."

"Oh yeah? Well, fuck them, then. Although it's true. I have gone to seed. I have too much money and too much fun, and I'm not willing to work with incompetents and nitwits anymore. I guess that makes me a malcontent."

"Apparently it does."

"Screw you, too. But let's cut the crap. What's your little case about?"

"I'm not sure there's any real point in going into it. You sound pretty burnt-out, to be honest. That's not what we're after."

"I *am* burnt-out, goddammit, and proud of it. I did a lot of burning in my day, which is more than you can say for most of your so-called colleagues. They're never going to burn out, because they're never going to get lit. You want another drink?"

"No. Like I said, maybe I should be going."

"What's the rush? This may be your only chance to see a genuine relic from the dinosaur age. Hold on, I'll be right back."

He visited the lavatory and returned with another glass of whiskey. "Let's stop playing games, huh? What's your case about and how do you think I can help you?"

"It involves Soviet nationalities."

"No shit?"

"No shit. They thought you might be worth talking to because you handled some cross-border operations in the 1950s."

"So I did. Total fuck-ups, as I recall. Got a lot of innocent people killed. Don't tell me they're going to do *that* again."

"Not exactly."

"What does that mean?"

"I can't give you details."

"So give me generalities."

"We're not going to *run* cross-border operations. We're going to pretend to run them. If you follow me."

"Deception."

"Yes."

"Make them think you're holding four aces when all you've got is a pair of twos."

"That's right."

"Hold on. I think I'm beginning to get the picture."

"What?"

"This has to be one of Stone's capers."

Anna said nothing.

"Edward Stone. You want me to spell it?"

Still she said nothing.

"This is one of his slick little games. Hootchie-kootchie. Now you see it, now you don't. And he wants me to help with the shit work. Except he doesn't have the balls to come see me himself, so he sends little Miss Dickless Tracy. Is that it, more or less?"

"You're out of line." She stood up.

"Hey, c'mon. Sit down. I'm sorry. About the Dickless Tracy part, I mean. I was joking."

"You're worse than they said. What's wrong with you anyway? What are you so angry about?"

"What's wrong with me is that I'm sick of watching us get our ass kicked from one end of the world to the other. It puts me in a bad mood and makes me say nasty things to nice young ladies such as yourself. If you want to know what's bothering me, just read the fucking newspapers. Do they still do that back at headquarters? Read the newspapers? They probably have a machine now that does that for them."

Anna said nothing.

"Here's one day's news, sweetheart," said Hoffman, picking up from the coffee table a copy of that morning's Athens *Post,* the local English-language paper.

"What's the front-page headline? 'Iranian Firing Squad Executes 21 of Shah's Officials.' Too bad. I probably know some of those guys. Okay, so we fucked up. What can we do about it? Look on the bottom of page one. Big headline: Leftist bombings in Turkey and Italy. There goes NATO. Ooops, we fucked up again. Turn inside and what have you got? 'CIA Agents in Greek Armed Forces, Socialist MPs Claim.' Which would be nice if it were true, but it isn't. And here's a gem on page three. You read this one." He handed the paper to Anna, pointing to a story in the middle of the page.

" 'Soviets Blame CIA for Italy's Violence.' "

"Go ahead," said Hoffman. "Read it."

" 'Moscow. The U.S. Central Intelligence Agency was blamed by a Soviet newspaper today for Italy's current wave of political violence. The daily *Sovietskaya Rossiya* said CIA agents were inspiring gangs of left-wing and right-wing extremists to throw bombs and shoot around corners at democratic leaders.' "

"Get that? 'Shoot around corners.' Finish reading."

" 'At CIA headquarters in Langley, Virginia, the agency's covert-operations section is working night and day on plans for provocations, murders and political divisions in Italy, the commentary said.' "

"Wonderful! The local paper in Athens, capital of one of our NATO allies, is printing raw KGB press releases. Oh well, another fuck-up. What can we do? So let's see what's happening on the home front, with the world turning to shit and us taking all the blame. Bingo, here's a story on page six. You'll like this one. 'Lesbian Policewomen Win Back Pay,' reads the headline. And I quote: 'Six former Boise policewomen fired by the city in 1977 for alleged homosexual activity have been awarded $103,000 in back pay, tax payments and attorneys' fees.' Isn't that nice? Aren't you glad to see our law-enforcement community worrying about the really important things?"

"You really are an asshole, Mr. Hoffman," said Anna. She stood up.

"Hey, sit down. We were just getting down to business."

"Not me. I'm leaving."

"Calm down."

"I am calm," said Anna. She walked to the door and opened it. "Boy, was Stone wrong about you. He said you were a crank, but that you were worth the trouble. I feel sorry for you, to be honest. You really are pathetic."

Hoffman countered with an obscenity, but it didn't matter. Anna was gone.

The phone rang in Anna's room the next morning at seven-thirty. "This is your wake-up call," said a male voice.

"I didn't leave a wake-up call."

"Okay, this isn't your wake-up call. It's Frank Hoffman. I'm calling because I owe you an apology."

"That's okay," said Anna. "Forget it. Goodbye."

"Don't hang up. I mean it. Let's have breakfast and we'll talk about it."

"No."

"You gotta have breakfast, honey."

"No, I don't."

"Yes. You do. I already ordered it."

"You what?"

"I already ordered breakfast for you. I hope you like scrambled eggs."

"You can't do that."

"I already did. I know people here at the hotel. It'll be up to your room in about fifteen minutes. So will I."

"You can't come up to my room."

"Why not? You have a suite, right?"

"How do you know that?"

"I told you. I have friends at the hotel. See you soon."

Anna was tired of arguing and hung up the phone.

Hoffman arrived bearing flowers, in addition to the breakfast tray. Not just a bouquet, but a whole trolleyful of orchids and gladioli and tulips. Anna wasn't sure she would open the door until he started singing. It sounded like an impromptu medley from *Kiss Me, Kate,* but it was hard to tell because Hoffman's voice was so gravelly and he dropped so many words. Anna decided to let him in—breakfast, flowers, Cole Porter and all. What else could she do?

"You were right last night," said Hoffman when he was seated and attacking his share of the breakfast tray. "I did act like an asshole. And I'm sorry. Really. I feel terrible."

"Stop apologizing," said Anna. "You'll make me feel guilty."

"Good," said Hoffman, shoveling scrambled eggs into his

mouth with a piece of toast. "I want you to feel guilty. Guilty enough that you'll renew your offer."

"What offer? I never made an offer."

"The offer you were going to make, to have me help you and Stone in your little Soviet caper, whatever it is."

"Why do you want to help?"

"Because I'm bored. And patriotic. And because you people need me."

"I thought you didn't like Stone."

"Stone's all right. Too smart for a dumb guy like me. But it's not his fault the world's fucked up."

Anna looked carefully at the large man eating breakfast so enthusiastically before her in the sitting room of her hotel suite. He was still wearing the same peculiar gold ornament around his neck that she had noticed the night before. It looked like a small life preserver.

"What's that?" asked Anna, pointing to the gold piece, changing the subject and giving herself time to think.

"A doughnut," said Hoffman.

"Why?"

"Because I like doughnuts."

"Oh."

"I tell some of my Saudi friends that it's an award I got from the agency. I say the 'O' stands for operations. They like that."

"But it's not an award."

"No, like I said, it's a doughnut. But it doesn't matter what it is. The Saudis like it because it's big and heavy and expensive. They're very size-conscious, the Saudis. One of them actually offered to buy it from me. Can you believe that? How can you respect people like that?"

"I see," said Anna.

"So listen. What kind of job do you have for me?"

"I didn't say I had any job."

"I know. But if you did, what would it be?"

Anna was thinking, as he talked, that since joining the agency, she had met only one person who was as outrageous as Hoffman, though in a much nastier and more dangerous way, and that was Ali Ascari. It occurred to her suddenly that these two gentlemen might make a perfect match, Frank and Ali.

"I can tell you a few things about the operation," said Anna. "The rest is code word."

"Yeah, yeah. Sure. Code word."

"We have an Iranian asset. His family is from Baku, in Azerbaijan. He claims to have contacts who are operating across the border, smuggling radios and VCRs and Korans. And maybe also some guns. We'd like to tap into his network and use it."

"For what?"

"For our operation."

"Remind me what that is again. I don't remember too much from last night."

"I didn't tell you much."

"Well, tell me some more. Can I borrow your jelly, by the way?"

"Sure," said Anna, handing him the jelly container.

"Go on, tell me. While you're at it, let me borrow a piece of your toast."

Anna laughed. Hoffman was impossible not to like, at least in the morning, when he hadn't been drinking. "Stone starts from the same place you do, actually," she said.

"Does he, now?"

"He thinks the agency is dead in the water."

"He's right."

"He thinks the only thing we can do, for now, is try to scare the Russians and buy some time."

"How?"

"By using people like the Iranian I was telling you about, to make the Soviets think that Central Asia and the Caucasus are coming apart."

"And you're looking for someone to run the Iranian and his smugglers."

"Correct."

"That's wild. It doesn't sound like Stone, though. It's too crazy."

"I don't know. Maybe Stone has gone to seed, too."

"What a happy thought."

"So? What do you think?"

"It's weird, and it's dangerous. And I have a sneaking suspicion that it ain't legal. But who cares. I like it."

"What do you mean, that it isn't legal?"

"Forget it. What do I know? I'm no lawyer. The point is, I like it. Count me in."

"But I haven't asked you yet."

"I know, but you will. Face it. You need a cranky old woman-hating son of a bitch like me."

"I'll think about it."

"What's the Iranian's name?"

"Ali Ascari."

"Where does he live?"

"London and Tehran. But he travels a lot, on three passports. One of them is Greek, as a matter of fact."

"Oh, is it really, now? That little detail ought to come in handy."

"As leverage?"

"Fuckin'-A right. When can you arrange a meet?"

"I still haven't offered you the job."

"Well, why don't you think about it while I get rid of the breakfast dishes."

Hoffman picked up the trays, knocking over a coffee cup, and walked to the door. He deposited them outside the room and returned. Anna didn't have to think very long. She recognized that Hoffman's raw energy—the crude, blunt, burnt-out rage of the man—fit the operating style of the odd little enterprise doing business as Karpetland. It functioned off the books, and so did Hoffman.

"So what's the verdict?"

"So how would you like a job, Frank?"

"I think I'm in love," said Hoffman.

27

⧫

FORTUNATELY HOFFMAN HAD TO LEAVE THAT AFTERNOON FOR a business engagement in Dubai, so he was gone before he could do anything that might have caused Anna to change her mind. This sudden conclusion of her business in Athens left Anna with a free day on the town before her flight back to Washington. Her first thought was to spend it sunning herself at the swimming pool maintained by the Athens Hilton. But after a stroll through the cabanas, which were filled with men in too small bathing suits and women falling out of their bikini tops, she decided that the Hilton pool was not her scene.

Anna's scene was something closer to a library. So after studying a map, she set off walking from the hotel in the general direction of the National Library, a place she had wanted to visit on previous trips to Athens but had never quite gotten around to. She made her way past Syntagma Square and its touristic jumble of airline ticket offices and tacky cabarets, toward Omonia Square.

The library was an immense neoclassical pile, just past the university and the Hellenic Academy. A little man in a uniform at the front desk asked where she was going; Anna, without thinking about it very much, said she wanted to see the Ottoman history collection. The oppressive burden of graduate school was by now far enough in the past that she actually did want to see the Ottoman collection. Other people collected ancient coins or catalogued species of bugs. Anna's area of useless specialization was late-nineteenth-century Turkish history. The guard at the front desk directed her to another guard, up a flight of stairs and down a very long hall, who in turn directed her to an owlish man who sat in the shadows of a large, cryptlike office. The man in question was the curator of the Ottoman history collection. His name was Jannos.

"What are you looking for?" he asked Anna dubiously. He spoke in a very precise, clipped English.

"Just browsing."

"This is not an area for browsing, madame. You have to know very much even to know what to look for."

Anna decided to lie. "I'm a doctoral candidate in Ottoman history at Harvard." It wasn't a big lie; more a change of tense.

"I see," said the curator, still dubious. "What is the topic of your dissertation?"

"Administrative Practices in the Late Ottoman Empire, with special emphasis on the management of ethnic conflict."

"I see," said the curator. He finally seemed convinced that she was legitimate.

"How extensive is your collection?"

"Very extensive, madame."

"Any new acquisitions?" she asked idly.

"No," said the curator. "Only the Albanian material, which is temporarily on loan to us."

Anna almost missed what he had said. "Excuse me," she asked. "Did you say the Albanian material?"

"Yes, madame. From the Bibliothèque Nationale in Tirana."

"You're kidding!"

He was offended. "I assure you that I am not kidding. Why are you surprised? We have reciprocal exchanges with many national libraries. We may not be Harvard University. But we are quite modern here, you know."

"I wasn't being critical. I was just surprised. The Albanians have some documents I was looking for—am looking for, I mean—for my thesis."

"And what documents might those be?"

"The Ibrahim Temo papers. He was one of the founders of the Union and Progress Committee."

"Ah! I am sorry."

"You don't have them?"

"Not anymore, madame."

"What do you mean?"

"We did have some of the Temo documents, but only very briefly. It was necessary to return them to Tirana, one month ago."

"Oh no!" said Anna. "That's awful."

"You see, we are quite a modern library."

"Now I'll never see them. The Albanians don't give visas to Americans."

"I am very sorry."

Anna was disconsolate, suffering under that special weight of regret that comes from discovering—too late—that you might have had something, had you only known it was available. Even the snippy curator could see that she was upset.

"Madame, if I may suggest. Perhaps you would like to see the Greek scholar who worked with the Temo collection while it was here?"

Anna's eyes brightened. "Yes, I suppose I would, if that's possible."

"Let me see if he is here. Please sit down."

The curator disappeared down a dark corridor and was gone for ten minutes. He returned with a tall, thin young man who had the colorless skin and sunken, affectless eyes that marked him as a denizen of the library.

"I'm Lucy Morgan," said Anna. The young bibliophile trembled slightly as he shook her hand. His name was Andreas Papadapoulos; it turned out that he was a doctoral candidate himself, whose dissertation—if he could ever finish it—was to be on nothing other than the life and works of Mr. Ibrahim Temo. Anna began to quiz the younger Greek about the documents, but the owlish curator put his finger to his lips.

"Silence in the library, please," he said.

But Anna was determined to share, at least vicariously, in the Temo archive. So with gentle prodding, she prevailed on the skittish Mr. Papadapoulos to join her for lunch.

"Did you really get hold of Sukuti's trunk?" Anna asked him when they were seated in an outdoor café near the university.

"Excuse me?" The poor young Greek looked as if he might jump out of his pasty white skin.

"Oh, come now, Mr. Papadapoulos. You know very well what I'm talking about. The trunk in which Ishak Sukuti kept the early records of the Union and Progress Committee. The trunk he tried to send to Temo, which Temo finally picked up at Yildiz Palace and took back with him to Romania, and which finally ended up in Albania."

"Oh, that trunk," said Andreas. "How do you know so much about Sukuti's trunk?"

"Because I spent a summer chasing it myself, in Istanbul. In Beykoz, to be precise, where Temo's daughter was living. I thought she might have it."

"Natalia Temo."

"Yes, Natalia." She nodded. Evidently he knew the whole story. Rationally, Anna knew that she had no reason to feel jealous. She wasn't a graduate student anymore. She had no academic subspecialty to protect. Still, it bothered her that someone—this frightened Greek scholar she had never met or known the existence of until a few minutes ago—had found and appropriated to himself something that ought to have been hers.

"So tell me. I'm curious to know what's in the great Temo archive."

"It is hard to say," he answered warily. "I am still working on my research."

"Don't worry, Mr. Papadapoulos. I won't steal your material. If you want to know the truth, I'm not really a graduate student anymore. I've dropped out."

"Oh," he said. He seemed slightly reassured. "Well, I can tell you a few things. The Albanians didn't let me have all the papers, and I only had several months to examine them. But I have found a few interesting things."

"Tell me whatever you can. I'm dying to know, actually."

"Yes, perhaps I can tell you a little," said the young Greek. He wanted so much to be nice, especially to an attractive, if slightly intimidating American woman. "What I have found is that the Tempo papers include most of the Young Turks' international correspondence from 1889, when they were founded, until about 1895."

"I already know that, Mr. Papadapoulos. That was the period I was examining in my dissertation."

"Yes, of course. So what is interesting about these papers is that they show the Young Turks had a network of contacts throughout the provinces of the Ottoman Empire, and even in many areas of the Russian Tsar's empire. I have found among the papers much correspondence among branches or affiliates of the Union and Progress Committee. They had branches in Salonika, in Izmir, in Paris, in London."

"What about the branches in the East?"

"Yes. I have found correspondence with them, too. With affiliated groups in Baku, in Tashkent, in Bukhara—all places that were at that time controlled by the Tsar. And most interesting of all, I have found correspondence with affiliates in Christian areas—in Yerevan in Armenia and Tbilisi in Georgia."

"So the committee had a network throughout the Caucasus and Central Asia?" asked Anna. As she spoke, she was thinking of another network. One that existed, for now, only in the mind of Edward Stone.

"Yes, that is right."

"And it cut across the ethnic boundaries."

"Excuse me?"

"I mean, the network included people who, in other contexts, didn't get along. Armenians and Azeris. Georgians and Tatars. Greeks and Turks."

"Yes. I suppose that is true."

"Hold on. Is it true or not?"

"Yes. On one level it is true. The Union and Progress Committee said that it was for equality of all ethnic groups that had lived within the boundaries of the Ottoman Empire. Armenians, Kurds, Greeks. Bulgarians. Copts. Even Jews."

"But on another level it wasn't true?"

"You must understand, Miss Morgan. These people in the Union and Progress Committee, they were spies. They always operated on several different levels."

"I don't follow you."

"They were spies. They were in a battle with Abdul-Hamid's secret police. They did secret things."

"I know what spies are, Mr. Papadapoulos."

"Well, these Young Turk spies would do strange things. They would start a newspaper in Paris or London, in the expectation that Abdul-Hamid's agents would bribe them to close the paper. They got 10,000 francs to close one newspaper in Paris. Then they would take the money and start another newspaper. They bribed the big European newspapers, too—*Figaro, Le Matin*—to write nasty stories about the sultan. They would deliberately plant false information in one capital of Europe, to make Abdul-Hamid's men chase after it, and plant different information in another capital. They were very clever, these Young Turk spies."

"But what about the network? You said the committee on one level supported equality among Armenians and Turks, Christians and Moslems, and all that. Was there another level?"

"Ah, I am sorry. That is the heart of my dissertation. I really cannot discuss it."

"Please," said Anna, touching the Greek man's hand. "The

documents are all yours. I won't do anything with them. Honest. I'm just very curious."

"I really should not discuss this, you know." He was softening. It was not in the nature of a Greek man, even a library dweller, to refuse the plea of a woman.

"Please," said Anna again.

"I will tell you, but only if you promise not to tell anyone else."

"I promise." She held up her hand, as if swearing an oath.

"Very well. The truth is that the Union and Progress Committee was a trick. They talked about equality, but it was not true. They had members—whole branches—that were Greek and Armenian and Coptic and Bulgarian. But from the beginning, there was an inner circle, controlled by Moslems. It was called the *Merkezi Umumi*. The Central Committee."

"How do you know that?"

"Because, Miss Morgan, it is in the papers of Ibrahim Temo."

"How? Did they describe two levels?"

"Not in so many words. But they did not have to. They did everything in code, these people. What I found was that they had two codes. One for everyone, including Christians. And one for the core group, which was Moslem only. I have found a letter, for example, that was sent in code to the Cairo branch. It warned the leaders—who were Moslems—not to share any secret documents with Copts."

"Why were the Moslems so suspicious?"

"Because they simply did not trust the others. They did not believe that the non-Moslem subjects of the empire truly wanted a modern and progressive Ottoman state. They suspected that the Greeks were really fighting for an independent Greece, the Armenians were really fighting for an independent Armenia, the Bulgars for Bulgaria, and so on."

"And they were right."

"Yes, of course. They were right."

"And did the Armenians and Greeks know that they were being treated differently within the committee?"

"Yes, probably."

"So what you are telling me is that, from the beginning, the members of this noble revolutionary network were at each other's throats."

"Not quite at each other's throats. But the seeds of hatred were there, 'from the Adriatic Sea to the Chinese Sea,' as they liked to say. Now you must remember your promise to me, Miss Morgan. You will not tell anyone about what is in these documents."

"My dear Mr. Papadapoulos, I promise you with all my heart that I will not tell anyone what you have found. My interest is in the present, not in the past. What I would like is to find a way to avoid reliving this history—not to retell it."

VI

WILLIAM GOODE

Washington / Athens
Istanbul / Tashkent

June–September 1979

28
◆

A REAL WAR WAS BEGINNING THAT SUMMER, IN A PLACE where the national sport was playing polo with a sheep's head. The place was Afghanistan, and like Vietnam and Algeria, it would soon become famous not so much for itself as for the folly into which it tempted a larger power. There was something about such places that subverted normal logic and common sense, that inspired the would-be conqueror to make an initial bold and foolhardy move, which soon would be lost without another such move, and then another, until the reputation and treasure of the giant power had been staked on swatting the geopolitical equivalent of a horsefly.

For decades Afghanistan had been a matter of pure indifference to the rest of the world, including the Soviets. The Peace Corps spent more time and effort there in the 1960s than the KGB. Even the British, who had once imagined Afghanistan as the fulcrum on which were balanced the Russian Empire and the British Raj in India, no longer paid much attention. But by the late 1970s, the Soviets had finally caught the virus that occasionally infects great nations and weakens their normal protection against stupidity and unreason. The Soviet media ruminated darkly about American meddling in that part of the world, which required a decisive Soviet response. "Sinister plots" by "certain Western agencies" were invoked.

The march of folly seemed inexorable. Moscow had installed a Communist government in Kabul in 1978, hoping to break the Islamic movement that was developing in the rural areas of the country. But the Afghan Communists only inflamed the Moslem resistance, leaving Moscow the unpleasant choice of intervening more decisively or admitting defeat. How familiar that sounded to the generation of CIA men who had watched the unfolding of Vietnam. Through the spring of 1979, the Soviet military presence in Afghanistan increased. Soviet military advisers, dressed in Afghan Army uniforms, were spotted throughout the country. One summer day the CIA station in Kabul sent an agent out to count the number of light-skinned men playing volleyball in the military compound at Bagram Air Base. The agent stopped counting at 400.

To a student of human folly, which Anna Barnes had considered herself for nearly a decade, the nature of the coming war in Afghanistan was obvious, without reading any intelligence reports. The essential facts were contained in a short newspaper story she read on the plane back from Athens. It described the fate of several Soviet advisers who had been captured by the *mujaheddin*. The Afghan rebels boasted that they had cut the ears and testicles off their Russian prisoners and then peeled off their skin, a strip at a time.

What struck Anna about this account wasn't the unusual barbarism of the incident, but its ordinariness. It might have been written about any war in that part of the world during the past millennium. For the history of that region was, on the simplest level, a theater of pain. The unlucky Russian soldier in Afghanistan, screaming in agony as another strip of pulpy white skin was torn from his body, might recognize in his tormentor the face of the Ottoman general Lala Mustafa. After the battle of Famagusta in 1570, the great Mustafa captured his Venetian opponent, cut off his right ear and nose, flayed and dismembered him alive, and then cured the empty skin, stuffed it with straw, and carried it about the city. Pain is timeless. Perhaps the Moslem *mujahed* recognized in his Russian adversary the face of the crusader Richard the Lionhearted, who put to death the entire population of Acre—2,700 men, women and children—after the town surrendered in 1191.

There had been times, reading her history books, when Anna had suspected that torture was the very essence of power in the Near East and Central Asia. The ability to inflict pain was what made a sultan a strong leader, and failure to do so marked him as a weak man. That was the tragedy of Ottoman history, that this noble and civilized people could also be so cruel. It was the same wretched story, from sultan to sultan, as if the heirs of Osman were all reliving the same bloody nightmare. The fourteenth-century sultan Murad I became so angry at his rebellious son Gunduz that he put out his eyes and cut off his head; then, as a test of loyalty, he ordered his lieutenants to blind and behead their own sons. Nearly all of them obeyed. A century later Mehmed II took a fancy to the handsome fourteen-year-old son of one of his ministers and demanded that the boy be brought to him; when the minister refused, Mehmed decapitated both father and son and had their heads carried to his dinner table. When Selim I took power in 1512, his first act was to have his two brothers strangled—an ordinary enough act by Ottoman standards—and also their five sons, some as young as five, while he listened to their screams from the next room. His successor, the peerless Suleyman the Magnificent, recorded in his diary that he routinely ordered his own troops beheaded for such offenses as "pasturing horses in unharvested fields." Calculated cruelty was the very essence of leadership. Murad IV, for example, was generally reckoned a strong and successful sultan. When he was bothered one day by a party of women dancing near the water, he had them all drowned; when his chief musician made the mistake of playing a Persian song, he was beheaded. And so history continued in the Near East and Central Asia, from massacre to massacre, from flaying to flaying. Periodically the "enlightened" forces of the West weighed in—from the Crusaders to the Red Army. They generally preferred to do their killing at a distance, with a longbow, or a rifle, or from an airplane. But they, too, were caught in the bloody chain.

29

ANNA BARNES RETURNED TO HER MOTEL ROOM IN BETHESDA to find two messages waiting for her at the front desk. Both said the same thing: "Please call ASAP." One was from Alan

Taylor. The other was from Margaret Houghton. Anna wondered how Margaret could possibly have discovered where she was staying, or even the fact that she was in Washington on temporary assignment. But her curiosity about Margaret was overcome by a longing to see Taylor, so it was his message that she answered first. She reached him at the office in Rockville and thirty minutes later he was in bed beside her.

"I missed you too much," said Anna after they had finished making love. She stroked the hair on his chest as she spoke.

"Impossible," said Taylor. "You can't miss someone too much."

"Yes, you can. A woman can."

"Not me. I missed you just enough."

"Just enough that you didn't sleep with someone else while I was gone?"

"Exactly."

Anna looked at his body, naked on the bed. "Did you know that the Arabs had thirty-seven names for it?"

"For what?"

"For the penis."

"Typical. The Eskimos have fifty words for snow. The Arabs have thirty-seven words for penis."

"Seriously. I read it once in a book written in the sixteenth century by Sheikh Nefzawi of Tunis."

"Christ! Where did you find all these bizarre books?"

"In the X cage."

"That sounds exciting."

"Not so exciting. It's the section of the Widener stacks where they hid all the dirty books. You needed a key, and permission from the Director of Library Services."

"Typical Harvard. So what were some of the fifty-seven varieties? Do you remember any?"

"Thirty-seven. And yes, I remember some of them. But they're pretty ridiculous."

"C'mon. Let's hear some."

"Okay. The bellows, because it inflates and deflates. The one-eyed man, for obvious reasons. The bald-headed man, also for obvious reasons. The sleeper. The knocker. The breaker. The weeper. The deceiver. The names go on and on."

"Which one am I?"

"I'm not sure yet. As we say in the library, it needs more research."

"What would Sheikh Nefzawi suggest?"

"He would say that a woman is like a flower that gives up its fragrance only when it is touched by gentle hands. He said that women are particularly like basil leaves in that respect, but that doesn't sound as sexy."

"I'm a willing pupil," said Taylor. Anna smiled and took his hand.

And so they gave it more research, spending most of the night making love, or drifting off to sleep after it, or waking up and wanting to do it again. It was a long night of love, in which these two strange bodies gradually became intimate. They would brush naked against each other, half asleep, until one or the other would reach out and caress the not quite familiar person sharing the bed, or blow a kiss in the ear, or tell a silly joke. They both woke up bleary-eyed, with the special feeling of exhaustion and bliss that is part of falling in love. They ordered breakfast from room service, ate heartily, and promptly fell asleep again.

Toward noon, Anna awoke and wondered aloud, "Should we go to work?"

"Fuck it," said Taylor.

That sounded exactly right to Anna. She slept for another two hours and was awakened by the sound of Taylor turning the crinkly pages of *The New York Times*.

"Can I ask you something?" said Anna after she had brushed her teeth, taken a shower, and gotten back in bed. "How many women have you slept with in your life?"

"I dunno. Fifty. Maybe a hundred. Do you care?"

"No. But that's a lot."

"Not when you think about it."

Anna pondered it a while. It still seemed like a lot. Anna had slept with eight men in her life. She could remember each one, each detail. They all seemed like boys, looking back. It occurred to her that Taylor might be the first man—real, grown-up man—she had ever slept with. She felt an immense curiosity about him, wanting to know the secret history and geography of his life in the same way that she was discovering his body. She knew he didn't like talking about himself, but she couldn't help wondering.

"Why did you join the CIA?" she asked after a while.

"Because it sounded like fun, and because I couldn't think what else to do."

"Honestly?"

"Honestly. I'm a nihilist at heart. A sentimental nihilist. I liked the agency because it sounded romantic, but it didn't really stand for anything. And I thought it would beat going to Vietnam."

"What was your first assignment?"

"Vietnam."

"Oops. What did you do there?"

"I was a counterintelligence officer in Saigon. I worked my ass off looking for North Vietnamese spies. But it was a joke, as it turned out. We didn't know it at the time, but most of the country was working for the NLF, including a lot of our so-called agents."

"And then?"

"Then Saudi Arabia, then Somalia, then Turkey. Then Rockville. Then in bed with you."

"Did you like the work?" pressed Anna. She didn't want to let Taylor change the subject yet.

"Less and less. It began to bore me, to be honest. And I was married to someone I didn't like, which made things worse."

"Dr. Marcus says people like you are the easiest for the KGB to recruit."

"Who's Dr. Marcus?"

"An agency shrink. He was one of my instructors."

"Oh yeah? Well, he's full of shit."

"What about now? Do you like your job better?"

"Until a few weeks ago I was ready to quit. Now, I like it. It gets the blood moving in the morning."

"Why? What's different? The work hasn't changed."

"I feel like I've finally found the inner chamber—the real CIA that's beneath all the layers of junk. You have to have watched things fall apart to understand what it means to find out that the core is still there. I thought it was dead."

"So what do you want to do next, after this Karpetland thing? Do you want to stay in Istanbul?"

"Stop asking so many questions. You're reminding me of my ex-wife." Taylor leaned over and grabbed the elastic waistband of Anna's panties, which she had only recently put on. "Let's make love," he said.

"I'm sore."

"Only one cure for that," said Taylor, pulling off her panties. And he was right. He was so gentle and so loving that it frightened Anna, momentarily, to think what it would be like without him.

Margaret called the next morning at the Karpetland office. Anna was embarrassed. In the thirty-six hours since first receiving Margaret's message, she had forgotten entirely about it. Margaret's voice was flat, noncommittal, as if there was something on her mind that she wanted very much to talk about, but not on the telephone. The older woman proposed that they have dinner that night. Anna said yes, even though she had been looking forward to another evening alone in bed with Taylor. They settled on a modest Italian restaurant in Bethesda, the kind that had an indoor fountain decorated with plaster cherubs, where the owner sang "That's Amore," on request.

Anna was glad to see Margaret, and more than a little curious. How *had* Aunt Margaret, the genteel spinster of the clandestine service, discovered that Anna was in Washington? And who on earth had given her the telephone number of the office in Rockville, which was supposedly under such deep cover? She wanted to ask Margaret who had spilled the beans, but was half afraid to find out. She tried instead to make small talk about London. Margaret didn't put up with that for very long.

"I'm worried about you," said Margaret after the waiter had brought them a bottle of cheap Italian white wine. "What have you gotten yourself into?"

"I can't really talk about it," said Anna. "It's code word."

"Oh, is it now? My, my! How quickly the little ones grow up."

"Come on, Auntie, That's not fair. You've been keeping secrets your whole life."

"I'm not prying. But I must tell you that what I've heard about your activities disturbs me."

"What have you heard?"

"That you've fallen into some scheme of Edward Stone's."

"How can you possibly have heard that? What I'm doing is supposed to be secret."

"Don't be silly, dear. There are no real secrets in the agency. In our line of work, secrets are a commodity. We produce them, we consume them, sometimes we trade them for something else."

Anna lit a cigarette. "So what do you know? Or think you know?"

"That you're working on a project for Stone that involves Soviet nationalities."

"No comment."

"And that there's a flap."

That got Anna's attention. "What flap?" she asked. "I don't know about any flap."

"There is an interagency committee that oversees CIA operations dealing with the Soviet Union. It's called the Soviet Working Group, or something innocuous like that."

"Never heard of it."

"Stone should have told you about it. But of course he didn't, for obvious reasons."

"What obvious reasons?"

"Because the interagency committee exists to keep people like Stone from going off the reservation."

"Don't play games with me. This is serious. You said there was a flap. What's the flap?"

"It's just a little one, for now. Someone from the State Department heard a rumor that the agency was running a covert action involving Soviet nationalities. They were concerned, because the State Department disapproves of that sort of thing."

"I know that."

"Then it won't surprise you to know that the State Department queried the agency through channels—meaning through this Soviet Working Group—and the official answer came back that the rumor was false. The agency wasn't doing anything new with Soviet nationalities."

"I see," said Anna.

"But that's nonsense, isn't it?"

"Please, Auntie. Don't push me. I'd talk about it if I could."

"Watch out, my dear. That's all I really wanted to say. Be very careful. This really is much more dangerous than you realize. Not simply to you and your career, but to others who may come to rely on you."

"Listen," said Anna gently. "I think you're more worried about this than you need to be. I can't talk about what we're doing, but I promise you that Stone has no real covert-action program of the sort you describe."

"What do you mean 'real'? Does he have a phony covert-action program?"

"I'm sorry. I told you, I can't talk about it."

"Well then, I repeat: Be careful."

"Why are you so upset, Margaret?"

"Because I can see it on your face. The look in your eye, the tone of your skin. You are suffering, my dear, from the exhilaration of working on something very secret and very exotic. And I'm happy for you. But I have to warn you: Men like Stone are at their most attractive when they are slightly out of control. But that is also when they are most dangerous."

"Really, Auntie. I think you're going overboard. If you can't trust men like Stone, who can you trust?"

"My dear," said Margaret, shaking her head, "I fear you are a lost cause. You've been in the business six months and you are already beginning to sound like Stone himself. Let's order dinner, shall we?"

"I'm not hungry anymore," said Anna.

But she stopped sulking after a few minutes and another glass of wine, while Margaret told a long, cautionary tale. It concerned a woman case officer whose husband had been killed in the line of duty. Driven by grief and a desire for revenge, she had studied Russian and volunteered for duty in the Moscow embassy. The mandarins had been only too happy to give her the chance. They were looking for women that year, to fill drops and service agents in "denied areas" like Moscow. What the woman didn't know was that Moscow Center had her made from the moment she arrived at Sheremetievo Airport. They finally nailed her as she was filling a dead drop for a putative agent. They held a press conference and showed off the goodies: one-time code pads; secret-writing equipment; even a poison capsule. It was a great show. The poor woman went home in some embarrassment.

"Somebody should have warned her," said Anna.

"Of what?"

"Not to get caught."

30

◆

THE EMPTY DESOLATION OF THE KARPETLAND OFFICE IN ITS early days had disappeared. The fluorescent-lit showroom was now stacked with boxes—books, cassette tapes, manifestos and handbills printed in the various Turkic languages of Central Asia—that were arriving every few days from clandestine printshops and audio labs around the Washington area. The provenance of this material was something of a mystery. Taylor hadn't ordered it, nor had Anna, and Marjorie certainly hadn't ordered it. That left Stone, who as usual was conducting most of his activities out of view.

Marjorie moved the boxes from the couches at the back of the showroom, clearing an area for her colleagues to sit. Stone would be arriving shortly for a meeting to discuss what he vaguely described as "Phase II." Anna mounted the stairs, then Taylor a few minutes later. The artifice was lost on Marjorie, who was too busy tidying to notice whether they were arriving separately or together. Taylor and Anna parked themselves on separate couches, in the shadow of a stack of boxes of Korans that had arrived the previous week from Pakistan.

Anna looked tired and preoccupied. In the days since her dinner with Margaret, she had been brooding about her personal and professional life. She had put up a brave front at the Italian restaurant, but the conversation had unstopped a mental dam of some sort, and she had slept uneasily ever since—tossing and turning, wondering where her noiseless steps were carrying her. Taylor had been away in New York much of the past week, which had given Anna more time to brood, and to contemplate her world in the cold, flat light of day. To pass the time, she had done some reading about Abdul-Hamid's intelligence service, the *hamidiye*, hoping it would give her some ideas about organizing networks in Central Asia. But it seemed, reading the books, as though Abdul-Hamid's only notable success had been in organizing pogroms against Greeks and Armenians. She found that worrying, too.

Anna wasn't frightened, or even all that worried; she was mostly confused, and she had decided, in the middle of one of these restless nights, that it was time to voice her uncertainties to her two male colleagues. And if they didn't like it, or thought her weak and feminine for asking questions, then tough shit.

"Hello, my friends," said Stone cheerily when he arrived.

"Hello, boss," said Taylor.

Anna didn't say anything. In addition to her other concerns, she was becoming tired of Stone's relentless politeness.

"Today's the day," said Stone when they were all seated on the two fat couches in the back.

"For what?" asked Anna.

"For reviewing the order of battle, my dear, and deciding where we go next. The time has come to talk of many things, as the Walrus said to someone or other."

"The Carpenter," said Anna.

"Thank you. Now then, Alan, where do you stand with Mr. Munzer?"

"Munzer's on board," answered Taylor. "I've made three trips to Brooklyn to see him, and we have reached an understanding."

"What are the arrangements?"

"He'll be a contract agent, on a six-month contract. We'll pay him six thousand a month, plus expenses."

"What about termination?"

"He'll get an annuity of a thousand dollars a month when he reaches sixty, which is next year, on condition that he signs a quitclaim and keeps his mouth shut. He says we owe it to him anyway because of the work he did for us in the 1950s, although Marjorie says personnel doesn't have anything in its files about a pension. I say fuck it. Let's pay him."

"Fine. Have you promised him anything else?"

"Not financially, no."

"I meant, spiritually."

"I went through the usual bullshit about the cause."

"What particular bullshit was that?"

"About liberating Turkestan from the Russians, and how we'll never betray him and all that. He was pleased when we got the radios to broadcast his poem, but he was still skittish about working with the agency again. So I arranged a dog-and-pony show for him last week with a buddy from the Near East Division who owes me a favor. He gave Munzer a briefing on Central Asia, all about how the Moslems are rising up to overthrow the atheists and infidels. Munzer loved it."

"What does he think he'll be doing for us?"

"Liberating Turkestan."

"And he assumes it's all for real?"

"Of course."

"How loudly will he scream when we pull the plug?"

"He won't be very happy, but so what? He's been claiming the CIA betrayed him for the past twenty-five years anyway. Why should anyone pay any more attention to him now?"

"Um-hum," said Stone coolly. "Well, that sounds reasonable enough, Alan. Thank you."

Anna bit her tongue. She wanted to say something, but it wasn't her turn, and Munzer Ahmedov wasn't her agent. Stone seemed to sense her uneasiness and turned to her.

"Now, what about you, Anna? Are you all set with Frank Hoffman?"

"I think so. He's signed a contract, but he refuses to accept any money from us. He says he's too rich already."

"And when will you be handing Mr. Ascari over to him?"

"Next week in Athens. Ascari is flying in from London."

"And what do you think of Hoffman?"

"I like him better than I thought I would at first. He doesn't play games." She meant it to sound cutting, but Stone seemed not to hear.

"So the pieces are in place, then. Which means that it is time for us to move on to the next stage."

"Mr. Stone?" said Anna. Her heart was racing.

"Yes, my dear."

"I'd like to ask you a question."

"Certainly. What is it?"

"What does the State Department have to say about our operation?"

"The State Department? Why do you ask?"

"I was just wondering. I thought they had a policy against stirring up Soviet nationalities. In fact, during the first conversation you and I had, at that motel off I-270, I remember you saying that the State Department was worried that anything involving the nationalities would cause problems with Moscow."

"Nuclear war, I think I said. They fear it could lead to nuclear war. That's nonsense, of course. But you're entirely correct. That is what they think."

"Right. So given that, you'd think they might object."

"I'm sure they would, if they knew about it. But fortunately, they don't."

Anna tensed. She was afraid that if she pushed, Stone would lie to her, which would force her to make a decision. But she had to ask; she had promised herself that much.

"Are you sure," she said, "that the State Department hasn't objected?"

"Let me think," he replied, studying her face. Anna held her breath. "There is one thing, now that I think about it. One of their people apparently heard a rumor that the agency was up to something and asked the front office about it. They responded, in all candor, that it was rubbish. Why? Are you concerned about who's authorizing all this?"

"A little."

"Of course you are," he said gently. "And you should be. But we're not some rogue elephant operating on our own, I can assure you of that. We're operating under explicit guidance from the White House."

"From the President?"

"From his National Security Adviser, which amounts to the same thing. We have authority from the highest level. It's not a straight line, I grant you, but it's there."

Anna let go a deep and genuine sigh of relief. "That's great. I hadn't realized that."

"I'm sorry. I thought I had mentioned it before."

"No. I don't think so."

"Well, I'm glad you brought it up. Because we need to be very careful about this legal business. We unfortunately are living in a land of pygmies, who would like nothing better than to catch us violating one of their rules. So we must be very careful, especially from now on. No more special requests to the radios in Munich, please. Alan briefly required the services of a friend of mine there, but I'm afraid that's the last of it."

"Why?" asked Taylor. "The radios could help us a lot."

"Because the management in Munich has issued a new order forbidding broadcast of anti-Russian tracts."

"How did they find out?"

"Someone was clumsy, or perhaps the Russians complained. How should I know? But the whistle has been blown, officially."

"What else can't we do?" asked Taylor.

"Oh, goodness," said Stone. He straightened his tie, making sure the ends were the same length. "Let me see. There was a phase of the operation I never mentioned to either of you, because it was too boring. It involved gathering data on Soviet nationalities. I wanted to collect underground religious and political material from Central Asia and the Caucasus, to give us a better idea of what was already happening there, so that our propaganda material would fit. But I'm afraid that won't be possible now."

"Why not?" asked Anna.

"The usual reason. Someone in the front office began asking questions."

"But what's wrong with that? Why shouldn't the front office know, if the project has the blessing of the White House?"

"Because it is a covert program, my dear. And because of its extreme sensitivity, it is being handled outside normal channels. As I told you, the line of authority is there, but it wiggles and waggles a bit. Some people know, and others—whom you might expect to know—do not. Do you follow me?"

"I guess so," said Anna.

"Good. Then let's get on with it." Stone rose from the couch and gestured to the showroom, now cluttered with boxes. "You have undoubtedly been wondering what the accumulating stack of debris in your office is all about. So I will give you a brief tour."

Stone led them to a stack of six boxes in the center of the room, next to Karpetland's modest display of Oriental rugs. He opened one of the boxes and took out a small pamphlet, five by seven inches. The title on the cover was in a Cyrillic script. He handed it to Taylor. "This is for you, Alan."

"What the hell is it?" asked Taylor.

"This, my friend, is a classic of sorts. It is a manifesto called 'Turkestan Under the Soviet Yoke,' written in 1935 by a man named Mustafa Chokay. I have taken the liberty of reprinting it in a format that could fit into the pocket of a Caspian Sea boatman or a shepherd in the wilderness of the Tien Shan mountains."

"How in God's name do you know about Mustafa Chokay?" asked Taylor.

"I just do. I am not entirely an idiot, you know."

"Chokay is Munzer's hero. George Washington and Abraham Lincoln rolled into one. Did you know that?"

"I'd heard that, yes."

"From who?"

"Let's not get bogged down in details. You're not the first case officer who's ever dealt with Munzer Ahmedov, for heaven's sake."

"So what do we do with the propaganda?" asked Taylor, pointing to the stack of boxes.

"I would like you and Mr. Munzer to take one box with you to Istanbul, where you should distribute copies in such a way that a few of them will come into the hands of your old friend Mr. Rawls. These will be your bait, these little tracts of anti-Soviet propaganda. I guarantee you that Rawls will swim toward them like a fish toward a floodlight."

"What do we do then?"

"That's the hard part, so obviously I intend to leave it to you. Rawls must discover Munzer, and he must imagine that he has stumbled across a Turkestani underground organization previously unknown to him. Munzer should make it known that his 'organization,' among its other activities, is smuggling thousands of these pamphlets into Turkestan. You figure out the details. I'm sure you're cleverer at this sort of thing than I am. My only advice is that you shouldn't stick things under Rawls's nose. Make him work. Let him assemble the puzzle himself. Otherwise he'll never believe it's real."

"What happens to the rest of the boxes?" asked Taylor. "You said we should send one to Istanbul, but there are five more."

"The rest, dear boy, will be going into the Soviet Union."

"How?"

"Through Afghanistan, most probably. We have friends in Pakistan who are quite active with the rebels there—have been for months. It shouldn't be any trouble to get them across the Afghan border. A box to Dushanbe, in Tajikistan. A box to Tashkent, in Uzbekistan. A box to Ashkhabad, in Turkmenistan. They tell me that the Afghan border is quite porous. And if the Soviets should catch our little smugglers on the way, so much the better."

"Slick."

"Thank you. Let's continue our tour, shall we?" Stone walked a few steps across the room to a smaller stack of boxes, next to the table that displayed the showroom's samples of wall-to-wall carpeting. As before, he opened a box and removed one of the books. It was in pamphlet format, like the first, but had on the cover, in Arabic calligraphy, the first sura of the Koran. Below that was the book's title, written in Cyrillicized Turkic.

"Here," said Stone, handing the pamphlet to Anna. "This one is for you. Read us the title, if you would."

" 'Guide to the Holy Places of Azerbaijan and the North Caucasus,' " read Anna.

"These are for your friend Mr. Ascari. It's a guide to Islamic shrines. Wondrous places! A rock in the village of Buzovna in Azerbaijan that supposedly contains the imprint of Ali's foot. Mount Shalbuz Dagh in Daghestan, from which the Prophet is supposed to have ascended into heaven on horseback, leaving behind a hoofprint. Glorious! The book also lists the tombs of various Sufi martyrs who died fighting the Soviets. It's a lovely little book. A better version of the one you gave to Ascari in Istanbul several months ago, which I gather he quite liked."

Anna nodded. "Mr. Ascari likes to think of himself as religious."

"Well then, he'll love this. We have five thousand of them. I would like you and Frank to arrange with Ascari to get these over the Iranian border into Azerbaijan. For a man of Mr. Ascari's commercial acumen, that shouldn't pose any great problem. And again, if he's caught with the goods, it may actually suit our purposes."

"How are you going to backstop it?" asked Anna.

"We'll be sending in, via a separate channel, some handbills calling for demonstrations at several of the shrines in Azerbaijan. We'll be doing the same thing in Uzbekistan, by the way, Alan."

"Will people actually go to the demonstrations?" she asked.

"A few, I hope. Enough to make it all look plausible."

"What will happen to them?"

"They will get arrested, I suspect."

"Does that bother you?"

"No. Should it?"

Before Anna could answer, Stone had opened the box again and was handing several dozen of the pamphlets to Taylor.

"Alan, you'll need some of these in Istanbul. Munzer might leave a few of them in places where they will be discovered by someone industrious."

"Good old Munzer," said Taylor. "He'll think he has died and gone to heaven."

"Now let's see. What else do I have for you?" Stone walked over to a group of smaller cartons set against the side wall. He opened a carton and removed two cassette tapes, packed in cheap plastic containers with Russian labels. "You'll love these," he said, handing one to each of his colleagues.

" 'Siberian Folk Chorus,' " said Anna, translating the label. "You've got to be kidding."

"Of course I'm kidding. They are actually tapes of a sermon by a Wahhabi mullah in Riyadh, preaching the downfall of Communism. Great stuff! Fire and brimstone. Sinners in the hands of an angry God. My Pakistani friends will take a thousand of these tapes in-country, via Afghanistan. I have a bunch more for Alan to take to Istanbul."

"Allahu-akhbar!" said Taylor. Anna cringed. The Islamic mania of the operation was beginning to bother her.

"The Korans!" exclaimed Stone. "I almost forgot! We have small-format Korans, from Pakistan. Thousands of them. We're actually piggybacking on our Saudi friends, who've been sending Korans into the Moslem republics covertly for the last few years. They do it mostly by giving the books to Moslem sailors, I gather, although I'm not sure I've ever met a Moslem sailor. In any event, the Saudis will be increasing shipments during the next several months. Back in Moscow, it's going to look like someone has declared a jihad!"

"Mr. Stone," interrupted Anna. "I'm sorry, but something is bothering me."

"What, again?" Stone didn't sound quite so genial this time.

"Why are we only working with Moslems in the Soviet Union? There are lots of other national groups that would like to be independent."

"Because those are the cards in hand, Miss Barnes. The game is being played at present with a Moslem deck. The Soviets are making our lives unpleasant in Iran, in Afghanistan, in Pakistan, in Turkey and from one miserable end of the Arab world to the other. And we are going to remind them that the Islamic card can be played in two directions."

"But it's a rotten game!"

"How so?" Stone put his hand to his ear.

"I don't want to give a sermon, but religious extremism is the problem in this part of the world, not the solution. Christians and Moslems have been at each other's throats for centuries. The reason is that each ethnic group always goes for a unilateral solution. Turkestani Moslems only care about Turkestan. Christian Armenians only care about Armenia. Nobody ever tries to bring them together."

"I'm sure you're right, my dear. It's a dreadful business, pogroms and all that. But I don't see what we can do about it."

"We can draw some Armenians into our operation. Or Georgians. But Armenians would be better."

"That's not realistic."

"Why not?"

"Because Uzbeks and Azeris don't like Armenians."

"So what? If we go against what's traditional, so much the better. That will frighten the Soviets even more."

"Why would it do that?" asked Stone, his eyes brightening. He was willing to consider anything that would give the Soviets heartburn.

"Because Moscow's biggest fear is that someday these ethnic groups will all get together and start shooting Russians. That's why the KGB works so hard to keep them suspicious of each other. The Ottomans were the same way. Divide and rule. If you really want to scare the daylights out of Moscow Center, then make them think there is an underground movement that links Armenians and Azeris."

"What do you have in mind?"

"Re-create the golden age, before 1914. Back when all the people in that part of the world were rising together against their imperial masters. It's not impossible. There are historical precedents."

"It sounds so . . . utopian." Stone said the last word as if it had a sour taste.

"What's wrong with that? If we're going to create an imaginary network, why not make it perfect? And as I said, that's the best way to give the Russians a heart attack."

"An appealing thought. But it's late in the day to add something new to our kit, I'm afraid. Why don't we save this for another time."

"There won't be another time."

Stone shook his head, like a bemused father. He looked at his watch. "We've got other matters to deal with. Do you really care about this?"

"Yes, sir. I've been worrying about this problem, one way or another, for nearly ten years. It matters to me. And I know what I'm doing."

"Very well," said Stone, tiring of the discussion. "Suppose we make you head of the Armenia desk? Would you like that?"

"What would it mean?"

"It means that if you can come up with a plausible way to

draw an Armenian into our little charade, then I will try to accommodate you. Is that fair enough?"

"I guess so."

"Any objections, Alan?"

"Nope."

"How will I find names of Armenians we could try to recruit."

"I'll have Marjorie get you traces on any live prospects that are in the registry. We'll pull their 201 files and get you the vital statistics. It will take several weeks. You can deal with it when you get back from Athens. Is that agreeable?"

"Fine," said Anna. She felt that she had won at least a temporary victory, a chance to paint on her own canvas, rather than simply carry out Stone's design. She excused herself and went to the ladies' room.

"Alan," said Stone, when she was out of earshot. "I wonder if you could stop by my house this evening."

"Sure. What for?"

"A little business I'd like to discuss privately with you."

"What's the address?"

Stone wrote out his address on N Street in Georgetown and handed it to Taylor. "Come around seven. Cocktail time."

Anna returned, still smiling from ear to ear. She sat down on the couch and put her feet up on the coffee table—a first.

"I have one more little surprise for the two of you, and then I must go," said Stone.

"Uh-oh," said Anna.

"Not to worry. You'll like this one. I've been thinking about it for weeks."

"Fire away."

"Alan, do you remember the Ottoman chair purchased by the Soviet consul general in Istanbul, into which you and the TSD man from Athens inserted the bug?"

"Of course I do. How could I forget that stupid fucking chair? What a waste of time."

"Now, now. Don't be so harsh. The chair helped bring us together. But the consult general sent it home, as I remember. To Alma-Ata."

"Correct. He sent it to the party first secretary in Kazakhstan as baksheesh."

"And so you forgot about it."

"Sure. What could we do? The transmitter only broadcast a half mile. And who really cares what the party first secretary in Alma-Ata has to say?"

"We do," said Stone. "Or at least we might want people to think we do. We might very well want people to think that a covert operation in Central Asia is so extensive that the Central Intelligence Agency has taken the trouble to install a very sophisticated bug in the office of the Kazakh party leader. And if people wonder how it got there—and that puts the Soviet consul general in Istanbul and his wife under a cloud—then we've accomplished a good day's work."

"That's diabolical," said Taylor.

"You flatter me. In any event, my friends, this is how I propose to terminate our piece of theater. In a few months, at an appropriate moment, we'll find a way for the KGB to discover the bug in Alma-Ata. We'll let them do the rest of the work for us, and sit back and watch the fun."

"From a safe distance, I trust," said Anna.

"Of course, my dear," said Stone. "I wouldn't have it any other way."

That evening, Taylor made the slow passage down Wisconsin Avenue's corridor of traffic lights in the white Karpetland van. He parked several blocks from Stone's house and walked the rest of the way. When he reached the address he stopped and studied the house. It was an architectural equivalent of Stone himself: an elegant red brick building, four stories tall, built at least two hundred years ago but lovingly maintained, as if in defiance of the passage of time. Taylor peered inside the leaded-glass window. There was an elegant front parlor, decorated with antique furniture. Down the hall, in what looked to be the study, sat Stone in a leather easy chair. Taylor rang the bell, and up padded the old man.

"Do come in," he said. He was wearing a cardigan sweater and smoking a cigar. He escorted Taylor back to his book-lined study, which overlooked a deep garden. When they were seated, Stone offered his guest a cigar, which Taylor eagerly accepted. It was a Davidoff No. 1, smuggled in by one of Stone's legion of friends.

"Miss Barnes is a marvelous woman, isn't she?" asked Stone as Taylor was lighting his cigar.

"Absolutely," said Taylor. "Great kid."

"And she's doing extraordinarily well, wouldn't you say, given how little real experience she's had?"

"Yup. She's hit the ground running."

"Do you think she's entirely comfortable with the operation? I wondered a bit, listening to some of her comments today."

"She's okay. She had a couple of problems, but once she got them off her chest, she seemed to lighten up. I wouldn't worry about her. She's a tough cookie. She's not going to bail out on you now."

"I'm glad to hear you say that," said Stone. "Certainly she's a strong-minded woman, with ideas of her own about how things should be done. But perhaps that's all to the good."

"All to the good, definitely," agreed Taylor. What's this all about? he was wondering. But Stone was, in his fashion, getting around to the point.

"What did you think about her plea for Christian-Moslem amity?"

"It's harmless," said Taylor. "I wouldn't worry about it. It might even be a good idea."

"One advantage is that it will keep her occupied, which will leave you free to do other things."

Taylor cocked his head. "Such as?"

"How shall I put this? In managing this operation, Alan, you shouldn't feel limited to the particular items that we discussed today."

"I'm not sure I follow you, Mr. Stone."

"I mean you don't have to limit yourself to the things that I sent over to Karpetland. The books and pamphlets and cassettes. You can try other things with Munzer as well, if you think it makes sense."

"Like what?" Taylor suspected that Stone was about to open a new door in the inner chamber, but he hadn't a clue where it led.

"The sky's the limit, really. In putting together this imaginary underground network, you can use whatever materials a real underground would use."

"Not just pamphlets and cassettes, but other things?"

"Yes, other things."

Taylor finally began to understand. "Like guns," he said.

"Yes. Like guns. And other things."

"Explosives?"

"Yes, indeed, surely. That would be appropriate for an underground organization that wanted to have an impact in Central Asia."

Taylor examined his nails for a moment, giving himself time to think. He was an impulsive man, but he wasn't a fool. And he knew Stone was proposing something extraordinary, even by the standards of his inner circle.

"Sounds like you're declaring war," he said eventually.

"I'm turning up the heat," replied Stone. "I'm tired of the Cold War, to tell you the truth. At this rate it's going to last forever."

Taylor studied Stone's face. He knew enough about how the government worked to understand that this part of the operation wasn't authorized by anybody, anywhere.

"What happens if we get caught?" he asked.

"A flap. But we won't get caught."

"Right. But suppose we do."

"Trust me," said Stone. "I have more friends in this city than any of the politicians. You won't suffer for it, unless your greatest ambition in life is to become a GS-18 before you're fifty. That I cannot promise you."

Stone knew his man. Just as there are some adolescent boys who can never refuse a dare, no matter how foolhardy, there are some middle-aged men who would rather die than acknowledge they have reached that stage of life. And with Stone's last remark, Taylor lost whatever remaining inhibitions he still had about the project. He leaned toward Stone.

"So how would we go about it, assuming it made sense?"

"You and Munzer could drop some hints in Istanbul that this Central Asian network isn't just a bunch of religious fanatics, that it also has a military wing. And I would follow up from here."

"Hot stuff."

"Very hot," agreed Stone.

"Who would do the shipping?"

"We'd handle some of it through Pakistan, have Frank Hoffman do the rest with this Ascari fellow. But it seemed to me, as we were talking today, that Miss Barnes might not feel entirely comfortable with this part of the operation."

"So you'd like me to do it?"

"Yes. That's right. I thought it might make sense for you to go see Frank in Athens, after he has met with Miss Barnes. Would that be possible?"

"I'd be screwing Anna. It's her case."

"Oh, that's all right," said Stone with a wink. "You're getting used to that, aren't you?"

Taylor was going to protest. Stone could blow up half of Central Asia if he wanted, but snooping into Taylor's love life was going too far. And it worried Taylor, too, in a vague sort of way, that Anna seemed to have moved in Stone's mind from being part of "the team" to some other, indeterminate status. He wanted to say something, at least to register his concern. But just then Stone gave him another conspiratorial wink and handed him a snifter of fine old brandy.

Anna stayed up late that night waiting for Taylor. They hadn't set a formal time to meet. Taylor had mumbled something about having a drink with a friend, and Anna had said she would see him when he got back. Reliability about such matters had never been a quality Anna valued much in men. It was such an ordinary, middle-class virtue. Solid, reliable, on time. It was one step away from boring. Dentists had to be reliable. Bankers had to be reliable. Lawyers had to be reliable. Reliability was a turnoff. The men Anna had fancied were the would-be poets and adventurers, the ones with frayed shirt collars and a hint of self-destructive recklessness in their souls. They didn't have time to be on time.

But now that she had actually found such a man, Anna wondered if she shouldn't revise her views. Excessive tidiness wasn't sexy in a man, it was true; but neither was sloppiness. Punctuality wasn't sexy, but neither was lateness. And there was nothing sexy at all about staying up till midnight in your motel room waiting for Romeo to come home.

Taylor finally returned at twelve-thirty, thoroughly looped, talking a blue streak about a scheme he'd hatched with Stone over late-night brandies to go boar hunting in eastern Anatolia. He gave Anna a wet kiss on the mouth and put his big hands on her breasts, and it appeared that somehow, despite all the booze, he intended to make love to her. But when they were nestled together in bed, and Anna was waiting for him to caress her, she realized that he had fallen sound asleep.

31

◆

IT WAS HIGH SUMMER WHEN ALAN TAYLOR RETURNED TO ISTANbul. The city was painted in the bright haze of July; the Sea of Marmara shimmered beneath his approaching airplane like a still salt lake. Coming in from the airport, Taylor asked the embassy driver to let him out at the ferry terminal at Eminonu, on Seraglio Point just below Topkapi Palace. It was Taylor's favorite spot in Istanbul—perhaps on the planet—capturing in a few hundred square yards the unruly human comedy: the barking chorus of vendors selling lottery tickets and bread; the arterial flow of travelers surging aboard the afternoon ferries to Uskudar and Besiktas; the churning black water beneath the ferries as they jostled offshore, belching smoke, waiting to dock; and just across the Golden Horn, the steep hill of old Pera, capped now with neon signs advertising Turkish banks and Japanese televisions. If there is a black hole on Earth, a place into which the matter of the universe is irresistibly drawn, thence to disappear into oblivion and eternity, it is surely the ferry dock at Eminonu.

Taylor moved through the crowd with the easy grace of a fish thrown back into his favorite pond. He crossed the Galata Bridge, passing the restaurants strung along the walkway below the main span, filling his nostrils with the smell of fresh fish cooking on the makeshift charcoal grills. The narrow walkway was filled with people pushing in both directions, and Taylor lost himself in the eastward flow, emerging a few minutes later on the Pera side. He began climbing the hill, still borne along by the human tide, joining with the Turks as they pressed their faces against the windows of small shops selling radios, batteries, plumbing fixtures, linoleum tiles, electrical switches, power drills, videocassette recorders—a veritable Noah's Ark of commerce arrayed item by item, shop by shop. Thinner now, the crowd moved up the last steep incline, where the younger men quickened their pace and turned toward Giraffe Street and the red-light district. By the top of the hill, the human stream had dispersed. Taylor walked alone the rest of the way to the consulate, refreshed by his reimmersion in the Orient, savoring the sense of anonymity and surrender that is the true religion of the East.

Taylor's colleagues were glad to see him back at the office, all except the deputy chief of base, who had a taste for bureaucracy and had actually enjoyed doing the paperwork while Taylor was away. He seemed worried that Taylor might remove these comfortable manacles of responsibility from him. Taylor summoned his deputy for a brief meeting in the bubble and reassured him that his own special assignment would be continuing for several more months, which meant that the D-COB could remain as A-COB. That pleased him immensely. He turned over to Taylor a neat stack of papers he had been saving, most of them not worth reading. On top of the stack was an invitation to Stanley Timmons's farewell party, which would be held in several weeks at the Ankara Golf Club.

Munzer Ahmedov arrived the following day from New York and went directly to an apartment in Aksaray, whose address and key Taylor had provided. It was an out-of-the-way place, down a dusty side street off the Ataturk Boulevard. The CIA base in Istanbul had acquired it a decade ago as a safe house but had used it sparingly in recent years because of fears that the location had been blown. That didn't matter so much in Munzer's case; indeed, allowing interested parties to guess at his links to the agency was part of the game.

Taylor had drilled Munzer on arrangements before he left America. They would meet at the apartment in Aksaray at ten o'clock the morning after Munzer arrived and at regular intervals thereafter, at times and places Taylor would specify. If

Munzer needed to contact Taylor urgently, he should go to a pay phone, call Taylor's home in Arnavutkoy, and leave a message on the answering machine that Mr. Sukru was calling and the rug was ready to be picked up. In that case, Taylor would meet him the next morning in the gardens of the Sultanahmet mosque. In a real emergency, Taylor could receive telephone calls at the consulate. And Munzer could always crash the American compound. He was, after all, an American citizen.

Munzer's job in Istanbul, Taylor advised, would be to set up the headquarters for a new Turkestani independence movement. The Uzbek came prepared. He brought with him from New York his framed portrait of Mustafa Chokay and a similar portrait of Ali Merdan Topcubasi, one of the leaders of the Moslem rebels who fought the Red Army in the 1920s. Munzer hung these icons on the wall of his new living room the night he arrived. He also displayed a large map he had brought from home, a sort of Turkestani version of the famous Saul Steinberg cartoon that shows the world ending just the other side of the Hudson River from Manhattan. In this case, it was a map of Central Asia that showed a vast expanse labeled Turkestan, dwarfing the neighboring regions of Russia and China. The final item decorating Munzer's new headquarters was the strangest. It was a favorite quotation from a Naqshbandi sheikh from the North Caucasus named Uzun Haji, who had fought fanatically against the Russians—both sides, Red and White—in the first years after the Revolution. The quotation, written in the Arabic of the Koran, read: "I am weaving a rope to hang engineers, students and in general all those who write from left to right."

Taylor knocked on the door at ten the next morning. "Is Mr. Yakub there?" he asked, following the prearranged script.

"No, this his brother," came the almost grammatical reply.

Taylor waited a few moments, trying to remember if there was another phrase in the recognition code. He didn't think so, but he had thrown away the index card on which the dialogue was written. He knocked on the door again. Still it didn't budge.

"Open the door, please," he said gently. He could hear the

rustle of a human body on the other side of the portal, but it stayed closed.

"Open the goddam door."

Munzer opened the door a crack, just enough to see that it was Taylor, who quickly entered the apartment and closed the door behind him.

The Uzbek had a look of reproach on his round face. "You not say password," he chided.

"What did I forget?"

"You forget to say at end: 'May I come in?' "

"Oh shit. Was I supposed to say that?"

"Yes, my friend. I say: 'No, this his brother,' then you say: 'May I come in?' Then I open door. You forget, maybe."

"Maybe," said Taylor. "But it doesn't matter. Here we are. It's nice to see you in Istanbul. I'm glad you arrived safely." He shook Munzer's hand.

"Welcome to house of Munzer," said the Uzbek. With a flourish, he ushered Taylor into the living room, newly hung with posters and portraits. "Welcome also to new headquarters of Turkestani Liberation Front."

"Very nice," said Taylor, surveying the room. He nodded respectfully toward the portraits of Mustafa Chokay and Ali Merdan Topcubasi, and then pointed to the quotation from Uzun Haji. "That looks interesting. What does it say?"

"Ah, that," said Munzer, smiling warily in a way that Taylor would have recognized—had he known him better—meant he was about to tell a lie. "It says: 'Long live heroic struggle of Turkestani peoples.' "

"Bravo."

"Come, Mr. Goode. Sit down, please, you are my guest. I do not have tea or coffee, sorry. You like water maybe? Or I go out and buy coffee? Or cigarettes?"

"I'm fine," said Taylor, smiling at Munzer's earnest attempt at hospitality. "We have business to do."

"Yes. Okay. Munzer is ready."

"Let's start by setting the time and place for our next meeting. That way, if we have to break off suddenly, we'll know how to make contact."

Munzer nodded.

"Our next meeting will be in three days. We'll meet at the

same time, ten o'clock, in Yildiz Park. You know where that is?"

"Yeah, sure. I find."

"I'll be waiting for you at the fountain above the entrance. If I have my arms crossed when you see me, like this"— Taylor folded his arms—"that means there's a problem, I'm being followed or something, and you shouldn't approach me. You should come back to the same place the next day, an hour later. Got that?"

"No problems. Munzer remember this spy talk from before."

"And on your way there, check to make sure you aren't being followed," said Taylor. He omitted the usual admonition not to be too obvious in watching your tail. In this case, what did it matter?

Munzer nodded gravely. "Okay, okay."

"Are you comfortable here?"

"Oh yes!"

"Did you find someone to take care of your store in Queens while you're gone?"

"My sons. One son is engineer. He take leave. One son study to be lawyer. He take vacation. One son in medical school. I let him stay. Business is doing. No problems."

"Good. Now I'd like to talk to you about your assignment."

"I am ready for anything. Climb mountains, swim Black Sea. Whatever you say. This is big chance to help my dear peoples."

"Glad to hear it. But right now, all I want you to do is establish contact with some of your old Turkestani friends here in Istanbul. Can you do that?"

"Yes. Okay."

"Who will you go see?"

"Editor of *Great Turkestan* magazine is friend of Munzer from old days. His name Hasan Khojaev. Maybe I go see him?"

"Is he trustworthy?"

"Of course. He friend of Munzer's. What I can tell him about new Turkestani movement, please?"

"Not much for the time being," said Taylor. He knew that was impossible. Munzer would say something to the magazine editor. But this way, it would probably come out mumbled and garbled, which was about right for now.

"I be careful," said Munzer.

Taylor reached into his briefcase and removed several copies of the Mustafa Chokay pamphlet that Stone had prepared back in Washington.

"Give your friend Khojaev some of these," he said, handing Munzer the copies of "Turkestan Under the Soviet Yoke."

"Allah! What is this?" asked Munzer, turning the pages.

"Some of our material. Your material now."

"This is Mustafa Chokay book! You make this for Munzer?" Taylor nodded.

"Show these to the editor, Khojaev, and to any other friends you trust, and see what they think."

"I show to Kirdarov and Nemir Bey. These two honest peoples. No bullshit."

"Fine. Whatever you say."

"What I tell them about Mustafa Chokay book?"

"You can tell them there are lots more of these on their way into the Soviet Union."

"Where from I tell them, please?"

"From Riyadh," said Taylor with a wink.

"Yes, okay. Riyadh," said Munzer, trying to wink back at Taylor. His eyes were so narrow it looked more like a squint.

"That's enough for now," said Taylor. "You get settled and talk to your friends, and I'll see you in three days in Yildiz Park."

On his way back from Munzer's apartment, Taylor drove down Yeniceriler Street. He studied the apartment on the third floor, right-hand side, looking for signs of life. But there was nothing. No lights, no movement, no sign that anyone had ever lived there at all.

Taylor's next stop was to see Sonia—the Circassian beauty who sang Oriental love songs at Omar's place. She was a better bet than Omar himself, who was an estimable man but talked too much. Sonia was smart, she was discreet, and best of all she had once been in love with Taylor, and might be still. He called her that afternoon and asked if he could stop by her apartment in Cihangir. She was surprised, and pleased.

Taylor kissed Sonia on the lips when she answered the door. It seemed spontaneous, like most of Taylor's calculated gestures. Sonia looked more beautiful than he had remembered. She was a slender woman, light as a feather, so delicate that she seemed to float a few inches off the floor. No wonder the Circassians had been the preferred bedmates of the Ottoman sultans for four hundred years. They were reputed, in the East, to be the most beautiful women in the world. Taylor had broken off with Sonia when he realized he was becoming infatuated with her, back in that distant other lifetime before his wife packed up and left Istanbul, when his only stipulation for a love affair was that nothing serious should come of it.

"I need your help," said Taylor when he was seated on Sonia's couch with a glass of vodka in his hand. During their affair, he had spent many happy, boozy hours drinking vodka and looking out her window at the ceaseless transit of boats and people along the Golden Horn.

"I hope you do not want me to escort another one of your American friends."

Taylor shook his head.

"I would do it if you asked me to, but I hope you won't."

"Not this time. I need something much simpler. An Uzbek friend of mine has just arrived in Istanbul. He's a nice old guy, loves to reminisce about the old country. He's bound to show up at Omar's one of these nights. When he comes, take good care of him. Treat him like someone special. You'll like him. His name is Munzer."

"He is a friend of yours?"

"Yes. A special friend. He's a freedom fighter."

"Okay, my darling. But this is too simple. What else do you want?" The light was streaming in through the window, illuminating her face so that she looked like a Byzantine angel.

"Nothing," said Taylor.

"Please want something. I would like to make you happy."

Taylor shook his head. It hurt to hold back from her. He could almost feel that slim feather of a body in his arms as he carried her to bed.

"Why do you stay away from me?" she asked quietly.

"Because," said Taylor.

"Why because?"

"Because I like you, and I don't want to hurt you."

Sonia closed her eyes. It was as close as she would ever get to a declaration of love from Taylor. He leaned forward. Not toward Sonia, but toward his briefcase. He took out a picture of Munzer and showed it to her.

"This is a picture of my friend. If he goes to Omar's, treat him nice. But don't tell anyone he's my friend."

Taylor put his finger to his lips. Sonia did the same.

"Shhhh," they said together. Taylor left a few minutes later. This time he kissed her on the cheek.

Taylor sent a cable to headquarters late that afternoon, asking for traces on one Hasan Khojaev, editor of *Great Turkestan* magazine. The response came back late the next day. A 201 file had been opened for a man with that name and description twenty-two years ago, but it had been closed a month later because of evidence that he had occasional contacts with Turkish intelligence officers and perhaps others. Hasan Khojaev seemed to be a peddler, a man who worked hard to stay in touch with everyone and sell off small pieces of what he knew. He sounded perfect.

Munzer showed up on schedule three days later at Yildiz Park. He was wearing black-framed sunglasses, apparently in the belief that they would make him less conspicuous. In fact, they made him look like Mr. Potato-Head. Munzer took off the sunglasses when they sat down on a park bench, and Taylor could see that there was a glint of curiosity and suspicion in his eye.

"Business first," said Taylor. "Our next meeting will be on Tuesday, five days from now. Got that? Next Tuesday. We'll meet at two p.m. at the ferry dock at Kadikoy, on the Asian side. I'll give you the same signal if there's danger, with the same fallback plan. Okay?"

"Munzer will write this down, please," he said. He took out a pen and carefully noted: Tuesday, Kadikoy, two o'clock. Taylor should have made him memorize it, but he suspected that Munzer might actually forget it without a written reminder.

"So how's it going?" asked Taylor when Munzer had finished writing.

"Okay, okay. I show Mustafa Chokay book to friends and they very happy. They say thank you, Mr. Munzer, our brother. This book must be part of big plan."

"What big plan?"

"That is Munzer question. Listen, Mr. Goode, you not pull Munzer's leg, okay?"

"What are you talking about?"

"You sure you tell Munzer everything?" He leaned over and gave Taylor a playful tap on the shoulder.

"Everything you need to know. Why? What's bothering you?"

"I ask you question, okay? You not have to answer, but maybe you answer."

"All right."

"Do you have CIA team in Istanbul?"

"Team? What do you mean?"

"Maybe another American man working with you?"

"Why do you ask?" Taylor tried not to smile, not to blink, not to hint at any particular interest in this subject.

"Because my friend Khojaev say another American man has been talking to Turkestani peoples in Istanbul sometimes."

"What about?"

"Free Turkestan. He is always talking about Free Turkestan. So I think maybe he is working with you."

"What does he look like, this American?"

"Khojaev say he is tall man, blond man."

"It's possible. I'll be honest, Mr. Ahmedov. There are other people working on this project, but I don't know all of them. Where is this other American now?"

"Khojaev say he gone now."

Oh shit, thought Taylor. "Did Khojaev say whether he would be coming back?"

"Maybe he come back. Khojaev not sure."

"Did Khojaev like him?"

"Khojaev never meet him. His friend Mr. Abdallah from Tashkent meet him, and he tell Khojaev about it. He say this American man talk all about freedom and independence of Turkestani peoples, talk about big help from America, but pssst, nothing. Sound to Munzer like old days, but I know from my friend Mr. Goode these is new days."

"Listen, Munzer," said Taylor confidentially. "I wish I could tell you all the details, but I can't. Some I don't even know myself. You just have to trust me."

"Yeah. Okay. Trust."

"Good. It will all work out. Believe me."

"So what should Munzer do now? Khojaev say Munzer should talk to other American man when he come back. But Khojaev not know Munzer already working with Mr. Goode."

"That's right, and don't tell him. Let me know when the other American comes back, and maybe we'll have you meet him."

"Okay. Munzer understand spy business. Nobody knows nothing."

"Right," said Taylor. "Forget this other stuff for now. I have something important I want you to do. For me."

"Munzer is ready."

Taylor reached into his pocket and removed a well-worn handbill, printed in the Cyrillic characters of Uzbek Turkish. He handed it to Munzer.

"What is this, please?"

"It's a leaflet, announcing a demonstration at a Sufi shrine outside Tashkent in ten days. One of our people in Moscow picked it up during a trip down there and sent out a copy."

"Allah! A demonstration? Uzbek people very brave, but this is too dangerous. What it means, please?"

"We're not sure. If it's for real, we should try to hook up with it. Ask around, will you? See if anyone in the émigré community knows anything about it. Give me a report the next time we meet."

Munzer folded the handbill carefully—lovingly—and put it in his pocket, next to his heart.

Where the hell was Rawls? Taylor drove again that night by his old apartment in Beyazit. The apartment was still dark and apparently empty. Taylor returned during the next few days to make sure, but there was still no sign of him. Maybe he had changed apartments. Maybe he had left Istanbul for good. All Taylor could do was put more chum in the water and wait for something to bite.

* * *

"Nobody know nothing about no demonstration in Tashkent," reported Munzer the following Tuesday. He had shed the sunglasses and was wearing a traditional Uzbek cap, embroidered in black and white. It rested on his head like a box top.

"That's too bad," said Taylor.

"No. Is good."

"Why? I want some information about these people in Tashkent, so we can decide what to do."

"No, no. Up-down side you have. If people talk in Istanbul, then no good. Must be phony. If nobody know, then maybe this real thing. Nobody here know nothing, so Munzer is happy. You tell friends maybe this demonstration by real Moslem men in Tashkent."

They walked slowly down the street, away from the Kadikoy dock. Just north of them was the Haydarpasa train station, the old gateway to Asia. Across the way stood a small caravan of buses, waiting to take travelers to the teeming suburbs of the Asian side; they belched out noise and smoke even while they were idling. And darting in every direction were the *dolmus* group taxis, most of them lovingly maintained old Buicks and Chevys, their rearview mirrors bearing colorful totems to keep away the evil eye. Munzer looked entirely at home amidst this scene; a man of Asia, walking toward home with each step. Taylor strode along with him, carrying a plastic bag in one hand.

"Listen, Munzer," said Taylor. "You're a Sufi brother, aren't you?"

"You know I am, so why you ask?"

"You're a Naqshbandi, right?"

"I am sorry. This for me is something not for talking about. You have secret things. So does Munzer."

"They're strong in Central Asia, aren't they? The Sufi brotherhoods, I mean."

"The strongest. They are the only real Islam. Official mosque is bullshit, run by KGB. Only true Islam is underground, with the *tariqat*. But you ask somebody else about these things. Munzer not talking."

"Okay, but one more question. Why are they so strong?"

"Because they are real brotherhood. Closed to outsiders. Never tell secrets. If Naqshbandi find out a member is KGB informer, that man is finished. No one speak to him. No one marry his daughters. He is alone. Better he should be dead. Same thing if member of brotherhood tells secrets to CIA, my friend, so you don't ask Munzer no more questions about *tariqat.*"

"Sorry. I only brought it up because I want to give you something that would interest your Naqshbandi brothers."

"What you talking about, please?"

Taylor reached into the plastic bag he had been carrying, pulled out a cassette tape, and handed it to Munzer. "This is for you. I have lots more of them. Thousands of them."

Munzer read the Russian label: "Siberian Folk Chorus." He snorted. "What I Need this for?"

"It's not the Siberian Folk Chorus, Munzer. It's a sermon from a Naqshbandi sheikh in Saudi Arabia. He talks about the duty of all Moslems, especially members of the Naqshbandi brotherhood, to liberate Samarkand and Bukhara and Ferghana from the atheists."

Munzer looked at the tape carefully, as if he expected to see a little sheikh inside. "You have more of these?"

"Thousands of them."

"Munzer can take this and listen to it, please?"

"Sure. Take a bunch of them. Your friends can listen, too."

"What you do with these?"

"We plan to send them where they will do some good. To Samarkand and Bukhara and Ferghana."

"You getting serious now, my friend."

"Yes," said Taylor. "We're getting serious."

32

FRANK HOFFMAN SAT LIKE A FIREPLUG ON THE COUCH OF ANNA Barnes's hotel room in Athens, waiting for Ali Ascari to show up. Anna had taken a suite at the St. George this time, a smaller and less conspicuous hotel above Syntagma Square. The room was at once dark and noisy, thanks to Hoffman's precautions. He had swept the room carefully for bugs and then, for good measure, he had unplugged the television and the lights, unscrewed the mouthpiece of the telephone to remove the speaker, and turned on a small portable noise machine. These prudential measures had given the room an otherworldly feel, somber and shadowy without the electric lights, echoing with unintelligible white noise.

Anna couldn't quite imagine it, but Hoffman seemed nervous. He was fidgeting under his coat with the two revolvers that were parked below his armpits, checking to make sure that they were still there. With his guns in place, Anna had noticed, Hoffman walked in a peculiar way, swinging both arms forward together at the same time, rather than alternating them. Perhaps he wanted to be able to draw both pistols at once.

Hoffman stopped fiddling with his guns after a while and began munching chocolate-covered peanuts, popping them into his mouth one at a time from a bag in his coat pocket. In five minutes he consumed the entire pack and reached into his attaché case for another. He had a half dozen more packs lined up in a row, in the compartment usually reserved for pens and pencils. He opened a new one and resumed munching.

At last there was a knock at the door.

"Is this Miss Bigelow's room?" asked a singsong nasal voice.

"You are early," replied Anna. Actually he was late, but that was the recognition code.

Anna opened the door and in walked Ali Ascari, wobbling his head ever so slightly. He was dressed soberly for the occasion, in a pinstripe suit with wide lapels and a striped tie that was nearly six inches across at the bottom. His mullah's beard looked as woolly as ever.

"Hello, nice lady," he said to Anna, standing on tiptoes and clicking his heels.

Hoffman rose from the couch and walked toward the Iranian, swinging his arms in that odd, two-handed gait.

"This is Mr. Block," said Anna. "He's the man I mentioned to you."

"Very nice to be meeting you, Mr. Block," said Ascari, extending a limp hand.

"Sit down," said Hoffman.

"Okay. I am happy to sit down."

Hoffman grunted and sat back down on the sofa.

"You are a CIA man, Mr. Block?"

"No comment."

"This nice lady, Miss James, tell me that next time I will be seeing CIA man. So I think you must be him."

"Listen, my friend," said Hoffman. "Let's get something straight before we go any further. I ask the questions. You answer them. Got it? Otherwise, take a walk."

"Okay," said Ascari warily. "You sound like CIA man. That is good enough for Ali Ascari."

"Drop it."

"Okay. No problem."

"You got a passport, so I can make sure you're who you say you are?"

"For sure. Not just one."

"Give them to me."

Ascari reached into the pocket of his suit coat and handed his Iranian passport to Hoffman.

"Where's the other one?"

The Iranian pulled the Spanish passport from his side pocket and handed it over.

"Cut the bullshit," barked Hoffman. "Where's the Greek passport?"

"No problem," said Ascari with a little smile and a wobble of the head. He stood up and removed the third document from the back pocket of his trousers.

"Thanks," said Hoffman. He laid the passports on the coffee table in a neat stack, with the Greek one on top. "I'll look at these later."

Anna spoke up. "I have told Mr. Block about our previous meetings, Mr. Ascari. I've told him every detail, including your appalling behavior in Istanbul. Mr. Block was not amused."

"Nope," said Hoffman. "To be honest, you sound to me like a real asshole."

"Please, Mr. Block," said Ascari. "I do not like bad languages."

"Is that right? Well, as we say in the U.S. of A., tough shit."

Ascari looked offended. "I am not liking this conversation. Maybe I leave now."

"Stay a while. I'm just beginning to relax."

"I am not so relaxing." He was looking over his shoulder to the door.

"Hey, lighten up. Take your coat off. It's a little hot in here, don't you think, Miss James? Maybe I'll take off my coat, too."

Hoffman stood up and slowly removed his suit coat, a sleeve at a time, so that one snub-nosed revolver became visible, and then the other. Ascari shook his head and took a deep breath. Now he looked genuinely frightened.

"Wait a minute, please," said Ascari, extending his arms plaintively. "There is big mistake here. I am very sorry for what happen in Istanbul. You want me to apologize? So I apologize. No problem. Okay?" He had a phony let's-be-friends smile on his face.

"Thank you," said Anna coldly. "But it's a little late."

"Save your apologies, pal," growled Hoffman. "Because I honestly don't give a shit whether you're sorry. I'm only interested in one thing from you."

"What is that?"

"My friend Miss James says you have some friends who are shipping guns across the Iranian border into Azerbaijan. Is that right?"

"Yes. I tell that to nice lady."

"If you say 'nice lady' one more time, I'm going to cut your dick off and stuff it down your throat. So stop saying it! It bothers me."

Ascari reached protectively for his crotch. "Very sorry. Please."

"Now, tell us about the guns."

"What you want to know?"

"Everything."

"We buy guns. We take them across border. We leave them in Azerbaijan. That is it."

"I want the details, dipshit."

"Excuse me, please?"

"I said I want the fucking details."

"What is in this for Ali?" asked Ascari, sensing that the eagerness of this crazed American for information might give him some momentary bargaining leverage.

"Money," answered Hoffman.

"How much?"

"That depends on whether you deliver. If you do, a lot."

"What does that mean?"

"Fuck you. You know what 'a lot' means."

"Maybe I not interested."

"Oh, you're interested. You just want to jerk me around. But you gotta understand, my friend, I've been dealing with assholes like you for most of my life."

The Iranian crossed his arms. "Ali not so sure he want to do business with you."

"Don't push your luck," said Hoffman. He scooped up the Greek passport from the table and leaned toward the telephone. He quickly screwed the mouthpiece back on and began dialing.

"Hey. What you doing?"

"I'm calling a Greek friend of mine at the Ministry of the Interior. He'll be mighty interested to know that an Iranian con man is traveling on a phony Greek passport."

"You are bluffing."

"Oh yeah?" said Hoffman. "Try me." He held up the phone so Ascari could hear it ringing. A voice answered, speaking Greek.

"Hello, Mikos? This is Frank. I've run across something that might interest you."

Ascari, convinced now that Hoffman was not bluffing, stood up suddenly and looked as if he might bolt for the door. Anna moved to block his exit, but Hoffman was quicker. He put one hand over the phone and removed a pistol from its shoulder holster with the other.

"Sit down, asshole," he said. Ascari backed down into his chair, and Hoffman resumed his conversation.

"Mikos, you still there? Here's the deal. I've heard about a guy who's traveling on a false Greek passport. He sounds like a pretty suspicious character. Gunrunning, smuggling. That sort of thing."

Ascari was making frantic hand motions, but Hoffman ignored him for the moment.

"That's right. A phony Greek passport. . . . No, I don't know where he got it. . . . What's his name?"

He looked at Ascari.

"Stop!" whispered the Iranian. "No more bullshit."

Hoffman gave him a wink, and then resumed the conversation. "Sorry, Mikos, but I don't know the guy's name yet. That's my problem. I just wanted to know if you'd be interested. If I find out, I'll get back to you right away. Okay? . . . Right. Bye. *Ciao.*" He hung up the phone.

"No more fucking around, please," said Hoffman. "Because as you have just discovered, I have got you firmly by the balls. And I would take genuine, personal pleasure in turning you over to the Greek police."

"We be friends, please," said Ascari. "I play ball game." He looked genuinely shaken.

"Hey, listen," said Hoffman, reaching over and putting a meaty hand on Ascari's shoulder. "I'm not really a prick. I just act like one sometimes. You'll like me when you get to know me better."

"Will you put gun away now, please?"

"Sorry. I forgot." Hoffman returned the pistol to its holster. Ascari relaxed slightly. "Thank you. You worry Ali a little bit. I thought CIA men play by rules, but you not playing by rules."

"You got it. I have one big advantage over my colleagues, which is that I'm crazy. I don't give a shit about the rules. So watch it."

"I hear you. For sure."

"Good. So let's start again, about the guns."

"Yes. I am ready to talk."

"Honey," said Hoffman, turning to Anna. "Leave us alone for a while, would you? This next part is agency business."

Anna nodded. Her departure was part of the scenario they had worked out earlier. They had agreed that once Hoffman had established control, she would check out—in the hope that this might help preserve at least a small shred of cover. She didn't like having to leave the conversation just when they were finally getting down to business, but there was one consolation. With luck, she would never have to see Ali Ascari again.

* * *

"Okay, pal," said Hoffman when Anna had left. "Let's take it from the top."

"Ali know too many things. What you want to know, exactly?"

"The whole shooting match. We want to move some things across the border, and we think maybe we'd like to piggy-back on what you're doing. So tell me the whole thing."

"Not much to tell. Most smuggling is run from Tabriz, in the north. Some of it go through Khvoy, into Nakhichevan. Some go through Ardebil, across mountains to Astara and Masally and Pushkino. Some go by boat on Caspian Sea, from Bandar-i-Anzali to secret ports in Azerbaijan."

"How do they get across?"

"This depend. Most smugglers just simple tribespeople. Half of family lives on one side of the border, half on the other side. They come and go, all the time. All of them are Azeris, so what is border to them? They hate Russians and they hate Iranians. Same difference."

"Do they get caught?"

"Not so often. They know special routes in mountains, special hiding places, special ways to escape KGB border patrols. They been smuggling long time. Sometimes this is business of family for many generations. They leave some cousins in Azerbaijan as part of family business. But these ones are the little smugglers."

"Who are the big smugglers?"

"Big crooks. They do it a different way."

"How's that?"

"Money. They pay off Soviet officials. They pay off border guards, or commander of border guards, or local KGB official who runs border guards, or local party official who is big boss of everybody. Once in a while they catch somebody, to pretend they are doing job. This is big business. I am telling you."

"I like the little guys, the family operation. You know people like that?"

"Sure. Some of them are my cousins."

"Could your cousins take a load of stuff across for us?"

"Why not. Business is business. What you got?"

"Books, mostly."

"Books? Books is bullshit! You listen to Ali. If you smart,

you send VCRs and porno tapes. That is what they want in Baku. *Debbie Does Dallas.*"

"We're sending books, you horny son of a bitch. Books and tapes. Religious stuff, nationalist stuff."

"What for?"

"To make a fucking revolution, that's what for!"

"Okay, but porno tapes better bet. Honest. Even old ones. *Deep Throat. Behind Green Door.*"

"Forget the goddam tapes! How soon can your cousins get a shipment moving?"

"Right away. You give to Ali. We get it there a few weeks later. But it cost you plenty. This not cheap. My cousins very greedy."

"I'll bet they are. How much do you want?"

"As you like."

"Cut the crap. Name a price."

"A hundred thousand dollars."

"Fuck off. I'll give you twenty thousand, if you make it."

"Ali cannot ask cousins to risk lives for less than seventy five thousand. In advance."

"Thirty thousand. Tops."

"For you, Ali will do it for sixty-five thousand. At this price, no money for Ali himself. But okay. We are partners."

"Forget it. No deal."

"You hurt me too much. Sixty thousand."

"Maybe I'll go to thirty-five thousand. If you can promise to get it there in two weeks."

"No. Sorry. Find someone else. Go ahead, turn Ali over to Greek police. I don't care. Pride is all I have."

"Forty thousand. Final offer."

"Fifty-five thousand."

"Forty-five thousand. Absolute final offer. And I keep the Greek passport for insurance."

"Why do you hate Ali? Fifty thousand. Best price. You can take out gun and shoot Ali, but still not less than fifty thousand."

"My friend," said Hoffman, extending his hand. "You have a deal."

Anna returned several hours later to find Ascari gone and Hoffman asleep on the couch. A messy tray from room service was on the table, along with a half dozen empty beer bottles. Hoffman had been celebrating, apparently.

"Wake up, Frank," said Anna.

"Whaaa?"

"Wake up!"

He roused himself and sat up on the couch.

"You were magnificent," she said, giving him a kiss on the cheek.

"What are you talking about?"

"With Ascari. That was a textbook lesson in how to establish control. It was worth a whole year of training, just to watch you."

"Aw, bullshit," said Hoffman. "That kind of thing only works with a real slimeball like Ascari. Otherwise, it's useless."

"Come on! As somebody once said, if you have them by the balls, their hearts and minds will follow."

"Baloney. Don't listen to all that macho crap. Fear is a lousy way to motivate people."

"You're too modest. What's better than fear?"

"Positive control," said Hoffman. He reached over to one of the beer bottles and drained the last few drops. That seemed to refresh him.

"Meaning what?"

"Meaning that when you're trying to recruit someone, you want him to do things because he's going to benefit from the relationship, not because you're about to bust his balls. Except in the case of someone like this guy Ascari, who's just an asshole and only wants money."

"It's funny. But you sound like a woman case officer I know. She tried to tell me the same thing a few months ago."

Hoffman smiled. "Margaret Houghton," he said.

"That's right. How did you guess?"

"Because there ain't that many women case officers, sweetheart. At least not ones that know the business. How do you know Margaret anyway?"

"She's an old family friend. She knew my father years ago, when he was starting out in the foreign service. I've known her all my life."

Hoffman thought to himself a long moment. "Remind me

what your real name is. I have trouble remembering real names."

"Barnes. Anna Barnes."

"That's what I thought."

"Why do you ask?"

"I knew a guy in the agency with that last name once, in Germany. I can't exactly remember his first name. Frederick, I think, or Philip."

"My father's name was Philip."

"Maybe it was the same guy."

"Probably not. My father spent most of his career in the State Department."

"He became an ambassador, right?"

"Yes. To Kuala Lumpur, then to Helsinki."

"Same guy. He worked with me in OPC, right after the agency was formed, in 1948 or '49. Then he joined the striped-pants set."

Anna shook her head. She had suspected it, imagined it. But still, it was a shock to hear someone say it. "My father was in the CIA?"

"Yup!"

"What did he do?"

"A shit job. That's why he left."

"What was it? I've always wanted to know what my father did after the war. He never talked about it."

"I'm not surprised. What he did was send a lot of poor Russian sons of bitches off to get killed."

"What are you talking about?"

"It wasn't his fault. That was the job. We were prospecting for Russian agents in the DP camps, looking for people we could play back into the Soviet Union. The Russians were terrified. They had fought with the Germans in Vlasov's army, a lot of them. Or they had just deserted. Stalin wanted them back. Your dad's job, if I remember rightly, was to decide which ones were usable."

"What did he do with the rest?"

"He sent them back to Russia."

"To get killed?"

"Most of them. It was a bad scene. These poor guys would hang on to us, pleading, sobbing. Anything to keep from getting on that train. A lot of them would throw themselves under the wheels rather than go back to the Soviet Union. It was an awful job."

"What did my father do about it?"

"After a while, he decided it was all bullshit. The agency, I mean. So he left. Didn't he ever tell you about it?"

"Just once, sort of," said Anna. "Before he died."

"What did he say?"

"He told me never to be a spy, but I couldn't figure out why."

"So why the hell did you join up? You should have known better."

Anna thought a minute. "I wanted to do something that would make a difference."

"Make the world a better and safer place?"

"I guess that's right. I know it probably sounds ridiculous."

"No, it doesn't sound ridiculous," said Hoffman. "It sounds dangerous."

33

BACK IN ISTANBUL, TAYLOR WAS RUNNING OUT OF BAIT. He continued to meet Munzer at least once a week, feeding him pamphlets and leaflets from his dwindling supply and waiting for the Soviets to surface. A new box arrived from Washington in mid-July, shipped via ordinary parcel post. It contained copies of another reprint from Stone's Central Asian library, this one titled "Dar ul-Rahat Musulmanlari," or "The Moslem's Land of Happiness," by the Crimean Tatar writer Ismail bey Gaspraly. First published in Bakhchisarai in 1891, it was a sort of Moslem science-fiction story, outlining life in a perfect Islamic state of the future. Munzer was delighted with this new piece of subversive literature and proudly distributed copies among his friends. But "The Moslem's Land of Happiness" failed to draw even a nibble.

The date of the Tashkent demonstration came and went. Munzer was curious about what had happened there. So, for that matter, was Taylor. He sent a query to Stone. Because of the old man's ban on using cables, he sent it by ordinary airmail—what used to be known in the old days, before international postage rates increased, as the "ten-cent pouch." According to Stone, it was still the most secure method for international communication. A week later Taylor received a reply. Stone didn't explain how he had obtained his information, but Taylor suspected from the wealth of detail that the old man had somehow gotten an agent into Tashkent at the time of the protest. Either that or he was making it up.

According to Stone's account, a small group of perhaps twenty people had gathered after Friday prayers in front of the Moslem Religious Board of Central Asia, near Chorsu Square in the old Islamic quarter of the city. The board was a Soviet-sponsored operation, and for that reason ordinary people were generally suspicious of it. A few leaflets announcing the demonstration had circulated in the bazaar the previous week, but most of the people gathered outside the gates appeared to be curious onlookers, rather than actual demonstrators. Apparently the local KGB office and the militia had also seen copies of the leaflet, for they were waiting nearby in large numbers.

The motley group of demonstrators then marched from the gates of the board to the ramshackle ruins of a mosque about a hundred yards away. The mosque was a shrine to Abu Bakr Mohammed Khafal Shasti, and to members of the Qadiri brotherhood it was a sacred place. As the little group reached the shrine, overgrown with weeds, one man—perhaps a provocateur—unfurled a simple banner proclaiming in Arabic the Koranic invocation: "There is no God but God and Mohammed is his Prophet." The protester was promptly arrested—along with at least ten others. The party newspaper in Tashkent made no mention of the demonstration or the arrests in the days that followed, Stone advised, and the poor Uzbeks were still languishing in jail while the local KGB tried to figure out what was going on.

At his next meeting with Munzer, Taylor summarized the events at the Qadiri shrine, embellishing Stone's account only slightly. He urged Munzer to have his friend Khojaev, the émigré journalist, investigate the story and publish an account in *Great Turkestan.* If that could be done, Taylor said, he might be able to help smuggle copies of the magazine into the Soviet Union. That seemed to rouse Munzer's curiosity.

"How you do that, my friend?" asked the Uzbek. "Soviet border not New Jersey Turnpike."

"No. But it's not the Berlin Wall either. There are ways of getting across."

"Yeah, sure. What ways?"

"Pakistan."

"What Pakistan, please?"

"Peshawar," confided Taylor. "You can buy anything in Peshawar, anything at all."

"And then over borders?"

"Yes. By truck. By horseback. By foot."

"Munzer understands. No more question."

Taylor was going to leave it there. But it occurred to him that it was odd, really, for Munzer to be asking such a specific question about operations. That wasn't his style. Taylor suspected that he was repeating a question someone else had put to him. Which might mean that someone, somewhere, was finally getting nervous.

"Why did you ask me about border crossing anyway?" pressed Taylor. "Has anybody been asking you for information about that?"

"Oh, you know. Is many questions."

"No, I don't know. Tell me."

"Khojaev ask me. He say his friend Abdallah from Tashkent want to know about these pamphlets we getting."

"Oh, really? Why did Abdallah want to know? Did someone ask him, like our other American friend?"

"Maybe. But Munzer think that don't make no sense. Why would American man ask Abdallah from Tashkent to ask Khojaev to ask American?"

"Don't worry about it, Munzer," said Taylor with a thin smile. "It makes sense."

Munzer was the toast of Omar's. He arrived one Thursday night, the night before the Sabbath, when Moslem men like to go out on the town. Sonia noticed him right away, a cute, round-faced man sitting in the corner, nursing a Coca-Cola.

"You are Mr. Munzer?" she asked.

Munzer nodded shyly. Even after twenty-five years in Brooklyn, he still wasn't fully accustomed to strange women introducing themselves in bars. But when she mentioned that she had heard of Munzer's exploits as a freedom fighter, and asked if she could sit down for a few minutes with him and hear stories about the old country, Munzer felt entirely at ease. He ordered a beer, and then another, and when Khojaev showed up an hour later, a bottle of champagne. Sonia introduced Munzer to Omar and to some of the regulars—a few Kazakhs and Turkmen and a dark-eyed Chechen who looked ready to slit someone's throat. And they had a grand time, talking and singing. The older men sat against the wall, holding hands and popping worry beads and talking politics. Just after midnight, Sonia led them all in a chorus of Turkestani songs. It was a glorious evening. Everyone seemed to be there, except the tall blond filmmaker from British Columbia.

Jack Rawls had returned to Istanbul in late July. It was almost by accident that Taylor learned for sure he was back in town. During the weeks of trolling and waiting, Taylor had asked the Turks to put a light surveillance on Silvana Kunayeva, the wife of the Soviet consul general. She didn't lead them directly to Rawls; she was too careful for that. But she did pay a visit one morning to a businessman in Beyoglu, a certain Mr. Guztepe, who had a prosperous import-export business with the Eastern bloc. This worthy gentleman made a trip the next day to a real estate office near Taksim Square. And the proprietor of the real estate concern, after much bullying from one of Serif Osman's Turkish agents, disclosed that one of his salesmen had just rented out an apartment in the district of Zeytinburnu, overlooking the Sea of Marmara. It was, if nothing else, a good place to hide. The city's leather tanneries were located there, and the district was permeated with the smell of chemicals and animal carcasses.

Once Taylor had the address, it was relatively easy to maintain a fixed surveillance of the apartment. And eventually, one morning, the camera recorded a tall blond man putting his key in the lock and letting himself in the door. So they finally had a fix on Rawls. But Rawls, alas, still did not have a fix on them.

Taylor's next move was to try to wire Rawls's new safe house in Zeytinburnu. He first attempted to do it the easy way—by renting an adjacent apartment and running in a probe microphone. But that proved impossible. The apartments above, below and on either side were already rented, and trying to bribe the sitting tenants or having them evicted seemed too risky. Taylor did find an empty apartment across the street—with a direct, line-of-sight view of Rawls's living-room window—and he had his deputy rent the place immediately, through a Turkish cutout.

Now Taylor needed a wireman. Stone had forbidden any use of regular agency personnel, but surely this was different—especially when Taylor had a friend who could solve technical problems and also keep his mouth shut. So he had his secretary call George Trumbo in Athens with the message that Sonia from Omar's place wanted to see him urgently. George suspected that his leg was being pulled, but he agreed to come anyway. When he arrived the next day, Taylor took him the short distance from the airport to Zeytinburnu and showed him the layout of the two apartments.

"This place smells like dog shit" was George's first comment.

"Forget how it smells" said Taylor. "Just tell me how to bug it."

"It's easy, if you've got the hardware," said the lumbering technician.

"Explain it for your dumb friend, please," said Taylor.

"You just use this guy's window as a microphone. Bounce an infrared laser off it from your apartment, pick it up with the right kind of optical gizmo, and feed the signals into an audio receiver. Bingo! You can read the vibrations of the windowpane as easy as if you had a needle in the groove of a phonograph record."

"Great," said Taylor. "So do it."

"Are you kidding? I don't have that kind of gear."

"So go back to Athens and get it."

"Al, you don't understand. I don't have it back in Athens either. They don't give that stuff to field engineers. They keep it back at headquarters. It's classified so secret you can't even be in the same room with it alone. I couldn't get hold of it without a lot of paperwork."

"Haven't you got friends back at the TSD front office who could help you get it without all the bullshit?"

"Maybe. But I'm not sure I want to ask for this stuff on the sly. Maybe you hadn't realized, but I'm still in hot water for fucking around with you a couple of months ago."

"What do you mean?"

"I mean that someone from the Inspector General's office came by a couple of weeks ago asking questions about you, and what were you up to, and had I done any work for you recently, and how did I like having a regular paycheck?"

"What did you tell him?"

"Nothing, except for stuff he already knew."

"Thanks. I owe you one."

"Forget it. What are you up to anyway that makes the IG's office so interested in you? Those guys are bad news."

"You don't want to know, Georgie. Believe me."

"Why don't you just go through channels and have someone from headquarters come out and install the hardware? They'll have it done in a day. What's the problem with that?"

"That's what you don't want to know."

"Okay, Al. Sorry I asked. But a word to the wise: Watch your ass. Somebody back home is mighty curious about what you're doing."

Taylor thanked his friend for the warning. He wasn't sure what was going on— what was prompting the IG's office to ask questions— but fundamentally he didn't care. The salient point, for the moment, was that wiring Rawls's apartment wasn't worth the hassle. Taylor would just have to wait a bit longer for the Russian from Vancouver to show his hand.

Munzer reported at his next meeting that Khojaev had finally introduced him to the mysterious Mr. Abdallah from Tashkent. Taylor had been hoping for several weeks that such a meeting would take place, but Abdallah wouldn't be rushed. Evidently he had been admonished by someone or other to be very careful about talking to people. Munzer had a twinkle in his eye as he described the encounter.

"Abdallah ask me for literatures," he said.

"So you gave it to him?"

"Yes, I give to him, like you tell me. I say to him: You are patriotic Uzbek man. You want to see what Munzer doing, so I show you. We all working together for same cause."

"What did you give him, exactly?"

"I give him 'Turkestan Under Soviet Yoke.' I give him 'Moslem Land of Happiness.' I give him 'Siberian Folk Chorus,' which is really Naqshbandi sheikh. I give him special Pakistan Koran, small size, very nice."

"What else? Did you show him the leaflet from Tashkent and tell him what happened there?"

"Yes. Abdallah very sad with me."

"Did you give him the new leaflet we got about the demonstration in Baku?"

"No. Munzer not give this one."

"Why not?"

"Because Abdallah not Azeri man. Munzer not Azeri man. What do we care? You leave this thing for Azeri men."

"You're all working together, for chrissake. Abdallah and Khojaev and your other friends should realize that this movement is bigger than just Turkestan. Other Soviet nationalities want their freedom, too. The Azeris, the Armenians, the Latvians, the Ukrainians."

"Who cares about Armenians and Azeris?"

"We do. The next time you see Khojaev, show him the Baku leaflet and tell him it's all right for him to give it to Abdallah. Okay?"

Munzer nodded, not entirely happy at the thought that the independence movement of Turkestan would have to coexist, even momentarily, with the desires of any other people on the planet.

A courier arrived at the consulate the first Tuesday in August with an entirely new sort of cargo. The man wasn't from the regular diplomatic courier service, based in Frankfurt, which carried sensitive material to and from Moscow and other hot spots. In fact, he didn't identify himself as a U.S. government employee at all when he checked in at the main gate. He just said that he had an important package to deliver personally to Alan Taylor. The Marine guards were about to send him packing when he handed them a sealed envelope with Taylor's name typed on it and asked that they deliver it to him immediately.

When Taylor opened the envelope a few minutes later, he found inside one of his own Karpetland business cards. "Send him up, with whatever he wants to deliver," he said. "And don't examine the box."

The courier, accompanied by a Marine, carried his cargo across the courtyard and upstairs to Taylor's office in the annex. It was a large box. The courier had carried it all the way on the Pan Am flight from New York on a reserved seat next to him. Taylor dismissed the Marine guard and closed the door. The courier, meanwhile, was studying Taylor's face, checking it against a photograph he had been shown. When he was convinced he had the right man, he placed the box on Taylor's desk.

"This is for you," he said. He was a tough little man, with the body of a circus roustabout and a manner that suggested he could keep his brain idling in neutral for indefinite periods.

"Who sent you?" asked Taylor.

"The boss at Karpetland."

"Oh yeah? And who the hell are you?"

"I work for the boss."

"Prove it," said Taylor. "I never heard of you."

The courier removed from his pocket a second sealed envelope, also addressed to Taylor, and handed it to him.

It was a note from Stone, written in his neat handwriting. "Alan," it began. "I am sending you this box by courier. When you receive it, give the courier one of your Istanbul business cards, with your signature, which will serve as a receipt. Sealed instructions are in the box. Be well." The letter was unsigned.

Taylor did as instructed, handing the courier a signed card in a sealed envelope. He walked him back to the consulate gate and shook his hand. The courier turned and walked off down Mesrutiyet Street. Where did Stone find these people? Taylor wondered.

Back in the office, door closed, Taylor opened the box. It was tightly and carefully wrapped. Inside was a smaller box and a large envelope sealed with wax. Taylor broke the seal and removed from it another letter from Stone, also handwritten. Taylor read it with astonishment: "My dear

Alan, the time has come to pull the chain, as hard as possible. To this end, I am sending you several new items. You'll find the first in the same envelope as this letter. It is a set of eight hand-drawn maps which show the location of potential targets in the Soviet Union."

Taylor stopped reading and removed a packet of material from the envelope. It was just as Stone described. A series of eight carefully drawn maps, with letters and notations in the Cyrillic Turkic languages of Central Asia. Taylor continued:

"The list of targets includes the headquarters of the Moslem Religious Board in Tashkent; a militia office in a suburb of Samarkand; the Tajik party headquarters in Dushanbe; a military barracks in Margelan, in the Ferghana Valley; the Turkmenistan KGB office in Ashkhabad; an all-union cultural center in Baku; an oil-pumping station in Sumgait; a militia office in the suburbs of Alma-Ata."

Taylor counted to make sure he had all eight maps. Then he resumed the letter.

"In addition to the maps, you will find a small cardboard box. Inside this box is a type of plastic explosive that is quite potent and well regarded by people who are familiar with such matters. I have included four bags of it. These are for show only. For God's sake, do not under any circumstances use any of it. Someone might get hurt. My intention is that the maps and the explosives should find their way into Soviet hands in Istanbul. Presumably you'll want to give them to Ahmedov, but I leave the details to you. Don't dally, because in a few weeks an actual bomb attack will take place in one or more of the Central Asian republics, though obviously not at any of the named targets.

"The final item is a suitcase, with a letter inside for Frank Hoffman. The suitcase, for your information, contains in its lining a substantial amount of the same plastic explosive contained in the box. Don't worry about the suitcase, by the way. The explosive can't be detected, and it's quite unlikely to explode. Please deliver the letter and the suitcase to Frank at your earliest convenience. Good luck!"

He's out of his fucking mind, was Taylor's first thought. That was also his second thought. But his third thought was that he had better get moving.

Late that afternoon, Taylor made a crash visit to Munzer's

apartment in Aksaray. He drove himself in one of the consulate cars, bringing with him the box of explosives and the envelope with the drawings. He fought the rush-hour traffic
across the Ataturk Bridge and up the boulevard toward
Aksaray. He parked his car at the corner of Munzer's little
street just as dusk was falling. The parked car was a giveaway, but what did it matter? For all Taylor knew, the Soviets
had already wired Munzer's apartment.

Taylor knocked loudly on Munzer's door.

"Kim o?" asked Munzer in Turkish. Who is it?

"Arkadas," answered Taylor. A friend.

"Who friend?" demanded Munzer in English.

"Come on, for chrissake, open up!"

Munzer opened the door. He was dressed in his pajama
bottoms and a sleeveless T-shirt. He looked puzzled.

"Why for you come?" he asked sleepily. "Is okay everything?"

"Yes. Everything is fine. But I need to talk to you about
something. I want to store some things here, where they'll be
safe."

"What things, please?"

"Why don't you sit down, Munzer. This is pretty important."

"Okay, okay." He walked to the living room and sat down
in a chair.

"Now listen, my friend. I told you back in Brooklyn that
we were getting serious about liberating Turkestan, and I
meant it. And don't forget, that's what you wanted."

"I no forget. What you got in there?" He pointed to the
box.

"Some surprises. For the Russians." He opened the box
very carefully and took out a fat sack containing a whitish
substance.

"What is this?"

"Explosive," whispered Taylor.

"Allah!" Munzer's sleepy eyes suddenly lit up. Taylor
couldn't tell whether it was from fear or joy.

"Don't touch it. Don't look at it. Don't think about it. Just
put it somewhere out of the way. Do you have a closet?"

"Yes. Here is closet." Munzer opened a door at the back of
the room.

"Let's put it there, then."

"What this is for, please?" asked Munzer as Taylor carried the box across the room and gingerly laid it down.

"For operations."

"Where?"

"Can you keep a secret, my friend, until the day you die?"

Munzer pounded his heart and growled an unintelligible oath.

"I trust you, Munzer. So I'm going to show you some of the targets."

He took the large manila envelope in his hand and removed the drawings, handing them one by one to Munzer. With each piece of paper, Munzer breathed a sigh of amazement, adding an occasional oath of battle.

"I am showing you these things because I need your help. It's not safe to keep them at the consulate, so I want to leave them here for a few days. Is that all right?"

"Yes, please."

"What's the safest place in your apartment?"

Munzer thought a long moment. "Under mattress," he said.

It was an obvious hiding place, the place a good thief would check first, but Taylor didn't mind. He walked solemnly to the bedroom with Munzer, raised the mattress a few inches, and slid the manila envelope into the box spring. Taylor glanced at Munzer and noticed that the round-faced little Uzbek man was standing at attention, like a soldier.

"I have to go soon," said Taylor. "Any questions?"

"This very big secret," said Munzer.

"Yes. Very big."

"Munzer can talk about it with anybody?"

"No," said Taylor.

"Can I tell my Turkestani brothers, please, that at last we have real army?"

"Do you really trust any of them?"

"My friend Khojaev maybe?"

"But he's a journalist. They all talk too much."

"There is Kirdarov."

"Where's his family from?"

"Kirgizia."

"Too dangerous. He may have contacts with the Chinese."

"What about Abdallah? He keep some big secrets, I think."

"Are you sure you trust him?"

"Yes, why not?"

"Okay. You can tell Abdallah we're planning operations. But that's it. And no details."

"Okay. Promise."

"One more thing, Munzer. Come here a minute." Taylor motioned him toward the bathroom.

Taylor led Munzer into the john and turned on the water faucet. Then he leaned toward Munzer and spoke quietly, under the sound of the running water.

"Don't you touch either of these containers, under any circumstances. Do you understand me? I have marked each of them so that I will be able to tell if anyone other than me has opened them. And if that person is you, you're finished. Got it?"

"Okay. Munzer understand."

Taylor turned off the water and walked back to the entrance hall. At the door, Munzer gave him a hug and a kiss on both cheeks.

It took just a week. Taylor returned to Munzer's apartment the following Tuesday with a device that would show whether anyone had tampered with the parcels. And to his great satisfaction, he found that both had indeed been opened. The hand-drawn maps had undoubtedly been photographed, one by one. One bag of explosive had also been opened, presumably so that a tiny sample could be removed and analyzed back in Moscow. Taylor didn't let on that the parcels had been opened. But he did badger Munzer once more about security, just to make sure that he hadn't snuck a peek.

"Are they all right, please? Nobody touching?"

"They're fine," said Taylor. "No problem. I'll take them back now."

"Why? Is time now for operation to begin?"

"Yes, it's time. I have to get this stuff to the people who will actually be using it."

"Munzer can go?"

"No, my friend. Not yet."

"Soon, please. Munzer want to be there when war start."

34

◆

THE FIRST BOMB ARRIVED IN TASHKENT IN LATE SUMMER, CARried in the hand luggage of an Indian businessman from Delhi. He had been in the city five days, negotiating an agreement to purchase cotton from the vast collective farms in northwestern Uzbekistan, and he was scheduled to leave that night on a flight to Kabul and thence back to Delhi. His name, so far as it mattered to Stone and his friends, was QRCOMFORT. His passport identified him as Ramchandra P. Desai.

It was a bright summer afternoon, the sort of day when Uzbek party officials like to show off the capital of their republic. Tashkent was a city of broad boulevards, tree-lined streets, a splendid park bisecting the center of the city, with rose gardens and graceful fountains. The Paris of Uzbekistan, you might say. The great advantage Tashkent had was that the wretched buildings thrown up in the time of Stalin had mostly been destroyed in the great earthquake of 1966. The authorities claimed that only nineteen people had died in the quake—proof of the sublime virtues of the socialist system. The actual death toll was closer to two hundred, which was still a surprisingly small number. Perhaps the authorities couldn't help themselves. They had to lie. The system required it.

The Indian traveler left his room in the Hotel Uzbekistan just before five in the afternoon, carrying his small travel bag on a strap over his shoulder. He was a quiet little man, neatly dressed, with that strange combination of servility and arrogance that is characteristic of many Indians when they travel abroad. All week long, he had treated his Russian counterparts with elaborate politeness and the Uzbeks with condescension. They tolerated his behavior because he was a buyer with real money, as opposed to rubles, and because the Indians were known to pay "commissions" if they received a favorable price. It helped, too, that he was a fussy and fastidious man, for as the week wore on and he became more and more nervous, nobody thought to question why. That was just the way these finicky, high-caste Indians behaved.

Now, as he walked out the front door of the hotel, Mr. Desai felt an acute sense of anxiety. He had done things for the Americans before, but this was different. The man who had given him the bag back in Delhi wasn't his usual case officer, but someone else. And the mission itself was peculiar: Deliver a bag, contents unknown, to another courier, identity unknown—in a strange city that was, really, no more than a pimple on the backside of Asia.

The Indian's skin was prickly, then clammy, then numb; he wanted to climb out of it and hide his quivering body in a new shell, like a hermit crab. Indeed, he thought for a brief moment that he would do almost anything to avoid completing the assignment. Step in front of a car perhaps. At the bottom of the hotel promenade, the cars were whizzing around the traffic circle surrounding Karl Marx Park. But that was no solution; they would still find the bag, and they would torture him, and then kill him.

Resignedly, Mr. Desai did as he had been told—turned right and walked a short block from the hotel to the entrance of the subway. Yes, the case officer had said, that's right—Tashkent had a subway, and a damn good one; the perfect place to get lost for a while, and shake off any surveillance. So the Indian paid his five kopecks—which he had been holding in his sweaty palm since he left the hotel—and boarded the subway at the stop called October Revolution. It was a fancy, gilded showpiece, just like the metro in Moscow. How fitting, thought the Indian, that the only thing the Soviets could build competently was underground.

"Don't look over your shoulder for surveillance," the case officer had said. "It's a dead giveaway." Mr. Desai resisted his intense desire to do just that; he stared instead at his shoes, then at the faces of the Uzbeks waiting for the train. They all looked like policemen; every moon-faced one of them. After several minutes a train roared into the station and the Indian stepped haltingly aboard.

He went one stop, to the inevitable V. I. Lenin station, all decorated with glass chandeliers, and walked to the door as if to get off. He put one foot out and then retreated back into the car as the door was closing, just as the case officer had told him. He didn't see any obvious KGB ape banging on the door to get back in; but then he wouldn't, would he?

The Indian rode two stops and exited at Navoye station, decorated with hideous medallions of the hammer and sickle. He walked across the platform to the other side—doubling back on himself to make sure he wasn't being followed. When the train arrived heading in the other direction, he scanned the passengers boarding it, to make sure that none of them had exited with him, and then hopped aboard. Now, in theory, he was "clean."

Two more stops and Mr. Desai got off, feeling the travel bag against his side. The case officer hadn't told him what was sewn into the lining—hadn't said a word about it—and the Indian, in truth, didn't care. He just wanted to get rid of it, get on his plane, and get home.

The Indian surfaced into the afternoon sun and walked down Karl Marx Prospect as casually as he could manage. It was a long, tree-lined pedestrian walkway, flanked by open-air restaurants, theaters and shops. It was crowded with Uzbeks out strolling, thank God. Who would notice a small Indian man with his travel bag, taking one last look at the city before leaving? He inched past the cafés, his legs shaky as wobbly stilts, looking for a particular open-air restaurant called Krokodil, where he was to have dinner.

Eventually he found it, and stood in line for the house specialty, indeed the only dish they served, which was pilau—a greasy concoction of rice, carrots and spices, topped with a few pieces of gristly meat. He paid his one ruble, took his plate of rice, and sat down at an empty table in the back. The flies seemed to find him instantly. Struggling to maintain his dignity, the Indian removed his handkerchief from his pocket and wiped clean his spoon. He might be heading for Lubyanka Prison, but he would not eat with a dirty spoon. He put the travel bag under the table, just as he had been told, and took a bite of the rice. The grease and the aroma made him feel nauseated.

After several minutes, a fat Uzbek sat down at the next table and began digging into an immense pile of pilau, smacking his lips as if he hadn't eaten for weeks. This most certainly was not the man the Indian was waiting for. *That* man arrived soon after. He shambled over to the table, approached the Indian, and said, in soft-spoken English: "May I join you, please?" just as he was supposed to. The Indian managed to answer: "I will be leaving shortly," just as instructed, but he was suffering from a terrible shock. For he could see that his counterpart in this clandestine meeting, the man to whom he was entrusting his life, was an African—as black as the mud at the bottom of the river Ganges. Now I am dead, thought the Indian businessman. Very definitely, I am dead. He stared at his plate for twenty seconds and then got up and walked away, leaving the travel bag behind.

The black man was a student from Tanzania named Vladimir Ilyich Mbane. He had been recruited by the chief of station in Dar es Salaam three years before, just as he was heading off to university in the Soviet Union. It had seemed like a sensible enough recruitment—an extra body to have on hand in Moscow or Leningrad or Kiev, or wherever the young man ended up. But the Soviets assigned the Tanzanian to a university in Tashkent, and there he sat idly for two years before the SB Division finally dropped him from the payroll. At that point, he had come to Stone's attention, and he had begun another sort of life, considerably more interesting.

Mbane ate his dinner slowly, with a genuine calm. He was the sort of man who made a perfect liar, and a perfect agent. In place of the nerve endings that, in most people, became sharp and brittle in times of stress, the African was all syrup and soft cotton. You could have hooked him up to a polygraph at that very moment and gotten a reading as flat as the waters of Lake Victoria on a windless day.

The Tanzanian finished his meal, hoisted the travel bag on his shoulder, and headed up Karl Marx Prospect toward Lenin Square. You might have thought he would stand out, a black man walking the streets of Tashkent, but the opposite was more nearly true. That was the great blessing of racism. Uzbeks and Russians disdained Africans as part of the baggage of socialist internationalism. A black man in the streets was, in many respects, invisible. People didn't look at him, didn't talk to him, didn't imagine that he could possibly be doing anything of consequence.

He walked up the prospect, past hundreds of unseeing eyes, to a broad square bordered by an arc of fountains. A ten-lane boulevard cut through the square—the ceremonial route used for May Day parades—and across it stood a towering statue of Lenin. The young African stared up at the visage of Lenin, nearly a hundred feet above. It had a particular look, this Tashkent version of Lenin. In the same way that each Christian community will give its figure of Jesus a touch of the national character—hair color, skin tone, the set of the eyes—this was an Asian Lenin. His eyes had the tight slant of the East, the cheekbones were as high and prominent as a Mongolian's, and the arm brandished a scroll, as if he were a socialist imam extending a firman toward his people.

The African's instructions were to leave the travel bag in the bushes directly behind the marble reviewing stand that stood on either side of the statue. He was ambling in that direction when a jeep carrying two militiamen stopped directly in front of the statue. The officers got out and surveyed the boulevard with hawks' eyes. One of them said something into his walkie-talkie. That was a bad sign, one that would rattle most people—certainly the Indian businessman—and cause them to abort the mission, run away and hide.

But the young African was a different cut entirely. He knew that his problem was plainclothes KGB surveillance, not the blue shirts. Without looking at the militiamen, he strolled casually down the boulevard, past the party administration building displaying the huge portraits of Marx and Engels, and down a long row of steps to a park below.

Mbane saw a park bench, set against a row of bushes, and settled his long body onto the seat. And without thinking about it very much, with the pure instinct that is a kind of genius, he swung the travel bag behind him, over the rail of the bench, and let it slide off his shoulder into the evergreen bushes. He took a cigarette from his pocket, lit it, and contemplated the situation.

The bench was a few dozen yards from the entrance to the Lenin subway station. From where he sat, the Tanzanian could see the large bas-relief mural gracing the station entrance. It showed Lenin leading the peoples of the East out of bondage. The figures beneath the great liberator were all Oriental—a team of Turkic men in four-cornered hats pounding metal and threshing wheat; Moslem women arrayed like the three Graces, holding aloft brooms!

This is close enough, thought the young Tanzanian. If you can't hit the Lenin statue, hit the Lenin subway station. He finished one cigarette, lazily smoked another to the let the early-evening sky darken a bit more, and then rose from the bench—checking to make sure that the bag was concealed by the overhanging branches of the bushes. Then Vladimir Ilyich Mbane, cool and calm, strode off into the subway station, five-kopeck piece in hand, disappearing into the summer evening.

And so it was that the first act of sabotage inside the Soviet Union by an agent of the West in many years blew up much shrubbery, a few dozen rose bushes, four park benches, a concrete walkway, and the coolie hat of a figure on a bas-relief sculpture. It happened in the middle of the night, hours after Tashkent had gone to bed, and many hours after the Indian businessman had landed in Kabul. The KGB let it be known that a gas line had ruptured. When KGB officers began questioning black men at the university, for several blacks had been seen in the area where the bomb was placed the day before, the young Tanzanian sent an anonymous tip implicating a suspicious fellow from Kampala who lived in an adjoining dormitory.

Taylor's mission to Athens was considerably less dangerous than the Tashkent affair. He took the morning flight from Istanbul, checking the bag Stone had sent him containing the plastic explosive. Nobody gave him any trouble at either the Istanbul or the Athens airport—he certainly didn't look like a bomb carrier—and he went directly to Hoffman's apartment at the foot of Lykabettos Hill. Taylor assumed that he would be expected, since he had asked Marjorie, back in Rockville, to let Hoffman know he was coming. He rang the doorbell, holding the bag full of explosive in his hand.

"Who the fuck are you?" asked Hoffman when he opened the door. He was unshaven, and dressed in a blue silk bathrobe trimmed in black satin that looked as if it might have once belonged to a professional wrestler.

"William Goode," said Taylor.

"Oh yeah?" said Hoffman, looking Taylor up and down. "So what?"

"Didn't anyone tell you I was coming?" asked Taylor.

"No," said Hoffman. He looked as if he were about to close the door.

"They were supposed to call you."

"Who?"

"Stone's people."

"Bullshit."

"No. Really."

Hoffman squinted his eye. He didn't like the looks of Taylor. He was too handsome. "Bullshit," he said again.

"Fuck you," said Taylor. "Let me in the goddam door."

Hoffman liked that a little better. "Who sent you?"

"Stone, for chrissake. Edward Stone."

Hoffman considered the situation and began to relent. "Maybe they tried to call," he said. "I left the phone off the hook for a while."

"How long?"

"I dunno. A couple of days. What does it matter? You're here now. You might as well come in."

"Thanks," said Taylor. He carried the suitcase in with him and set it gently atop the coffee table in Hoffman's living room.

"What the hell is that?" asked Hoffman, pointing to the suitcase.

"Stone told me to deliver it to you. There's a letter inside that explains everything."

"Cut the crap, sonny boy. What's your real name anyway?"

"Taylor."

"Well, cut the crap, Taylor. What's in the fucking suitcase?"

"Explosives."

"Say what?"

"Explosives. You know. Boom!"

"Jesus Chriminy. Explosives! Has Stone lost his mind? What does he think he's doing anyway? Starting a world war?"

"Read the letter," said Taylor. "Maybe that will explain."

"I don't have to read the goddam letter. I know what it

says. He wants me to give this portable nuclear weapon, or whatever it is, to a crazy Iranian asshole by the name of Ascari, and have him transport it to some fleabag town somewhere in the middle of the Caucasus or Central Asia—so that Big Ivan back in Moscow will think that Uncle Sam is still a tough guy. Is that the general picture more or less?"

"Probably. I haven't read the letter. But that sounds about right."

"Sure it does. Of course it does. That's the basic play book. Think of ways to scare the shit out fo the Russkies. And here's a new way. Bombs!"

"You don't like it?"

"No. I do like it. I just think it's a little nuts. What's gotten into Stone anyway? He used to be so conservative."

"I'm not sure," said Taylor. "I think he got fed up with all the bullshit and decided to wing it for a while. He's got a strategy."

"Does he, now? And what might that be?"

"He thinks that if we give the Soviets a good hard push, they'll fall over."

"Well, I certainly do hope he's right. Yes, indeed. Because if he isn't, we're all in deep shit."

"What do you mean? War?"

"Fuck no. Nothing as trivial as that. I'm talking about legal trouble."

"What legal trouble?"

"Someone from the Athens station came to see me a few days ago asking a lot of questions. Did I know Edward Stone? What was he doing? Did I know a woman named Anna Barnes? They may even have asked me about you."

"What did you tell them?"

"I told them to fuck off. I don't work for the agency anymore. I told them that if they wanted to talk to me, they should get a subpoena."

"What happened? Did they, get back to you?"

"I don't know. That's why I took the phone off the hook. I didn't want to hear any more of their bullshit. When you showed up, I thought you were a process server."

Taylor laughed and shook his head. "Nope. I'm a co-conspirator."

"That sounds neighborly," said Hoffman. "Let's have a drink."

Hoffman made sure the phone was still off the hook and opened a new bottle of scotch. By the time the bottle was finished, late that evening, they had drunk many toasts to the estimable Edward Stone, pledged unshakable loyalty to each other and to the cause, whatever that might be. Hoffman had even offered Taylor a job with Arab-American Security Consultants, should he ever find himself in difficulty with his present employer.

The second bomb exploded in the Uzbek city of Samarkand. It arrived there in the luggage of an Iranian architect. Or at least that was what he claimed to be. He certainly had a big Persian nose and spoke a sweet, musical-sounding Farsi. He liked to tell Uzbeks that he was a descendant of the Persian architect who built the Bibi Khanum mosque in Samarkand—an immense, crumbling wreck next to the bazaar that had collapsed of its own weight centuries ago. The Uzbeks would laugh when he said that and ask if he knew the tale of what happened to the architect.

Oh yes, said the Iranian, he knew the story. Tamerlane hired the architect to build a mosque in honor of his beautiful Chinese wife, Saray Mulk Khanum. Then he went away on one of his conquests. The wife wanted to surprise him with the completed mosque by the time he returned, and urged the Persian to hurry his work. The architect agreed, on one condition. He wanted to kiss the lovely queen on her cheek. She consented. But when the Persian planted his lips on the woman's veiled cheek, they burned through the material and left a red mark of shame upon the lady's face. Tamerlane, needless to say, was not amused when he returned. He had his faithless consort thrown from the highest tower of the new mosque and was going to do the same to the Persian architect. But when the architect reached the top of the minaret, the legend had it, he sprouted wings and flew home to Persia.

The Iranian loved retelling the story of his putative kinsman. He shared it at several places in the bazaar. He even went through all the details in the little bookstore on Akhunbabayev Street, across from the university dormitory and next to the militia barracks. They interrogated the manager of the bookstore at length the next day, and he remembered it clearly. The man was an Iranian, an architect. He came into the shop and asked to look at an engineering textbook, a standard one for sale in nearly every bookstore in the Soviet Union. He looked at the book and then said no, he already had that one, and pulled an identical book out of his bag to show that it was so.

No, the bookstore manager didn't think the Iranian could have switched the two books. He had watched so carefully, the man being a foreigner. But perhaps it was possible. There were other customers in the shop. And yes, the manager had put the engineering book back on the wall, on the side of the shop that adjoined the militia barracks. Of course it hadn't felt strange, he told the comrade inspector. It was the same engineering textbook. Otherwise the bookstore manager wouldn't have put it back on the shelf.

The bomb wrecked the bookstore. But what made a considerable impression on the local people was that it also blew a sizable hole in the wall of the militia barracks. The militiamen like to imagine that they are invulnerable—strutting about in their high leather boots—and they are widely disliked, especially in a simple out-of-the-way place like Samarkand. So the local residents were almost glad it happened, and more than a little admiring of the Persian architect who had done the dirty deed and then—as it were—flown away.

The Persian architect had most certainly disappeared vanished into thin air despite an elaborate search. But as the authorities checked their records, they discovered, to their chagrin, that they had no record of any such person entering or leaving Uzbekistan. The Persian identity, it seemed, had been a ruse.

Despite these setbacks, the KGB knew what to do. A new rumor began making the rounds in the bazaar. The bombings in Uzbekistan—for everyone knew there had been another, in Tashkent—were the work of an Armenian terrorist organization based in Yerevan. The Armenian merchants in the bazaar wanted more money, and they were trying to frighten honest Uzbeks with their bombs. That made perfect sense. It was the Armenians' fault.

VII

LUCY MORGAN

Washington / Paris
Istanbul

September–November 1979

35

"**H**ULLO, MR. ANTARAMIAN."

"Hullo, hullo! How glad I am to meet you. I have not seen you for a long time."

"Where are you going?"

"I am going into Henry Seigle's new store to buy a suit of clothes to wear in my work. Won't you come with me?"

"Yes, I think I will. I have not seen that store yet."

"It is a magnificent building—the largest in Boston."

"Here it is, let us go in."

Anna Barnes read the dialogue in her American-English grammar, trying to follow the Armenian version that was printed alongside the English. She had bought the book years ago at a rummage sale in Somerville and had kept it as a curiosity, a charming piece of flotsam that had washed up from a distant shore, never imagining that she would have any practical use for it. Now, as she searched for a possible Armenian recruit among the dozens of names in 201 files and spotters' reports that Marjorie was stacking on her desk, it seemed possible that she might actually find some use for the old grammar. She turned to a passage marked "Meeting a Lady Friend on the Street."

"Hullo, Agnes, where are you going?"

"Hullo, Mr. Giragosian, I am going to church. Won't you accompany me?"

"No, thank you. I am going to the beach."

"Oh, please, do come with me. There is nice singing in our church, and the pastor will speak on the subject of 'The Wages of Sin Is Death.' He is an elegant young man and an elaborate speaker. Come, I will introduce you to him."

"Yes, but I am not a Protestant, I am a Grigorian."

"It makes no difference, we are all Christians. Come for my sake."

The dialogues went on like this for many pages, with advice on every facet of life for the new arrival in America. The author, one E. A. Yeran, had provided suggestions for what to say to the immigration office ("Are you going to any address in particular?" Yes, sir, I am going directly to my uncle"), how to rent a furnished room (three dollars a month is too much, even for a room with three windows, steam heat and electric lights), how to buy a suit for under ten dollars (tell the salesman: "I want a dark color, so that it will not show the dirt, as I will wear it in my work") and even a sample dialogue for use in the Chinese laundry:

"Hello, John. Give me my laundry."

"You got checkee?"

"Oh, say, I have lost my check. It is not in my pocket."

"No checkee, no shirtee. You 'Melican man loozee checkee oli time."

Anna combed the files, looking for a modern-day Mr. Antaramian or Mr. Giragosian who could be drawn into the operation. Each morning Marjorie arrived with a new collection of paperwork from the registry, to be returned to Langley that afternoon before four-thirty. Anna was curious how Stone had arranged this flow of material. The files, bearing the true names and histories of agents, were among the most sensitive documents the agency maintained; their removal, even if only for a few hours, could have been done only with the connivance of the most senior people in the Records Division.

The Karpetland office was empty these days, except for Marjorie. The boxes were all gone, shipped to Istanbul and Peshawar and Dubai, and from there to still more mysterious places. Taylor was gone, too, and that, for Anna, was a more serious problem. She missed him. She had forgotten that unreasonable aspect of love, the change in your body chemistry that made you ache when the connection was lost. It offended Anna. How could a feminist daughter of the 1960s feel this way—like an empty glove, limp and useless when it wasn't filled up with someone else's flesh and bone and life? How absurd.

After several weeks the emptiness became a dull ache,

which was better but also worse, because it felt less like love. And into this new valley of lovelessness fell questions about Taylor. Why didn't he call or write? Why didn't he send a silly message, like the NOC from San Francisco who translated songs from *My Fair Lady* into Chinese and sent them home by mail during a long TDY stint in Beijing, to amuse his beloved and perplex the Chinese authorities. And then: Who was he sleeping with? Anna believed in trusting people, especially people she loved, but in Taylor's case, that emotion seemed almost beside the point. To kill the questions, there was work—the narcotic of choice for modern career women—and it became Anna's protest against the unfairness of having to care so much about someone else.

In her self-created post as head of the Armenia desk, Anna had to decide what she was looking for. Her first thought had been to find an Armenian equivalent of Munzer Ahmendov—an émigré who was living in the West but was in touch with nationalist sentiment back home in his native republic. But that proved harder than she had expected. Most sensible Armenian émigrés in the West were devoting themselves to the rational pursuits of making and spending money.

Anna sampled the various outposts of the Armenian diaspora, looking for plausible candidates. The agency had records on a handful of Lebanese Armenians who had worked with the Beirut station in the 1950s and 1960s as contract agents. One of them, a gold merchant on Hamra Street, had even been recruited in the 1950s to try to set up a network in Soviet Armenia. He claimed that he traveled there once a year to visit members of his family, and had apparently promised a case officer from the SB Division that he could recruit his cousins— who were party members—to spy for America. But nothing ever came of it. The gold merchant, like many of the Armenians in the agency files, proved to be a better talker than a spy. When he returned from Yerevan to Beirut, he was full of apologies. One cousin had moved to Novosibirsk; another was sick. Very sorry. Maybe he would try again next year.

But the agency lost interest. The Lebanese Armenians didn't seem worth the trouble. Their ranks were undoubtedly penetrated by the KGB; worse, many of them actually seemed to sympathize with the Soviet Union—which after all had sustained an Armenian homeland of sorts since 1920. Moreover, since the early 1970s, many of the younger Lebanese Armenians had been following their Palestinian neighbors into the netherworld of terrorism. The Lebanese émigrés were best left alone, Anna concluded.

Then there were the American Armenians. Unlike the Lebanese variety, they tended to be conservative people—Republicans, most of them—whose chief ambition was to assimilate successfully in the life of America. A few Armenians had worked for the agency as case officers, some of the highly respected, but Stone had ruled out using any additional CIA people. The main Armenian-American organizations were out, too, for much the same reason. Their leadership had been close enough to the government over the years so that the first thing any of them would do, on being contacted, would be to call someone in the front office and ask what was going on.

Two possibilities surfaced in the files of the Domestic Contacts Division. One was a second-generation Armenian physicist from Stanford who traveled often to international scientific conferences and provided regular reports on what his Soviet colleagues had to say. But according to the file, he spoke no Armenian and had no strong interest in Armenian causes. He hardly seemed the man to organize an underground movement. The other was a journalist with one of the newsmagazines. The agency had opened a 201 file on him because once, during the early 1970s, he had agreed to take a close look at a Soviet COMINT facility outside Budapest during a reporting trip to Hungary. He had performed a few other one-shot assignments over the next several year and then had gone inactive. He spoke good Armenian and was described by his former case officer as something of a hothead when he had a few drinks. In short, he sounded perfect. But there was one insurmountable problem. The agency had been banned, ever since the great flap of the mid-1970s, from recruiting American journalists as agents. The same rules must surely apply to Stone's operation, Anna reasoned.

That left a final capital of the diaspora, the Armenian exile community in France. And it was there—amid the Armenian booksellers and jewelers and travel agents—that Anna at last found someone who sounded like a good candidate—almost ideal, in fact, except for one rather serious flaw. The man in question wasn't an émigré. He was an actual Soviet citizen, a doctor who had been doing postgraduate research at the Sorbonne medical school for the past two years and was due to return home to Yerevan in the fall.

His name was Aram Antoyan, and he had entered the CIA computer files a year before, as a result of a rather silly mistake. The French counterintelligence agency, the Direction de la Surveillance du Territoire, had routinely informed the CIA station in Paris of his arrival in 1977 to study "nuclear medicine," which sounded exciting but simply meant using radioactive dyes as a diagnostic tool to monitor the functions of the kidney, bladder and other internal organs. Some idiot in the Paris station, however, had assumed that "nuclear medicine" must have something to do with bombs. A false-flag operation was duly approved to find out more details and see if Dr. Antoyan could be recruited. A NOC made a pass at him in Paris, posing as a Belgian anesthesiologist, but he came away convinced that the Soviet doctor was just that—a medical researcher, with no apparent knowledge of military matters.

The only unusual thing about young Dr. Antoyan, reported the NOC, was that he talked fervently about Armenian issues—to the point of criticizing official Soviet nationalities policy. The file concluded with a brief exchange of cables between Paris and headquarters on the advisability of further development of the case. The anti-Moscow talk was encouraging, but headquarters concluded that Dr. Antoyan's likely access to classified information when he returned home would be close to zero, and that recruiting him wouldn't be worth the time and effort.

"I think I've found my man," Anna told Stone three days later at the office in Rockville. Stone had tried to put off the meeting, and had agreed to come only when Anna threatened that otherwise she would pay him a visit at Langley.

"What man are you talking about, my dear?" he asked. Stone was wearing a striped bow tie that day, which made him look especially clipped and precise.

"My Armenian agent. I've found someone in Paris who would be perfect for the part."

"That's nice. But I still haven't decided to add another body. We're having enough trouble with logistics as it is."

"This person wouldn't present any logistical problems. Quite the opposite, in fact. He'd be self-contained."

"How's that?"

"Because he's a Soviet citizen, not an émigré. And he's on his way back to Yerevan soon, so we won't need any extra plumbing."

"Sorry. Out of the question."

"Why, dammit?" She was peeved. The Armenian project was her own small piece of ground, and Stone was cutting it out from under her.

"Too dangerous."

"For whom? Him or us?"

"Both, but especially for him."

"You're wrong," said Anna.

Stone bristled. He wasn't used to having his judgment questioned.

"He'll know how to take care of himself," she explained. "And we're not asking him to do anything very risky. According to the file, he's already quite outspoken about his Armenian sympathies, so he may be in hot water anyway."

"I'll think about it. But my initial response is no."

"There isn't time to think about it, Mr. Stone. He's going home soon. All I'm asking is that you let me check him out."

"What makes you think you can recruit him?"

"Intuition."

"That's bullshit, my dear, if you don't mind my saying so."

"I don't mind, so long as you let me give it a try."

"I'd like to, honestly. But it's a delicate time, more than you realize. I won't bore you with the details, but we're having some difficulties with the front office. We don't need any more baggage."

"I'm not baggage," said Anna. Her voice had a tremor of anger.

"I'm not talking about you, Anna. I'm talking about the Armenian."

"Alan will back me up. So will Frank Hoffman, if I ask him."

"How stubborn you are. I must say."

"You gave me your word that you would let me explore this, Mr. Stone. If you back out now, it's going to make me reevaluate a lot of other things."

"What is that supposed to mean?"

"It means I want to go to Paris."

"I see." Stone thought about it a good long while, long enough for Anna's resolve to crack, if it was crackable. But she sat there nearly motionless, convinced of the righteousness and good sense of what she was proposing. And Stone, it must be said, knew when to fold a weak hand.

"Very well," he said. "Before you go, I will insist on a plausible scenario for recruitment and termination. I'll want all the usual paperwork and then some. After that, you'll be on your own."

Anna nodded, and allowed herself a modest, chaste smile of triumph. Stone studied her handsome face. There was a fierce look in her eye that Stone, had he been feeling less harassed, would surely have recognized as the product of his own tutelage. It was, in a way, a victory for his methodology, another triumph for the old boys.

36

◆

THE ARMENIAN DOCTOR LIVED IN THE SOUTHERN SUBURBS OF Paris, in one of the dormitories for foreign students known as the Cité Universitaire. He worked during the day at the Faculty of Medicine of the Sorbonne, just off the Boulevard St. Germain. Young Dr. Antoyan was a creature of habit: He caught the Métro each morning at eight-thirty, changed at Denfert-Rochereau, got out at St.-Germain-des-Prés, and walked the four short blocks to the Rue de l'Ecole-de-Médecine. The best thing about him, from Anna's standpoint, was that the files showed no trace of any KGB connections. He was, quite simply, a young research doctor—a very bright one, apparently— who had been sent abroad for advanced training.

Anna decided that the best recruitment scenario was the simplest and closest to life. She would present herself to the

Armenian doctor as a former Harvard graduate student in Ottoman history, now working with a foundation that supported cultural and historical research on the Near East and Central Asia. She would informally solicit his views on Armenian issues, ask him to do a short research paper (for which she would pay him handsomely), then ask him if he might be willing to do additional research when he returned home to Yerevan. And then—if all had gone well up to that point, she would pop the question. Stone couldn't really argue with what she proposed. It was a standard recruitment scenario—used with minor variations on hundreds of Eastern bloc and Third World students over the years.

As an intermediary in setting up the rendezvous, Anna chose a young French journalist named Danielle Marton. She found Marton's name in the files summarizing the development work that had been done two years before. Marton was a perfect access agent. She was a more or less witting asset of the Paris station, carrying the cryptonym UNWILLOW, who had met Antoyan through her husband, a doctor, when the Armenian first arrived in Paris in 1977.

Anna, banned by Stone from working through the local station, simply called Danielle Marton on the telephone and invited her to lunch. She never quite explained how she had gotten Marton's name—and certainly never said she worked for the agency—leaving all that to the French journalist's imagination, which was much more powerful and persuasive than anything Anna could have said. Anna dropped a few leading questions about the Soviet Armenian doctor; by the end of the lunch, Marton was volunteering to arrange a meeting.

They met at five-thirty one afternoon in a quiet café several blocks from the Boulevard St.-Germain. Anna and Danielle had arrived early and were animatedly discussing one of the great questions of the twentieth century—why had the feminist Simone de Beauvoir fallen so slavishly in love with Jean-Paul Sartre?—when up walked Dr. Aram Antoyan. He was a handsome man in his early thirties—medium height, with dark features, jet-black hair and a thick black beard. He was wearing blue jeans and a tweed sports coat over his blue linen doctor's tunic. He might have been a resident at an American hospital, except for one unmistakably Armenian features—the large black eyes that appeared to be deep pools of memory and sorrow, even when he was smiling.

Danielle made the introductions. The young Armenian doctor, though obviously tired from a day at work, tried his best to be charming. He flirted with his friend Danielle, complimented her on her dress, asked her about her latest article. He was more reserved with Anna, obviously curious about what she wanted but waiting for her to take the lead. They conversed in French, but even in that sometimes mannered language, he spoke with a directness and clarity that was almost like English. Danielle excused herself after a few minutes, saying that she had to make dinner for her husband, the doctor. Anna let the conversation meander for another twenty minutes before making a move.

"I'm interested in the Armenian question," she said eventually, by way of explaining why she had arranged the meeting.

"La question arménienne," repeated Antoyan, turning the French words over in his mouth. "A ruinous topic. I suppose it is our fate, we Armenians, to be not a people, but a question. Why are you interested in this sad subject?"

"I work for a foundation," said Anna.

Antoyan looked at her skeptically, his thick black eyebrows arching upward.

"My foundation studies contemporary issues in the Near East and Central Asia. We work with universities, American corporations. That sort of thing."

"May I please ask you a question?"

"Of course," said Anna, hoping that her face didn't betray the anxiety she felt.

"Do you work for the Turks?"

"No," said Anna, relieved that this was his principal concern.

"Good," he said with a trace of a smile. "I would be concerned if you were working for the Turks. But if you're not a Turk, and not an Armenian, I must ask you again, why are you interested in the Armenian question?"

Anna spoke from the heart. She told Dr. Antoyan about her freshman roommate at Radcliffe, Ruth Mugrditchian, with her stories about a great-aunt who crawled across the Syrian desert with a Bible in her hand and another relative who survived because he was hidden at the bottom of a well. Those stories, she explained, had gotten her interested in Ottoman history.

"Yes, yes," said the Armenian doctor. "That is why everyone becomes interested in the Armenians. We are such perfect victims." He closed his eyes. Like every Armenian child, he had grown up hearing similar stories of the genocide. But that evening, sitting in a café in St.-Germain, talking with an attractive American woman, it was obvious that he did not want to hear them all over again.

"I'm sorry," said Anna. "I'm not interested in Armenians only as victims."

She was angry at herself for being too direct, too clumsy in her opening. She tried to remember the advice of her instructors, so many months ago. Go slow, let your quarry set the pace of the conversation. Let him tell you, in his way, what matters to him. But Aram didn't seem to mind her clumsiness. He had a wry smile on his face, the look of a man determined to make merry at a wake.

"If you really want to know about the Armenian question," he said, "you must listen to Armenian Radio. They have the answer to everything."

"Glad to, but what's Armenian Radio?"

"Impossible! You mean you have never heard of the famous Armenian Radio and its answers to listeners' questions?"

"Sorry, but I haven't."

"This Armenian Radio distills the ancient wisdom of our people. I will give you an example. Armenian Radio is asked: What is the most ancient and beautiful city in the U.S.S.R.? Armenian Radio answers: Yerevan is the most ancient and beautiful city in the U.S.S.R.

"And how long would it take a nuclear bomb to destroy Yerevan? the radio is asked. Armenian Radio answers: Tbilisi is also a very ancient and beautiful city."

Anna realized that her leg was being pulled. "So what does Armenian Radio say about the Armenian question?" she asked.

"Armenian Radio answers that the Georgian question is also very important."

* * *

It was a soft September evening, and Dr. Antoyan didn't seem in any rush, so they ordered another round of drinks and talked about America, the movies, modern medicine, the writings of Solzhenitsyn. There was no topic, it seemed, that Dr. Antoyan wasn't willing to discuss. He was in that respect typical of the new generation of Soviets that was beginning to travel overseas in the late 1970s. They were curious and surprisingly self-assured—especially the scientists and research doctors, who like their Western colleagues considered themselves members of the international republic of the intellect and disdained petty rules. After two hours of this charming conversation, Anna felt that she really ought to get back to the subject at hand. She tried to think of an artful transition, but couldn't.

"Tell me about Armenia," she said. "What is it like?"

Aram smiled. "It is simply a place, with the ordinary pleasures and problems of any other place. Plays, restaurants, theaters, parks. To me, that is its triumph. Armenia is ordinary and alive, rather than special and dead."

"But what makes it different from Moscow or Kiev? Or Paris?"

"It is more corrupt."

"But corruption is everywhere in the Soviet Union these days, isn't it?"

"Yes, but that is workmanlike Slavic corruption. In Armenia it is an art form. It is the soul of the economy."

"I'm not sure I understand," said Anna. "Can you give me an example?" She hoped she wasn't sounding too eager, too hungry for information. But the Armenian doctor seemed happy enough to talk.

"Take the cognac factory in Yerevan," he said. "It is one of our greatest economic enterprises, located in a great stone building atop a big hill as you enter the city. Some people assume it must be the parliament building! Now you might think that the goal of this enterprise would simply be to produce fine cognac, since ours is renowned throughout the Soviet Union. But that is not quite right."

"What is it really there for?"

"To create surplus production, which can be sold illegally for private benefit. Let's say the monthly production quota is five thousand bottles of cognac. The factory will claim to make six thousand bottles, to overfulfill the quota and receive its bonuses. But in fact, the factory has really made seven thousand bottles."

"What happens to the extra thousand bottles?"

"Precisely the question! What happens to the extra thousand bottles? Let us assume that I am one of the managers. I send a hundred and ten bottles to my Armenian friend in Leningrad. He signs for receiving a hundred bottles, the amount he actually ordered. He sends me money for the extra ten bottles and sells them. Or maybe he and I develop a swap system. I send him cognac; he sends me leather. And maybe I swap some of the leather with another Armenian friend in Tashkent, who has some cotton. The thousand extra bottles are all disposed of in a similar way. You understand?"

Anna nodded. She thought of all those vanishing bottles, and of the difficulty of managing an entire economy that ran on two sets of books.

"The system is rotten at every point," said Antoyan. "The only thing that is alive is the rot."

"That's fascinating," said Anna, "and very helpful to my foundation." The Armenian seemed almost recklessly frank in his description of how the system worked. She wondered to herself whether she should make her move, push him to venture across the invisible line, toward cooperation. But Dr. Antoyan was smiling again.

"You know what Armenian Radio says on this subject?" he said.

"No, what?"

"Armenian Radio is asked: Is it possible to build Communism in Armenia? Armenian Radio answers: Yes, but we would prefer that you build it in Georgia."

Anna laughed, but in truth her mind was somewhere else. She felt like a salesman, trying to get that first toe in the door. Being friendly and polite wasn't enough; in the end, you had to push your way in.

"Listen, Dr. Antoyan," she said. "My foundation is very interested in this subject."

"What subject?"

"Corruption in the Soviet Union."

"I see."

"And we would love to know more about it. Maybe you could write a brief paper for us about the economic situation, summarizing what you have told me. Just a few pages. We would offer you a small research stipend, of course, if you could accept it."

Aram smiled, as if he knew exactly what Anna's foundation was all about. Anna plunged ahead.

"How does that sound?" she asked.

Still there was no answer from Aram. He just sat there looking composed, a smile still traced on his lips.

"What do you think?" pressed Anna again, this time almost in a whisper.

But the Armenian doctor kept his silence. After a few more agonizing seconds, he looked at his watch, remarked on the lateness of the hour, and said he must be heading back to the dormitory at Cité Universitaire. As he stood up to go, Anna felt sick to her stomach. She was convinced that she had bungled her first, and probably last, chance at recruiting the young Armenian. This feeling was in no way lessened when Dr. Antoyan, in parting, gave her a gentle and affectionate kiss on the cheek.

Aram Antoyan's response came back a day later. It was a single typed page placed in a sealed envelope that he dropped off at the office of Danielle Marton. Anna was surprised when Danielle called to say that Dr. Antoyan had left a message for her; she had feared she would never hear from him again. But when Anna read the message itself, she was even more surprised. It read, in its entirety, as follows.

Some Observations on the Soviet Union

1. Armenian Radio is asked: What is so strange about Rooms 1714 and 2114 at the Rossiya Hotel in Moscow? Armenian Radio answers that they are adjoining rooms.

2. Armenian Radio is asked whether a commissar should close the door of his office when making love to his secretary. Armenian Radio advises no, as people will think they may be drinking.

3. Armenian Radio is asked: What happens to Italians who stay too long in the U.S.S.R.? Armenian Radio answers that when they go home, all the bras seem small.

4. Armenian Radio is asked: Should a woman marry a man who has been sent to prison for murdering his

first wife? Armenian Radio answers that this is not a problem, as he is single.

5. Armenian Radio is asked if it is all right to make love to a woman in Lenin Square in Tbilisi. Armenian Radio says it's all right, but people will probably stop and give advice.

6. Armenian Radio is asked: Can we create socialism in France? Armenian Radio answers: Probably, but who needs it?

Anna's first thought was that it was a code, pregnant with hidden meaning, or a ruse of some sort. Nobody in his right mind would send a simple list of jokes in response to her query. But as she thought about Antoyan, and the seductive look in his eye when he talked, it seemed possible that the only hidden meaning of his message was that he wanted to sleep with her. Good, she thought. An innocent motive. She called Danielle and asked her to contact the Armenian doctor.

"Call him yourself," said the French journalist. "His number is 537-17-77." There was a note of pique in her voice.

Anna called Dr. Antoyan that afternoon at his laboratory and suggested that they meet for dinner. "Why not," was Aram's response. Anna deliberately chose a fancy restaurant, one that Aram couldn't possibly afford on his research stipend. It was a small and elegant spot on the Ile St. Louis, which had been a favorite of her father's many years before. Anna dropped the name of Ambassador Barnes when making the reservation and was promised a table outdoors, overlooking the Seine. She was on her way back to the hotel, to get ready, when it occurred to her that she was sick of everything in her wardrobe. She was staying at the Bristol Hotel, near the fancy dress shops along the Rue du Faubourg-St.-Honoré, and on a whim she stopped and browsed in one of the most stylish boutiques. She emerged thirty minutes later wearing a new tweed suit, with a tight skirt and a short, tailored jacket. She also let the salesgirl talk her into a new silk blouse, suggestively open at the neck.

"Why are you so frank with me?" asked Anna when they were halfway through their first glass of wine. "I thought Russians had to be very careful with foreigners."

"I'm an Armenian," he said. "Not a Russian."

"I meant 'Soviets.' But it's the same thing. Aren't you afraid that someone will see you talking to an American and report you or call you in for questioning?"

"Not at all. I am a scientist. Working with foreigners is part of my job. I don't know any secrets, so why should anyone care? My job in Paris is to learn how to diagnose a condition called 'reflux' in the urinary tracts of little children. That is why they sent me here. The rest, pfff. Anyway, as I said, I am an Armenian. Everyone in Moscow knows we're unreliable."

"Why are you unreliable?"

He tilted his head, as if it were a question he didn't really want to answer, but then went ahead. "There is an old proverb which the esteemed George Orwell quotes in one of his books. 'Trust a snake before a Jew, and a Jew before a Greek. But never trust an Armenian.' "

"That isn't fair."

"Of course not, but it's funny. And there is a strange way in which it is true. Armenians are not very trustworthy."

"Why not?" asked Anna. She had no idea where the conversation was heading, but she was determined to let him set the pace this time.

"Because we have suffered too much. We begin with the assumption that the rest of the world hates us, so we don't care too much about making a few more enemies. In fact, I suspect that Armenians have come to like being so universally despised. It is part of our national identity."

"That sounds absolutely crazy," said Anna. "Have some more wine."

"It isn't crazy. We Armenians are the victims of an accident of geography. It is our great misfortune, a nation of people who like reading Shakespeare and the sonnets of William Wordsworth, to exist on the barren steppes of eastern Anatolia and the Caucasus. Think of it! A nation of craftsmen and merchants and poets surrounded by people whose idea of science is inventing new degrees of bastinado to torture their prisoners. What an absurd geographical mistake! But I am sorry. I am talking like an Armenian."

"Have some more wine," she repeated. "What on earth do you mean, 'talking like an Armenian'?"

"I mean that I am talking like a victim. That is our great national failing. We Armenians are in love with victimhood. We love it the way an amputee loves his stump. It is our excuse, our reason for being."

What a bizarre notion, thought Anna. It occurred to her that nearly everyone she had encountered the last few months was possessed by some crazy idea or another. Stone. Taylor. Now this Armenian doctor. Perhaps even herself.

"If my friend Ruth Mugrditchian heard you, she would want to punch you in the nose," said Anna. "She would tell you how the Turks shot her great-grandfather in cold blood and left her great-aunt to die in a ditch on the road to Aleppo. And don't tell me her grandparents were in love with their victimhood. That's sick."

"Perhaps it's hard to see in each individual case," answered Antoyan. "But you must stand back from this pathos and think of all the cases together. It simply isn't possible for a million people to be destroyed in a few months' time unless they acquiesced somehow in this fate, unless they embraced martyrdom and death. That is the danger for a nation of romantic poets, like Armenia. Its people fall in love with the idea of suicide. And I am telling you, the Armenians are in love with their pain. They hate to give it up."

"But not you?"

"No, not me. I don't want to be a victim, and I am not a victim. My father was not a victim, nor his father."

"What did they do?"

"They were fighters. My father fought at Stalingrad against the Germans. My grandfather fought with General Antranik when the Armenian militia and the Red Army stormed Baku and Kokand. He shot many Moslems. I am sure that to Azeris and Uzbeks, he must have seemed like a ruthless Armenian-killer."

"Does that bother you? That he killed so many Moslems?"

"Not very much. I would rather be hated as a killer than as a victim."

"But people don't hate victims."

"Oh yes, they do," said Antoyan. "For victims, they actually feel something crueler than hate. They feel contempt. And I want none of it."

Anna was going to protest again, but the Armenian had

risen from his chair. A family of gypsies had approached the restaurant, hoping to sell flowers to the diners. The maître d'hôtel was trying to shoo them away, and the ruckus was getting louder. Antoyan reached over the maître d' toward the gypsies with a ten-franc note in his hand and retrieved a bunch of day-old carnations.

"Please don't encourage them, monsieur," said the maître d'.

The Armenian ignored him and returned to his seat. He handed the flowers to Anna.

"Back home in Yerevan," he said, "on a pleasant evening like this, the road into the city would be crowded with women selling carnations from their gardens, far more beautiful than these. So I give them to you as a symbol of what is alive and graceful in my native city. Perhaps you will come there one day and buy some yourself."

"Perhaps I will," said Anna, trying to imagine this strange republic of cognac makers and flower sellers and brooding tragedians. "But I doubt it."

Anna paid the bill, without protest from Antoyan, and they set off for a stroll along the Seine. The tiny Ile St. Louis was awash with people. Anna and Aram joined the stream heading toward Notre Dame and the Place St.-Michel. The river twinkled with the lights of the city and the moonlit sky: a sleek *bateau mouche* slid by underneath the Petit Pont. Aram put his arm around Anna. She let it rest there. Let him believe that he was seducing her, if he liked, she thought. She could still control the relationship and use it for her purposes.

Antoyan led her to a bench along the Quai des Orfèvres, away from the crowd of evening strollers. He took Anna's hand gently in his, opening the palm toward him.

"I will read your fortune, my dear Miss Morgan," he said.

"You are a palm reader?"

"That is one of my Oriental skills. The reading of palms. The casting of spells. The divination of water. If I were not a medical doctor, I would be a shaman. Here. Relax your hand and I will look."

Anna let her palm go limp, while he studied the lines creased across the soft flesh. As he was examining her, Anna looked at his own hands. They were a doctor's hands. Confident, strong, deliberate. She imagined what his body must look like, without clothes. He was not a lean Thoroughbred, like Taylor. More like a Caucasian horse, close-footed and compact, adept at the narrow paths of the mountains.

"You are a beautiful woman," he said.

"Thank you," answered Anna. "But what does that have to do with reading my palm?"

"Everything," he said. "I can read this hand, and this face, like an open book."

"All right, Svengali. Go ahead."

"I see in your hand that you have had many love affairs."

"Not so many," said Anna defensively.

"But the men were all too weak for you. They were selfish boys. They wanted a mother, or a sister, or maybe a girl for one night. But they didn't want a woman."

Anna wanted to pull her hand way, not because he was wrong, but because he was right. "That's true," she said. "But you're not reading it in my hand."

"You want to be in love with a man who is mature and confident," he continued. "A man who knows what love is."

"Yes."

"But you are not in love now."

Anna thought for a long moment about Taylor. "I guess that's right," she said.

Antoyan studied her hand for another twenty seconds. The only sounds were the rush of wind in their ears and the honking of far-off car horns at the Place St.-Michel.

"You are worried about something," he said eventually. "In your work."

"Yes," said Anna, becoming more interested and curious. "But what am I worried about?"

He studied her hand, and then looked up at her from under those black eyebrows. On his face was that trace of a smile that seemed to come over him when they veered toward the true nature of her work.

"I don't know," he said. "But you are caught in something from which you cannot escape, from which you do not want to escape. And gradually it is becoming your destiny."

Anna felt a chill, as if from a sudden gust of wind along the river. "Let's go," she said. "I'm cold."

The Armenian removed his coat and put it over Anna's

shoulders. They walked in silence along the quay for fifty yards.

"You're no fortune-teller," she said after a while. "You're just a good guesser. You could have said those same things about anybody. Everybody wants to be in love. Everybody worries about work."

"Perhaps that is true," said Antoyan. "But the art of the palm reader is to speak to the heart of one person only. And that is not so easy."

Anna looked at him, tenderly and warily. In some mysterious way, he was transforming the nature of their interaction, so that it was coming within his control, rather than hers. She could feel the ground slipping from under her feet, and she wanted to reestablish her balance.

"Listen, Aram," she said. "When are you going home?"

"Two weeks, I am sorry to say."

"When you get back to Yerevan, would you be willing to stay in touch with me?"

"Why do you ask?"

"Because I'm interested in what you say about Armenia. So is my foundation. And we'd like to pay you for the help you've given us."

The Armenian was silent for a long while. He looked at the ground as he walked, lost in thought.

"Come have dinner with me tomorrow night, and we will talk about it," he said eventually. "I have some things I must discuss with you also. But no more talk of money, please. I want something from you, but it is not money."

"Where shall we meet? At the Cité Universitaire?"

"No. That is not the place. We would be seen. Perhaps we could meet at your hotel."

"Ahh. So you do care whether someone sees us."

"Of course I care," said Antoyan. "I told you, I do not want to be a victim."

37

___◆___

Anna was staying in a small suite at the Bristol. The rooms were simple and stylish, decorated with fine fabrics in shades of beige and taupe. The suite cost nearly 2,000 francs a night—a small fortune in 1979—but the money seemed to flow endlessly from the bank accounts back in Rockville, and over the past few months Anna had fallen into the comfortable habit of traveling first-class. It was one of the many small corruptions that had entered into her life as she had moved deeper into the realm of unaudited covert operations.

Aram Antoyan rang from the lobby and proposed that he come upstairs. Anna promptly agreed; she had been hoping he would do just that. Meeting in the room would be more secure, and also more intimate—which Anna reasoned would be good tradecraft on both counts. She had initially taken the precaution of unplugging the lights, just as Hoffman had done in Athens, but then decided it was too dark and turned them back on. She had also, in her ladylike way, tidied the room and dressed herself in another newly purchased outfit from the Rue du Faubourg-St.-Honoré, this one a simple black chemise. And finally, she had opened the mini-bar and poured two glasses of vodka, one for Aram and one for herself.

As she waited for the knock on the door, Anna ran through her mental agenda one last time. The essence of any successful recruitment was control, of her own emotions and those of the target. She recalled what Hoffman had said back in Athens, and what Margaret Houghton had told her so long ago at the restaurant in Washington. The task for a good intelligence officer as to sense what the other party wanted out of life, and then to help him to achieve it. It was, in a strange way, like what a seductive woman tries to do with a man: contrive a world, partly of illusion, in which he can realize his deepest hopes and desires. At first that had sounded to Anna like a very feminine definition of intelligence work, but if she had learned anything in the past year, it was that Margaret's initial guidance had been right. The male mythology of intelligence was bunk. Except for the occasional bad apple like Ali Ascari, the spy business wasn't about "burning" people, "busting their balls" or "turning the screws." It was about stroking people, coaxing them, entering into their dreams and nightmares and translating these private visions into the language of the world; it was about leading people along a path toward a mutually agreed destination, albeit sometimes by a circuitous route.

Anna's reverie was interrupted by a sharp rap on the door. Despite her calm rehearsal, she felt a sudden rush of anxiety like an actress about to perform a new play. She needn't have worried quite so much. For, unknown to her, Dr. Antoyan had come to the Bristol Hotel to act out a drama of his own invention.

When the Armenian was seated, glass of vodka in his hand, he leaned earnestly toward Anna. The characteristic look of bemused reflection was gone from his face. He was there to talk business. Anna was thinking about how to begin, but Dr. Antoyan beat her to it.

"There is something I must tell you," he said.

"That's interesting," said Anna. "Because there is something that I must tell you, too."

"I will go first, if you do not mind. That may make it easier for you, or harder. I don't know. But I haven't been entirely honest with you."

Oh shit, thought Anna. This crazy Armenian is going to tell me that he's a KGB officer, and that he wants to recruit me.

But that was not it at all. Antoyan began in a roundabout way—which was unusual for him but, under the circumstances, understandable.

"How much do you know about the Soviet Union, Miss Morgan?" he said.

"Some," she answered. "Not very much." As she looked at his face, she noticed that he had trimmed his black beard since the previous night. It no longer seemed a mask of creativity, but of camouflage and control.

"To the rest of the world," he continued, "the Soviet state

probably looks like a colossus that is impregnable and invulnerable. But if you live there, you know that it is quite different. We have, throughout the country, people who are known in the West as 'dissidents.' They are everywhere. You cannot find anyone my age, anyone who is the least bit sensible, who does not understand in his heart that the great Soviet Union is a sick and dying animal."

Anna nodded. She thought of what Edward Stone had said, back at the beginning of this strange quest. He had used almost the same words in describing the decay of the Soviet state.

"They are everywhere in the Soviet Union, these dissidents," he went on, "and they are especially numerous in my own republic. But in Armenia, they are not called dissidents. They are called patriots."

"And you are an Armenian patriot," said Anna. She could feel the first ripples of what was coming.

"Yes. Despite some of the things I said last night, I am an Armenian patriot. I am no politician. In fact, I hate politics in the way that any honest scientist does. But I love my country in a sense that is beyond politics."

Anna nodded again. "I suppose I knew that about you," she said.

"That is why I am going home in two weeks. I could arrange to stay here at the Faculty of Medicine for another year. Perhaps longer. I am very good at my work. But I feel that I must go home, to be with people who feel as I do."

"Who are they, your fellow patriots? What do they want?"

"I will tell you a little history, so you will know who we are. Our dissident movement began in April 1965, on the fiftieth anniversary of the genocide of our people. The apparatchiks running the Armenian republic weren't planning any ceremony to mark the event. It wasn't convenient, as the Russians like to say. But the ordinary people wouldn't stand for it. This pain was their identity, and they wanted to scream—so that the world would know they still existed. They took to the streets, by the thousands, in a great tearful march that lasted all one day and into the next. The local KGB and the militia went crazy. But they could not stop it."

"Did you march?"

"Yes, of course I marched. I was sixteen years old. I wanted to scream, like everyone else. But after we had stopped scream-ing, my friends and I wanted to do something more."

"What was that?"

"We wanted to build a real country. In 1968, some of my compatriots started a group called the Armenian Self-Determination Movement. They argued that no government in Yerevan could be legitimate without free elections. That was quite a revolutionary idea in 1968, and many of them were put in prison. A few who weren't arrested went underground. Some even went to Beirut to join the secret Armenian organizations that were starting there in the early 1970s."

"What about you?"

"I was careful and cautious. Perhaps I was also frightened. I won a place at the university in Moscow, and everybody told me that I was destined for great things. I didn't want to destroy my chances. You see, a clever scientist in the Soviet Union can live a very good life. It is not something to throw away. But all the while, as I worked and studied, I stayed in touch with my old friends. They had become very excited about the campaign to assassinate Turkish diplomats. All the hotheads wanted to run off to Damascus and join ASALA and kill Turks. But I thought this was a terrible mistake."

"Why?" Anna was letting the waves of his argument lap against her, waiting to see the source from which it flowed.

"For all the reasons I explained to you last night. We are a people caught in the past. We want the world to see our old wounds, to celebrate our suffering with us, to commemorate, to apologize. But I think this approach is wrong. It keeps us chained to this dead animal of the past. And it will lead us to make the same tragic mistake as before."

"What is that mistake?"

"We are looking for the world to save us. We want the Turks to apologize to us. We want Moscow to protect us. We want America to love us. We are looking for someone else to give dignity and definition to our race. But I am finished with that. When I came here to Paris and had a chance to think for myself, I realized that I am tired of the Armenian past. I want to build the Armenian future. I want us to be an ordinary part of the modern world, just like everyone else. And I have found a small group of people who feel the same way I do."

"Bravo," said Anna. "But you can't do it alone. You need help."

"I know. That is why I am here, with you. I don't know exactly what you do, you and your 'foundation,' but I have a feeling that you can help us."

Anna took a deep breath. So here it was. He had walked across the line on his own, without so much as a push. Did he really know what was on the other side?

"I want to tell you about what I do," she said, "so that there will be no misunderstanding between us later. My foundation works closely with the government . . ."

"Don't tell me," he interjected.

"I must tell you some things. I represent . . ."

"Don't tell me!" he said again sharply. "It is better left unsaid."

Anna stopped and thought. There was no requirement, certainly, that she tell him all the details. But it bothered her to be side-stepping the central fact of their relationship.

"Sometimes," she said, "it's better to know exactly what you're getting into. Things can happen later."

"And sometimes it is better to leave things fuzzy. In this case, I want something very specific from you. And if you can get it for me, the rest is irrelevant."

Anna had a strange feeling of disorientation, as if the huntress was also the prey. "What do you want from me?" she asked.

"My friends and I have decided that we want Armenia to join the revolution."

"What are you talking about?"

"The revolution of one world. When you come to a place like Paris from the Soviet Union, you realize that there is something happening in the world which doesn't have anything to do with capitalism or socialism, or even with politics. It has to do with communication. The world is becoming one, and we Armenians want to join. Now."

"Join what? I still don't understand what you mean."

"We want to sit around the same fire with you at night. We want to watch the same news on television, watch the same movies on Saturday night, dance to the same music. We want to share in the same conversation. If we can do that, the rest will take care of itself."

"How can I possibly help you do that?"

"It is simple, really," he said, stretching his hands out toward her. "It is just a matter of obtaining the right sort of antennas."

She thought at first that he was putting her on. "What antennas?"

"Television antennas."

"What are you talking about, Aram? Are you crazy?"

"Please! This is the most serious thing in the world. The Kremlin is terrified that the United States someday will launch a satellite that can broadcast television pictures across the Soviet Union. I know that from a friend of mine who works at Central Scientific Research Institute No. 50, in Bolshevo outside Moscow. He says that a few years ago the Politburo ordered his entire laboratory to stop work on anti-satellite weapons and find some way to prevent a television satellite from transmitting its pictures."

"Is that so," said Anna, trying to commit to memory the name and location of the institute. "What did they recommend?"

"Nothing. They said it was impossible, without shooting the satellite down."

"But there isn't any TV satellite over the Soviet Union."

"No, but there is a television satellite over Europe, and there will be more."

"Maybe so. But what good does it do you? You couldn't pick up the signals in the Soviet Union. The KGB would spot a satellite dish in a minute."

"Of course they would. But, my darling Miss Morgan, you do not need a satellite dish. You can use something else, no bigger than the top of this table." He pointed to a small end table beside the couch.

"Nonsense."

"It is called a phased-array television antenna. You can tune it, like a dish, to receive satellite pictures. But you point it electronically, rather than physically. You can hang it flat against the wall, or lay it on top of the roof. It's practically invisible."

"Are you serious?"

"I am completely serious. This is a very simple device, but unfortunately it is not yet sold commercially. I thought that perhaps your foundation could help us obtain one."

"What would you do with it?"

"We would use it to connect Yerevan with the world. We would do it in secret at first. Set up the antenna with a video recorder, somewhere the KGB could not find it. Each night we would monitor the news of the world, and send a summary to our friends at the television station in Yerevan. After a while, maybe we would send them a bit of videotape, with pictures of some of the places in the news. And then, if they could be trusted, some more. And then we would send the whole cassette over, to use on Armenian television.

"And not just the news. Our people want to know what the world is reading, and what it is watching at movie theaters, and listening to at the concert halls. We want to learn about a world that is not bounded by the Caucasus, or the absurdities of Communism, or the tragedies of Ottoman history. We want to live in the present, with the rest of the world, without Turkish ghosts at the door. Then we can join the world of Europe and America, at last."

"It's a wonderful dream, Aram," said Anna. "But you would never get away with it. The authorities would discover what you were doing and stop you the minute the foreign pictures were broadcast on Armenian television."

"Don't be so sure. Armenians are patriots. That is the thing about a people who have truly suffered. There is not one of us who would stand with Moscow against the Armenian nation."

"But ultimately you would need the cooperation of all the people who produce Armenian television, and all the people who watch it."

"So? To be an Armenian is to be a member of the conspiracy. It is that simple. We are ready. All we need is your help in obtaining the right kind of antenna."

Anna wasn't sure whether to take him seriously. It still sounded crazy, although somewhat less so than she had first thought. But it occurred to her, looking at Aram, that it didn't really matter what she thought of the idea. It was his dream. Her only job—as an intelligence officer—was to help him realize it.

"Assuming we were willing to help," she said, "what would you want us to do?"

"Aha!" answered Antoyan. "I hoped you would ask that."

He rummaged in his coat pocket and removed a sheet of paper covered with a handwritten wiring diagram.

"One of my friends prepared this," he said. "It is simplicity itself."

"Who is your friend?"

"I am sorry. I cannot tell you. He is an Armenian scientist, like me, but I cannot say more than that."

"Is he a Soviet citizen, or French, or what?"

"Shhhh," said Antoyan. "No more. You do not need to know anything about the man, because you have here the product of his research." He pointed to the diagram and its precisely drawn circuits.

"Each of these points is a tiny antenna," he explained. "There are many hundreds of them, all interconnected. When they are coordinated by a computer, they can be tuned to receive television signals with great precision, even when the antenna is not perpendicular to the waves."

"I'm sorry," said Anna, "but this is lost on me. I failed physics."

"Take my word for it. The circuitry is simple. The only hard part is the computer. If your people build it, it will work. The real problem isn't building it, but getting it into the country. Now, the question is: Can you do it?"

"Maybe," said Anna. She was trying to be tough, trying to hold on to some measure of control.

" 'Maybe' is not enough. Can you do it?"

"I will try. I can't make any promises. I work for an organization. I have to get the approval of other people. This is the kind of thing they've approved in the past, but I can't be sure."

"Trying it not enough. I must have an answer."

Anna stared out the window of her suite toward a small green garden, enclosed in a narrow courtyard. She desperately wanted to say yes. In a sense, this was the moment she had dreamed of when she joined the agency, a moment in which idealism and activism fused together.

"What is the answer?" he pressed.

"Yes."

"What does 'yes' mean?"

"Yes, I will take this drawing to my colleagues and urge them to do what you want."

"And if they say no?"

"They won't say no. It's not worth the trouble it would cause them. Don't worry. When I make a promise I keep it."

Aram closed his eyes. He looked completely exhausted, his face drained of energy and emotion. He rose slowly to his feet and looked around the room.

"I must go now," he said.

"Stay for a while," she said softly. She was embarrassed at the thought, but she wanted this young man of the Caucasus to sit with her a while, hold her in his arms; it wasn't sex she wanted, exactly, but something softer. She wanted to touch his face, massage his back, watch his large, sad eyes close and feel his body fall asleep next to hers.

"I must go," he said again. "It is dangerous for me to be here. And for you."

She looked out to the enclosed garden again and turned back to him. "You know, Aram, I've had this wrong in my mind. I thought that I was seducing you, but you have been seducing me."

"You are still wrong. Nobody is seducing anybody. This is real."

Anna nodded.

"I will have to meet with my colleagues," she said.

"Yes."

"That will take a week or so."

"Yes."

"If they agree, it will take at least a month to prepare one of these things." She pointed to the diagram. "By that time you'll be back in Yerevan. How will we get it to you?"

"There is a way. Your people will know how to do it."

"What is it?"

"I will tell you when we meet again, in a week. If the answer is yes."

Anna sighed. "All right."

"How shall we arrange the next meeting?"

"The same way as before. I will call you at the laboratory. We'll make a date. You come meet me. The only difference is that, this time, come to the place two hours before the time I mention. If I say eight, come at six."

He nodded and smiled that charming half smile, for the first time that evening. "You make a lovely spy, my darling," he said.

They embraced at the door, carefully at first, a kiss on each cheek. It was hard to know which of them gave way first, whose lips opened and whose eyes closed. It was a passionate kiss that dissolved any barrier that had remained between them. Aram put his hands on her breasts, and then on her thigh, and it was only then—as her body was curling toward his, strung so tight with desire that a string might have popped—that she pushed him away.

Aram smiled his delightful smile one last time as he turned and walked down the corridor. Anna knew she had made a mistake in becoming intimate with him. It was a gross breach of professionalism, irredeemable, unforgivable. But at that point, she honestly didn't care. Like her colleagues at Karpetland, she had some time ago jumped the tracks of appropriate behavior.

38

THE SUPREME PRIORITY OF THE CIA WORLDWIDE THAT September, Taylor discovered after his return to Istanbul, was a summit meeting of the Non-Aligned Movement in Havana, Cuba. The gathering was an empty propaganda exercise that had wisely been ignored in past years, even by most of its members. But not this year. The President, it seemed, had become interested in "North-South" issues, and headquarters was falling over itself trying to provide intelligence on his pet project. So the cables had gone out, to every station and base in Africa, Asia, Latin America and the Near East, requesting intelligence in minute detail about what would happen in Havana in early September. This was known in the trade as "tasking."

Taylor was tasked on Havana, along with everyone else. But otherwise, headquarters was unusually uncommunicative with the Istanbul base. It was as if they were giving him room, waiting for something to happen. That left him extra time to study the important matter of the Non-Aligned summit, as enumerated in queries stacked atop his desk:

"—Identify the various NAM subgroups, cores, meetings and roving delegations. Are certain members who should normally relate to a group being excluded?

"—Identify the delegations, delegates and outsiders who appear to have unique influence with NAM (the movers and shakers) and their positions.

"—Identify Cuban vulnerabilities in NAM issues and Cuban actions to thwart U.S. efforts to alter Cuban draft.

"—What particular NAM members are the Cubans trying to placate? How?"

It reminded Taylor of the final exam of a sociology course at college, complete with extra-credit problems. He could imagine young CIA careerists around the globe working overtime to provide the latest information on, say, the respective roles of Somalia and Indonesia in discussions of UNCTAD/G-77 economic issues as they affect LDCs.

Taylor initially sent home a cable apologizing that because of Turkey's non-membership in the Non-Aligned Movement, he would be unable to provide any information whatsoever about the Havana meeting. But it wasn't quite so easy. Headquarters fired back a cable asking Istanbul to check its Iranian, Kurdish and Arab assets for information, and reminded the base chief that "this campaign is of direct interest to the President."

Once the Non-Aligned summit had actually taken place, there was a new avalanche of cables from headquarters demanding answers to such crucial questions as: "Did Zambian working groups take any moderating actions or did their actions completely support Cuba?" And for the extra-credit types, there was this stumper: "How did individual country activity in committee sessions compare with their presentations in open sessions? What trade-offs were made by whom and how were they worked out? Countries of special interest in this regard are Kuwait, Nigeria, Somalia, Iraq, Tanzania, Mozambique, Jamaica, Peru and Guyana. (One night was described by delegates as a 'night of hell.' What happened that night?)"

Taylor was in the midst of composing a fanciful cable responding to this last query ("The 'night of hell' began when a member of the Haitian delegation arrived at the conference

center escorted by two female members of the Tontons
Macoutes . . .") when his secretary buzzed that he had a call
from America. That was odd. People rarely telephoned from
America. Odder still was when Taylor picked up the phone
and heard the unmistakable voice of Edward Stone. He
sounded as if he were calling from a pay phone near the Beltway. You could hear the rush of traffic in the background.

"Do you know who this is?" asked the voice.

"Of course I do," said Taylor.

"This is the person you think it is."

"Right. That's what I thought."

"Good. I need to see you immediately."

"What's up?"

"I'll explain."

"Okay. When do you want to meet?"

"Tomorrow night."

"Where? Back home?"

"No. Somewhere in Europe."

"Where were you thinking of?"

"I'll let you know," said the voice.

"Have you told our colleague?"

"Not yet. But I will. That's another thing."

"What?"

"Your colleague has been bothering me about something.
We'll have to deal with that as well."

"No problem. How will I know where to meet you?"

But Stone had already hung up. The message arrived a few
hours later by the simplest and most direct means—a cable to
Taylor from headquarters headed, like all such communica-
tions: "CITE: DIRECTOR." It advised: "MEETING DISCUSSED REF A
WILL TAKE PLACE 17 SEPTEMBER 16:30Z AT CEVDET PASA 93,
BEBEK." Needless to say, there was no "REF A."

Taylor had to read the cable twice before he was sure he
had it right. The address was that of a run-down, fourth-class
hotel up the Bosporus from Istanbul, a place where the paint
was peeling and they didn't bother to cover the cigarette
burns on the carpets and furniture.

Stone greeted Taylor late the next afternoon at the door of
his hotel room. For the first time Taylor could remember, the
old man looked untidy. His eyes were bloodshot and baggy

after a sleepless overnight flight; his suit was rumpled from the unsuccessful attempt to bed down on the plane; there was a spot on his tie; and the skin on his face had a soft, fleshy texture, as if it had been applied in layers. If it were anyone else but Stone, you would suspect that he had been drinking. Past him in the adjoining room, Taylor could see Anna, seated in a chair, and through the window, the twinkling lights of ships along the Bosporus.

"You don't look so good," said Taylor.

"Looks are deceiving," answered Stone. "I feel splendid."

"Have it your way, but you look like you haven't slept in a month."

"What is sleep, my dear friend, when we are on the edge of victory?"

"Which game are we about to win?"

"Haven't you been reading your cables? There has been a coup in Afghanistan. Moscow's man, Taraki, has just been deposed by an even more ruthless fellow named Amin."

"Swell. So the Soviets will be getting out?"

"Better than that, my boy. It means they will be getting in—even deeper. It means they are almost in the net."

Taylor was about to ask Stone what the hell he was talking about, but the old man took his arm and steered him toward the sitting room, and Anna. She stood up slowly and shook Taylor's hand, cool and correct, a perfect colleague. He tried to catch her eye, but her gaze was elsewhere. Something had changed, but Taylor for the moment didn't get it.

"Welcome to Istanbul," he said. "By the way, I think you need a new travel agent."

"No, we don't," said Stone. "This hotel will be quite adequate for our purposes. Miss Barnes and I will be leaving first thing tomorrow morning. And this place has ambience. I'm told Hitler's agents stayed here during the war."

"Classy joint. But why are we meeting in Istanbul anyway? Why not Paris or London?"

"Because we control this environment. Or to be more precise, you—as Istanbul base chief—control this environment."

"That will be news to the Turks."

"I'm not referring to the Turks. I am referring to our so-called colleagues at Langley."

"Oh, them," said Taylor.

Anna listened to this exchange in silence. Stone's machinations interested her far less at that moment than obtaining approval for her operation with the Armenian doctor, who was waiting in Paris for an answer. Stone had put her off when she had tried to raise the issue with him an hour before, when they first arrived at the hotel, saying that they would discuss it as a group. Now, as Anna looked at Taylor, she thought not of love, or even affection, but of how best to manipulate him. And as Taylor gazed back with his bedroom eyes, she concluded that the answer wasn't very complicated.

Stone, meanwhile, had opened the window to let in the breeze, and removed from his briefcase a small machine that made a babbling sound, like a roomful of Chinese talking at once in a dim sum restaurant. It served to cover their conversation from the eavesdroppers that Stone assumed were lurking in the next room, always and everywhere.

"I am sorry to summon you so suddenly," said Stone over the sound of the noisy machine, "but we have a problem."

"What's that?" asked Taylor.

"Termination."

"Of what?"

"Of our operation. I want us entirely out of business by the end of November. Everything shut down, no continuing operations, no agents running around looking for trouble. No nothing. *Finito la musica.*"

"What's the rush?"

"I wouldn't call it a rush. I would call it prudence."

"Cut the crap, Mr. Stone. What's up?"

"The pygmies are in pursuit, my friends. The little people in the front office and their legislative chums think they have discovered something naughty, and the Inspector General has been summoned."

Anna looked carefully at Stone. Oddly, she felt energized by the old man's disarray, rather than frightened by it. "What naughty business have they discovered?" she asked.

"Something in Afghanistan."

"And what does this naughty business in Afghanistan have to do with us?"

"They think I am involved in it. It's nothing that you need to be overly concerned about. It's just that once people start asking questions in one area, they inevitably begin snooping elsewhere, checking the laundry basket and counting the silverware."

Taylor cleared his throat. "Don't you think you should level with us, Mr. Stone?" he said.

"Frankly, no."

"I agree with Alan," said Anna. "You should tell us what you've been doing in Afghanistan."

"I promise I'll tell you all about it someday, when we have a few relaxed hours. It's quite an interesting story. But this really isn't the time."

"Give it a try," said Anna coolly. "What have you been doing in Afghanistan?"

Stone sighed. "Very well. A teaser. A war is beginning there, my young friends. On one side is the power and ferocity of the Red Army. On the other is a collection of men in funny hats. How do you suppose this ragtag force is getting the ammunition and training to challenge Moscow?"

"From us?"

"Not directly. Not through any channel that would require the sorry characters who inhabit the seventh floor to sign their names. But indirectly, yes. They are receiving support from us."

"From you?"

"From me, if you like. And from several liaison services. But I'm a suitable culprit."

"Who authorized it?" asked Anna.

"Ahh. The blessed authorization. What a wonderful notion we Americans have, that any action is moral and legal if someone 'authorized' it, and immoral if someone didn't. We Americans have become paper fetishists, idolaters of official stamps and seals."

"Who authorized it?" she repeated.

"In this case, if you must know, the National Security Adviser asked me in March to do what I could to demonstrate American sympathy for the *mujaheddin*. I am sure that there is some piece of paper somewhere attesting to that. Not that any reasonable person should care."

As Stone spoke, his bloodshot eyes widened and his voice rose. Perhaps it was the fact that he was so tired and unkempt, but it struck Anna, as she watched him, that he was a man at the limit of his physical and emotional resources.

"The Inspector General will care," she said.

"I wouldn't worry too much about the Inspector General. He happens to be an old friend of mine who owes me a great many favors. The problem is not the Inspector General but the director, Mr. Hinkle, who has developed the peculiar idea that he works for Congress rather than the executive branch."

"I hate to break this to you, boss," said Taylor, "but the IG's office is already asking questions. They visited my friend George Trumbo in Athens a few weeks ago."

"I am aware of that," said Stone.

"You already knew they called George in?"

"Oh yes. Not to brag, but there isn't much I don't hear about, one way or another."

"You should have told me."

"Why? Why worry you about something that doesn't matter? I would have let you know if your friend George had said something injudicious that might have caused problems. But he didn't. His mind seemed to have gone blank."

"Good old George," said Taylor. He made a mental note to send Sonia on a visit to Athens.

"Now then," said Stone. "Have we asked all of our little questions?"

Neither one answered.

"Good. Then let's talk about termination. As you young wizards of tradecraft are aware, this should be the first topic of discussion when you start any operation— how to turn it off. We're a bit late in getting to it, but not hopelessly so. Alan, what about your man Munzer?"

"He's thriving. The local Turkestani émigré community thinks he's the best thing to hit town since Tamerlane. But he shouldn't be hard to turn off. When the time comes, we'll just tell him that the movement needs him back in America and ship him home."

"What about money?"

"He's been a good soldier. You should definitely pay him the pension he says we owe him, and if you feel generous, you can keep him on contract for another year. But I wouldn't worry about him."

"Will he talk if people begin asking questions?"

"Nope. Not if I tell him not to."

"How can you be sure?"

"Because Munzer likes me. And he's afraid of me. He thinks I'm slightly nuts."

"Clever fellow."

"There's one thing I'd like to know," said Taylor.

"Ask away."

"What have all our machinations accomplished in Uzbekistan?"

"They have stirred the pot."

"What's that supposed to mean?"

"Surely you understand, both of you, that this little drama of ours is playing on two screens. One is Central Asia. The other is Afghanistan. The two reinforce each other. Together, they suggest to the men in the Kremlin that they have a 'Moslem Problem,' a rather serious one. The delightful thing, from our standpoint, is that Moscow's cure for this problem will only make it worse."

"What's their cure?"

"Invading Afghanistan. When the Soviet troops march in, your Mr. Munzer will know that the real battle has begun. And when they straggle out a few years from now, defeated, he can congratulate himself for having played a small role in one of the great triumphs of the twentieth century."

He's possessed, thought Anna. He's so locked on his target he can't see anything else.

"What if the Russians win?" she asked.

"They won't," said Stone. "I guarantee it."

He leaned gingerly toward Anna, as if she were a newly frisky animal that had discovered it had teeth and claws. "Now, my dear, what about Mr. Ascari, the Iranian. How are we to terminate him?"

"It shouldn't be a problem," said Anna. "He doesn't like me, and he isn't afraid of me either. But he's absolutely terrified of Frank Hoffman. He'll do whatever Hoffman tells him. If we say stop, he'll stop. If we say keep going, he'll keep going."

"What about severance payments or an annuity?"

"He has nothing to complain about. Frank is paying him a flat sum for each trip across the border. It's good money, even for a hustler like Ascari."

"What shall we tell London?"

"About what?"

"About whether to retain Ascari as a regular DDO agent. The last they knew, you were preparing to hand him over to an inside case officer."

"You want my opinion?"

"Of course."

"Dump him. He's a jerk. The best thing to do is throw him to the wolves."

"I'm not sure they would have him," said Stone. He smiled amiably. There was a long pause, and Stone seemed about ready to end the discussion.

"Hold on," said Anna. "What about my Armenian agent?"

"That is the last item on our agenda," said Stone.

"What Armenian agent?" asked Taylor.

Anna was about to answer, but Stone raised his hand.

"You will recall," he said, "that some weeks ago we agreed to let Miss Barnes explore the possibility of engaging an Armenian operative for our enterprise. Now she has found an appropriate person and proposes to do just that."

Taylor looked at Anna, who was leaning forward in her chair as if ready to spring. She was, in some subtle way he didn't yet understand, a different woman from the one he had left in Rockville. "Isn't it a little late for something like this?" he asked.

"No," said Anna. "I don't see why."

"Because we're closing up shop at the end of November," replied Taylor, "and it's almost October now."

"That's enough time, so long as we really do have until the end of November. We're not going to fold up before then, are we, Mr. Stone?"

"No," he answered. "I shouldn't think so."

"Then there's enough time for what I want to do."

"Perhaps you should explain for Alan and me just what that is."

Anna nodded, took a gulp of air, and began her pitch. "The Armenian is a doctor, a medical researcher who has been studying in Paris for two years. He's part of a small network of Armenian activities, inside and outside the Soviet Union. He's going home to Yerevan in ten days, and he wants us to help him with something, which happens to fit perfectly with what we're trying to do."

"What does he want?"

"He wants us to give him a device that will allow his friends to pick up satellite television signals from the West. He says it would change everything in the Soviet Union if people could see how the rest of the world works."

"He may be right. But what is it, exactly, that he wants from us?"

"A phased-array television antenna."

"What on earth is that?"

Anna removed the wiring diagram from her purse and handed it to Stone.

"This," she said, pointing to the drawing, "is a phased-array television antenna." Stone studied it for a few moments and then handed it to Taylor. He turned it one way, then the other, held it up to the light, turned it backwards, and then handed it back to Stone.

"This doesn't mean a fucking thing to me," said Taylor. "But I know someone who'd understand it in a minute."

"Who's that?" asked Anna.

"George Trumbo, my friend from the TSD office in Athens. He's a genius with this stuff, when he isn't drunk."

"Could he build one of these?"

"Probably. If someone got him the hardware."

"Would he keep his mouth shut about it?"

"Definitely. But are you sure this makes sense?"

"Yes," she said. "Absolutely positive."

"How would your Armenian pick this thing up, assuming George could make it?"

"He says we could find a way, over the border. We're supposed to talk about the details next week, assuming we agree."

"I don't know," said Taylor. "It seems kind of half-assed. It bothers me."

Stone didn't offer any opinion for the moment. He studied the wiring diagram again, and then rubbed his eyes. Anna had expected strong opposition from him, but across his exhausted face had fallen a look of calm equanimity. It was a shadow cast by some new idea that was working in his brain.

"I think it's an intriguing idea," said Stone eventually.

"You do?" said Anna. She smiled.

"Have you made a formal recruitment pitch to this Armenian fellow yet?"

"Not exactly," she answered.

"What does that mean?"

"I haven't told him who I work for."

"Have you paid him money?"

"No."

"Do you have any sort of contractural arrangement with him?"

"Not really. I've only met with him three times. It didn't seem appropriate."

"That's unfortunate," said Stone.

"Why?

"Because the bond between you is personal rather than professional. As such, it carries an awkward element of moral obligation. Contracts are so much easier. Still, it's an intriguing idea."

"It bothers me," said Taylor again.

Anna wanted to kick him. Why was he sabotaging her chance at the very moment Stone seemed willing to agree? She couldn't tell, looking at him, whether he was genuinely concerned for her welfare or whether he was simply jealous.

Stone apparently was growing tired of the discussion.

"I'm hungry," he said. "Let's eat."

They broke for dinner at nine-thirty. Taylor suggested that they eat at a fish restaurant called Urcan, up the Bosporus in a town called Sariyer. He thought a change of scene would do everyone some good. So they all piled into a taxi and headed upstream. The custom at Urcan was for customers to choose their dinner from among the fish swimming in the tanks by the front door. Stone selected a flounder that was lying motionless on the bottom of the tank, trying to blend into the sand. He later pronounced it delicious, and lingered long over the dinner, the wine and the Greek brandy. It was a merry evening, with everyone doing their best to avoid serious conversation. By the time they left Urcan, all three were quite tipsy, especially Stone. He held Anna by the arm as he walked unsteadily toward his suite, and gave her a kiss on the cheek at the door.

"Let's resolve this Armenian business tomorrow morning, before we leave," he said. "Breakfast in my room at eight-thirty." He closed the door.

Anna looked toward Taylor, who was leaning against the wall a few feet away.

"How about a nightcap?" she said, hoping it didn't sound too calculating.

"You're on."

"I'm in room 9. Give me ten minutes to get ready."

39

WHEN TAYLOR KNOCKED ON THE DOOR TEN MINUTES LATER, Anna pulled it back just a crack. The smooth skin of her cheek was visible through the opening. So was the outline of her breast beneath the gauzy fabric of a loose shift, the sort of garment that Istanbuli ladies wore after the bath. "I'm not ready yet," she whispered. "Why don't you come in and wait while I get dressed."

She beckoned Taylor to come in, as if inviting him to join in a secret revel. As he entered the room, he saw that Anna's body was naked under the translucent folds of her dressing gown. He was aroused immediately, and moved forward to embrace her.

"Don't touch!" said Anna. "It's not polite to touch a lady while she's dressing."

She retreated toward the bed, where she had laid out her clothes in a neat pile. "Why don't you sit down," she said, pointing toward the chair. "I'll just be a minute." She stood by the bed for a long moment. The light on the bedside table was behind her, rendering her thin shift completely transparent. Taylor could see the roundness of her breasts, the supple curve of her thighs and a few wisps of pubic hair.

"That's quite an outfit, Mata Hari," said Taylor.

"A local couturier," said Anna. "The harem girls wore this sort of thing in the seraglio to amuse the sultan."

"I'm amused."

"As I recall, there was one sultan who liked to hide behind a window overlooking the baths. He gave his women gowns like this, but with the stitches removed. They were held together only with a little paste. When the women got near the steam bath, their clothes would fall off."

"What did he do then?"

"He watched." Anna smiled coyly and picked up her panties from the bed.

Taylor changed position in the chair so that his trousers didn't bind him so tightly. He was spellbound. There was something overwhelmingly erotic about seeing this well-bred woman act like a tart.

"Which way do these go?" asked Anna, holding up her panties and turning them backwards and forwards so Taylor could see. It was quite obvious which way they went. There was nothing but a thong in back and a small triangle of white lace in front. Anna slipped them on, one leg and then the other, leaving herself open to Taylor's view.

"Forget the nightcap," said Taylor, rising from the chair. "Let's make love."

"Uh-uh-uh!" said Anna, wagging her finger at him. "I'm not dressed yet."

She extended one slim leg, arched her toe, and began putting on her panty hose, pulling one leg of the hose up a few inches at a time until it was at the top of her thigh. Then she did the other leg, just as carefully, until the panty hose were straight and taut at the waist. She gave him a little wink.

"Stop it!" said Taylor. "You're driving me crazy."

"Good," said Anna.

She turned toward the bed and slipped off the sheer dressing gown. Taylor could see the thin string of her panties running down the tight crevice of her ass. She picked up her bra from the bed, a lacy number not much bigger than the panties, and cupped it under her breasts.

"Do me up, would you?" she called over her shoulder to Taylor.

Taylor walked toward her and didn't stop until he was pressing hard against her. His hand reached not for the fastener of the brassiere, but around her body to her breasts. Anna slapped his hand, playfully but hard enough so that it stung.

"Naughty boy!" she said. "No touchee-feelee until we talkee-talkee."

Taylor dutifully fastened her bra, fumbling with the clasp

just as he had as a teenager, trying to undo his first girlfriend's bra in the back seat of a car.

"Why do men have such trouble with bras?" she asked coquettishly when the strap was fastened. "Do they think bras are sexy?"

"Stop it," groaned Taylor again. "What's gotten into you?"

She put on a simple linen dress, letting it slip over her breasts and hips, and next her high heels. Then she walked over to her suitcase and removed a bottle of Johnnie Walker Black from a duty-free bag marked "Aéroports de Paris."

"Actually, there's no reason to go out for a nightcap," she said. "I brought a bottle."

She went to the bathroom and retrieved the lone glass perched in front of the cracked mirror. She poured several inches of whiskey into it and gave it to Taylor.

"We'll have to share," she said.

Taylor took a sip. He looked at Anna, now fully clothed and sitting catlike on the bed, and shook his head.

"What's this all about?" he said. "What do you want from me?"

"I want you to say yes," she said. It was somewhere between a purr and a pout.

"To what?"

"I want you to tell Stone tomorrow morning that you think my Armenian operation is a good idea and you're all for it."

"But I don't think it's a good idea."

"Why not? It makes a lot more sense than handing out Islamic literature in Uzbekistan."

"Maybe so. But that still doesn't mean you should do it."

"Why are you so conservative all of a sudden, now that it's my turn to try something?"

"Come off it. That has nothing to do with it."

Anna sighed and put her head in her hands. "I feel like I'm playing 'Istanbul Gentleman,' " she said.

"What's 'Istanbul Gentleman'?"

"It's a game the harem women used to play. One of them would dress up like a man, paint a mustache on her lips, put a watermelon rind on her head as if it were a fez. Then the others girls would make her sit backwards on a donkey. And then somebody would give the donkey a kick, and she would go bouncing around the courtyard until she fell off."

"And that's what you feel like?"

"Yes. That's exactly what I feel like."

"That's crazy."

"Please, Alan. Tell Stone you think it's okay. He doesn't really seem opposed to the idea. In fact, he would probably have said yes already if you had kept your mouth shut."

"Don't trust Stone. He's operating on six levels at once. If he decides to let you do this, it will be for his reasons not yours."

"What are his reasons?"

"I haven't a clue. But I know Stone. He's devious."

"I didn't think that bothered you."

"It doesn't."

"Please say yes. Let me be as crazy as Stone if I like."

"How do you know this Armenian isn't working for the KGB?"

"I just know. He's as pure as the snow on Mount Ararat."

"Give me a break."

"If he was a phony, the seams would be visible. But there aren't any. And if it's any reassurance, they did a CI workup on him two years ago and didn't find any intelligence connections."

"CI makes mistakes. So do case officers."

"Come on, Alan. You know what I'm talking about. You've recruited dozens of people. Don't you just know when someone is for real?"

"Sometimes. But sometimes you get so caught up in a case that you lose your judgment. It's called 'falling in love with your agent.' "

"That's a cheap shot."

"Is it? Then explain to me why you're so determined to do this."

"Because it matters to me. And it's the right thing to do."

"Did you sleep with him?"

"What's that supposed to mean?"

"Just what it sounds like. Did you sleep with him?"

"That's an outrageous question. But the answer is no."

"I only ask because you're acting so strange. Something has happened to you. You're different."

"What's different is that I'm trying to get serious about my job. And for some reason I can't understand, that bothers you."

"Let's make love," said Taylor gently.

Anna paused. She was flustered. Her seductive bravado had been punctured by Taylor's questions.

"What about you?" she asked. "Have you slept with anyone since we were together?" She wished she hadn't asked the question the moment the words were out of her mouth.

"Yes," said Taylor.

She took a deep breath. "Do you feel guilty about it?"

"No. Why should I? It was just recreational sex. It doesn't change the way I feel about you. I can pretend to feel guilty if you want."

"Fuck you."

Taylor sat down beside her on the bed.

"I'm sorry," he said. "The last thing I wanted to do tonight was argue with you."

He put his arm around her. She was going to remove it, but let it stay.

"Tell Stone you like my operation," she said.

"Okay," said Taylor. "If that's what it takes to get you in bed."

"Tell him you think it's the best idea anyone's had since Allen Dulles."

Taylor smiled. "Okay."

"Promise?"

"Yes."

"I need a drink."

Taylor handed her the glass of whiskey. She finished what was left and poured some more. As she drank it down, it occurred to her that she had never felt more like a whore.

"Now you can take off my clothes," she said.

It took Taylor far less time to remove Anna's ensemble than it had for her to put it on. He pulled the garments hurriedly from her body, pushing her dress up, pulling back the flimsy brassiere, peeling the panty hose from her legs and tugging her tiny panties so hard they bit into the soft flesh between her legs. And then he was on top of her, only half undressed himself. Usually his lovemaking was gentle, but now, for the first time, he was rough with her. He pushed into her hard, and when she cried out, he pushed in hard again. He turned her over on her hands and knees and entered her from behind, slapping her bottom with his open hand as he went in and out. He made love angrily, like a man who had something to prove. And Anna, for her part, did something that she had never done before with Taylor. She faked an orgasm.

Taylor left a few minutes after they had finished. He mumbled something about going home to change clothes. Otherwise, neither said very much. What was there to say? Taylor drove home to his apartment in Arnavutkoy and slept a few hours.

The next morning, before returning to Bebek to meet with Stone, Taylor stopped by the consulate to check the overnight cables. One cable in the stack caught his eye. It was addressed to Amy L. Gunderson, from the chief of the European Division. The cable ordered her to return to London immediately or contact her case officer at the embassy there. Taylor wondered for a moment what he ought to do. But there wasn't any real question in his mind. He drove to the hotel in Bebek as quickly as he could and knocked on Stone's door at eight-fifteen.

The old man looked somewhat more composed than he had the night before. "You're early," he said.

"You had better read this," said Taylor. He handed the cable to Stone, who read it carefully, paying special attention to the time, date and routing by which the message had been sent.

"I'll handle this," he said evenly. "This isn't a time to be worrying Miss Barnes. She has a lot on her mind."

He took the paper in the palm of his hand and crumpled it into a ball.

"I'll need that back," said Taylor "For the files."

Stone handed the wad of paper back to Taylor. "It was never received."

Taylor nodded.

Anna knocked on the door a few minutes later. She didn't look at Taylor. "Good morning, gentlemen," she said.

"Good morning, my dear," replied Stone. He was at his most courtly. "Sleep well?"

"Just fine."

"We haven't much time, I'm afraid. Your plane leaves at ten-thirty, mine at noon. So let's finish our business. Are you still keen on this Armenian operation?"

"Yes," said Anna. "Very keen."

"What about you, Alan? Do you have any reservations? You sounded a bit skeptical last night."

The room was silent for a moment. Taylor looked at Anna, but she was avoiding his glance, gazing instead out the window, toward the Bosporus.

"I don't have any problem," said Taylor. "If Anna wants to do it, it's fine with me."

"That leaves me," said Stone. Anna turned back from the window and looked the old man in the eye. "I've given it some further thought overnight and I think your project makes a good deal of sense. It's quite enterprising on your part. Certainly it will put your man in some jeopardy, but as you say, he's asked for our help. All we're doing is satisfying his request. So I wish you good luck."

"Thank you," said Anna. Her face was flushed. She had won, but she felt no sense of release.

"When will you see the Armenian again?"

"When I get back to Paris."

"Well then, you can tell him that your friends at the foundation have agreed to support this worthy venture in international communications—and that we will supply him with one prototype, one only."

"He'll be pleased."

"No doubt. Now, Alan, I want you to take the wiring diagram to your friend Mr. Trumbo in Athens. He'll need help in getting the components in a hurry, so have him contact an old colleague of mine in Technical Services back home. I'll make the necessary arrangements." Stone wrote a name and telephone number on a piece of paper and handed it to Taylor.

"As for delivery," continued Stone, "I'm afraid we can't leave this to the uncertain devices of your Armenian friend. We'll need to do it ourselves. My Transcaucasian geography isn't the best, but I suspect the only sensible way to get it in is across the Iranian border, through Nakhichevan. So I suggest we engage the services of Mr. Ascari and his smuggling network one last time. They shouldn't have any trouble with it. We'll tell them it's a new kind of VCR."

"Okay, I guess," said Anna. She hated the thought of any aspect of her venture falling into the hands of Ali Ascari, but she was in no position to argue.

"The pickup will be the most delicate part. Before your Armenian friend goes home, you'll need to set a precise time and place for him to collect the shipment. I assume Ascari and his chums can suggest a delivery spot, but we have less than ten days to get all this set. So I would like Alan, when he's in Athens, to meet Hoffman and Ascari and work out the details. Alan can send the information to me, and I will relay it, in turn, to you so you can tell the Armenian before he gets on his plane. Is that agreeable?"

Everyone nodded.

"I have one final request for you, Anna," said Stone. "I want you to be very careful in Paris. The KGB may have your Armenian friend under surveillance. So I want you to change hotels when you get back. Call me directly, at home, with the telephone and telex numbers of your new hotel."

"All right."

"Several other precautions," said Stone evenly. There was not a hint of deceit in his voice. "You should stay away from anyone in the Paris station, or anyone who might have any dealings with it. You should under no circumstances try to contact your old case officer in the London embassy. That would be insecure. I'd also like you to stop using your old credit cards and stop writing checks on the Rockville bank account. They leave too obvious a paper trail."

"What will I use for money?"

"This," said Stone. He walked over to his luggage and returned with a red vinyl travel bag that said "TWA."

"What's in it?" she asked.

"Fifty thousand dollars," said Stone. He looked at his watch. It was after nine.

"You'd better get going, or you'll miss your plane," he said. Anna hoisted the flight bag over her shoulder and shook Stone's hand.

Taylor, who had watched this exchange with a growing sense of unease, turned to Anna. "I'll walk you down," he said.

"That's okay," she answered. "I can manage by myself." She shook Taylor's hand, coldly, and walked out the door.

Taylor turned to Stone. "I ought to give her a hand with the bags," he said.

"She can manage. You heard her. Stay a few minutes. I'd like to talk with you."

"All right," said Taylor.

"When you see Frank in Athens, tell him to send something extra with that last shipment to Armenia."

"What should he add?"

"Explosives."

"Christ! What the hell for? This Armenian doctor won't know what to do with them."

"They won't be for the Armenian doctor. They'll be for someone else. The British have some Armenian friends, if memory serves. They can help."

"Do what?"

"I'm not sure yet. But it seems to me that if we're going to do this Armenian business, we ought to do it right."

Taylor nodded dumbly, but he was troubled. "Can I ask you something?" he said.

"Certainly."

"Why did you agree to this silly idea of Anna's?"

"Because she wanted to do it."

"Come on. That's bullshit."

"I have my reasons."

"What are they?"

"Cover."

"Cover for what?"

"For all of us. In the worst case, if things really fall apart over the next several months, it may be quite useful to have an additional iron in the fire—another face of our operation that doesn't look quite so menacing. Miss Barnes would make quite a compelling witness before a closed session of the Senate Intelligence Committee, if it ever came to that, God forbid. I can imagine her testimony—one world, satellite television, plucky Armenians. There wouldn't be a dry eye in the house."

"But she could get hurt."

"She's a big girl. As a matter of fact, she's really been quite self-reliant lately. Almost headstrong. Perhaps you haven't noticed the change because of your . . . personal interest in her."

"I've noticed."

"There is one more thing about Miss Barnes that makes me inclined to let her do what she wants."

"What's that?"

"I won't call it disloyalty, but she simply doesn't know when to accede to authority. I find that troublesome in any subordinate. But to be candid, I find it especially unattractive in a woman."

* * *

Anna's final meeting in Paris with Dr. Antoyan didn't last long. She was staying in a small hotel in the suburbs now, out near the American Hospital in Neuilly. She had met with the Armenian once, when she first arrived back in town. Then she had waited for a message from Stone, with the necessary details, before seeing him again. She hadn't heard from Taylor, but she neither expected to nor wanted to.

She met Aram at a suburban café near the outer edge of the Bois de Boulogne. The Armenian had shaved off his beard completely by now. His face looked thinner and more vulnerable without it. He was dressed in an ill-made gray suit, which hung from his body like a sack. He looked as if he were already halfway home.

Anna carefully explained the procedures for delivering the equipment. In early November, it would be transported over the Iranian border into Nakhichevan, an Azerbaijani enclave bordering Armenia, and from there to a small village at the southeastern edge of Armenia. The village was called Kiarki, and it was populated by ethnic Azerbaijanis. On November 10, Aram should go to the house of a man named Sadeq Shirvanshir. He should say: "Hamid sent me."

Anna wrote the address on a piece of paper, along with the time, date and password, and asked Antoyan to memorize the information. He studied the sheet for thirty seconds, closed his eyes, and repeated the words to himself several times. Anna retrieved the paper and put it in her purse.

"I will be there," he said.

"Come back to my hotel with me," said Anna when they had done their business. "I'd like to spend a few more hours with you."

"That would not be wise," the Armenian answered softly.

"Why not? I'm tired of wisdom. Wisdom is for old men."

"If I spend more time with you, I will not want to leave. And it would put us both in danger. They may be watching me more carefully, now that I'm about to go home."

Anna felt a wave of sadness flow over her. "When will I see you again?" she asked.

"The next time I come to the West."

"When will that be?"

"I don't know. It could be a few years."

"How will you know where to find me?"

"That should not be hard. I think I know how to contact you." He had that sly half smile which once would have charmed Anna but now just made her anxious for him.

"How can we contact you in Yerevan?"

"I thought we agreed at our last meeting that you would not try to use me for any other purpose."

"We did agree. This is just for emergencies."

Antoyan wrote an address and phone number on a paper napkin and gave it to her. "This is the hospital where I will be working. But people should be very careful if they ever try to contact me. The Soviet Union is not like the West. There is no such thing as an innocent meeting."

"Do you have a home address?"

"Not yet. But I can give you the address of my parents' apartment." He took back the napkin and wrote the address in English and Armenian script. "Be careful," he said again.

Anna tried hard not to show it, but she was frightened for him. She had worked so hard to arrange Antoyan's mission, but now on the eve of his departure, she didn't want him to go. She had brought along her airline bag of cash and tried to give him some money, to buy gifts for his relatives at least, but he dismissed her with an abrupt wave of his hand.

"Don't be silly," he said.

The waiter came and asked if they would like anything more. Aram shook his head.

"Let us say goodbye now," he said. "Otherwise it will be too hard." He embraced Anna, kissed her on both cheeks, and let her go. Her eyes were full of tears. Anna had heard that when Russians don't want someone to leave, they sit on their bags at the train station and refuse to move. But she couldn't do that. She was Aram Antoyan's case officer.

"If anything goes wrong, we'll contact you," she said.

"Nothing will go wrong."

"But if something does, we'll make sure you get a warning in time. I promise."

"Goodbye, my darling," he said. He kissed her a final time on the cheek, turned, and walked toward the Métro station. He never looked back. Dr. Antoyan, as he had said so often, had no desire to be a victim. Not even of love.

VIII

ANNA BARNES

Washington / Istanbul
Yerevan / Boston

October 1979–December 1980

40

THE ROOF OF EDWARD STONE'S CANTILEVERED HOUSE OF CARDS fell in one morning in mid-October. Stone was as usual a step ahead of his pursuers, but in this instance it did him little good. He received a telephone call just after seven-thirty from Harry Peltz, his friend and informant in the European Division. Peltz said he had received a tip from a neighbor in Falls Church who worked for the Office of Security. At ten-thirty that morning, Peltz confided, a team of investigators from the Office of Security would raid the headquarters of an unauthorized CIA proprietary in Maryland that traded under the name Karpetland, Inc. The bust was part of a larger dragnet, Peltz said. Very secret, very closely held. He thought Stone would want to know.

"Thanks so much, old boy" was all Stone said. But he was as close to panic in that moment as a controlled and composed man can be.

Stone left his blue pinstripe suit and black wing-tip shoes on the valet stand. He pulled on a pair of corduroy pants, a polo shirt and a sweater and headed out the door. The traffic was slow all the way out Wisconsin Avenue, but Stone managed to reach the office in Rockville just before nine. He was there when Marjorie arrived, punctual as ever. He got right to the point.

"We're closing up shop, Marjorie," he said. "Immediately."

Marjorie stared at Stone, hearing the words but not really taking them in. She had never before seen her boss quite so disheveled, but the detail that disturbed her most was that he wasn't wearing any socks. She stared for a long moment at his white wrinkled insteps.

"Is everything all right, Mr. Stone?" she asked.

"Yes, of course it is," he said, looking at his watch. "Everything is just fine. But we must close this office. Right now. Do you understand?"

"When?"

Stone exploded in exasperation. "Right now! Today! This morning! Are you deaf?"

He was almost shouting. Marjorie, who was even less accustomed to hearing Stone raise his voice than to seeing him without socks, began sniffling and looked as if she might burst into tears.

"Get a grip on yourself," said Stone. "We have a lot of work to do in a very short time."

That quieted her. "Now unlock the desks and the filing cabinet," he said. "Quick!"

Marjorie fumbled with her keys a few moments but managed to open the various locks. The filing cabinet didn't contain much. Travel records for Taylor and Anna; the rental agreement for the office; insurance documents for the white Karpetland van; junk mail received at the office the past six months, which Marjorie had neatly filed away; back issues of a carpet-industry newsletter called "Wall to Wall." Stone scooped it all up and dumped it in a large cardboard box that had once contained Pakistani Korans.

"Where are the checkbooks?" he asked. Marjorie brought them from her desk. "And the credit-card receipts? And the phone bills?" Marjorie fetched those items as well.

"Where's the petty cash?"

"In the safe."

"How much do we have?"

"Eighty thousand dollars."

"Open the safe, please. Now." Marjorie turned the combination lock but failed, twice, to get it open. Her hands were shaking.

"Goddammit! Tell me the combination, and I'll open the bloody lock."

She called out the numbers to Stone in a quavering voice. Stone ran through the sequence, pulled the handle, and opened the safe door. He removed several thick stacks of bills, a cash ledger, some blank air tickets, a classified CIA telephone directory, a classified report titled "Kurdistan in

Perspective" and a jar of instant coffee that Marjorie inexplicably had kept locked up in the safe.

"This must be yours," said Stone, handing the coffee to Marjorie. He took the money and the classified material and dumped it into the cardboard box. He looked at his watch again.

"Jesus Christ!" he said. It was almost nine-thirty. "They'll be here any minute."

"Who?" whimpered Marjorie. "Oh, Mr. Stone, what's wrong?"

Stone fixed his gaze on her. "A hostile raid will take place here in less than an hour."

"Who?" she said, still mystified. "The Russians?"

"Not the Russians themselves," said Stone. "Their friends."

"Blessed Mother Mary," said Marjorie. She looked frightened, but also galvanized.

Stone surveyed the room once more. He rummaged hurriedly through the desks of Taylor and Anna, removing whatever bric-a-brac he found. A carry-out menu from a bar called McGillicuddy's in Rockville; stationery from the Athens Hilton; a Turkish-English dictionary; a dog-eared copy of *The Forty Days of Musa Dagh*. Stone grabbed them all and threw them into the cardboard box. He searched all the desk drawers one last time, to make sure he hadn't missed anything, and then turned to his faithful secretary.

"My dear Marjorie, how would you like to take a vacation?"

"I've already had my vacation," she answered. "Two weeks in August."

"How about another vacation, on the company? How about Cancún? Or Rio? Have you ever been to Rio?"

"I haven't had my shots."

"What shots?"

"Diphtheria. Malaria. Don't they have a lot of diseases there?"

Stone rolled his eyes. "Perhaps somewhere in this country would be better. Where would you like to go?"

"I could visit my mother in Florida."

"Where does she live?"

"Lakeland."

"Fine. Do you know the address and telephone number?"

"Oh yes. I call my mother every Sunday." She wrote out the

address and phone number. While she did so, Stone reached into the cardboard box and counted out ten thousand dollars.

"Now then, Marjorie," he said. "I'd like you to take this money and use it to pay for your airline ticket to Florida and your expenses while you're there. Please don't use your own checks or credit cards. We'll take care of the accounting later."

Marjorie nodded earnestly.

"I want you to stay at your mother's house until you hear from me," he continued. "Don't contact anyone else until then, not even your best girlfriend. It's very dangerous. I can't tell you the details, but you must trust me."

"I will. I promise," said Marjorie. She took the cash and began stuffing it into her purse. Fortunately, it was a very large purse, and when she removed a fat Danielle Steele novel, the money just fit. Stone looked at his watch one more time.

"We'd best be going," he said. "I want you to go directly to National Airport and take the first available flight to Florida, no matter where—Miami, Tampa, Orlando—then go to Lakeland. Can you do that?"

"I don't have any clothes. I'll have to go home and pack."

"There isn't time. Buy yourself some new clothes when you get to Florida."

"But I don't even have a toothbrush."

"Buy yourself a new toothbrush, goddammit!" said Stone. He was almost shouting again, and it looked for a moment as if Marjorie might resume her sniffling. Stone reached into the cardboard box and handed her some more bills, not even bothering to count them.

"I'll keep the receipts," she said.

"Yes, you do that. Keep the receipts." He took her by the arm and escorted her to the door.

"The keys, please," he said. "That's a good girl."

They climbed down the stairs together. Stone scanned the parking lot carefully before opening the door and, seeing no sign of surveillance, led her by the arm to the Rockville Pike. After a few agonizing minutes, he managed to hail a cab.

"Take her to National Airport," Stone ordered the driver. He opened the door for Marjorie.

"Remember!" he said. "Do exactly what I told you. Don't leave Lakeland or talk to anyone until you hear from me. I'm counting on you!"

"Yes, sir," said Marjorie, voicing the unquestioning and automatic loyalty that is the mark of a disciplined soldier in any service.

The cab sped off. Stone jogged back to the Karpetland office as fast as he could manage. He made a last quick tour of the room and then carried the cardboard box down to his car, leaving the parking lot just after ten. He drove west toward the Potomac River, to a park and picnic area on the Maryland side of Great Falls. The park was deserted on this October morning. Stone parked next to an outdoor barbecue grill. He removed the cash from the box and crumpled the remaining files and papers into a small bonfire. He patted his pockets for matches and cursed loudly when he realized he didn't have any. He decided to use the cigarette lighter from the car instead, which worked admirably. Within a few minutes the records of the sham enterprise known as Karpetland had been reduced to ashes.

Stone's next stop was back at his house on N Street, to make two urgent telephone calls. It seemed imprudent to make them from his own phone, so he knocked at the house across the street, owned by a genteel old Georgetown matron. He explained that his own phone was unaccountably on the blink. Could he possibly use her phone to make several overseas calls? Of course he could. She was flattered that tho great and mysterious Mr Stone would think to ask.

The first call was to Taylor in Istanbul. It was late afternoon there by now, but he was fortunately still at the office, haggling with the consulate's chief administrative officer about the housing allowance for a new CIA officer who would be arriving in December. Taylor loathed such housekeeping details, but for some unexplained reason, his deputy—who normally handled them—had been absent the past day and a half.

"We have a problem," Stone said when he reached Taylor. He didn't bother to identify himself.

"What's that?"

"A certain rug dealership is going out of business sooner than expected."

"How soon?"

"Today. It may be under new management at this very moment. The parent company was planning to take possession this morning."

"Is that so?" said Taylor. He knew he should feel devastated, or at least frightened, but at the moment he felt a weird sense of relief that the inevitable had finally happened. Still, he knew he should try to register concern. "Oh shit," he said.

"Just so," said Stone. "It's important to do what we can quickly to tidy up the loose ends. I'm thinking of a certain gentleman of your acquaintance who normally resides in Brooklyn."

"Yes, indeed, I know him well."

"Is he still in your part of the world?"

"Last I knew. I saw him several days ago."

"I suggest you pay him a visit immediately, and urge him to do a bit of traveling, on the first available flight."

"For how long?"

"A month or so. Then he can go home. Find some money for him somewhere or other, and I'll reimburse you."

Stone rang off. Taylor apologized to the administrative officer that something had come up, and they would have to resolve the matter of the housing allowance the next day. Then he headed off to Munzer's flat in Aksaray, taking a Turkish taxi rather than one of the office cars.

Taylor was too late. When he opened the door of Munzer's flat, he found that a burly young man from the Office of Security was already there, standing next to the Uzbek. The security officer had arrived the previous day from London and, with the connivance of Taylor's deputy, had obtained the address of Munzer's safe house and spent much of the past fifteen hours trying to interrogate him. Now he loomed over the old Uzbek gentleman like a sheriff's deputy guarding his prize witness.

"Allah sukur!" said Munzer as soon as he saw Taylor's face. "Thank God you are here!"

"Who are you?" demanded the security man. He had his hand under his coat, as if reaching for a gun.

"None of your fucking business," said Taylor. "Who are you?"

The security office flipped open his wallet and displayed some sort of badge along with his CIA identification. He looked like the sort of fellow whose favorite bedtime reading was *Guns and Ammo.*

"That doesn't mean shit to me," said Taylor. "They sell those at Woolworth's?"

"Fuck you!" snarled the security man. He took a menacing step toward Taylor, but Munzer moved in front of him, appealing to Taylor with his palms outstretched.

"Please, my friend. This man is telling so many lies about you. Big lies. You must tell him he is wrong."

"What did he say?"

"Yesterday he come here to my house and says he is your friend, so I tell him some things. But today he begin to say lies about you. He says your name not Mr. Goode but Mr. Taylor. Okay. No problem. That is spy business. Then he say you not really working for agency at all and you make up whole story about big American plan to liberate Turkestan. He say nobody is doing nothing for Turkestan, so forget about all that. But I tell him no. This is big lie. My friend Mr. Goode promise me. CIA not break promise to Turkestani people again. This is impossible."

"You come with me, Munzer," said Taylor, taking him by the arm. "I'll explain everything to you. Pack some clothes in a suitcase, and I'll tell you on the way to the airport."

"Not so fast, asshole," said the security man, withdrawing his revolver from the shoulder holster. "Neither of you is going anywhere."

"Put that gun away," said Taylor, who hadn't thought to bring one of his own. "Do you know who you're talking to? I'm the Istanbul base chief. You're on my territory."

"Not anymore."

"What's that supposed to mean?"

"As of yesterday, your deputy is chief of base. I'm operating under his authorization."

"That little shit," said Taylor.

Munzer, who was beginning to get the picture, let out a low moan. "What about Turkestan?" he said. "What about my dear Turkestani peoples?"

"Shut up, gramps!" said the security man.

Munzer's round face reddened, and his almond eyes narrowed to slivers. It is a cardinal principle among Uzbeks always to treat elders with respect. This ill-mannered young American had insulted not just Munzer Ahmedov but the soul of Uzbekistan. The old man tightened his hand into a fist, and he looked for a moment as if he might throw a wild punch at the security man.

"Calm down, Munzer," said Taylor.

The Uzbek turned to Taylor with an imploring look in his eyes. "Tell me this man is lying. Tell him Turkestani Liberation Movement is real thing."

Taylor said nothing. He could not bear to lie to the old man anymore.

"Tell him, please." Munzer's large round head was wobbling like a ball knocked off center. "Do not break the heart of Munzer twice in one life."

Still Taylor was silent. Munzer looked at him imploringly, then warily, then angrily. His face grew redder and he began to curse bitterly in Uzbek.

"Listen to me, Munzer," said Taylor. "Don't fight with this security guy anymore. It's not his fault. Just be honest with him. Answer the questions he and his friends put to you, and everything will come out fine. You haven't done anything wrong."

But Munzer barely heard him. He was still muttering Uzbek curses.

Taylor was formally placed on administrative leave the next day and ordered to return to Washington. Before he left the consulate for the last time, his deputy asked to speak with him. He was elaborately apologetic, in a way that only highlighted his pleasure at the prospect of replacing Taylor. Still, something impelled the deputy—whether genuine concern for Taylor's operation or a desire to hedge his bets back home—to confide a final bit of intelligence. There was one thing, he said, that Taylor and his friends should probably know. The Soviet consul general and his wife had been called home suddenly to Moscow, and a special team of KGB headhunters had set up shop in the salmon-pink palace on Istiklal Avenue. Taylor nodded. Stone had evidently played his last card.

Stone's other calls that day proved no more successful than the one to Taylor. He tried Anna, but she had left her hotel in Paris a week before. The assistant manager there said she had gone to Deauville for a brief holiday. The assistant manager thought that was very strange—going to the Normandy coast in October—but yes, the American woman had left the address and telephone number of the hotel where she would be staying. Stone tried the number and asked for a Miss Morgan. Nobody by that name was registered. He asked for Anna Barnes. Yes, said the desk clerk, a woman by that name was staying in the hotel, but she was out. Stone left his name and said he would call back.

Stone's final call that day was to Frank Hoffman in Athens. A tape-recorded message said that all calls were being handled by Hoffman's administrative assistant, a certain Mr. Panos. Stone telephoned this gentleman and demanded, in his most authoritative tone, to know where Hoffman was.

"Are you from the embassy?" asked Mr. Panos.

"I'm from higher up, in Washington," answered Stone.

"I tell you same thing I tell embassy man today," said the Greek. "Mr. Hoffman is not here. He is gone. Traveling."

"Where?"

"He is gone traveling to Saudi Arabia. Mr. Hoffman has a Saudi diplomatic passport, you know."

"Remind me of the name on that passport."

"Rashid al-Fazooli."

"What about the Iranian gentleman who has been working with Mr. Hoffman. His name is Mr. Ascari. Do you have any idea where he might be?"

"He is gone, too."

"Where?"

"Back to Tehran."

"What happened to him?"

"Mr. Hoffman fired him. He got very angry, Mr. Hoffman."

"Why?"

"I am not sure I should tell you," said the Greek.

"Yes," said Stone crisply. "You should tell me. Mr. Hoffman would be angry with you if you didn't." There was something hypnotic about Stone's voice that commanded respect, even from strangers.

"Mr. Ascari wanted more money," explained Mr. Panos, lowering his voice even on the phone. "He want to be vice president of Arab-American Security Consultants. Open Tehran office. But Mr. Hoffman said no."

"Then what happened?"

"Ascari try to get even, and Greeks find out. They tell Mr. Hoffman that Ascari no good."

"How's that?"

"Ascari no good. Rotten apple."

"How did they know? Did he do something?"

"They photograph him going into Russian embassy in Athens, and they tell Mr. Hoffman. That's why he fire him. Then Mr. Hoffman leave real quick. He decide this is good time to go to Saudi Arabia, visit clients. You got any message?"

"No. No message. I'm sure Mr. Hoffman can fend for himself quite adequately."

41

◆

STONE CONTINUED TO COME TO WORK EACH MORNING, REPAIRing to his small office hidden amid the maze of Langley. The day after the big raid, several people from the Office of Security stopped by to ask about the missing Karpetland files. Stone said he didn't know what they were talking about. He retained a lawyer later that afternoon, from a Washington law firm whose leading partners were, like Stone, fanatical tennis and squash players and, perhaps as a consequence, had a reputation as especially fierce negotiators. Stone's lawyer advised him to say nothing to anyone. Everything would work out. That advice cost $250 an hour, a reduced rate since Stone was a friend.

The Inspector General himself paid a visit after several days, looking very embarrassed. He said he had recused himself from the case, owing to his long-standing friendship with Stone, but he wanted to ask one favor. The director was planning to request the French police to issue an arrest warrant later that day for Anna Barnes, unless Stone agreed to help find her.

"How unpleasant," said Stone. Of course he would help. He wrote out the address and telephone number of Anna's hotel in Deauville, and by the next morning she was on her way back to Paris, accompanied by a woman case officer from the Paris station.

Then things were quiet for several days. It was as if the solons of the seventh floor, having come this far, were unsure what to do next—unsure what might come unraveled if they began pulling hard on this particular string. A few of Stone's most loyal friends took to calling him at home in the evenings and meeting him in parking lots to pass along whatever rustlings of gossip they had heard.

As best Stone could piece it together, the operation had been compromised not so much by one sudden leak as by a long, steady drip of information. In midsummer, the director's office had instructed the Inspector General to investigate rumors from Radio Liberty's headquarters in Munich of an unauthorized CIA operation involving Soviet Central Asia. The investigation had been perfunctory at first—people going through the motions, building the necessary alibi files, but not really digging for the truth. At some point, it had become more serious. Apparently, an ambitious young officer in his early forties, who had recently been transferred to the IG's office after a disappointing tour in Latin America, had heard about the investigation, begun asking questions—and gotten what he correctly perceived as a runaround. Sensing an opportunity to ingratiate himself with the seventh floor, he had mentioned the investigation to one of Hinkle's beady-eyed special assistants.

The probe might still have been contained had the special assistant not mentioned it to his girlfriend, who worked on the staff of the House Intelligence Committee. She told her boss, who asked the director during his September testimony on the FY 80 supplemental budget whether the agency was conducting a rogue operation in Soviet Central Asia. That did it. From that moment on, the machinery of official investigation was fully engaged and ground inexorably forward.

Taylor returned home from Istanbul a week after the big bust. He felt an enormous indifference toward the agency—past, present and future—and was already beginning to think about a new career. None of his ideas went much beyond the standard fantasies of the CIA burnout: becoming a free-lance writer; starting a restaurant in Northern California; becoming a risk arbitrageur on Wall Street and making a bundle of money. The clearest measure of his lassitude was that he thought seriously, on the plane back to Washington, of calling his ex-wife. As for Anna, he tried not to think about her. He had a sense that he had done her a great injury, but he had no idea what to do about it.

Taylor didn't want to see Stone, but he knew he must, if only to pass along the information from his deputy about the sudden withdrawal from Istanbul of Kunayev, the Soviet consul general, and his wife, Silvana. He called Stone at home the night he arrived and made a date to have breakfast with him the next day at his house in Georgetown.

Stone received Taylor with his customary courtliness the next morning. It was one of those perfect Washington fall days, like spring except that the air was crisper and the sky a sharper blue. Stone's wife had set breakfast in the garden, which was bounded by neatly trimmed evergreens and enclosed by an old brick wall that seemed to have stood there since Federal days. The garden was a place out of time, removed from the noise and commerce of Georgetown.

Stone appeared not simply unfazed by recent events but, in a strange way, buoyed by them. He saw himself, in the twilight of his career, as a relic of what was best and most enduring about the America that had grown up so quickly during and after World War II—namely, the Central Intelligence Agency. The fact that he was under attack from the agency's current management—people he considered amateurs and dolts—only confirmed his sense of rightness and well-being. It bothered him not at all that he was accused, in effect, of subverting the values and institutions the agency had been created to protect. Those were legalisms, in Stone's mind. They were drawn on a different template from the one that had guided Stone's life and work.

Taylor accepted Stone's hearty greeting, but found it impossible to reciprocate with his usual bravado. He had spent much of his career wanting to be one of the Stones, but he wasn't sure that morning that it was any longer possible, or desirable.

"How are you holding up?" asked the old man.

"Adequately," said Taylor. He made no effort to disguise his unhappiness. He had resolved, in general, to stop pretending.

"Suck it up, my boy!" admonished Stone. Taylor wasn't

sure what he was supposed to suck up, so he didn't respond. He wanted to do his business and leave.

"I have something important to tell you," he said.

"How do you like your eggs?" asked Stone, as if he hadn't heard.

"I don't eat eggs. Cereal would be fine."

"Cereal?" answered Stone. "I'm not sure we have any, but I'll check with my wife." He padded inside and conferred with his gracious spouse.

"She says we have something called Cheerios, but that they're very old. Is that all right?"

Taylor nodded. "I have something important to tell you," he began again.

This time Stone managed to hear him. "Good news, I hope," he said.

"I guess so. You predicted it, so I suppose it's your doing."

"Sorry, but I'm drawing a blank. What are you talking about? Here. Have some fruit." He ladled some berries into Taylor's bowl.

"Remember Kunayev?" asked Taylor. "The Soviet consul general in Istanbul and his wife. The fun couple."

"Yes, indeed. The elusive Madame Kunayeva."

"They've been called home. I assume the Soviets have also pulled out Rawls, but I couldn't check it before I left. A KGB team has flown into town to sort things out. Evidently they realize we've been diddling them and they're trying to figure out how. Like I said, it's just what you predicted."

Taylor had expected to see the usual look of genteel self-satisfaction on Stone's face. Instead, it was a blank, as he struggled to make sense of what he had just heard. Taylor wondered if perhaps the old man was becoming forgetful, and needed a prompt.

"The KGB must have found the bug in the Ottoman chair, in Alma-Ata," Taylor said. "How did you arrange that anyway? I'm curious."

"I beg your pardon?"

"How did you tip the Russians off? You said a few months ago that this was how you wanted to finish off the operation. You were going to help Moscow Center discover that the CIA had bugged a chair belonging to the party first secretary of

Kazakhstan, and let them figure out how it got there. So how did you do it? How did you pass the message?"

Stone was shaking his head. "That's just it," he said. "I didn't tip them off. I never played that card. I didn't have time."

"Then who pulled the plug?" asked Taylor, beginning to realize that this was not, apparently, Stone's last triumph. "How did the Russians find out that something fishy was going on in Istanbul?"

Stone poured himself a cup of coffee. He wasn't about to get frazzled at this late stage. "I suspect that they discovered the nature of our game the same way half of Washington seems to have found out—as a result of gossip among people who are supposed to keep secrets, but don't; and through cable traffic that is supposed to be secret, but isn't. They may also have had a bit of help."

"From whom?"

"From that appalling fellow Ascari, the Iranian."

"How do you know?"

"The Greeks apparently photographed him entering the Soviet embassy in Athens. He was mad at Hoffman."

"Oh, Jesus," said Taylor. "How much to you think he told the Russians?"

"Quite a lot, I suspect. Though he may not have told them all the details about his cousins, the smugglers. For business reasons."

"Where's Hoffman?"

"He's gone to ground. I suspect that he's angry at me again."

Stone took a sip of his coffee and dropped in another lump of sugar. It disappeared with a kerplunk.

"Bad news," said Taylor.

"I suppose so," said Stone, determined to regain his happy equilibrium. "Although I'm not sure it really matters all that much. If Congress knows, why shouldn't the KGB? Anyway, I believe we've got our people out of harm's way."

"Not all of them," said Taylor. "You're forgetting Anna's man. The Armenian."

"So I am."

"He's got problems. When he goes to pick up that package

in a couple of weeks—with your extra goodies thrown in—he's going to get nailed."

"Quite likely. I agree."

"So shouldn't we try to call off Ascari's delivery service?"

"I suspect that's impossible. Ascari's friends and relations are probably already on their way. I doubt we could call them back now even if we tried."

"We could at least send a message to the Armenian, warning him to stay away from the drop site."

"Dreadful idea. Any message would be insecure. It would almost guarantee that he would get caught. This way, he at least has a chance."

"You had better tell Anna. This means a lot to her. She's going to be upset."

Stone looked at Taylor with that blank, affectless gaze that most people regarded as a mark of professionalism.

"Why do we have to tell her?" he said. "It doesn't matter, and she would only be tempted to do something silly."

Stone buttered a piece of toast.

Taylor stared at him. "I must not have heard you right," he said.

"You heard me fine. You're just getting sentimental."

"Fuck you," said Taylor. With this last, cold-blooded exchange, something had snapped in him.

"Worse than sentimental," said Stone. "You're becoming rude. And disloyal."

"Fuck you," Taylor said again. For him, the long seduction was over. He was, in that moment, sick to death of Stone and his fellow conspirators—people who, for all their noble pretenses, had their thumbs pressed permanently on the moral balance. He stood up from Stone's finely laid breakfast table, rattling the china cups and saucers.

"Sit down," said Stone.

"I'm sorry," said Taylor. "But I've had it. Find somebody else."

"Sit down," he said again, in that resonant voice that had parted the waters of life for so many years. Taylor ignored him.

"I'm leaving," he said. "You tell Anna about the problem with the Armenian, or you can count me as an enemy from here on out. And I warn you, I'm the wrong person to have as an enemy. I'm no pushover, like your country-club friends.

I'm as devious as you are, and I don't give a shit what happens to me. Or you. So you tell Anna. Got it?"

Stone didn't answer, but Taylor knew he would do it. If there was any consistently reliable aspect of Stone's character, it was his ability to discern and act upon his own self-interest. Taylor walked up the flagstone terrace of Stone's garden, through the French doors, and let himself out onto the early-morning commotion of N Street. It wasn't a new beginning. That would be unlikely for a man of Taylor's age and temperament. But it was at least an end.

42

◆

STONE PROPOSED TO MEET ANNA AT THE PLACE WHERE THEY had begun nearly a year before—the Holiday Inn off I-270. "How sweet," said Anna sarcastically when he suggested it. It seemed like one of Stone's typical ploys, and she wondered what the old man could possibly want from her now. But when she got to the motel, and saw the too bright wallpaper and the tacky furniture, she felt something like nostalgia. It was like the compulsion that brings people back to high school reunions; they might not care any longer about the place or the people, but they still want to mark the distance traveled.

The I-270 industrial park surrounding the motel looked the same a year later, only more so. A new Mexican restaurant had opened, along with several more office buildings to house the new companies that had come to feed at the federal trough. Many of them seemed to specialize in the defense establishment's latest obsession, known as "C-three-I," for communications, command and control, and intelligence. One of the newly arrived firms, headquartered across the highway from the Holiday Inn, proposed to build "hardened" facsimile machines that would be able to send messages even after a nuclear war. The machines would cost several hundred thousand dollars apiece, but as the company's executives liked to say, you couldn't put a price tag on the nation's security.

Stone was already in the motel room when Anna arrived. A year ago, he had seemed a figure of measureless mystery to Anna. Now she felt she knew him as well as her own father; rather better, in fact. Gone, too, was the look of intense fatigue that had struck Anna at their first meeting. In its place now was a kind of empty glow, like the look retired people get when they begin spending their time playing golf in Florida.

"This will all blow over," said Stone after shaking hands.

"I'm not so sure," said Anna. "They're asking a lot of questions, and they already seem to know most of the answers."

"They have to do that, make a show of it. But when they're finished, they will realize how awkward this whole business is for all concerned. Not just for you and me, but for the director, the President, even a few members of Congress. Then they'll come to their senses and the whole thing will gradually fade away. Take my word. I've seen it happen before."

"I'm sure you have."

"What questions did the interrogators ask you?"

"I'm not supposed to talk about it."

"Oh, they always say that. They want to isolate people and intimidate them. Don't worry. You can certainly tell me. I already know all the information."

"They wanted to know about the Armenian operation. They seemed to have most of the details about everything else."

"What did you tell them?"

"Not much. My lawyer told me not to, at least not yet."

"Lawyers always say that."

"Look, I don't want to talk about the investigation. Not because of the lawyers, but because it depresses me. The only reason I came to see you was because Alan said you had something you needed to tell me."

"So you've seen Alan?"

"No. I don't want to see him. I talked to him briefly on the phone."

"Did he tell you what I was going to say?"

"No. He just said it was important." She looked at Stone. He had that Palm Beach undertaker's look. It was obvious he had bad news.

"It's something that concerns you," he said softly.

"Let's stop beating around the bush. It's about the Armenian doctor, isn't it?"

"Yes."

"What's happened to him?"

"Nothing, yet. But it appears that the Soviets have learned a good deal about our activities. So there is every likelihood that your friend Antoyan will be apprehended when he tries to pick up the shipment we've sent him."

Anna shook her head, as if to shake off what she had just heard, but the words stayed in the air. It took a moment to match them with her memory of the real person, the deep brown eyes and determined voice of the man she had said goodbye to in Paris a few weeks before. For the first time since they came to get her in Deauville, Anna felt like crying. But not now, not in front of Stone. She struggled to control her emotions, so that she might do something useful to help the Armenian doctor. She cleared her throat.

"How did the Russians find out?" she asked.

"I'm not sure," said Stone, not quite truthfully. "Perhaps one of Ascari's smugglers got caught and confessed. Maybe Ascari himself defected. You always said he was unreliable. But I don't really know. All I'm sure of is that the KGB has pulled its people out of Istanbul, and that they're conducting an investigation."

"What can we do to help Antoyan?"

"Nothing, I'm afraid."

"That's bullshit, Mr. Stone. I knew you'd say that. But it can't be right. There has to be something."

"There isn't. I've checked with Hoffman. The shipment has already left Iran. It's on its way. There's no way to call it back."

"What about Moscow station? Headquarters can cable them and have them send someone down to Armenia to warn Antoyan."

"The director would never approve it. Why should headquarters help us? In any event, it wouldn't work. It might make you feel better, but it would only put your man in greater jeopardy."

"Why? Why can't Moscow station pass a simple message, for God's sake? Why is everything that's obvious always impossible?"

"Because our case officers in Moscow are all blown, my dear. The Soviets have identified every one of them. Anyone who tried to go to Yerevan would be under heavy surveillance the moment he left Moscow. It would only make things worse for your Armenian friend. The Soviets would think he was a real agent, rather than a young dissident who managed to charm an overeager young female case officer."

Stone's last remark silenced Anna. She wanted to curse him, to tear the seamless mask from his face. But she knew that what he had just said was true. The recruitment of the Armenian doctor was Anna's responsibility. She had no business asking Stone, or anyone else, to fix what had gone wrong. It was her problem to solve, and she would somehow have to do just that. Stone could continue circling forever in his moral cul-de-sac if he liked. But Anna wasn't chained to the seat with him.

"I need some air," she said. "I'm going to take a walk."

"I'll join you," said the old man.

"No, you won't. I want to be alone for a little while. I need to think."

"I'll wait for you."

"Suit yourself," she said.

She was gone for nearly an hour. She walked along the service road next to the interstate highway, oblivious to the rush of the traffic, turning over in her mind the situation facing Aram Antoyan and the possibilities for escape.

Anna found herself wondering, reflexively, what her father would have done. But that thought passed out of her mind. That yardstick, against which she had measured so much of her life and surroundings, no longer fit. A few months ago, Anna would have recast the question: What would Edward Stone do? How would the old boys, the glistening heirs of 1945, cope with such a dilemma? But Anna had discerned a truth about them. Over the years, while they were toasting their famous victories at the Athenian Club, they had tended to abandon the little people in places like Laos and Vietnam, the mountains of Kurdistan, the Bay of Pigs. They had a nasty habit of leaving their agents hanging. And Anna, however green she might be, didn't intend to make the same mistake.

A last model went fleetingly through Anna's mind. It was

ill formed, impulsive, full of daring but weak on delivery—all qualities shared by the person Anna had in mind. What, she wondered, would Alan Taylor do in a situation like this? Or more precisely, what would he think was the right thing to do, even if he was prevented by some missing spark plug of the soul from carrying it out?

Anna continued walking, moving her feet through the rough pebbles at the edge of the highway. She kept returning to two central facts: The first was that the Armenian doctor's predicament was almost entirely of her making; the second was that unless she did something to warn him, he would almost certainly walk into a trap on November 10, just over two weeks away. An idea began to form in Anna's mind, born of these two inescapable facts. You couldn't call it a plan, exactly; it was too ill formed and imprecise. Its only real virtue was its simple audacity; it was the sort of thing that no one in his right mind would consider, which meant, by Anna's calculus, that it had a modest chance of success.

Stone was doing the crossword puzzle from *The New York Times* when Anna returned. He looked up from it with a kindly twinkle in his eye, and that maddening look of perfect composure. He gazed for a long moment at her earnest and resolute young face.

"You're going, aren't you?" he said.

"What are you talking about?"

"To Yerevan. You've decided to rescue the Armenian doctor yourself."

"What makes you think that?" asked Anna unconvincingly. Her face was flushed.

"You are transparent, my dear."

"It's none of your goddamned business. I don't work for you anymore. For once, you are out of the loop."

"Fine," said Stone calmly. "But if you are planning some sort of mad adventure, you should listen to a few words of advice."

"I'm sick of your advice."

"I can't entirely blame you. But you had better listen to this last bit, because it could save your life, and his."

Anna said nothing. But she listened.

"If you go, you must go entirely on your own. Stay away

from the agency completely. Do you understand? Stay away from the embassy."

"What's your point?" She looked at her watch.

"The point is that nothing the CIA touches in the Soviet Union is secure. Nothing. There is no such thing as a secret conversation in our embassy, even in supposedly secure areas like the bubble and the communications vault. The KGB has penetrated everything. They have us wired, literally. They have a network of tunnels under Tchaikovsky Street. From there, they can run cables up the walls of the building, with microphones and even tiny cameras. They can tap into the grounding wires in the basement and read half of the electronic signals in the building. By listening to the sounds of electric typewriters and cipher machines—just the sound, mind you—they can reconstruct most of the classified traffic going in and out. Our people take the Russians for fools, people who drink too much and wear bad suits. But they are the best in the world at what they do. I'm telling you, nothing is secure."

"Okay," said Anna. "What else do you want to tell me?"

"I assume you're planning to go in as a tourist, on a regular tourist visa. I have no idea whether you're clean—whether the Soviets have tumbled to the fact that a woman named Anna Barnes with your passport number works for the agency. They may have, with all the recent commotion and cables whizzing back and forth. And then again, they may not have. Evidently it's a risk you're prepared to take."

"Evidently," she said.

"I must warn you that time is crucial. The Soviet consulate normally requires two weeks to grant a tourist visa. If you apply immediately and everything goes smoothly, you will just barely have time to get to Yerevan and warn your friend. So you'll need to move quickly. The Soviets require three photos, a brief application form and a photocopy of your passport. You'll also have to buy a package tour from Intourist. Fortunately, they send planeloads of tourists to Armenia every month. Half of Fresno has been to Yerevan. So it shouldn't be too hard."

"What else?" asked Anna, no longer bothering to maintain the fiction that she didn't know what Stone was talking about.

"I suggest you let a travel agent make the arrangements. That's what a tourist would do. And that way, you won't have a chance to say anything stupid to the Soviets at the consulate. They probably won't give you the visa until the day before you leave. That's one of their childish habits. They apparently think it puts visitors on edge and makes them easier to manipulate. When you do get the visa, disappear. It will take the agency a few days to realize you're gone, and by that time you should be out of the woods. Or into them."

"Go on," said Anna. By now, she had taken out a pen and begun to make notes. "Keep talking."

"You must embrace your cover as if it were the very skin you were born with. You are a tourist, first, last and always. You are not a spy, you have never met any spies, you wouldn't know what one looked like. Don't do anything—anything—that would suggest any familiarity with tradecraft. Don't look for surveillance, ever. Not even in the slick, hard-to-detect ways they taught you in training. Don't look in shop windows to see the reflections of people. Don't turn your head when you light a cigarette so you can casually check what's behind you. And for God's sake, don't play counter-surveillance games. Don't change cabs or buses. Don't ride the subway and reverse direction. Don't take the phone off the hook or run the water when you're having a conversation."

"Slow down," said Anna, struggling to keep up.

"In short, don't act like a spy. Because the Soviets are wise to these tricks. Every one of them is a tip-off that you may be on an intelligence assignment, and the Soviets routinely follow anyone who looks the least bit suspicious. And don't forget, they have virtually unlimited resources to throw at you. They have been known to use as many as fifteen cars on one surveillance. Don't try to beat them. It's impossible. If you think you're being followed, give up and come home. Any attempt to evade surveillance will only make it worse. Do you understand me?"

"Yes. Any more advice?"

"Not much. If you get to Yerevan, play it straight. You met Antoyan in Paris. He's a handsome young man. You've come to Armenia. Why shouldn't you pay him a visit? It's the most natural thing in the world. Don't try any elliptical code words on the phone. Don't try anything. Get in, get out. With luck you may make it."

"Is that it?"

"One last thing. Stay away from everyone in the agency, but especially Alan Taylor."

"Why Taylor?"

"Because he has a guilty conscience. If he finds out, he'll never let you go."

"It's none of your business, but Taylor is the last person I would tell."

"Good luck," said Stone. He shook her hand warmly. Anna reciprocated, but there was still a wary look on her face.

"I don't understand you," she said.

"Why not? By this time I should be an open book to you."

"Not quite. Walking back here just now, I was sure that if I told you what I was planning to do, you would try to talk me out of it."

"Why would you think that?"

"Because if there's one thing I have learned in working with you, it's that you always have an angle. You don't say or do anything that doesn't fit into a larger scheme. I haven't figured out what it is in this case. And to be honest, I don't care."

Stone smiled. "I was right about you, Anna, from the beginning. You really are a most remarkable woman. It has been a great pleasure to work with you."

43

ANNA AWOKE OVER THE NORTH ATLANTIC WITH THE SENSA-tion that she was choking. She struggled toward consciousness as if she were trapped underwater, trying to reach the surface before she ran out of breath. The terror ended only when she realized that it had been a dream, one that had afflicted her several times over the past ten years. The images of this dream were drawn from the pages of Ottoman history. It was the story of a particularly cruel sultan, who became convinced that one of his concubines had been unfaithful to him and interrogated every woman in the harem. When none of them confessed, he ordered that every woman in the household—more than two hundred of them—should be drowned. They were seized, tied into sacks weighted with stones, and thrown into the Bosporus.

In the dream each time, Anna was diving off Seraglio Point. As she dove deeper in the water, she heard a ghostly chorus of women's voices. When she reached the bottom of the Bosporus, she saw a vast underwater forest of sacks, each containing the body of a woman, swaying gently with the current. Anna swam in horror toward the surface, as the arms in the sacks reached toward her imploringly. She always made it, breaking the surface of the water just as she broke through to consciousness. But the dream was terrifying, every time. And never more so than that night on the plane, halfway to Moscow—sewn by her own hand into a heavily weighted sack and falling, with each second, toward the deepest abyss.

Anna had done everything Stone had advised. She had obtained her visa from the Soviet consulate in the necessary two weeks. She had booked the shortest available itinerary from Intourist: an eight-day trip with a brief stopover in Moscow on arrival; continuing on that night to Yerevan for three days; three days in Tbilisi; then back to Moscow for the return trip home. The schedule was tight, but not impossible. Anna left New York the afternoon of November 7. That meant that she would arrive in Moscow midday November 8, catch a flight to Yerevan that night, and have all of the next day, November 9, to track down Dr. Antoyan.

Her first clutch of fear had come at Kennedy Airport, when she checked her suitcase and realized it could be redeemed only in Moscow. Anna still had ninety minutes to kill before departure time. Act like a tourist, she told herself. A long line of people were crowding the newsstand and pharmacy, stocking up on life's essentials. She joined the queue, buying extra deodorant, tampons, chewing gum, Kleenex, sleeping pills. She bought magazines, a half dozen of them, on the theory that if she was too nervous to concentrate on a book, she could always read a magazine. But when she sat down in the departure lounge, she had trouble getting through *People*. She closed her eyes and heard loud Russian voices. A group of

Russian men had arrived in the departure area. They were dressed in leather jackets and tight blue jeans, smoking American cigarettes. They had a kind of rough sexuality, like blue-collar American men of the 1950s. Members of an athletic team maybe. Why shouldn't they be boisterous? thought Anna. It may be their last chance.

Anna was fortunately seated by a window in an otherwise empty row, which meant that she didn't have to talk to anyone. She took a sleeping pill after dinner, in the hope that she might get some rest. But all it brought her was the Bosporus nightmare. She didn't sleep at all after that. She listened to the hum of the engine against the bulkhead and thought about Aram, and his cart-horse body, and the way he had held her at the door of her room at the Bristol Hotel in Paris. She tried to read one of her magazines; then a Graham Greene novel about a leper clinic in Africa, which did her no good at all. Eventually they served breakfast, but the coffee was weak and the roll was stale. Moscow couldn't be far away.

She was fortunate, in a way, that she hadn't slept much. The fatigue dulled her anxiety as she approached her first encounter with Soviet officialdom at passport control. She didn't feel nervous until the last moment, when she moved into the booth and the KGB border guard gazed up at her with steely blue eyes. Anna looked away, certain that her own eyes would betray her, and handed the man her passport and visa. Then she waited. The booth, like so many things in the Soviet Union, had been designed to intimidate the individual. It was lit by an unforgiving neon tube, which made even the most robust person look pale and haunted. Overhead, across from the passport officer, was a long mirror. It was tilted downward so that the officer could observe his supplicants from behind—could see their hands shaking, or their knees quivering, or their feet tapping nervously.

Anna's hands were at her side, clenched in tight and sweaty fists. The officer was taking his time, examining her passport, then her face, then her visa. She caught his eye again, involuntarily, and she could feel her head twitch, even as she tried to hold it steady. The KGB officer looked at her passport one more time, studied another sheet in front of him, and then rose from his seat.

Oh, dear God, thought Anna. They've made me. I'm on a

watch list. She felt a sensation of pure terror, and a sudden surge in her metabolism—like a kettle boiling over. Stone had warned her about this moment. There would be no way to know whether the Soviets had identified her as an intelligence officer until she was on their doorstep, standing in the passport line at Sheremetievo Airport. The young, blue-eyed officer returned, accompanied by an older man. He looked at Anna's visa and passport, then at Anna, and then whispered something. Please, let it all happen quickly, thought Anna. Let the older one tell me in Radio Moscow English: Excuse me, Miss Barnes, would you come with me, please? That way, at least, it would be over.

But it was only beginning. The young clerk fixed his eyes on Anna a final time, closed them like a shutter, and stamped the visa. He handed it back to Anna. His face showed no emotion whatsoever. Anna was relieved, almost giddy, as she walked toward the baggage-claim area. It was only when she had retrieved her suitcase and was heading for customs that she realized her relief was premature. Of course they would clear her through passport control, even if they had a firm identification of her. Now that she was in their country, they owned her.

The first real harbinger of disaster came at the Intourist desk at the airport. Anna was supposed to go there on arrival, to arrange a transfer to Vnukovo Airport for her Aeroflot flight that evening to Yerevan. She handed her book of Intourist vouchers to the woman at the desk, who studied it for a long while, checked a list, and then looked up at her. Why am I on all these lists? wondered Anna. She felt the surge of anxiety welling up again.

"Well, I guess I have good news for you," said the Intourist lady, in that strange, too colloquial English that is taught in Soviet language schools.

"What's that?" asked Anna.

"I think you will have an extra night in Moscow, at Intourist Hotel across from Red Square, with no charge."

"What do you mean?" Anna was numb from fatigue and stress, but she could tell that something bad was happening.

"That was a joke, I guess. What I mean is that we have a problem with your flight from Vnukovo to Yerevan. Flight 837 has been delayed."

"How long?"

"Until tomorrow."

Calm down, Anna told herself. Keep cool. "What time tomorrow?"

"Maybe it will be in the morning."

"What time?"

"Nine, ten, eleven. I don't know. Maybe it will be in the afternoon."

"What's wrong? Isn't there another flight? I have to get to Yerevan. I'm really looking forward to Yerevan."

"I am sorry, but it is not convenient."

"What do you mean, 'not convenient'? I have a reservation for a flight tonight."

"That flight has been delayed," repeated the woman blandly.

"Could I please speak to the manager?"

Anna realized immediately that she had made a mistake. Russians have a huge chip on their shoulder in dealing with Americans, and are just waiting for someone to try to pull rank, demand special privileges, or otherwise embody the Soviet propaganda image of the pushy, grasping American capitalist. It is a losing game. The only thing that makes anyone special in the Soviet Union is the blessing of the Soviet government. And that, Anna certainly did not have.

"Well," said the offended Intourist lady, "I think probably you can talk to me, because I am the manager. And so I will tell you your program. You are going to Intourist Hotel tonight. Tomorrow morning, an Intourist car will take you to Vnukovo for your flight to Yerevan, which has been delayed. Now an Intourist car will take you to the hotel." The woman nodded in the direction of a burly driver, who did not offer to carry her bag. Anna realized there was absolutely no point in arguing further. She would leave for Yerevan the next day, November 9.

Anna settled into her room on the seventeenth floor of the Intourist Hotel, overlooking Gorky Street. The desk light didn't work; the window wouldn't open; there was a television set, but it was broken. She unpacked her bag and took a long shower. There wasn't any shower curtain, so the water sprayed all over the floor. Anna dutifully mopped it up. The city was like that; it reduced you to peonage in a few hours' time. As Stone had once observed, Moscow was a vast Skinner box that had been created to condition behavior—among foreigners and Soviet citizens alike.

Anna wrapped herself in a towel and waited for her hair to dry. She thought seriously of giving up. From the scene at the airport, it seemed possible that her identity had been compromised. A worse problem, in some ways, was the delay in her flight to Yerevan. Unless she arrived in time to find Dr. Antoyan, the whole trip would be useless. She decided to take a walk, to clear her head. It was midafternoon by now, and there was a November chill in the air.

She walked across Marx Prospect, watched the guards at the Lenin Mausoleum in the dying afternoon sun. A Soviet couple—just married, the bride in a white wedding dress—had come to have their picture taken in front of the Mausoleum. What a pathetic way to start a marriage, thought Anna. They must be party members. She followed them out of the square, toward a subway stop. On a whim, she entered the subway station, paid her five kopecks, and rode to Komsomolskaya. She changed trains and took the circle line all the way to Culture Park, on the other side of town, and then rode the red line back toward Marx Prospect. She wasn't looking for surveillance or trying to avoid it. She was simply trying to get a feel for a new city, the way any tourist might. Still, she had a pleasant sensation, sitting in some of the nearly empty cars, that she was not being followed. And that was enough to allow her to sleep, fitfully, the night of November 8.

Anna awoke early the next morning and took her assigned car to Vnukovo Airport, southwest of the city. She went to the Intourist desk there and confronted another stone-faced matron. No, there was no word yet when the delayed flight to Yerevan would be leaving. Yes, there was another flight for Yerevan leaving in fifty minutes, but there were no seats. It was a special flight. "Fully booked, fully booked," the woman repeated. She suggested that Anna go to the café and have something to eat; she would come and collect her when the flight was ready. That at least sounded like a plan of action. But an hour passed, with several cups of tea and a gooey chocolate éclair but no sign of the woman. Anna returned to the small wooden door of the Intourist office.

"Not time, not time," said the matronly clerk. Seeing Anna's distress, she took pity on her and motioned for her to sit on the couch in the office. Two other Americans were already camped there—Dickran and Marj Kazanjian from Glendale. They were also waiting for the delayed flight to Yerevan.

"Call me Dick," said Dickran Kazanjian. He lowered his voice. "They say this happens all the time with Aeroflot."

"They say there's nothing you can do except wait," added Marj Kazanjian. She, at least, had brought along some knitting.

So they waited through the morning and early afternoon. It was eleven o'clock, then noon, then one. Dick and Marj suggested lunch, but Anna wasn't hungry. A little after two, the Intourist lady announced that she had good news. Flight 837 would be leaving for Yerevan soon.

"What time?" asked Anna.

"Five o'clock."

"But that's when Flight 837 was supposed to leave yesterday," said Anna. "Why didn't you just tell us yesterday's flight had been canceled?"

"Flight 837 has been delayed," said the Intourist lady, and there was obviously no point in arguing.

Anna now began worrying in earnest about how to cope with the delay. The flight from Moscow was scheduled to take just over three hours; Yerevan was an additional hour behind Moscow, so they would arrive, at the earliest, a little after 9 p.m., Yerevan time. It would take at least an hour to get to the hotel and check in. So it would be ten o'clock before she could begin to look for Dr. Antoyan. By that time, his office would undoubtedly be closed. She had his parents' home address, but that was all.

The flight finally left at five-twenty. It seemed to Anna to take forever. She was wedged in a middle seat, between a gentle Armenian lady in her mid-fifties and a garrulous old Armenian man who kept dispensing loud opinions to his seatmates—including Anna, who didn't understand a word. She tried to pass the time by reading her Graham Greene novel about the leper colony, but she kept reading the same page over and over again. A Russian flight attendant came by, handing out pieces of chicken wrapped in cellophane. Anna passed up the chicken; the Armenians on either side devoured theirs and handed the greasy bones back to the stewardess.

Anna's first sense that they were nearing Yerevan came when people began crowding over to her side of the plane. The Armenian woman had her nose up against the window, but she backed away so that Anna could see. To the left of the plane, visible in the moonlight, was a ridge of snow-capped mountains.

"Ararat?" asked Anna. The woman shook her head. Not yet. But several minutes later, Anna saw the woman peer out the window again, and then put her palms together and say a quiet prayer in Armenian. "Ararat," she said, pointing out the window to a snowy moonlit peak, rising eerily out of a flat plain toward the heavens. Anna could see that there were tears in the corners of the woman's eyes as she gazed on this symbol of Armenia and its tortured existence. So here I am, thought Anna. I have arrived in the nation of victims, where people grieve even on airplanes.

Anna shared a car in from the airport with the Kazanjians, who chattered away with the enthusiasm of diasporan Armenians coming home. They were all staying at the Armenia Hotel on Lenin Square in the center of town. Anna stared out the window while the Kazanjians talked about Cousin Simpad and Uncle Garabed. It was a high, dusty city; most of the buildings had been constructed of the same pinkish stone. The city had a recurring architectural motif as well—a high, rounded arch with the graceful curves of the Armenian alphabet, which looked as if it was all "U"s and "M"s.

It was ten o'clock when they reached the hotel; the Kazanjians invited Anna to join them for dinner in the hotel dining room, but she begged off. By the time she had taken her bag up to her room, a depressing little cubbyhole with mildew stains on the walls, it was ten-twenty. Her best bet to reach Aram, she decided, would be to go directly to his parents' place and try to find out from them where he lived. But how? It would be folly to take a taxi from the hotel at this hour. Any hotel driver would undoubtedly also be a part-time police informer. She looked out the window of her room and saw the play of lights and fountains in Lenin Square. People were out strolling, which meant there might be a few taxis on the streets.

Move, Anna told herself. Don't waste another minute. She put the address of Aram's parents in her purse and headed for the square. There was a seedy-looking group of men by the door, and as Anna left the hotel, one of them came after her. He wasn't even subtle about it. When he called out something that sounded like "I love you, baby," Anna was relieved. He was just a hustler, trying to pick up a Western woman. Anna got more catcalls from the Armenian teenage boys who were sitting astride the fountains, smoking cigarettes. Fortunately, she also attracted the attention of a taxi driver. Anna handed him the address which Aram had written out for her in Armenian characters. The driver nodded and began chattering away in Armenian as he drove up the hill. He left Anna off at an apartment complex near the radio tower, overlooking the city. She asked him to wait, in halting Russian, but when she gave him the money, he sped off.

It was just after eleven when Anna knocked on the door of the Antoyans' second-floor apartment. A white-haired man shuffled to the door in his bathrobe. He had to be Aram's father. The eyes gave him away. He looked at the American woman standing on his doorstep as if she were a creature from another planet.

"*Vot Antoyan Aram?*" she asked. Is Aram Antoyan here?

"*Nyet,*" said the father. He might have closed the door on her if his wife hadn't padded up behind. She had a gentle, studious look that also reminded Anna of Aram. Neither of them spoke English, and Anna's Russian wasn't up to the task. But Aram's mother spoke passable French, so they conversed in that language.

"I met your son in Paris," said Anna. "We are friends."

Mrs. Antoyan smiled, as if she knew exactly what that meant.

"I have come to Yerevan on a visit. I would like to see your son while I am here."

"I am sure he will be very happy to see you," said the Armenian woman. "He talks often of his time in Paris and the friends he met there."

"Does he live here? He gave me this address in Paris."

"Oh no. He is a grown-up man now," he said with another motherly smile. "Too old to live with his mother and father."

"I would like to see him soon," said Anna.

"Very well. You can visit him tomorrow at the hospital. I will give you the address."

"No. I have that address. Actually, I would like to see him tonight if that is possible."

This request was a bit forward for Mrs. Antoyan. She blushed. Here it was, nearly midnight, and a complete stranger was trying to get in bed with her son. Evidently it was true what they said about American women.

"Perhaps it is too late tonight," said the Armenian lady, trying to preserve a measure of decency.

All things considered, Anna was pleased that Mrs. Antoyan had her pegged as a woman of loose morals. She did her best to reinforce that impression.

"Please," said Anna breathily. "I want to see him very much. Won't you give me the address?"

At this point, old Mr. Antoyan broke in and mumbled something in Armenian—which Anna suspected translated roughly as "Give the bitch Aram's address so I can get some sleep."

"I can give you his address," said the old woman. "But I don't think he's there now."

"Why not? Where is he?"

"With friends. You should not ask about these things. You should try tomorrow."

"I would like the address," said Anna.

Aram's mother rolled her eyes. She wrote out the address on two sides of the paper, in Russian and Armenian characters, and gave it to Anna.

"Thank you so very much," said Anna. "I have missed him terribly, and I can't wait to see him again. Perhaps we can all meet for dinner."

"Perhaps so," said Mrs. Antoyan. But she looked dubious. It was all right for her son to sleep with this loose American woman, but dinner was a different matter. In an Armenian household, dinner was a sacrament.

"Good night," said Anna, waving goodbye. Old Mr. Antoyan scanned her legs and gave her a wink before closing the door.

Anna walked back to the main road. Finding a taxi at this hour in a suburban neighborhood would be next to impossible. But she suspected that in Yerevan, as in most Soviet and Eastern European cities, a private car might be willing to take her for a few rubles. She walked downhill, toward a large petrol station a few hundred yards away, gesturing with her outstretched hand for a car to slow down and pick her up. She waved off the first driver who stopped. He was a heavy-set man, obviously intoxicated, who looked as if he wanted to screw her. The next car contained a young couple. They were passing Anna by, but she gestured frantically and they pulled over. She handed the address to the woman, with a desperate look on her face.

"Pazhalusta!" implored Anna. The woman whispered something to her husband, who thought a moment and then nodded. Aram's flat was back toward the center of town, near the Opera House. The couple sat in silence in the front seat, evidently wondering what on earth a foreign woman could be doing, alone, in a Yerevan suburb at midnight. Anna worried, for a moment, that they might be taking her to a police station. But after fifteen minutes, they pulled up to a four-story building on a narrow side street.

"Vot adris," said the woman, pointing to the apartment on the third floor.

"Spasiba, spasiba," said Anna, handing the driver a five-ruble note.

She got out of the car and looked around. The streets were empty and quiet. The city was asleep. She saw no sign that she had been followed, but then, in deference to Stone's advice, she hadn't been watching. She looked up at Aram's third-floor apartment. It was dark. Maybe he was asleep. Maybe he was with another woman. It didn't matter. She only needed to tell him two words: Don't go.

Anna looked carefully, left and right, and then stepped into the entryway of the building. She climbed the stairs as quietly as she could. When she reached the third floor, she stood on the landing a moment, letting her eyes get accustomed to the dark, and then tapped quietly on the door.

No answer. Come on, you bastard, open the door. She knocked louder, still trying to avoid rousing the neighbors, and then louder still. She heard a door open on the floor above, and saw the lights switch on across the hall. But still there was no response from Aram. She gave one last, loud knock, and then sat down on the stairs to ponder her options.

She had half decided to sit there on the steps and wait for Aram to come home. But that possibility faded when the door across the hall opened and a nosy-looking old woman in a frayed bathrobe stuck her head out and stared at Anna. She would have stayed there anyway—damn the old woman—but the door opened again several minutes later. It was the same old woman, but this time she was making a motion with her hands, as if to sweep Anna away. Anna suspected that if she stayed, the woman would summon the militia.

Hastily, Anna scribbled out a message on one of her traveler's checks, the only clean piece of paper she could find in her wallet. She wrote it in French, their lingua franca. She tried to compose it in a way that would be obvious enough for Aram to understand, but not so obvious that it would incriminate him if someone else read it first. It read: "Hello, my darling. I'm in town for a quick visit. The friend you were going to meet tomorrow has unfortunately caught a cold. I'm staying at the Armenia Hotel. I ache for you." She threw in that last phrase for cover, but she realized, as she wrote it, that it was also true. She did ache for him. She folded the check in half and slipped it under the door.

It was now almost one o'clock. Back at the hotel, the hall ladies who monitored each guest's coming and going would be waiting up for her. If she didn't come back soon, they would probably sound the alarm. Anna loitered a few more minutes across the street, hoping that Aram would show up, and then gave up. Where was he? Probably sleeping with some dark-haired Armenian woman. Or more likely, Anna decided, he was with some of his friends planning the next day's rendezvous.

Anna walked back to the main street, feeling very conspicuous. Fortunately, a cab drove up after several minutes, and Anna was back at the hotel by one-thirty. The night desk clerk gave her a naughty wink. She set her alarm for five-thirty but lay awake more than an hour, assembling the pieces of her plan of action.

44

◆

Aɴɴᴀ ɢᴏᴛ ᴜᴘ ᴀᴛ ᴅᴀᴡɴ ᴏɴ Nᴏᴠᴇᴍʙᴇʀ 10. Sʜᴇ sʜᴏᴡᴇʀᴇᴅ, dressed, and was downstairs by six-fifteen. Fortunately, the desk clerk was on duty. Unlike the stolid Slavic personnel who manned the Intourist hotel in Moscow, he had a friendly, slightly larcenous look about him. God bless the Armenians, thought Anna.

"Good morning," she said.

"Good morning," said the clerk. "What we need, please?"

"I would like to go sightseeing today."

"Intourist," he said, motioning down the hall. "Service bureau open nine-thirty."

"Yes, but I want something special," said Anna. "Not just the regular Intourist tour."

"Something special?" he asked, lifting his eyebrow.

"Yes. I want to see the old monastery at Khor Virap, where St. Gregory the Illuminator was kept underground."

"Not so good trip. Not permitted trip. Khor Virap near border. Restricted area."

"Yes, I know," said Anna sweetly. "But my Armenian friends said I could probably arrange a special trip. You know, for dollars?"

"For dollars?" He looked around to make sure that nobody had heard. That was a good sign, thought Anna. He was already a co-conspirator.

"Yes," she said. "If that's all right. Do you know anybody who could help me arrange a special tour like that?"

"Car we got," said the desk clerk. "My brother has very nice car. Maybe I call him. If it is a very special trip." He said the word "very" with some emphasis, as if it signified an extra twenty dollars.

"Could your brother take me in his car? That would be wonderful. I have a friend who may want to come along, too. Maybe we could stop and pick him up on the way."

"Why not."

"And one more thing. I would love to visit some of the little villages in the Ararat district. There is one I am told is very beautiful, called Kiarki."

"Why not," he repeated. He lowered his voice. "Not telling anybody, please. This business for us."

"Don't worry," she said. "I won't tell a soul."

"When you go?"

"Now," she said.

"Now?" He looked at his watch.

"Yes, please. I want to see Ararat at dawn."

The desk clerk shrugged his shoulders, picked up the phone, and called his brother. The only word Anna made out was "dollar." He showed up thirty minutes later driving a shiny red Zhiguli sedan. He was a burly man with a big mustache who spoke some English and said he worked at the cognac plant. A serious crook, thought Anna. His name was Samvel.

Anna got in the back seat, then realized that she would attract attention there and moved up to the front, next to Samvel. She gave him Aram's address. Her plan was to stop there first, to see if he had returned home. If he hadn't, she would go to the little village of Kiarki herself and try to head him off. She hoped the trip south wouldn't be necessary, that she would find Aram at home—bleary-eyed after a late night of drinking and scheming with his friends—and spend the rest of the day with him. In bed, perhaps.

Please be home, Aram, she thought as the Zhiguli turned the corner onto his street. Please be home. She got out of Samvel's car and walked up the three flights of stairs to the apartment. She pounded hard this time, not caring who heard her. But there was no answer. She crouched on all fours and peered under the door and saw that her note, written on the folded check, was still there. He's slept somewhere else the night before the pickup, for security, she thought. Anna took a deep breath, steeling herself for what she had to do next. She returned to the car and got in next to Samvel.

"My friend isn't here," she said. "Maybe he has gone ahead

of me. Let's drive south. There's a pretty little village I would like to see, called Kiarki, and then I want to go to Khor Virap."

"Fine and dandy," said the driver. Somewhere, he had learned a few such phrases of American slang.

It was now seven-fifteen. They headed south out of town, descending the hills of Yerevan toward the flat plain beneath Ararat. The sun was bright, warming the morning air. The driver sped along, past low-slung suburban houses and collective farms with numberless rows of grapevines. It was a tidy little world—the vines carefully maintained, the houses clean and decorated with ornamented metal rainspouts, each crowned with animal figures and other designs.

Samvel, the driver, kept up a steady stream of patter in a combination of languages. He seemed to be a kind of Armenian Sancho Panza, a genial rogue of the road. When they passed a militia station, he turned to Anna and said with a wink: "Permission for this we no got. If anyone stopping us, you my Armenian cousin from America. 'Very sorry,' you say, 'I come all the way from Fresno to see Khor Virap.' You give me dollars. I give to him. Everything hunky-dory."

"Hunky-dory," agreed Anna. She handed him a ten-dollar bill. He tilted his head in a gesture that said "more" in any language, and she gave him another ten. This commerce done, she began to relax slightly, whizzing along the open road on a sunny day with her fixer at the wheel.

They were heading down a four-lane highway, straight toward the great tufted cone at Ararat. Samvel gazed toward the brooding peak and began to wax poetic. He was, like many Armenian men, prone to make speeches at the slightest provocation. He gestured toward Ararat and put his hand on his heart. "This mountain is like a magnet to me," he said grandly. "In the shadow of this big mountain I feel immortal!" The big magnet of Ararat was actually across the border in Turkey, but never mind. The poetry of the Armenian soul overflowed from Samvel. He exhibited the national love of the grand gesture, the fatal romanticism. Anna wished that Aram could hear him.

The Soviet-Turkish border was visible a few miles farther on, as they neared the Aras River. "Don't look too close," said Samvel. "Border area closed."

But Anna couldn't resist. Every four hundred yards or so, she saw a tall tower, like the guard towers at prisons. As they got closer, she could see the frontier itself, half a mile away across the plain. What struck her was the fact that all the barbed wire faced inward; she had known it, intellectually, but it was still appalling to see that the fences had been constructed to keep Soviet people in, rather than to keep strangers out. And there were so many layers of them. First came a chain-link fence, with solid-concrete posts every few yards and what appeared to be insulation and conductors for electrified strands of wire. Next came a barrier of coiled razor wire, then another chain-link fence, then a patch of ground that had been raked smooth, so that it would show the slightest footprint, and then a paved road for the vehicles of the border guard. Across this road there was another barrier of razor wire, and than a last fence, crowned with that admission of national defeat—the inward-facing tier of barbed wire

The border looked utterly impassable, even to the wiliest smugglers. But Ascari's men weren't coming this way, across the plain from Turkey, Anna reminded herself. They were coming over the trackless mountains from Iran, where even border guards lost their way.

"And now we are coming to famous Khor Virap," said Samvel. "Maybe you would like to stop here first?"

"No, let's stop here on the way back," said Anna. "First I want to see Kiarki, the village near the border."

"But that is Azerbaijani village. People there are Turks. Why go there? It will be ugly."

"My friends say it is very pretty. I'd like to go."

Samvel grumbled but agreed to go. It was now past eight-thirty. Anna looked now at every car they passed, hoping she might see Aram's face. She was determined to get to the village before he did, but with each additional minute she became more worried that her plan wouldn't work. Samvel looked over at her, nervously drumming her fingers against the dashboard of the Zhiguli. Armenians don't like to see people anxious. It is an affront to the national character, which feels comfortable with laughter or tears—and abhors what lies in between.

"I will sing you a song," said Samvel.

"An Armenian song?"

"Of course. What you think I would sing, Turkish?" Anna laughed, and he began to sing in Armenian, in a rich bass voice that had an almost operatic resonance and filled the lit-

le Russian car with sound. He sang several verses full of
genuine if well-dramatized emotion.

"It's a beautiful song," said Anna. "What do the words
mean?"

"I am singing about my grandfather's village, called
Moush, in Turkish Armenia. Now there is no more Moush.
People all gone, all dead. But we sing this song to our sons,
so they will know what it was like. The song says:

> Get up, my boy, let us go to our homeland.
> We will drink from our own water and milk.
> I will satisfy your longing.
> Get up, my boy, let us go to Moush,
> the land of our fathers.
> Even if it is in a dream, let us go and come back."

Anna closed her eyes. The ribbon of asphalt rolled under
them, bringing them closer to the enclave where the borders
of Turkey, Iran, Armenia and Azerbaijan all meet. A highway
laid over the bones of the dead.

"Sing me another song," she said. "It makes me forget
about my problems."

"You bet. But this is a sad song."

"That's okay. I like sad songs."

Samvel's voice was even deeper and richer this time, like
the bass pipes of a great church organ. He sang only four
verses and then stopped, overcome by the emotion of the
song and the moment. "I am sorry," he said. "It is hard for
me to sing this song."

"Translate it for me," said Anna. The more she saw of
Samvel, the more he seemed to embody his countrymen—at
once so robust and so sentimental. These Armenians were
like small boats with too big sails, always in danger of becoming swamped.

"I should not have sung this song. The words will make
you too sad. It is a song about death. This song says:

> Everywhere you go,
> Death is the same.
> But I am jealous of the man,
> Who can die for his country."

"What is that song?" asked Anna. "I think I heard a frien
of mine humming it once in Paris."

"It is our national anthem," said Samvel.

A few miles farther, Anna saw a sign in Russian pointing
to the village of Kiarki. She looked around her. In the dis
tance, to the southeast, were the jagged sawtooth mountain
that marked the border with Iran. They were almost crimso
in the morning sun. Ahead was the border with the Azerbai
jani enclave called Nakhichevan. It was a ramshackle cross
roads marked by a traffic circle, an army garrison and, o
separate sides of the border, two derelict wineries. Anna fel
that she had come at last to the very armpit of the world, thi
remote place that was at once in the shadow of Turkey, Irar
and the Soviet Union.

"Kiarki," explained the driver, in case Anna had missed the
sign.

"Slow down," she said as they neared the village.

She looked around for signs of anything unusual. The
houses were small, one-floor bungalows, perhaps a bit mes
sier than those in the neighboring Armenian villages, but oth
erwise identical. Many of the houses had grapevines in the
front yard, growing up metal pipes that stretched from the
street to the roof. A few women sat in the shade of these
vines, preparing food. And there were children, dozens o
them, playing in the streets and in a small park near the cen
ter of town.

"It's dirty here," said Samvel as they neared the town
square. "Turks."

"Is this the only road from Yerevan?" asked Anna.

Samvel nodded. "There is small road, on other side of
town, but it only goes to next village."

"Stop the car," said Anna. "I want to get out here." Samvel
steered the car off the main street of the town and stopped
about forty yards from the square. From where the Zhiguli
was parked, Anna would be able to see any other car arriving
from Yerevan on the main road.

She covered her hair with a simple scarf and got out of the
Zhiguli. Samvel got out with her. She surveyed the road, up
and down. Behind them was only dust. Nobody seemed to
have followed them into this windswept little pea patch of the

Caucasus. She looked toward the town square—with its little bust of Lenin alongside a drinking fountain—and to the streets beyond. There was no sign of the militia, or the army, or the KGB. It was all calm and ordinary—as numbingly ordinary as only a border outpost in a remote region could be. She saw no sign whatsoever of Aram. The only odd thing was how few adults there were in the streets. Maybe they're all out working at the collective farm, thought Anna.

"What you want to look at?" said Samvel. He still thought visiting Kiarki was a stupid idea. Why spend a minute visiting Turks when there were so many Armenians nearby? But he was trying to cooperate.

"I'd just like to walk around," said Anna.

Her immediate problem, in fact, was how to stay put; how to contrive some way to stay right where they were until Aram arrived. She had an idea, one that would require good acting—especially to convince a histrionic character like Samvel—but was worth a try. She walked gingerly across the pavement, testing her ankles, toward the fountain and the bust of Lenin. As she climbed the stone stairs toward the monument, she took a sudden, terrible tumble—twisting on her left ankle, falling hard on her hip, and then rolling over on her shoulder.

Samvel was horrified. He came running over to Anna, calling out to her in Armenian and English. She lay on the ground, moaning and holding her ankle.

"You need doctor?" asked Samvel. "I take you to doctor."

"I don't think it's broken," said Anna. "It just hurts like hell. Let me try to walk on it."

She stood up and dusted herself off. Samvel offered his arm as a crutch, then his shoulder. Anna leaned on him and limped along, marking each step with an "ouch" or an "argh." The ankle did, in fact, hurt slightly, but it was the hip that had really taken a pounding. She walked back to the car, making just enough of a show of agony to impress Samvel, but not so much that she attracted people from the village.

"I'd like to just sit in the car for a little while, if it's okay," she said. "Then when I've rested my leg we can go to Khor Virap."

"They got Armenian doctor in next village, probably," said Samvel. "He fix you up good."

"No, I'd like to stay here for a little while. Maybe you

could get me a bottle of mineral water or something from the store. I'm thirsty."

"Jim-dandy," he said. "I bring back to you in few minutes. You stay in car. You not supposed to be here, according to rules. But everybody in Armenia break rules all the time, so don't worry. But stay here."

He walked off in search of a store. Anna scanned the streets, going and coming. Several trucks arrived from the direction of Yerevan, and so did a half dozen cars of various descriptions. A horse cart trotted down the street with an Azeri farmer and his son. A few bicycles whizzed by. But in none of these vehicles did Anna see anyone who looked remotely like Aram Antoyan. Down one side street, she thought she saw a tall man in a gray coat watching her from the shadows. But when she moved to get a closer look, he disappeared.

Samvel returned after a while with a fizzy cherry drink in a bottle, full of apologies. Most of the local stores were closed for some reason, he said. Typical Azeris. In an Armenian village the stores would all have been open, and they would have had Pepsi-Cola. Anna drank it slowly, scanning the highway. When the bottle was finally empty, she complained again of pain in her leg and asked if Samvel could perhaps get her something to eat. He looked at his watch. It was almost ten o'clock now.

"Food is better in Armenian village," he said. He wanted to leave.

"Please, Samvel, I need to eat something before we travel."

He nodded and went off again. Anna fixed her eyes on the Yerevan road and watched the same occasional parade of cars, still looking in vain for the face of Aram Antoyan. Where in God's name was he? she wondered. She was half angry at him and half worried. She turned and was scanning the streets in the interior of the village, wondering if maybe he could have come some other way, when she saw something that made her heart leap.

In the distance, nearly a hundred yards away, she could see the figure of a man emerging from a car that had parked on the small road that led away from town in the other direction. What made her think immediately of Aram was the man's gait, that close-footed step of the mountain pony that she had found so endearing in Paris. The man in the distance was heading toward a warren of houses. Anna wondered for a moment what to do, and then simply acted on impulse.

She opened the car door and walked quickly—forgetting the fake limp—toward the figure in the distance. She removed the headscarf, so that he would recognize her more easily. He was walking toward her—perhaps sixty yards away now—and was turning to his left. The closer Anna got, the more certain she was that it was Aram. He still hadn't recognized her.

Anna quickened his pace, until it was almost a run. He had stopped in front of a two-story house, slightly grander than most of the rest in the village. Oh my God, thought Anna. This must be the home of the smuggler, Sadeq Shirvanshir. In a moment, Aram would be in the house and gone.

"Aram," she called out to him, into the wind.

He turned and glanced at her briefly, so preoccupied with his own business that he didn't really bother to look who might be calling his name. He turned back toward the door of the house.

"Aram," she cried again.

This time he heard, looked, and looked again in disbelief. They were still forty yards apart. Anna began shaking her head and waving her arms, in pantomime, as if to say: Don't go in the house. Stay away from the house. Stay away from me.

He understood the first part, but not the second. In his shock and exhilaration at seeing the woman he thought he had left behind forever in Paris, he thought only of embracing her. He ran toward her, in short, tight steps, and put his arm around her.

"*Qu'est-ce que c'est?*" He was delighted and dumbfounded. "What can this be? Why are you here?"

Anna took his arm and walked quickly away from the house of Sadeq Shirvanshir, then stopped and looked at him. Aram had grown his beard back. He looked ruddy and healthy, not at all the worse for his return home.

"Listen to me carefully, Aram," she said in French. "There is a problem with the delivery. I don't think it's safe for you to pick things up. I promised back in Paris that I would warn you if something was wrong. This was the only way, coming here myself."

Aram was shaking his head and smiling. "But there is nothing wrong, you silly girl. Everything is okay."

"Yes, there is something wrong. Trust me. The KGB knows what my friends and I have been doing. They are probably waiting for you to pick up this delivery. You shouldn't take the risk. They will think you're a spy."

"But you are wrong. There is no danger here," repeated Aram. "I tell you, we are safe."

"Listen to me!" she pleaded. "I have come all this way to warn you, and you aren't even listening."

"No, you must listen to me," he said. He was trying to be calm and manly, in the presence of this anxious woman. "There is nothing to worry about. There is no danger."

"How do you know? What are you talking about?"

"I have already met the smuggler, Shirvanshir. I met him three hours ago, at first light. I stayed with friends last night in the next Armenian village, so that I could be near and watch and make sure there were no tricks. But it is just as you promised. He knew the password. There was no KGB. You are mistaken. We are safe."

"Why were you going back just now if you have already met with him?"

"To pick up the equipment. He has to bring it from a hiding place outside town. He told me he would bring it back in three hours. So now I am going to get it. Do not worry. There is no problem."

"Walk with me to my car," said Anna. The streets were empty, but still, she wanted not to rouse the attention of the local villagers. "I don't think you should go back," she said. "It could be a trap."

"Impossible. Anyway, if it is a trap, I have already fallen into it. They already know who I am. If I don't go, the only thing that happens is that I do not get the antenna. So I must go. I will not listen to any argument."

"Please, Aram. This is crazy. I have a bad feeling."

"This time you are wrong. I am the fortune-teller, remember? Do not be frightened. You come with me to the house, if you like. You will see."

"No," said Anna. "That would not be a good idea."

They were almost to Anna's car. Samvel had returned in the meantime and was holding a sandwich, stuffed with a spicy Armenian meat known as *basterma*. He evidently had walked to the next village to get it. He looked at Aram, then gave Anna a knowing look, as if to say: So this was what we were waiting for in Kiarki.

"How is your ankle?" asked Samvel sarcastically.

"Better," said Anna. She pointed to Aram. "I met my friend here. He has an errand to do. I'd like to wait here a few more minutes to make sure he finishes his errand, then we will go."

"Okay, okay," said Samvel, looking at his watch.

Anna held Aram's hand. "We shouldn't be seen together anymore. When you get the package, go back to Yerevan alone. I'll wait here until I know you're safe, then I'll go back, too."

"When can I see you in Yerevan?"

"We shouldn't meet again. It's too risky."

"Nonsense. You will come meet me tonight at my apartment. I will give you the address."

"I know where it is. I got the address from your parents."

"Nine o'clock," said Aram. "Bring your toothbrush."

He turned and walked back down the side street, toward the house of Sadeq Shirvanshir. Anna sat back down in the front seat of the Zhiguli.

"Nice guy?" asked Samvel.

"Yeah. Nice guy."

Anna watched Aram's clipped gait all the way down the street, till he reached Shirvanshir's house and knocked at the entrance. The door immediately opened and a hawk-eyed man drew the Armenian doctor inside. Anna couldn't see or hear any more. She could only sit and watch the empty space in front of the house.

The game inside Shirvanshir's house took only a few minutes. The Azeri smuggler brought out a large waterproof bag, the kind that can be dragged behind a boat making its way across the Caspian Sea or strapped to the back of a mountain goat on the snowy ridges of the Caucasus. He handed the bag to the Armenian, who reached inside and withdrew a rectangular frame. He looked at it carefully, opening the cover to examine the electrical components inside, and pronounced himself satisfied.

"What about the other shipment?" queried the Azeri with a half smile.

"What other shipment?" asked Aram, his warm relief of a moment ago turning to ice. "What are you talking about?"

"The other shipment my cousins bring from Iran." He opened the bag wide, so Aram could see what was at the bottom. There was a small pouch, containing a whitish substance.

Aram's eyes darted back and forth. He looked at the Azeri and saw the face of a mercenary. A smuggler who needed to maintain good relations with the border guards, and who didn't much like Armenians to boot. Aram looked about the room and saw nothing unusual, but he heard a loud creak in the floorboard behind the door to the kitchen.

"Who is the other shipment for?" demanded the Azeri. "Who will pick it up?"

"There isn't any other shipment. Only this one."

"You are wrong, my friend," said the Azeri. He reached into the bag and slowly withdrew the package of plastic explosive. "I think you are planning to kill some of my Azeri brothers."

"My God!" whispered Aram. Anna had been right. It was a double cross. He turned on his heel and ran for the door. As he did so the door to the kitchen burst open and a man with a pistol shouted for Aram to stop.

Anna watched the street, afraid even to blink. Aram had been inside one minute, then two, then three. She was counting every second. Finally she took a breath and looked away, toward the little playground near the center of the square. She didn't understand, at first, didn't think to ask the question: Where were the children? What had happened to the dozens of children who, an hour ago, were playing in the streets of Kiarki? They had disappeared. The streets were too empty; the silence was too pervasive.

Anna turned her eyes back to the door of Shirvanshir's house. Something was wrong. She got out of the car and took a step toward the house, and then another. She saw the door open. An instant later she heard the shot reverberate through the village. Then she saw Aram. He stretched one arm toward her, waving her away; the other was at his side, bleeding from the gunshot wound.

He was still on his feet, half running toward her, shouting something she couldn't hear. Two officers had emerged from the back of the Shirvanshir house, and two from across the street. They were trying to block Aram's way—trying to subdue him without killing him; trying to keep him alive for interrogation. Aram ran right at the closest one, knocking him aside, forcing the other officers to raise their guns in self-protection. Aram kept running. A second shot echoed across the little village, and a moment later, a third. Anna took cover behind a stone wall when she heard the shots. She was at midpoint between the car and the house—unable to save Aram, unable to save herself.

Aram's right leg, torn by a bullet, gave way under him and he fell to the ground. As the officers converged toward him to make their arrest, the Armenian doctor summoned a last measure of will and threw himself toward one of his would-be captors, flailing his arm toward the gun. When the final shot rang out in the village of Kiarki, it released Dr. Aram Antoyan from the danger of compromising himself or anyone he loved. It was an Armenian death. He had sought it, embraced it, added his name to the roster of victims.

45

◆

ANNA BARNES WAS TAKEN INTO CUSTODY IN THE VILLAGE OF Kiarki on the morning of November 10, along with her driver, Samvel Sarkisian. She protested that she was an American citizen, traveling in Armenia on a tourist visa, and innocent of any crime. The KGB major who arrested her spoke no English, so her protest was of little use. He took her to Yerevan, where she was held at the local KGB headquarters on Nalbandian Street while the higher-ups in Moscow tried to figure out what to do with her.

The next day, she was flown to Moscow and taken to a suburban KGB office in Yasenevo for interrogation. When she refused to answer questions, she was formally accused of violating Soviet border restrictions, a potentially serious charge for anyone lacking diplomatic immunity, since it carried a lengthy prison sentence. The Soviet Foreign Ministry notified the U.S. embassy that afternoon that an American citizen named Anna Barnes, passport number A2701332, had been arrested in the republic of Armenia and brought to Moscow. The Soviets did not make any public statement of the charges, however. Silence ensued on both sides, as Soviets and Americans tried to figure out what had happened in Kiarki.

Four days after Anna's arrest, a KGB colonel who maintained an informal, back-channel liaison with the CIA station chief sought out his American counterpart at a diplomatic reception. He remarked that the Barnes case was regarded as extremely serious by the Soviet Union, and one that could be very embarrassing for the United States. The investigation was continuing, he said, and the Soviet government would undoubtedly publicize the case soon unless it was resolved through diplomatic channels. The KGB colonel seemed to be inviting the American side to propose a deal—a swap of prisoners perhaps—but the Americans didn't respond, that night or during the week that followed.

The prevailing sentiment in Washington, among the few people who knew about the Barnes case, was a desire that it go away. Despite the official American silence, however, there was a steady patter of cable traffic with Washington and discussion within the embassy. The Soviets, listening in clandestinely to much of this debate, rapidly began filling in the missing pieces of the puzzle.

The Soviet Foreign Ministry finally issued a brief public statement eight days after the debacle in Kiarki. It said that an unnamed American woman had been arrested in a restricted border area of Soviet Armenia and would be tried under Soviet law. The State Department immediately protested. At the daily noon briefing, a spokesman called the Soviet charges "ludicrous" and said the American in question was a businesswoman who had been visiting the Soviet Union as a tourist. The spokesman demanded that the Soviets release her without delay. An article in *The New York Times* the next day quoted unnamed "administration officials" explaining that the unfortunate woman had been involved in a "close personal relationship" with a Soviet Armenian dissident she had met during a business trip to Paris and might have been lured unwittingly into the forbidden border zone. Press coverage of the incident lasted just two days. With no name or other identifying details about the woman, the media lost interest.

It was, for the moment, a standoff. The Soviets had no interest, at that point, in publicizing details of a case that raised the sensitive issue of Western contact with dissident Soviet nationalities. The American side was also happy to keep the lid on a case that, if it should be disclosed in detail, would cause an uproar—embarrassing the CIA and the White House—and almost certainly trigger a congressional investigation. Besides, both sides had bigger things to worry about at that moment. Soviet troops in the Central Asian military district were beginning to assemble around Samarkand for a possible move south across the Uzbek border into Afghanistan. And for the Americans, the only hostage problem that mattered that month was in Tehran, where radical students had seized the American embassy. So a lone American woman sat in a prison cell in Moscow, waiting for trial.

Anna's cell was small, but neat and relatively comfortable. She had better food and toilet facilities in prison than the average Soviet citizen had outside, the guards regularly reminded her. The interrogation was correct and controlled; it was not the KGB's style to use harsh methods on American prisoners. The interrogators visited her every day, sometimes for hours, sometimes for a few minutes. But they seemed only marginally interested in the actual facts of the case. Instead they quizzed her again and again about small details in her résumé.

The questions were clever probes, designed to elicit particular bits of information that could be matched with other facts already known. Who had Anna studied with in graduate school? Why had she left Harvard before completing her dissertation? What had her father done in the foreign service? Was she aware that he had previously worked for the CIA? How had she spent the year between leaving graduate school and joining the investment bank in London? Who were Halcyon's clients, and what services had Anna performed for them? Why had she been absent from London so much during her first year with the firm? Anna had appropriate answers for all these questions, most of them backstopped by cover arrangements back home, but as she repeated them, they began to sound ridiculous—even to her.

Anna had decided, from the moment they took her into custody, to admit whatever she knew they could prove and deny everything else. She had tried all along with Aram to build a plausible legend about their relationship, and now she repeated the story like a mantra. She had met him in Paris while she was there on business for the firm. Yes, she had known that he was a dissident; that was part of the reason she found him so attractive. Yes, she had come to Armenia to see him. No, she hadn't informed him she was coming, because she had wanted to surprise him. And yes, she had been in love with him.

She admitted, of course, that she had written the note to Antoyan that was found on the floor of his apartment. She couldn't very well deny it, since it was written on one of her traveler's checks. The interrogator kept returning to one phrase in the message: "The friend you were going to meet tomorrow has unfortunately caught a cold." What did that mean? From the moment of capture, Anna had worried how she would explain that phrase. She eventually settled on an answer, which she repeated over and over. The "friend" in question, she told the interrogator, was a reference to herself. She had gotten the sniffles during the trip from Moscow, and was forewarning Aram so he wouldn't be disappointed. It was lame, but the best she could do.

Explaining why she had traveled to Kiarki was the most awkward part. When she had met Aram in Paris, he had spoken often about the beauty of the Ararat valley, she said. He had urged her to see the monastery at Khor Virap and the little Azeri villages near the border. Aram had said he often went there himself, to relax, and when she couldn't find him in Yerevan the night she arrived, she had concluded that perhaps he had gone south and decided to follow him. She "admitted" after several days of questioning that one reason she had gone to Kiarki was jealousy. When Aram hadn't come back to his apartment that first night, she had feared he must be with another woman; and because he had mentioned Kiarki so often, she suspected they might be there. The interrogator listened politely to her and then laughed and said the story was preposterous.

They allowed a counselor from the U.S. embassy to come

see her after several days, and at regular intervals after that. But the visits were little comfort. Anna assumed that every word and gesture was being monitored, and when the embassy officer leaned toward her at one point, as if to hand her something or whisper in her ear, she pulled back. The Soviets also sent in the Moscow equivalent of a jailhouse stoolie to try to elicit information. Their candidate was a chatty woman about Anna's age with a New York accent who claimed she had been arrested in Leningrad with several grams of hashish. Anna, who had previously been denied contact with other prisoners, was now allowed to eat all her meals with the loquacious woman. The New Yorker tried every way she could to get Anna to open up, without success. She talked about boyfriends, she talked about clothes and makeup, she talked about the CIA. After a week, she disappeared.

The harshest tactic the Soviets used was simply to let time pass—and let Anna come to the recognition that nobody was going to save her; to the realization that, without cooperating, she might spend years in a Soviet prison. And as the weeks passed and Anna's sense of abandonment increased, her spirits inevitably began to ebb. Doing battle with the KGB in the early days had galvanized her and given her an identity. Now she was just a prisoner.

In January, after she had spent two months in custody, Anna was introduced to a new interrogator. His name was Viktor, and he was a different sort altogether from the functionaries who had visited her before. He was in his late forties, with sleek gray hair and the cool manner of a professor of mathematics, and he spoke near-perfect English. He made no pretense whatsoever of investigating the case and was, transparently, an intelligence officer. He began the first conversation bluntly.

"Do you know that Edward Stone has sacrificed you?" he asked.

"I don't know what you're talking about," bristled Anna. She had denied, from the first day, that she had any connection to the Central Intelligence Agency or that she knew any of its personnel.

"I don't expect you to answer," said the Russian. "In fact, I would prefer that you not answer. But if you must, please do not make stupid statements that insult my intelligence. Can we agree on that?"

Anna didn't speak. She had a vague recollection from some long-ago training session that this was a standard KGB interrogation technique—to tell the prisoner details about the case, using bits of information to gather more—and she tried to steel herself. But in this case, steel was blanketed by velvet.

"Stone sacrificed you," repeated the Russian. "That's why he let you go to Armenia to rescue poor Dr. Antoyan. And that's why you're still here, two months later. You are expendable. I am sorry to have to tell you these facts, but you should know them."

"I am innocent of the charges against me and I demand to be released to the custody of the American embassy," Anna said dully. That was part of her standard line, repeated in every interrogation session.

"Yes, of course. I will note that for the record. If it is important for you to say this, I am happy to listen. Although it is very boring."

Viktor's manner of bemused tolerance put Anna off balance. She was going to repeat the rest of her set piece, about being an innocent tourist who had come to see her Armenian boyfriend, but decided it was pointless.

"Would you like some coffee?" asked the Russian.

"No," said Anna.

"Pity. I am going to have some." He went to the door of the cell and called to a guard, who returned a few moments later with a steaming cup of coffee. Real coffee, not the dreadful watery stuff the Russians served. The aroma filled the cell.

"You know, really, you should relax," said the Russian. "It is such a pleasure for me to have a chance to talk with one of Edward Stone's operatives. For us, Stone is a kind of spectator sport. He is such a clever man, and his operations are so subtle. To finally sit in the same room with one of his people is like meeting backstage with one of the actors in a Broadway play."

"Give me a break," said Anna. It was an involuntary response to the Russians' flattery, but she regretted it instantly. It was a step toward confirmation and collaboration, and she resolved that she would not say another word of substance.

"Really, it's true. But never mind. Stone is a great man, but he betrayed you. That is a fact. I will try to be frank about what we know about your case, so you will know where you stand. Then you can make your decisions accordingly."

"Do whatever you like," said Anna. "I've told you that I'm innocent. I'm not a spy. I don't work for the CIA. I don't know anyone named Stone."

The Russian just smiled. When it was clear she had finished, he continued.

"We have spent a lot of time analyzing your case, as you can imagine, and particularly the question of why Stone decided to sacrifice you. The reason, we think, is that he was worried about getting caught—not by us, but by investigators from Congress and the agency—so he decided to create a diversion. And you were the diversion. What do you think of that?"

Anna stared at him impassively. This week, her guards were giving her cigarettes, and she took one and lit it.

"Stuff it," she said.

"Apparently you don't believe me. So I will pose for you a question. Do you know what your friend Mr. Stone sent to Kiarki that day for poor Dr. Antoyan?"

Anna blew a smoke ring in Viktor's direction.

"So cocky you are! You are thinking that of course you know what Stone sent. He sent that ridiculous television antenna that Antoyan wanted. But you have missed the most important fact. The antenna was there, but there was something else. I wonder if you know what it was."

Anna blinked and looked away, lest her eyes betray her. The Russian leaned toward her.

"Stone also sent a load of explosives in the same shipment. Czech. Very fancy. Enough to blow up half of Yerevan."

"Bullshit," said Anna.

"Poor thing. I think it is possible that you did not know anything about these explosives. I have always suspected that, contrary to some of my colleagues. And now looking at you, trying to hard to be brave and not give away any information, but also so obviously surprised, I am quite sure of it."

"Bullshit," she repeated.

"Yes, I agree. It is bullshit. But it is also true. I could show you the explosives, bring you the KGB guard who discovered them. But you wouldn't believe me. Maybe you would like to know how we found out about this shipment to your Armenian doctor?"

"Fuck off," said Anna. She was becoming tense and angry.

"We learned about the shipment from an old friend of yours. Can you guess who that might have been?"

Anna took another puff on her cigarette, closing her eyes as she did so.

"It was Mr. Ali Ascari," continued the Russian. "An Iranian gentleman. I believe you first met him in London. Not a very attractive man. Too mercenary. A peddler. But still, quite helpful. He told us all about you and your fat friend Mr. Hoffman, who got mad and tried to fire him. A mistake, I think. And he told us about the other shipments of explosives, to Uzbekistan and Azerbaijan."

"Stop trying to frame me!" exploded Anna. "I told you I'm innocent of all your charges. Stop inventing these ridiculous lies."

"Poor girl," said the Russian again. "I wonder. Can it be that you did not know about the deliveries of explosives to Uzbekistan and Azerbaijan? Your friend Mr. Hoffman knew. He gave them to Mr. Ascari, in a suitcase. But perhaps he did not tell you. I must say, honestly, I feel very sorry for you, Miss Barnes."

"Go away," said Anna.

"I really do feel very sorry for you. I think you did not know how dangerous your criminal activities were. But now that I have told you, you will understand why we take your case so seriously."

He took a sip of his coffee, which was by now cold. When he put the cup down, his demeanor had changed slightly—not so friendly now, no longer the bemused professor.

"You see, Miss Barnes, we regard you not simply as a spy, but as part of a terrorist network that has been operating against the Soviet Union. The fact that you may not have been aware of the full details of this terrorist plan does not lessen your guilt. For this reason, many of my colleagues want to make an example of you—as a warning to Mr. Stone and his friends—and to seek the maximum penalty when your case comes to trial. Which in matters of terrorism, under Soviet law, is the death penalty."

Anna shuddered involuntarily, once, then a second time.

She feared for a moment she might break down and begin sobbing, but no tears came. What she felt was not self-pity but a deep, dry despair—anger toward Stone and Taylor balanced by disgust at her own mistakes. Aram Antoyan had died because of her stupidity. Why shouldn't she?

"Let me say the obvious, please, Miss Barnes," said Viktor. "You have only one way to save yourself, and that is to cooperate with us. In that event, the prosecutor may be willing to reduce the charges, perhaps dismiss them altogether. But that is your only chance."

"Go away," said Anna. Her voice was brittle.

"I admire your loyalty and self-control, but it is misplaced. Your colleagues have betrayed you. You have been manipulated and abandoned. Frankly, there is little we can gain from your cooperation, since we already know all the important aspects of your case. But still, we give you this opportunity."

"Go away," she said again. "I'm not going to tell you anything."

And she didn't, not that day or in the weeks that followed. Viktor returned several more times, coaxing and cajoling her with new tidbits of information about Stone and Hoffman and even Alan Taylor; and then threatening her more directly. With each additional visit, Viktor reminded her more of Stone, which only stiffened her will to resist. When Viktor's smooth insinuations failed to elicit her cooperation, the Soviets got nasty. They moved Anna to a smaller cell—with a smelly hole in the floor rather than a toilet and a flat wooden board to sleep on rather than a mattress. They left the light on all night, and woke her up at strange times, and one day, after denying her food for twenty-four hours, brought in a piece of meat crawling with maggots. But still Anna refused to cooperate. She was, in her way, dead to the world—beyond grief over Aram's death or anger at Stone's betrayal. All the fires in her had been banked.

46

◆

IT TOOK MARGARET HOUGHTON ONLY A FEW WEEKS TO DIS-
cover what had happened to Anna. She wasn't supposed to
know, but Margaret was good at getting around such barri-
ers. That was what had made her career so successful. She
operated at the margins, standing quietly aside in the compartments where secrets were held, waiting to be helpful.
And people told her things. In this case, she pieced together
from a half dozen people how Anna had gone to Armenia
and been arrested. More important, she learned that the
agency had no clear plan about how to get her out. For once,
the old boys and the bureaucrats on the seventh floor seemed
to be in agreement. The sensible plan, they concurred, was
to do nothing.

Margaret thus found herself Anna's sole advocate and lob-
byist within the clandestine service. As she talked with colleagues who remembered other, similar cases involving
NOCs, she became convinced that it would take a significant
American concession to get Anna released—a trade for a Soviet spy, or something else that Moscow wanted—and she
pursued this strategy tirelessly.

She began by going to see Edward Stone one Saturday afternoon at his house in Georgetown. Her own house was on
Q Street, just three blocks away, and she walked the short
distance in a sleek black fur coat; her hair, in a neat bun, was
sparkling from a trip that morning to the beauty parlor. It was
a chilly December day, and Stone was sitting in front of the
fire in his library, drinking tea, when Margaret rang the bell.
Stone welcomed her graciously, with his usual protective
show of good manners. But to Margaret, who had known him
nearly forty years, he looked vaguely uneasy. She noticed

something else about him, which had never before occurred to her. He looked old.

"Shame on you," she said when they were seated in the library.

"That's not a very friendly greeting," he answered. "Perhaps you would like some tea."

"Yes, please."

Stone called to his wife to bring the teapot, but she had already retreated upstairs. Mrs. Stone generally tried to avoid Margaret Houghton's company. She had been convinced, for much of her married life, that her husband and Margaret had once been lovers. Stone waited for Margaret to volunteer to get the teapot, and when she didn't, he grumpily went out to get it himself. He set the tea tray down in front of Margaret and let her pour.

"I'm very sorry about what happened to Anna, if that's what you mean," he said.

"You should be. It's your fault."

"I can understand how you might think that, Margaret, but you're quite wrong. In fact, the opposite is true. Unfortunately, I am not at liberty to discuss the details."

"I already know the details."

"Then you should know that I opposed Anna's notion of recruiting this Armenian doctor, and agreed only because she insisted. When the operation went sour, I warned her against any attempt to rescue the man. Again, she didn't listen. I feel very sorry for Anna. She was a great favorite of mine. But it's not my fault, and I'm afraid there is nothing I can do at this point to help her. Except to keep quiet and play along with the cover story that she's an innocent tourist."

Margaret shook her head.

"That's nonsense," she said. "Of course there's something you can do. You can go to Hinkle and tell him to make whatever deal is necessary to get Anna out. She's a prisoner, for heaven's sake! You can't leave one of your troops behind on the battlefield just because it's inconvenient to rescue her. You of all people!"

"I've already been to see the director. To be frank, he is the one who insists that we do nothing. From his standpoint, this case is a potential disaster. Anna is a NOC. If we trade for her, we confirm to Moscow that we were running an illegal network inside the Soviet Union. Besides, there's an aspect of this case you may not be aware of."

"What's that?"

"This crazy Armenian friend of Anna's wanted explosives. They were part of what we sent in. We can't admit to the Soviets that we were involved in such an operation. It would be ruinous. And imagine what Congress would say."

"So what do you plan to do?"

"The director argues that we should do nothing and wait. The Soviets will eventually release her. They aren't stupid."

"And you agree?"

"Yes, actually. I do."

"You make an unlikely couple, you and Hinkle. I thought you didn't like him."

"I think he's a fool. But in this case, it's irrelevant."

Margaret looked at Stone, tight and controlled as ever. Hers was not the look of a colleague, or even a friend, but something more intimate and poignant. But Stone did not return it. He was looking at the floor, waiting for her to be done. Margaret turned and gazed at the fire, now flickering into coals, soon to be exhausted and barren of heat and light. There really was nothing more to say to Stone. She rose and retrieved her fur coat, and spoke only when she had reached the door.

"You really are a great disappointment to me, Edward," she said quietly. And she was gone.

Margaret Houghton made an appointment the next Monday to see the director. He was away that week, and the next week he was busy, and his secretary finally confided that Margaret was wasting her time, because the director didn't want to see her. Margaret went to call on him anyway, taking the elevator to the seventh floor, smiling and waving to the few friends she had left in the front office, flashing her badge at the others. She made it to the secretarial cordon sanitaire outside the director's office before she was stopped.

"I'd like to see Mr. Hinkle," she said.

"He's in conference, Miss Houghton," said the head secretary.

"I'll wait."

"It may take a long time."

"I don't mind. I've brought some paperwork."

"I'm afraid you can't do that. It's not allowed."

"Oh yes, I can," said Margaret. "You're going to have to have the guards come and remove me physically, which will be quite embarrassing for the director. But I'm not leaving until I've seen him."

Margaret looked so determined, and so perfectly confident of herself, that the secretary thought it best to reconsider. "Hold on," she said. She picked up the phone, buzzed Hinkle, and said in a muffled, apologetic voice that a Miss Houghton was waiting outside and wouldn't leave without seeing him. Anna heard Hinkle's unlikely curse through the phone.

"Fuck a duck!" he said. But fifteen seconds later the big door opened and a square-jawed, round-eyed man emerged. He had his suit jacket buttoned, even in his own office.

"I'll give you five minutes," said Hinkle, looking at his watch.

"I've come to see you about Anna Barnes," said Margaret when the door was closed.

"What about Anna Barnes?"

"What are you doing to get her out?"

"All of the usual procedures."

"What are they?"

"I can't talk about it. This case is very sensitive. You're not cleared for it. It's none of your concern."

"Mr. Hinkle, I have known Anna since she was a girl. I encouraged her to join the agency. I'm very concerned about her situation. I don't think we're doing enough to get her out."

"You're out of order."

"Excuse me?"

"I said you're out of order. This organization has rules, and you've violated them by coming to see me. The Barnes case is being handled by authorized people. You must leave it to them, and to me. That's all I have to say on the subject." He looked at his watch. "Your five minutes are almost up."

"Director," said Margaret. "I should warn you. I'm going to pursue this. If you won't listen to me, I'll find someone who will. As you know, I have that right under Executive Order 12333."

"What right?"

"Look it up in the rule book. The section on congressional oversight."

"Are you threatening me?"

"Yes, sir. I am."

"Fat chance!" he said, which struck Margaret as an inappropriate response under the circumstances, but somehow typical of Hinkle.

Margaret waited a few days to see if her threat accomplished anything. In truth, she felt uncomfortable with the idea of going to a member of Congress. It seemed like ratting to the teacher. But when the grapevine reported no movement on the Barnes case, she concluded that Hinkle must have thought she was bluffing. So she reluctantly made an appointment to see the chairman of the Senate Intelligence Committee, whom, as luck had it, she had met at a wedding in East Hampton the previous summer. He agreed to see her the next evening in his office at six-thirty, and when she arrived, he had already poured himself a tall glass of whiskey. Perhaps he had remembered her from East Hampton as a younger woman.

She began summarizing the details of the case, shyly at first, for she was unaccustomed to discussing such things with anyone outside the charmed circle. She explained that a young woman case officer—a constituent of the senator's, as it happened—was in prison in the Soviet Union because of blunders made by agency officials back home. The senator nodded. He seemed to know the vague outlines of the case, but no more.

"I thought Hinkle was handling all that," he said.

"No. He's not doing anything."

"Why not?"

"Because the case is a can of worms, and he doesn't want to open it."

"What's inside?" asked the senator with a sly look. Like so many of his colleagues, he harbored the secret conviction that he—not the incumbent—should rightfully occupy the White House, and therefore took special pleasure in making life difficult for the executive branch.

Margaret told him the story, every sordid detail, as she had pieced it together. She spun the tale of Stone's plotting so artfully that by the end the senator believed he had glimpsed the outline of a conspiracy at the very heart of the CIA, one that had cruelly manipulated a young woman—a constituent!—and left her to rot in a Moscow prison.

"Promise me one thing," said Margaret when she was done. "You must conduct your investigation in secret, within the Intelligence Committee. If you go public, Anna will never get out."

The senator, chivalrous and courtly and very drunk, put one hand on his heart and the other on Margaret's shoulder and promised that he would not rest until Anna was safely back home.

A week later, the CIA station chief in Moscow called his KGB liaison and requested an urgent meeting. At that hour in New York, he said, the FBI was arresting a Soviet citizen who worked for Aeroflot in New York. The man would be charged with espionage, the station chief advised, and since he lacked diplomatic immunity, he would be tried in federal court—unless the Soviets were prepared to negotiate a swap. It took just three days to work out the details. The Soviets were eager to strike a deal. The Barnes case was a nuisance, even for them.

Anna Barnes was released in February 1980. Her case received no further publicity in the Soviet press. The State Department issued a short statement noting that the American woman—still unnamed—who had been accused of border violations in November had been released. In the continuing commotion over Iran, the press ignored the story. It rated one paragraph in the "World News" roundup in *The Washington Post*.

Anna returned home to Washington via Frankfurt. A DDO officer met the plane there and accompanied her back to Dulles, and from there to another crummy motel room in the Washington suburbs for debriefing. The motel was only marginally better than Anna's prison cell in the Moscow suburbs. It had a telephone, but Anna assumed it was tapped and didn't call anyone. She ordered fattening food from room service, drank all the little bottles in the mini-bar, and, her second night there, picked up a nineteen-year-old college student who was working as a bellhop and sent him home exhausted early the next morning.

The debriefing was desultory, as if the agency didn't really want to know the details. It became evident to Anna that her case was an embarrassment. That was fine with her. She had no interest in reliving it. They asked whether she had disclosed classified information to the Soviets during the interrogation. When she said no, they nodded and smiled. She was a woman. Of course she had cracked. A senior DDO officer arrived at the last session and presented her with a medal. Actually, he only showed it to her—a fat bronze medallion, embossed with the CIA eagle, encased in a rosewood box.

"We can't let you keep the medal," apologized the DDO man. It might reveal to unauthorized persons that she had been a CIA officer under non-official cover, he explained. So they would keep the medal for her in a box at Langley, and if she ever wanted to see it, all she had to do was send a letter to a postal box in Arlington asking for an appointment.

The DDO man then turned to the awkward question of Anna's career, or what was left of it. She was no longer useful as an operations officer overseas, he said, since her cover had been blown to the Soviets. The Office of Personnel could try to arrange something for her in the Domestic Contacts Division, in a pleasant spot like Boston or San Francisco, if she wanted to stay in the clandestine service. Or perhaps Anna would like to work as an analyst in the Directorate of Intelligence. That could also be arranged. But if she was prepared to leave the agency immediately, a special one-time settlement would be provided, augmented by a generous contribution from the director's contingency fund. All she would have to do was sign a quitclaim, promising never to sue the agency or any of its officials, along with a supplementary secrecy agreement and various other waivers and indemnities.

Anna signed the paperwork. It had never occurred to her to stay on with the agency. Her plan for the moment, she said, was to go back to Harvard and finish her dissertation. The DDO bureaucrat opened the rosewood box to give her one last peek at her medal, and then departed. Anna checked out of the motel an hour later and caught the first shuttle to Boston.

47

◆

Anna's days began as before, with a slow climb up the steps of Widener Library. Little seemed to have changed in the two years she had been away. The course catalogue was virtually identical. "The Bildungsroman: The Novel of Education, from Fielding to Joyce." "The Theory of Interpersonal Relations." "The Making of Modern Europe." That was the virtue of places like Harvard, and also the curse. They were impervious to the passage of time.

The stone steps up to the reading room still passed beneath the same bizarre mural, commemorating the death of the benefactor's son, Harry Elkins Widener, during World War I. The mural showed an impossibly voluptuous woman sticking her breast in the face of a dead soldier. "Happy those who with a glowing faith, In one embrace clasped death and victory," said the inscription underneath. Anna had read those words several thousand times, trudging to and from the stacks in the old days, without ever being clear what they meant. She had a faint notion now, when she thought of Aram in Kiarki, of what the epigrammist must have had in mind. But it still seemed like nonsense. The dead weren't happy. They were simply dead.

The Director of Library Services, one Joseph S. Mellanzana, assigned Anna a new stall, this time on 4E, near Numismatics, Heraldry and Graphology. Her desk looked out through a small window at Harvard Yard, and she could watch the undergraduates throwing Frisbees and dry-humping their girlfriends on the grass. It was early summer by the time she settled in, and the stacks were sweltering. Anna cracked open her small window, but it made no difference. Even the books seemed to be sweating in their bindings. She filled up her shelves with the same tomes as before. *Jon Turklerin*

*Siyasi Fikrleri 1895–1908. Turkiye Tarih Yayinlari Biblio-
grafyasi, 1729–1955. Al-Aral wal-Turk fi al-Ahd al-Dustur
al-Uthmani, 1908–1914. Deutschland und der Islam.* Mr.
Mellanzana sent her the same timely reminders: Handle
older books carefully, lest you break the spines. Contact the
Office of Library Services if you wish to renew stall privileges for the fall term. Anna didn't mind any of it. She was
on autopilot.

Anna's old department chairman asked her to teach a section of his survey course on Near Eastern history in the fall.
It seemed easier to say yes than no, so Anna accepted. The
course work bored her, but she found some of the young men
attractive. They were neater than she remembered, shorter
hair and better dressed, and also more frightened of women.
She slept with several of them that first term and enjoyed
it, in a recreational sort of way. They were so eager and
clumsy, and she was tired of proficient men. She didn't take
offense when one of the undergraduates confided, after a
frantic few minutes of passion, that he thought older women
were sexy. He was right. Older women were sexy.

Taylor called in October. He had sent several letters before,
via the agency. Anna had recognized his handwriting and
thrown them away, unopened. When Taylor finally reached
her on the phone, she wasn't surprised, even though the
number was unlisted. Taylor was good at things like that.

"How are you anyway?" he asked in his rough-and-ready,
how-ya-doin' voice.

"Fine," said Anna.

"What are you up to?"

"Teaching. Getting my doctorate. Taking it easy. Starting
over."

"Me, too."

Anna didn't say anything. She wasn't especially curious
what Taylor was doing.

"Really," he said. "I'm starting over. I quit. Moved to California, bought a place in Santa Monica. Nice spot. You
should see it."

"How are you paying the mortgage?"

"The movie business. An old college friend of mine is a
vice president at one of the studios. He likes listening to my
spy stories, so he signed me up to write a script."

"You're a screenwriter?" asked Anna. She laughed aloud. "That's perfect."

"Why fight it? It's the eighties."

"I suppose so."

"Listen," said Taylor. "I'd like to see you."

"Really?"

"Yes. Definitely."

"Why?"

"Didn't you get my letters?"

"I didn't open them. I threw them away. What did they say?"

"That I feel bad about what happened. Not just the end. The whole thing."

"You shouldn't. It wasn't your fault."

"I love you."

"Come off it."

"Seriously. Maybe I really do love you."

"So what? That's nice of you to say, but it doesn't matter. We're starting over. You said so yourself."

"You sound pissed off. And sad."

"I'm sorry. I'm just trying to be honest."

"Do you want to see me?"

"Not really."

"Do you hate me?"

Anna shook her head. It's a little late, she thought. But at least he wants to connect. That was something.

"No," she said. "I feel sorry for you. You're an overgrown kid."

"I wouldn't blame you if you did. I should have warned you about Stone. I knew he was out of control, but I couldn't do anything about it. It was my fault."

Anna was sick of the call. He was shameless, even in his apologies. She wanted to hang up, but she was still too polite for that.

"What is your problem, Alan?" she said at last. "You've got some part missing, but I still don't know what it is."

"I'm a neggo. That's my problem."

"What does that mean?"

"Nothing. It's prep school slang. Forget it."

"I have to go," said Anna.

"Are you sure you don't want to see me?"

"Yes. I'm sure. Thanks for calling. It was a nice thing to do. But don't call me again."

Taylor took a deep breath. He was about to say something.

"Goodbye," said Anna. She hung up the phone. Taylor had it wrong, again. It wasn't anger that she felt. He was part of a life that was dead. Cold. The fire had gone out. What was there to say?

The presidential election was held in November. The winner was the Republican candidate, an amiable conservative who promised, among other things, to restore the CIA to its former glory. Anna read an article in the newspaper several weeks later about the "transition team." In agate type, among the people listed as advising the President-elect on how to revitalize the agency, was one "Edward Stone, retired intelligence officer."

Anna corresponded regularly with Margaret Houghton, and tried very hard to sound cheery when they talked on the telephone. But Margaret was no fool. She sensed that all was not well and in December, a week before Christmas, she made a surprise visit to Cambridge. She invited Anna to dinner at Locke-Ober's, her favorite restaurant in Boston and a place, she confided, where two different men had proposed marriage to her, in two different decades.

Margaret looked more refined and birdlike than usual, her hair sprayed precisely in place, her nails lacquered and buffed. She was a picture of elegance, frozen in a perpetual late middle age. Anna, in contrast, had the look of a slightly shopworn graduate student. She had let her hair grow long, wore no makeup, and was wearing a simple white dress. She was no longer dressed to kill, or even to wound. Most worrisome of all, to Margaret, was that when the waiter arrived to take orders for cocktails, Anna requested a club soda.

"Outrageous," interjected Margaret. "I won't hear of it. This is Locke-Ober's, for heaven's sake, not Tommy's Lunch. A bottle of champagne, please. The best you have."

"A half bottle," corrected Anna. "I'm not going to drink much."

Anna politely sipped the champagne when it arrived and, despite Margaret's urging, ordered grilled trout and a salad for dinner. She made conversation amiably enough, but it was like a verbal meringue. Mostly air, with nothing solid or substantial inside.

"What's come over you?" Margaret asked eventually. "You seem to have lost your edge."

"I suppose that's true," said Anna, ever pleasant and agreeable. "I think I have lost my edge. I don't have anything to prove to anyone, which is fine with me. I like it this way."

"Well, I don't. I'm worried about you. You seem to have lost your appetite for life."

"Maybe I'm not hungry."

"Fiddlesticks. You're not the anorexic type. The problem with you before was that you were voracious. You threw yourself into things, and you believed too much what other people told you. Now you don't believe in anything, so far as I can tell."

"Yes, I do. I believe in myself."

"In my book, that's the same as not believing in anything. It's mere selfishness. I had expected better from you, my dear."

Anna was stung. However little she cared about the opinion of most of the world, she wanted to maintain Margaret's respect.

"That's not fair!" she said. Without thinking about it, she reached for her champagne glass and took a healthy swig.

"Do you like graduate school?" queried Margaret.

"Not particularly. It's the same as before."

"Why don't you leave?"

"Because it helps pass the time. And for the moment, I can't think what else to do."

"That's pathetic, my dear, if I may say so."

"Why? Most people feel that way about their jobs. Why should I be any different?"

"Because you're not most people. You have special gifts, and therefore special obligations."

"Whatever you say." Anna said it with a tone bordering on indifference.

"Stop feeling so sorry for yourself!" Margaret said sharply. "You're not the first person in our line of work who ever had a rough break, and you're certainly not the first to have been manipulated by Stone and the old boys. The corridors at

Langley are full of people like you. But at least they have the gumption to stick it out."

"He's dangerous, Margaret. I've had it with him."

"Of course he is. I tried to tell you that a year ago, but you wouldn't listen. Now you think you've invented the wheel."

"He's more dangerous than you realize."

"Possibly. But do you know something?"

"What?"

"Our old friend Edward is also right, in his way."

Anna sat up straight in her chair. With this remark, Margaret had gone too far.

"Are you crazy? What could Stone possibly be right about?"

"About the Soviets. He's right to think that for all their bullying, they're terribly weak under the surface, and he's right to think that we should give them a good hard shove, rather than accommodate them forever. And he is especially right about Afghanistan. If it weren't for him, the *mujaheddin* would still be on their horses, batting around a sheep's head."

"Maybe so. But he's also a liar and a shit. I don't want anything more to do with him, or any of them. No matter how right they may be, they're still wrong."

"My goodness, dearie. You've become an undergraduate again."

"I have not." Anna drained her glass and poured another.

"Yes, you have. You want everything to go in one direction, and when it doesn't, you decide to check out. In the real world, you'll discover that much of the time, good people do bad things and bad people do good things. That makes moral choices rather more difficult."

"You've been in the business too long."

"No, my dear. The problem is that you haven't been in it long enough. Which brings me to my point."

"What point?"

"I want you to come back."

"Where?" Anna looked toward the door.

"To the agency," whispered Margaret.

Anna laughed aloud, not quite spontaneously or convincingly. "Are you kidding?" she said.

"No," said Margaret softly. "I'm serious."

"But I just told you. I think the business is amoral. The

people in it are either con men or drones. Not that I care. It's not my problem anymore. I'm finished."

"Of course you care. That's why they need you. You're one of those rare good people who are strong enough to do good things. There aren't enough of you at headquarters anymore. They've all gone. The old guard has left, and the new one hasn't arrived yet. They need you."

"Stop it."

"I mean it. They need you. And if it's morality you're interested in, then I don't see anything particularly admirable about parking yourself in graduate school. You're about as moral here as a potted plant. This life is not worthy of you, my dear. It shows on your face. You're bored stiff."

"Still the recruiter. I would have thought you'd learned your lesson, with me at least."

"You were a questionable recruit before, but not now. Now that you've had all the nonsense burned out of you, you may actually be able to accomplish something."

"This is ridiculous, Margaret. No matter what I might or might not want to do, they wouldn't take me back. Not for anything interesting at least. I'm trouble. I was part of a flap that everyone would rather forget. They were delighted to see me go."

"Not so. Hinkle was, but he's already packing his bags, and the new management would welcome you back with open arms. They know Stone played a dirty trick on you. I've talked to them about it. They think you're a heroine."

"They're fools, then."

"Tell me that you'll think about it. They need you. And the fact is, you need them. You're miserable here, and you know it."

"Then I'll do something else."

"Like what? Go to law school? Sell municipal bonds? Don't be silly. Once you've been in the intelligence business, you're no good for anything else. It gets under your skin."

"My skin is thicker now. Let's drop the subject. It's giving me indigestion."

Margaret sighed. "All right, my dear. I just hate for you to give the old boys the satisfaction of saying they were right."

"About what?"

"About women in the intelligence business. They're all

telling each other how your case proves that women can't handle the stress of operations. They get the jitters, and then they quit."

"I didn't get the jitters."

"Of course not. but you know how the old boys are. It wounds their vanity to imagine that a woman could actually do the job. They're even claiming that you betrayed CIA operations to the Soviets during interrogation."

"That's a fucking lie."

"Of course it is. That's why I hate to see you give them the satisfaction."

"Margaret, you are infuriating. How do I get you off my back?"

"By telling me that you'll think about going back."

Anna shook her head. "Why would I want to go back to all the lying and manipulation and secret mumbo jumbo? Explain that to me again."

"Because you want to do something useful with your life. And because you want to play the game."

"What did it get you, after all these years?"

"A moral challenge. A chance to sit here with you tonight. Life itself."

Anna picked up the half bottle of champagne and found that it was empty. She called the waiter and ordered another.

"Tell me you'll do it," said Margaret.

"Will it make you happy if I say I'll think about it?"

"Yes. Very happy."

"Okay," said Anna. "I'll think about it. But we both know what the answer will be."

Author's Note

— ◆ —

THIS BOOK IS A NOVEL, DRAWN FROM THE AUTHOR'S IMAGINA-
tion. Readers will search in vain for real counterparts to the
events and people described. They do not exist. This is not a
roman à clef or a veiled description of real events. it is a
work of fiction, as will be evident to those who know the true
details of the period I have described.

I would like to thank those who helped nurture this book:
my wife and once again my first reader, Eve Ignatius; my
parents, Paul and Nancy Ignatius, and my sister, Sarah Ignatius, who read and commented on the manuscript; my friends
Garrett Epps and Lincoln Caplan; my peerless agent, Raphael
Sagalyn, and especially my editor, Linda Healey, whose en-
couragement and wise advice helped shape every page of this
book. She is the sort of editor writers dream about.

Thanks finally to my guides across the terrain of this
novel: in Istanbul, Thomas Goltz and Stephanie Capparell; in
Moscow, Yorevan, Tashkent and Samarkand, a series of Soviet and American friends who helped me see the nationalist
revolution that swept the Soviet republics in 1990. I am also
grateful to Rusi Nasar of Central Asian Affairs Consultants
for sharing his knowledge of Uzbekistan and to Colonel Bar-
ney Oldfield for his store of Armenian Radio jokes. Special
thanks to three Ottoman historians: Sukru Hanioglu, who described his research into the Ibrahim Temo papers, and Serif
Mardin and Yvonne Seng, who were kind enough to read and
critique the manuscript but are in no way responsible for its
errors and biases. I am also grateful to many others unnamed,
who generously shared some of their insights into the Great
Game.